“I thought all the beasts were safely in their cages,” she said, looking directly into that amber gaze.

The surprised laugh burst out of him, crinkling his eyes and stretching his mouth wide. He grinned down at her. “I never did enjoy cages, my lady. Or tolerate any form of restriction.”

Lilwen gave a small, involuntary moan of desire. “Oh, how I agree with you!” Then, in case she had sounded a little mad, she continued, “That is, women have so many cages, layers and layers of them. You burst out of one, only to find there is a bigger one around that, and a yet bigger one around that one too.”

The stranger took her arm, placed it in his, and began to stroll with her around the shady landscaped gardens. “So you have been bursting your stays?” he asked conversationally.

Lilwen blushed, stopped. She lowered her eyelashes as her mind whirled. Too late for a polite lie. His fingers had gripped the soft pliancy of her skin and muscle rather than a corset.

Praise for Maryanne Ross

"Fast and teasing at first but all satisfied by the end."
"Finding the courage to seek adventure."
~Romance Writers Australia Judges

"Emotional and adorable. Ross hits all the right notes."
~Bestselling author Ebony McKenna

Bouncing the Bustle

by

Maryanne Ross

Victorians Unlaced

This is a work of fiction. Names, characters, places, and incidents are either the product of the author's imagination or are used fictitiously, and any resemblance to actual persons living or dead, business establishments, events, or locales, is entirely coincidental.

Bouncing the Bustle

Contact Information: info@thewildrosepress.com

Cover Art by *Debbie Taylor*

The Wild Rose Press, Inc.
PO Box 708
Adams Basin, NY 14410-0708
Visit us at www.thewildrosepress.com

Publishing History
First Edition, 2021
Trade Paperback ISBN 978-1-5092-3746-3
Digital ISBN 978-1-5092-3747-0

Victorians Unlaced
Published in the United States of America

Dedication

For Graeme
and for all those who care for Australian forests
and their flora and fauna

Acknowledgement of Country

I wish to acknowledge the Palawa people of
Lutruwita/Tasmania, on whose Country
most of this novel is set.

Chapter One

January 1901, Melbourne Zoological Gardens

Lilwen Jones wriggled her shoulders, trying to ignore the itchy heat of her black mourning costume in the strong sunshine. She ran her fingertips over the Melbourne Zoo's famous flower displays as she strode along. Unable to resist, she took a quick peek around and pinched off a segment of a gorgeous rose-scented geranium.

Lilwen jerked guiltily as a pair of vivid amber eyes pinned her with a lethal stare. The tiger! The beast's tail flicked and twitched with restlessness. She saluted the tiger with her pilfered plant. How well she knew that burning urge to escape.

The animal growled, and Lilwen stepped back, slamming into a hard body behind her. Two strong hands encircled her small but uncorseted waist. Warmth leached through her bodice, her petticoat…to her skin. She hitched a breath.

She swiveled, embarrassed, and the apology died on her lips. Another tigerish gaze skewered her: dark honey and predatory, bright with intelligence. Dark curling hair, streaked gold by the sun, flopped over an elegant-boned face. A bony nose perched above a mobile, curving mouth. A disreputable hat shaded the man's right eye, and his long leather overcoat hung open over a robust torso, completing her impression of disheveled grace.

"*Tyger, tyger, burning bright*." His voice rumbled deep and low in his chest. Lilwen imagined his tail swishing behind him. His lips twitched up and his eyes glinted, sardonic and amused. She sniffed: leather and clean sweat.

She wriggled a little to evade his grasp, but those long-fingered hands tightened on her waist. Not so tight that she couldn't break free, more of an invitation, a firm caress. For one long moment, Lilwen remained within the tiger's clutch, transfixed by the tiger's spell.

"I thought all the beasts were safely in their cages," she said, looking directly into that amber gaze.

The surprised laugh burst out of him, crinkling his eyes and stretching his mouth wide. He grinned down at her. "I never did enjoy cages, my lady. Or tolerate any form of restriction."

Lilwen gave a small, involuntary moan of desire. "Oh, how I agree with you!" Then, in case she had sounded a little mad, she continued, "That is, women have so many cages, layers and layers of them. You burst out of one, only to find there is a bigger one around that, and a yet bigger one around that one too."

The stranger took her arm, placed it in his, and began to stroll with her around the shady landscaped gardens. "So you have been bursting your stays?" he asked conversationally.

Lilwen blushed, stopped. She lowered her eyelashes as her mind whirled. Too late for a polite lie. His fingers had gripped the soft pliancy of her skin and muscle rather than a corset.

This half-savage gentleman called forth a reckless

urge swelling within her. She would give him the daring truth.

"As you no doubt felt when you laid hands on me just now. While my father lay ill, I bounced my mini-bustle down the cellar stairs. When he died, I crushed my corsets."

That deep laugh rumbled through him again. "And may one enquire, has there been a corresponding release of social behaviors?" The corners of his mouth pressed in. Those dark honey eyes had mischief lurking in their depths. She caught the quick glance down at her figure.

She said, serious now, "Changing my dress seems right: the first step to adventure, to finally being my own woman. The old queen lies dying, and the new century will soon blaze forth and extinguish the shadows of the old." She paused, wriggling as a trickle of sweat crept inside her bodice. "However, I fear that long habits of obedience are not easily broken. Sadly, I am entirely respectable."

"Then the respectable thing for me to do, having so mishandled you, would be to procure you refreshment. No doubt you enjoy those foolish ices?"

"No doubt! But what luxury, sir."

Sitting at a tiny ironwork table, trying to eat their ices with a modicum of manners, he offered his name: Sawyer Thane. "Lilwen Jones," he repeated, drawing out the syllables, his lips pouting on the *w*.

He is not tame. Not this vital man, with his air of danger, of fast reflexes and instant activity. He wore his freedom as carelessly as his hat. She couldn't tear her gaze from his person.

Normally, she would have lowered her eyes, kept

an outward semblance of virtue and modesty. She had long ago learned to hide her blaze of intelligence and her impatience with the littleness of women's days.

"Perhaps you are an explorer?" she asked. Her heart quickened within her. "I can hardly think of a life more exciting. To see all those far-flung countries. To brave the jungles of the Americas, to visit the beautiful gardens and forests of the Far East, to see firsthand the strange animals of Indochina."

"You are interested in explorers' tales?"

"No!" Lilwen, laughed, blushed. "That is, yes." She fiddled with the tiny spoon. "I wish to be an explorer myself—of a kind."

He was silent. She risked a glance up; his face bore no judgment, no conventional shock. His toffee eyes were fixed on hers. A strange expression enlivened his countenance. Wonder? Hope? Something thawed deep inside.

"A plant collector," she whispered, breathlessly. There. Spoken out loud.

She gazed at him. Was it possible he could understand her dream? "To travel to distant lands, collecting plants I have never before seen, in places one must have desperate courage to venture. I wish…I wish I were that person. Could be that person."

"How very unusual you are, Miss Lilwen Jones. May I ask what is stopping you? Apart from society's certain disapproval?"

"So like a man!" Lilwen laughed, and his fierce grin warmed her through. "I have worked for years in my father's plant nursery. Since he lost nearly everything in the crashes of '93. I adore plants, but as I tend them, they…"

"Yes?" He leaned forward and one long brown curl spiraled over his left cheek, until he tilted his head to regard her. A long finger hooked the errant curl back behind his ear.

His hands, his fingers, Lilwen thought. So different from other men's manicured, cultivated hands. "My plants speak to me," she confessed. She took a breath. "Oh, not literally, of course, but as I stroke their shining leaves and touch their velvety petals, nurture their soft new furry shoots, they whisper to me of exotic locales, climes far away, of adventure and strange peoples."

"Traveling can be very rugged."

"Do you think I don't know?" she retorted. "Mr. Partridge has sat at our table many times, recounting exciting tales of his youth. He was a famous botanist and explorer, you know. But what is your work?"

"I fear you would not approve, should I tell you what it is."

"And why should you care about my approval, sir?"

"Perhaps your fascination with my tiger has given me pause."

He stared at her steadily, narrowing his eyes as though making a decision. "My work is not respectable. I catch wildlife for zoological gardens, here and around the world."

Everything stilled in one frozen moment. Lilwen slammed the remains of her ice to the table. Stared at him. Spiky feelings rose in her gullet, choking her throat. Disgust and crushing disappointment tasted bitter on her tongue. "You are a *poacher*? You catch these magnificent animals and then…*imprison* them? And you were laughing at my talk of women's cages and prisons?"

Sawyer stood up. "Miss Jones, no! Not at…"

Lilwen stood too. Smacked a coin onto the table, which bounced and fell off. She noted with a pang the silver gleam of a shilling, too much for a small refreshment, but she was so enraged and disappointed, she simply could not bend and retrieve it.

"A hunter!" she hissed. "Debasing those proud, wild, free animals."

She spat on the ground, in probably the most unfeminine exhibition of behavior she had indulged in since she was two years old. "That's what I think of your ice! That's what I think of your work. It's cruel and wrong."

Sawyer stretched out a long, tanned arm.

Unaccountable tears rose in her throat, burning the backs of her eyes. She turned and strode off, dodging in and out of the shrubberies like a demented child, her skin shivering with anguished rage. Fast footsteps scrunched on the gravel paths. His voice sought her, calling her. He could track wild animals; of course he would find her.

She went where no even half-civilized man would go and retired to the ladies' ablutions.

****

Lilwen sat in her tiny kitchen, toying with her small plain meal. Just for a few minutes, life had ripped into vivid color, full of possibility and adventure. Meeting the man-tiger had made her crazy dreams seem almost possible. An explorer, she had thought. A plant collector.

But what was she really? A child of 1880s Marvelous Melbourne, that decade of gold, glitz, and glamour, when Melbourne boasted the greatest riches in the entire world. And then, in the early 1890s, came the Great Bust, the fall of the stock exchange, and the banks all shut their doors on their screaming investors, and everything turned to dust.

"What's the matter with you, lass?"

Lilwen jumped. "Oh dear, I was in a brown study, Flora." She forced a smile for her far-too-observant nursery assistant, a doughty elderly Scots woman with the steel of hardship in her veins.

"My life is full of impossible choices!" Lilwen paced the kitchen in an unconscious echo of the tiger, frustration fizzing under her skin.

"Yes, Sweet Pea, it's part and parcel of being your ain woman."

Lilwen laughed. "You are very wise, Flora. You know, when my father died—"

"A miser and a bully and no mistake! May his wicked shade never darken these doors."

"I thought I could be whatever I wanted to be." She smiled at Flora. "I never told you. I found his stash of sovereigns hidden under his bed, and do you know, I threw them all in the air so they streamed all around me like golden promises."

Lilwen danced a few steps around the kitchen. "I could have brilliant adventures! Collect new plants from exciting places and turn our fortunes around once more. But then I discovered…money disappears, like that!" She snapped her fingers. "And I am so ignorant. How does one actually become an explorer?"

Flora began to make tea, rattling kettles and cups, with an air of weathering a storm. Lilwen lifted their housekeeping money tin from the mantelpiece and surveyed their dwindling hoard of silver shillings. She gave it a shake.

"The very thing that kept me and my father alive—my common sense—is my enemy now. All I can feel is fear. I can only see the problems, looming too large: what if all the money is spent, with no new plants, what would happen? What terrible things might happen to a young woman alone?" She knew, of course. All women did. "And what would happen to you, Flora?"

"Don't fret yourself, Lilwen lass. Your nursery is making enough and more to get by."

"But not by much. I must do more."

"What has upset you, normally so calm and canny?"

"Nothing, I promise. But I wonder. Should I be thinking instead about getting myself a husband?"

Flora made one of those expressive noises indicative of how she regarded the lowly male of the species.

Lilwen said, "I do have suitors, you know. One of my merchant buyers has long been expressing rather clumsy attraction. He is two decades older, fat and jowly, with a wet mouth." She twirled and curtsied. "And Mr. Partridge, the distinguished botanist, is showing interest. He has gained an invitation for me to attend a society ball this Friday evening. It will be so delightful to attend a ball for once."

"Your father never let you go into society because he did not want to lose his workhorse."

"Yes, I understand that now. He always said we were no longer rich and we lacked money for gowns and girlish fal-lals."

Flora said, her tone severe, "As for the

distinguished Mr. Partridge, that man is sixty if he is a day. It is a young man you need, to match that energy and sparkle. Not another shackle like your father, to keep you from your ain youth."

"How you do go on, Flora! Very governessy. But I am aware what an unusual governess you were. I didn't know then that girls were not taught proper science and botany! It broke my heart when my father decreed you had to go, and I must work."

"Well, lass, I thank all the stars we found each other again. You may be an orphan, but you will always have your Flora…now, now, enough of that."

Lilwen released Flora from the embrace and began to tidy the kitchen. That new life she had dared to imagine for herself was most likely a girlish folly. An impractical dream.

But a tiny, vital spark of hope still flared.

****

On the night of the ball, Lilwen donned a dress shaded the exact rich violet of a rainbow. Half mourning—and she could restrict herself to the quieter figures. She could not entirely refuse the enticing prospect of dancing! Within minutes of her arrival, names decorated her dance card, and she spun and twirled around the ballroom like one of her more dizzying fantasies.

While circling in a staid polka, she glanced around the decorated room. Her mood dipped when she spied no infuriating man-tiger prowling the floor with lithe grace. A foolish curiosity flamed within her: would Sawyer Thane yet attend?

She wanted to banter with him again. To bask in his ready understanding of her dream…To feel those steady hands on her tingling skin.

Despite his appalling occupation.

"My dance, I believe." The imperious voice grating in her ear was not at all the rumbling tones for which she had been listening. A veined, spotted hand emerging from a pristine white sleeve latched onto her arm. She smelled the speaker before she saw him: faint, stale body odor overlaid with scent.

The polka had finished. Her partner hesitated, waiting for Lilwen to signal acquiescence.

"Mr. Partridge," she said. "How do you do, sir? Are you sure you would not rather rest on those comfortable couches with your friends? I have invitations enough to dance, as you see, and am quite amused for the present."

Mr. Partridge scowled at the young man still clasping her hand and moved his bulk to quite cut her dancing partner off from the conversation. "Miss Jones." His little mouth screwed up like a bad-tempered baby's. "Would you be so kind as to do me the honor?" He gave a slight sideways bump to further disengage the other man. Lilwen squashed a laugh.

She smiled, curtsied to her previous partner and resigned herself to Mr. Partridge's rather too enthusiastic attentions. He was one of those who spoke to the creamy swell of her breasts pillowing from the top of her gown.

She danced twice with Mr. Partridge, and then after mopping his brow, he popped a cool beaded glass of sparkling wine into her hand. He took hold of her arm and steered her toward a convenient alcove. His smug and slimy expression called to mind a slug on wet morning grass.

A pair of honey tiger eyes flashed in her mind. She cut a glance over Mr. Partridge's padded, powdered shoulder. No mysterious hunter at this ball. Yet.

Mr. Partridge was speaking and apparently had been for some time, as he was in full flow, reveling in the sound of his own pompous vowels. "So naturally, as my wife, you will continue to oversee the plant nursery, without sullying those lovely hands any further—"

"Mr. Partridge!" How impolite to reveal she hadn't been listening to his proposal of marriage. She couldn't very well ask him to repeat it. "Sir, the greatest desire of my heart is to travel, as you did in your youth..." *Worse.* Now she reminded him of his years. "Travel. Collecting plants..."

"Nonsense!" He cut her off. "You will be more comfortable in my manor. With plenty of *other* nursery work in the future, I pray." He positively leered.

Lilwen's fabulous new life faded to beige. She clenched her fists. A bright coal of survival stirred to flame within her.

"Sir. I am honored by your proposal, but it appears you expect me to go on as I have before. What then, is the advantage of the married state to me? Currently, I have a little money, I have autonomy, and I can order my days as I wish."

Mr. Partridge's face purpled. "I had not thought you so! To go on in this unwomanly way—it must be grief!"

"Oh, aye," Lilwen said. " 'Tis certainly grief—sorrow that I have not fought for my true wishes long before this!" She shook him off, ran across the ballroom and into the garden, lit for the evening with hanging lamps and candles, creating a magical, golden paradise.

She stood by the sparkling fountain, her chest heaving with a glorious compound of rage and unfurling elation. A flash of movement caught her eye. A figure striped in golden light and deep shadow stalked through the bushes. Sawyer Thane loped closer, parted a gardenia bush, and arrowed straight to where she stood, silver moonlight pooling all about her.

Lilwen's heartbeat accelerated. She was outwardly respectable. No wonder poor Mr. Partridge labored under a misapprehension—but inside! Oh inside! How her traitorous heart leapt at the sight of Sawyer striding toward her.

"Do not importune me, sir! I am currently wallowing in strong emotion—anger—forbidden to the female sex. You must leave me to eat my chagrin and swallow it down in pieces, like a good woman."

"Again? But indeed, there is nothing better than indulging in a lovely fit of choler once in a while."

Lilwen laughed.

He stepped close. He was a creature made of the lantern's glow and shifting shadows. He placed his hands around her waist. Those parts of her skin that he had touched before remembered his touch: the heat and strength in his hands. The delicate, questioning touch of his fingers. Her body cleaved toward him. She must be holding her breath; her throat tight, she could only gasp in small, fast gulps of air.

His size, the darkness, the leap of her heart as they drew close—her skin skittered with fear and a strange thrilling hunger. His intent gaze, burning dark in the shadows of his face, trapped her own. His steady touch, the very size of him, anchored her, like a safe center in the whirlwind of her mind.

"Lilwen," he said. She opened her mouth. He stared at her lips. In the half darkness, his head bent. His lips almost grazed hers. "I have been waiting for you. I hoped—not so foolishly as it transpires—that you would be in attendance."

His teeth gleamed as he released her. "I made one lap of the ballroom, bowed to all those pastel misses, and effected a bold escape. And lurked here, guessing you too would seek the garden."

Her skin shivered with delicious tremors. Just so did a tiger hunt its prey, all concentrated grace and total focus on the object of its desire. "Stalking me, sir? I am not one of your unfortunate beasts, to be hunted and trapped in a cage for your amusement." Her voice husked.

"Lilwen, please listen." He put gentle hands on either side of her face. "I save animals that are injured or sick. They would die if left in the wild. The zoos care for them and keep them safe."

Her mind reeled. Her mental image of him cartwheeled.

His voice gritted. "My work is perilous. Wildlife poaching is worth much money. It involves desperate, dangerous men."

"So you, too, say it is no activity for a woman." The surge of bitter feeling surprised her, as though Sawyer had betrayed her.

"It depends on the woman." Sawyer's smile glowed in the golden lamplight. "Lilwen Jones, why do you not go exploring, if that is the desire of your heart? I have no wish to see a brave female pacing and chewing at her cages."

She stared at him, her world spinning in colored

glass, the pieces of her life rearranging in a fabulous design.

He searched in his pocket. An exquisite gemstone balanced in the palm of his hand, flickering brown and tawny gold.

"How lovely," Lilwen breathed.

Sawyer put his fingertips delicately on her wrist. Her entire body thrilled to his touch. "The gem is called tiger's eye. It gives emotional healing, career success, courage, and…passion in the loins!"

His eyes burned in the lamplight as he placed the gemstone into her hand, curling her fingers around it. "I chose it because you loved my tiger."

"I cannot accept it, sir." But her hand kept clutching the gem.

"Please. A token of my esteem. And something more: a tiger's eye to remind you of the wildness within."

He bent toward her, hesitated. Her lips parted as she gasped in a breath. Large calm hands descended gently on her shoulders. The heat and strength of his muscular body enveloped her. His male smell of leather and bitter herbs mingled with the perfumed night garden.

He brushed her lips with his own. The soft pliancy of his lips pressed with tender dips, then harder, more urgent. His tongue tickled her top lip, then flicked inside her mouth, flirting and tangling with her own.

A sizzling flush of heat melted her within. His hands and arms were on her body; her own fingers sought the broadness of his shoulders, sliding down hard, corded arms. Under her questing fingers, he seemed both strongly connected to the ground like a great tree, and ready to explode into action.

"Miss Jones!" The upper-class male voice was peremptory. Mr. Partridge.

The spell broke. Lilwen blushed in the darkness and stepped back.

"I will find you again," said Sawyer and vanished into the gold-hued garden.

Lilwen dealt with Mr. Partridge with vague, polite attentiveness.

Poor Mr. Partridge.

For the second time that night, she didn't hear a word he said.

Chapter Two

Sawyer stalked the confines of the heavily brocaded, pomaded, and buffed dining room. He had only just got back to town, with his life, his health, and the injured tiger, but already suffocation squeezed his chest and the itch to escape hammered in his veins with every beat of his blood.

"Darn it, Chip, sit down! You're making me dizzy with all that manly pacing."

Sawyer stopped. He heaved a breath before casting a glance at his elder brother, who was as brocaded, pomaded, and buffed as the dining room, like some kind of human cushion sitting fatly in his upholstered chair. Sawyer gave a short bow. "I beg your pardon." Even he heard the icy boredom in his tone.

"Are you even listening?" his brother said.

Sawyer quirked a brow. "Are not the funds I bestow on you and our esteemed father adequate? You know our agreement. There is no need to involve me further in your schemes."

"I take exception to your tone, lad," growled his father, as he took a huge pinch of snuff, sprinkling the foul stuff over his coat lapels and liberally over the wing chair. "No need for you to be well breeched, the line you're in. Best leave the blunt to us."

To waste, gamble, and lose.

"Beg pardon, sir." Sawyer leaned an elbow on the

mantelpiece. He would give them ten more minutes. He pasted an interested expression on his face and returned to calculating how soon he could get his next expedition together, mentally itemizing each detail of equipment, firearms, and food.

A single name snapped his attention back to his admirable family.

"Miss Lilwen Jones…" his father drawled. Sawyer cut him a look. His father's greedy eyes gleamed as he literally rubbed his hands. His brother smiled like a cream-filled cat.

Sawyer went on full alert, as though he had spotted a panther stalking the antelope. "What about Miss Lilwen Jones?" he asked through gritted teeth.

"Oh ho!" said his brother. "Thought you wasn't in the petticoat line, Sawyer?"

"That's right!" said his father, tripping over his words in his haste to be heard. "Such a life you lead! No decent woman would have a bar of it—nor an indecent one! Ho ho, hear that, Bertram? None decent nor indecent!"

"Oh ho! Super funny, Father. True too."

"Best you keep your interests with your dear family, Sawyer my lad. Your dear father and brother and nevvies have the best use for those paltry funds you bring home. Best to leave it all to me to guide the use of your glitters and blunt."

"Speaking of glitters," his brother chimed in, "where's those black opals you mentioned once, Sawyer? The wife's nagging and whingeing about a bigger home, and you know I can't put up with that noise in my ear morning, noon, and night."

"I'm sorry to hear it," said Sawyer stiffly and,

before he gave in to the temptation to smother his brother with the fat cushion and throttle his father with his florid silk necktie, banged his way from the room.

He had better warn her. Whatever plan they brewed, it could not be in her interests to be involved in any of their business, and most particularly not his father's moneylending.

Sawyer strode through the inky evening streets, relief of movement calming his restlessness a very little. And as he strode, a rosy fantasy grew of Miss Lilwen Jones' vivid features glowing in gratitude as he protected and assisted her.

Sawyer withdrew his left boot from a cold soaking in a glimmering rain puddle, and his fantasy shattered. He grimaced and laughed at himself. The fiery Miss Lilwen Jones would no doubt give him a resounding telling off for daring to stick his nose in her business.

His humor faded. The fact remained that his father was hatching an unsavory scheme that concerned her. He would hunt her down and protect her, whether she cared for his help or no.

His disreputable parent and brother were right about one thing. What decent woman, what woman worth having, would have *him*?

Sharp longing stabbed his guts as a vision of a misty, sunlit home floated in his mind. Half blind with yearning, only his sharp reflexes saved him from planting his dry boot in a squelchy pyramid of reeking horse dung.

He snorted. Thick iron fences clanged up around his imaginary house while he tugged on the bars, choking with restless boredom. He shrugged. He was better alone.

As for his fortune and the money he made rescuing wildlife…his father and brother were welcome to it.

Sawyer loped through the rain-glittering, empty streets for much of the night, searching for a plant nursery with Jones above the door.

****

Sawyer rose before dawn and strolled down to the great river flowing through the city. He paid the bargeman and took the ferry a few stops down the river to Burnley, standing holding onto the rails and letting the brisk fresh wind whip his face in the cold morning air. Never for him a comfortable interior; no, he always wanted weather on his face, motion, and a view of the horizon.

Once at the plant nursery, Sawyer picked open the locked door and eased inside, smoothing himself through the half-dark nursery rooms, filled with plants of all kinds on tables and tables. Their sweet green breath thickened the air.

She was here.

He stood back in the shadows of the nursery, hidden behind two tall potted palms, absorbing the sight of her. She threw dirt and plants in energetic fashion, her skirts hitched up, her cheeks rosy, and her beautiful eyes bright with exertion.

A round bosom balanced broad shoulders. A slim waist curved into slender hips, which wriggled enticingly as she bent and straightened, stacked and threw.

She radiated a kind of electrified presence and wild energy which drew him even more than her beautiful face and shapely figure.

He clenched his fists in his pockets.

This moment had to be one of his worst. How could he warn her of impending doom, when everything within him wanted to take her in his arms? He could embrace her, now, this instant, before the expression in her intelligent gray eyes turned to hatred, once his father arrived.

He took a step. But such behavior would make it so much worse. A betrayal.

His father. His impossible father. Sawyer had made it his practice to cover for him with an appearance of respect. He made up the shortfall in manners which his business-smart father lacked, failing to see the point of politeness if it garnered you no reward. But now? He faced an impossible choice: pay loyalty to his father or rescue the damsel?

Wary indecision was so foreign to his temperament that he froze in confusion.

****

Lilwen had arrived in the nursery early, well before opening time and even before Flora.

Her nursery, now, although really it always had been. Her energy, brainpower, and determination powered this business. It had drunk her blood, taken her flesh, eaten years of her youth. She was twenty-two: almost eight years since the infamous crash of 1893. Eight years since as a fifteen-year-old, she had forced this nursery into being with their last reserves of cash and a cartload of gumption. This nursery *was* her.

She wanted hard work this morning, to release her mad energy and churning thoughts. She potted up the last of the summer flowering roses, heaving pots and potting mix, dragging hoses and hefting plants.

She bent closer, drinking in the loveliness of the

roses, salving something bruised inside her. Vibrant petals folded around each other in the most exquisite colors: bright blood reds, moody crimsons, sunny apricots and yellows.

Restlessness and yearning sizzled under her skin. She couldn't get the ball, and Sawyer, out of her mind. His eyes, his physical presence, his athleticism and power combined with gentleness. That kiss! His mouth! Her thoughts skittered. She knew nothing about him. The man was a mystery. Where did he live? Would he be going away soon? Who were his family? Why had he given her the gemstone? Could there be any future with a man like that? What exactly did he feel about her?

Work. That was always the answer. Hard, physical work.

Lilwen moved to the back area and began separating old dead plants with their attendant root balls of dirt from still useful pots. She threw the lumps into a large pile, harder than necessary, enjoying the enlivening sensation of using her back and shoulder muscles, testing the range and speed of her throwing arm.

Thwack! A lump of soil made a dull thumping sound.

"Still angry, I take it?" rumbled a deep voice, the laugh in it thrilling Lilwen to her core. She jerked upright, a multitude of emotions warring within her, a pot dangling from one hand and a lump of dirt in the other.

Sawyer Thane emerged from the shadows, his good suit liberally sprinkled with loose soil and plant debris.

"You! The nursery is not yet open, sir." A giggle threatened to overtake her.

"It has taken me since dawn to find the correct establishment. You have an unusual way of greeting customers."

Lilwen laughed like a bird breaking free and taking flight.

She dropped the pot and root ball and stepped closer, reflexively, to brush the soil away. Her fingers touched his lapel. He stood calmly, allowing her, his eyes glinting and a smile flirting in and out.

Her fingers were dirty, smearing on his coat; her hand fell away. He caught her hand in his own, and his gaze trapped hers, his dark honey eyes searching. She slowly put her palm back on his chest, feeling his muscular strength and heat, the deep, hard beat of his heart.

"You are alone in life?" his voice croaked. "No relatives? Suitors?"

"But yes, I have suitors!" She put up her jaw and backed away. Picked up the pot and stood holding it in front of her, turning it in her hands. "I am very much admired by a corpulent but wealthy merchant, with ginger side-whiskers and the grace of four or five decades of life. And Mr. Partridge, the famous botanist, has been most attentive of late."

The air hummed.

"And you, sir?" she asked. "No wife? The proverbial girl in each port, perhaps?"

"Miss Jones. Lilwen…" He looked away, grimaced. "I am come to warn you…"

"Of what?" A thousand, a million ideas rushed through her mind. Married? Promised? Engaged to someone he hated? Mad wife in the attic?

But she had not, it emerged, imagined the correct hazard.

"My father comes. Prepare yourself. I will stand by you."

"What can you mean?"

Lilwen was shortly to remember her desire to know more of Sawyer. Foolish, foolish woman.

Within an hour, all she wanted was never to set eyes on him again.

****

Lilwen did not suffer in suspense for long. A loud banging on the locked front door of her nursery caused her to look enquiringly at Sawyer, who grimaced, rolled his shoulders as though preparing for a fight, and then held out a polite arm to gesture her toward the door.

Lilwen glared at him and went to see who demanded entry in so peremptory a manner.

A tall, portly man occupied the doorway, fist raised to hammer once more. He stood very erect and was dressed in the formal morning attire of a generation ago, complete with fobs, chains, seals, and a small folded handkerchief in his breast pocket. His expression was choleric and his cheeks suffused with an angry purple red that looked nigh permanent. Broken veins disfigured his nose and cheeks, and long jowls quivered with emotion.

"Yes?" said Lilwen, barring the way, leaning forward aggressively with hands on her hips and elbows jutting to take up more space. She had seen off angry men her father's age more than once over the years.

The man pushed her left arm back and barreled through into the nursery. He stood there, mopping his face with a large handkerchief retrieved from a pocket, looking around him with a judging, proprietary air.

"How can I help you, sir?" Lilwen sharpened her tone. The man ignored her, looking to Sawyer, his expression becoming even more cross, if that were possible.

"This man is nothing to this place, sir. I am the proprietor. Please direct your attention to me, and explain this uncouth intrusion."

The man looked at her and sneered. "Are you now? Are you sure, missy?"

Lilwen stared at the man, and a terrible premonition began to grow within her. Nausea collected in the pit of her stomach.

Sawyer stepped forward. "Father, please. This scene is unnecessary. I begin to imagine you enjoy inflicting misery on people."

Lilwen's attention snapped to Sawyer. "Father? *Father?* Will someone please enlighten me? Immediately, if you will!"

Sawyer placed a hand on her arm, and she shrugged it off. She stared at the older man, her lips compressing in burgeoning anger, the breath coming faster in her chest. "Either state your business or leave this establishment forthwith. I do not tolerate bullies, nor men who would think to take advantage of a lone woman. You have exactly one minute." Lilwen theatrically consulted her watch, attached to her waist by a slim chain.

The man preened, stuck a finger in his waistcoat, strutted around a little. "High ceilings. Gives the place a bit of tone. Good bit of glasswork, those tall windows at the front and sides." He stamped several times on the floorboards. “Solid timber, even if it is Australian hardwood and not good English oak.” He cast another glance around, taking in the work areas to the rear of the nursery. “Well set up, I’ll say that for it.”

Sawyer lounged against a pole, his forehead resting in one elegant hand. His voice, when it came, was muffled, and possibly contrite. “Miss Jones, please excuse my parent. We shall unravel this tangle.”

“We’ll sort this out, certainly we will, my son,” said the man. “Easily done. I gather you have explained all to the young lady here.” He snapped his fingers at Lilwen. “Keys!”

Lilwen sidled over to the fern section, which she had been watering that morning—this hot summer, all her plants were very thirsty. Keeping watch on the men, she reached a hand back, gripped the faucet. She waited.

Sawyer shook his head at his father.

“This all now belongs to me,” said the portly man. “The esteemed Emrys Jones borrowed—”

Lilwen didn’t wait to hear any more.

She turned the tap and grabbed the hose in one smooth motion.

Lilwen sprayed Sawyer first, who yelped and then let out a great shout of laughter. Before his companion could adjust his thinking, she treated him to a good drenching. It didn’t seem to cool his temper any.

Sawyer’s father spluttered, an unhealthy purple color mantling his cheeks and neck. His wet clothes clung to his thick, bulky shape. “I came prepared to be fair,” he roared. “But I see you are not a suitable person at all. At all.”

“You will remove yourselves from *my* nursery.

This instant."

Mr. Thane held out an embossed white business card. "Here is my direction. You must attend me today, or the bailiffs will be here tomorrow."

Lilwen merely waved the hose at them. Grinning, Sawyer bundled up his father and manhandled him to the entrance. The card fluttered to the ground. Spluttering and choking noises receded as Sawyer hustled his horrible parent through the door and away down the street.

Lilwen locked the nursery door. She picked up the damp card, looking at the inscription. *Mr. Thaddeus Thane. Investor. Money Lender.*

Her legs and knees lost all their strength, and she sank onto the wet ground. She put her head on her knees, ignoring the cold water seeping through her skirts, as nausea swirled through her innards.

What was to become of her now?

Sawyer Thane…his strange behavior. Was he trying to help her, or had he made her acquaintance simply to look over his new acquisition, *her* nursery? Her brain clouded and cracked. Her throat thickened, and her stomach curdled. The fact she was alone in the world slammed into her with the force of a broadside.

Her impossible father. He was at the bottom of all this. Everything looked very black indeed.

Chapter Three

Let him wait! She needed time. Seesawing emotions battered her body in tumultuous waves. Bright solutions rose like shimmering mirages in her fevered brain, only to be cast away as impracticable, implausible, impossible. Her hands trembled with fear and fury until she dug them hard into potting mix.

A Brilliant New Idea for earning extra shillings hovered: botanical drawings and illustrated catalogues to promote her nursery.

She spread watercolor paints and colored pencils across her desk, along with magnifiers, tweezers, short rulers, and a tiny cup of water. Quality parchment, pristine white, lay before her, covered in a sheet of translucent tracing paper. One of her treasured glasshouse orchids cheekily poked out its tongue as it reposed in a vase.

She took a breath and, with a lead pencil, carefully drew the first lines of her botanical illustration onto the tracing paper. When the drawing was accurate and finished, she would reverse the tracing paper and redraw over the back, transferring the outline onto the precious parchment. Then she would paint and color the image until a faithful rendition of her enchanting orchid bloomed from the page.

The door creaked. “Good morning, Flora,” she called.

Silence.

Lilwen twisted in her chair to meet a familiar, mocking amber gaze. Sawyer's long lean body reposed against a pillar, his hands in the pockets of his dark gray flannel trousers, stretching the fabric across the front, revealing the long planes of his muscular thighs as he stood. His dark brows rose in quizzical enquiry.

A blush coursed through her body. A thrill of alert anger shot through her. "You are fond of trespassing in this establishment, Mr. Sawyer Thane."

He surveyed the blank paper placed neatly on the desk before her, with the paints, pencils, small rulers, and drawing equipment. Sauntered toward her.

She clutched her desk. Her chest constricted. Every cell in her body tracked Sawyer as he came closer. What was he about to do? What would he say? She struggled for composure.

Reminded herself: this man and his father were about to ruin her. Ruin everything she had strived for and built over eight long, hard years.

He pulled up another chair and sat next to her. Lilwen sat as straight and stiff as her old governess Flora could have wished. She jammed her elbows tight against her ribs. She hardly knew where to put her hands. She stared straight ahead, as though her eyes were as fixed in her head as those of a china doll.

Sawyer squinted at the drawing title and plant parts labelled in her careful copperplate. "The orchid *Cymbidium tigrinum*. How lovely, and how apt. You do seem to love tigers!"

She huffed a small laughing breath.

He said, "The sprightly petals, so erect and sweet, flushed with green and pink, form the entrancing outside of the flower. The bottom petal, suffused with dark rose, is the labellum. It protrudes like an inviting tongue, open and ready to lick, leading inside to the special, secret parts of the flower."

Lilwen swallowed. Her lips parted. She was melting into the warm tone of his voice, the heady waft of his breath brushing the lobe of her ear as he spoke, warming the tender hollow where her jaw met the column of her neck, sending shivers through her.

His words held her spellbound. He must love plants too.

She said, "Each orchid emits the special scent preferred by a particular wasp species. The floral structure echoes the mating parts of the wasp and is exquisitely designed to attract and harbor just one specific wasp. A beautiful and unique partnership."

He put out a finger and, very gently, stroked the petals and sepals of the orchid. Lilwen could swear the flower opened a little more. She exhaled, fascinated, as his long fingers stroked side to side on the lower petal, the labellum, tracing its shape and contours.

He said, "Deep within, the sensitive column stands tall, its sticky tip nestling under the tiny cap. Waiting. Ready." A fingertip stole inside the flower. Touched.

Something loosened inside Lilwen. Her skin heated.

He bent his gaze on her—dark and intent. The shape of his mouth spoke desire.

"Lilwen." He touched her bottom lip. Her lips parted under his fingers as he stroked along the sensitive curve. He tapped her top lip. "I love this plumpness here," he growled. His fingers trailed down her chin and around to her ear, tracing the tender skin.

He placed a fingertip in the hollow of her shoulder.

His eyes burned molten copper. He was so close. She secretly breathed in the scent of vital man, soap, and sage. *Perfect.* He towered over her yet enfolded her in a protective presence. At that moment, he was so beautiful. Beautiful like a dangerous predator.

A beast claiming her as his own.

Sawyer's deep, low tones caressed her. "I'm going on a voyage soon. I ask you to come with me. We will go to Siam, or French Indochina, or to the Dutch East Indies, all those places your heart desires, and collect plants."

A whole new world of possibilities opened up in Lilwen's mind. Her imagination stretched toward it, as though she had been locked in a closet for years and now could see a slash of sunlight through a high window into a garden.

Why did she allow this man to spellbind her so? She met his gaze as clearly and bravely as she could, her heart pounding in her chest. "I cannot. I must not. I must stay here and fight for what is left of my nursery. This is my work. My future. And…I barely know you, Sawyer Thane."

"But that will be remedied as we travel!" Sawyer regarded her, his expression intense. Then something in him lightened. "Can you not start another nursery when we return?"

Lilwen laughed, the bitter note evident. "Just like that? Nurseries are an investment. They require infrastructure, benches, hoses, equipment. Plants."

She hesitated, as the sharp, familiar pain of loss teased at her edges. "This nursery holds the last memories of my mother. She was quite hopeless at the physical labor, but she loved flowers and spent hours arranging them in huge, scented, radiant bunches all over the shop."

Sawyer's face softened, but she didn't want his pity. She took a breath. She must make herself say this. She was fighting for her own dignity, her own life. "I am beholden to your father. The very last thing I want is to be beholden to you too."

The words gave her courage. More words blazed out of her. "As if…as if I would entrust myself to you when your family is bent on ruining me? As if I need to dig myself deeper into whatever mess my father has generated?"

She stood. Removed herself from immediate danger of more physical contact. "Please, leave. Go now."

"I will buy your debt from my father."

"You will not. Besides, I doubt he will sell it to you. He hates me now."

The words thickened into a solid ball, choking her throat. She rose from her desk and walked quickly away. She did not look back.

****

Lilwen's day was only to worsen.

She had barely collected her thoughts, straightened her dress and hair, when Mr. Partridge arrived, all bustle and self-importance. After Sawyer's masculine presence, she almost laughed, but courtesy demanded she present a seemingly acquiescent and polite façade.

She would get rid of him as soon as she could. She needed to smooth her mind, her wildly swinging emotions, her disordered imagination. There was only herself now. She had to use her brain, not her…what had Sawyer termed it? The sensitive column with the sticky tip under the little cap. She smothered a wild giggle.

Mr. Partridge bowed and presented Lilwen with a crisp bunch of red hothouse roses, the ones all vibrant color, uniform buds, and very little smell.

"My dear Miss Jones," he began. "I come to pay my respects. I trust you are enjoying your usual robust health?"

"Yes sir, and you?" Lilwen seated herself, prepared to endure the man for a polite fifteen minutes or so.

"You will know why I am here." He leered. "Perhaps I have been remiss in not coming immediately after the ball? One does hope you have not been kept in suspense, fretting your heart away, hmm?"

"Ah, no, I…"

Mr. Partridge cut across her. Came and took her elbow. "Allow me to escort you to my club for a little repast, a little celebration, perhaps?"

A snake of suspicion uncurled in her breast. "Is it your birthday, Mr. Partridge?" she asked, all eyes and innocence.

"Birthday! Ha ha! Birthday!" he chortled. "My, you are a one! We shall have some games!"

"Mr. Partridge, I am unsure of your meaning."

"Oh ho! Naughty puss." Lilwen shrank back as he slapped her cheek. She didn't miss the glance he cast at her buttocks as he did so.

"Marriage, my dear! Oh, dear me. Wait one moment."

Lilwen watched in paralyzed horror as Mr. Partridge creaked his way down onto one knee. Was there any stopping him? "Please, sir, don't…please, get up."

"But I am about to propose to you."

"Well, even if you are, I don't want you on your knees. The men so ready to fling themselves on their knees in a proposal are often the very men who subsequently ensure they never prostrate themselves ever again. Should I ever marry, I want equality. I don't want someone on their knees to me. I want to be loved and respected. Not this false mark of adoration."

Mr. Partridge froze in his uncomfortable kneeling position, rendered immobile by her forthright speech, or perhaps by his lumbago. He hauled himself to his feet and said with bad grace, "Well then, well, then. Miss Lilwen Jones, will you—"

"Mr. Partridge, please, let us end this charade. I have already declined to marry you, as you well know. I thank you for the honor. And I hope your rheumatics are not the worse for kneeling on my damp ground."

She turned, as though to continue with her work. In truth, her mind whirled. Perhaps she *should* marry him? Was she throwing away her only chance to redeem her father's debts and make a life for herself? Was she a fool, holding onto her pride, and those dreams, so barely emerged from their cocoon into harsh daylight?

Would marriage to Mr. Partridge be so very dreadful? She would not, could not, tolerate the kind of poverty again that they had endured in the years following the crash, when she was but a very young woman.

A fat hand plucked at her shoulder. She whirled to face him. His face reddening and his features twisting with malice, Mr. Partridge said nastily, "I have bought up your father's debts. You are not in a position to refuse me."

More debts? Had her dreadful father run up loans all over town?

She pushed down the terror threatening to swamp her. "Why, sir, would you want a reluctant bride? Attempting to coerce me will not alter my feelings; rather, they will be less warm than now."

"Reluctance is easily cured in the bedroom," he replied baldly. "Won't be long before you will be glad to stay home. No more of this waltzing about town. Running off, leaving me on the dance floor. In fact, marriage is an honorable offer. You'd best accept."

Lilwen blanched. Horrid man.

The hose in the fernery glistened like a beacon.

But no. She must end this fight now. Face him and send him on his way.

"Sir, you will oblige me by leaving these premises. Allow me the courtesy to fully consider your offer. I will want to see the details and the evidence, if this is to be a business arrangement."

"It is not suitable for a woman to know aught about business."

Mr. Partridge stepped forward and tried to push his fleshy mouth onto hers.

Revulsion shot through her. "We are not married yet, sir." She held open the door and kept her head sideways, away from his face, as he brushed heavily and slowly against her body as he walked past.

Once she was sure he had departed, Lilwen sat next to her lemon trees and inhaled their clean, astringent scent to breathe Mr. Partridge and all the attendant extra worry he had brought with him, right out of her lungs.

****

Much later, Lilwen put down her paintbrush and regarded her drawing dispassionately. Disappointment bit her. The picture looked clumsy and amateurish, with blocky colors and mangled perspectives. Botanical art was so much harder than it looked. Her drawing did not at all resemble the intricate and colorful illustrations in her plant books and herbals. No doubt she lacked a sufficiently patient temperament.

It seemed all her ideas were foolish and impractical, with no foundation in solid reality.

Just like her scorched dreams of financial independence and liberation.

Chapter Four

The next day, Lilwen decided she could delay no longer and caught the tram to Thaddeus Thane's office located in a lane depending from Collins St. Not the best address, but nor was it the worst.

As she entered the tall, narrow building, climbing the steep stairs, she avoided glancing around for a familiar silhouette. Despite her best intentions, her ears still pricked for Sawyer's voice and clues to his presence. She had a strong suspicion she would be glad of his sardonic, whimsical person. In the event, he proved as elusive as his tiger, somehow camouflaged in this most unlikely setting: a city moneylender's office. He did not appear.

Lilwen straightened her slumping shoulders and shrugged off the disappointment weighting her limbs. Her mouth and nose screwed up in a fleeting private grimace at the care she had taken in her morning toilette: curling her hair, wearing a fashionable mourning costume, with lace at neck and wrist, gold and pearls in her ears, and a long string of shining jet beads adorning her torso and hanging to her waist.

Mr. Thane spent some time fussing, seating her, and calling his staff to provide tea and biscuits, which came promptly in the best Staffordshire china. His friendly demeanor surprised her; Lilwen watched his eyes carefully for vengefulness or spite. She perched on the edge of her seat as he waffled about weather and the vagaries of the Melbourne Stock Exchange.

She shook her head at a proffered biscuit. "You will have my gratitude if you will cease prevaricating and tell it to me plainly."

Mr. Thane senior tut-tutted, rubbed his hands, and smirked.

"What has my father done?" she asked dully, her spirits dragging as though his dread hand had reached from the grave to squeeze her heart in its bony fist. "Would you oblige me by giving me your tidings forthwith?"

Sawyer's father sat back in his chair and regarded her, the malice she had been dreading flashing through his snapping dark eyes. "Gratitude, is it now? Oblige you? Found your manners suddenly?"

Lilwen put up her jaw. Waited.

"You were not aware that your father took out another mortgage on his establishment, the nursery? Made an agreement to supply me with monthly payments, of which you are now in considerable arrears?"

Her stomach clenched. "Show me the paperwork."

"Aaah, it is couched in very businesslike and lawyer-like language, I am afraid. Rest assured, I speak truth."

"Nevertheless, I wish to see the papers. My father, though embittered and grieving for his departed wife, was not a fool. He taught me well."

"Not how to be polite and womanly, however."

"If you mean weak, vacillating, and easily imposed upon, then no, I am not."

A snort of laughter emanated from the doorway.

Sawyer. She turned wrathful eyes upon him.

His father rose and began to take a turn around his office. His great belly nearly knocked aside several objects on the table and shelves as he paced.

Lilwen swallowed. “If what you claim is true, then what is the amount of these arrears? The entire amount that is due?”

He named a sum which made Lilwen’s heart stop in her chest. She would take two years, scrimping and saving, to even come close to the principal, let alone interest.

Mr. Thane turned dead eyes on her. “If you fail to provide this amount within three weeks, then my company has no choice but to foreclose.”

The clangor of the great doors of the debtors’ prison, closing hard on her freedom, rang in her ears. A cold heavy stone lodged in her stomach.

She looked wildly around her. It seemed her position was impossible. “Mr.…Mr. Partridge, the famous botanist, you know, visited my nursery yesterday. He said he had letters affirming that my father owed him money too.”

The atmosphere stretched until Lilwen felt like screaming just to break the tension.

Mr. Thane smiled like a crocodile might—cold and avaricious, ready to swallow her whole. “Well, now. Well, now. We *may* be able to consider loaning you a sum to defray that debt. What collateral do you have?”

Lilwen’s hand went to her beads. Her mother’s beads. Mr. Thane’s greedy eyes followed her hands. His gaze went to her ears. Why had she been so stupid as to wear perhaps the only items of value that were hers? To an unscrupulous moneylender.

She faced an impossible choice. Marry Mr. Partridge? Never! Borrow yet more funds from the grasping Mr. Thane? Unthinkable!

Hope fluttered in her breast like a new-minted butterfly. She coughed, said, "I can come about. There is a way…"

He snorted.

"Give me a year…" She looked at his triumphant face. "Six months. I will find a plant that will turn my fortunes around."

"What is this marvelous plant?"

"That is my secret, sir."

"A shaky proposition. You give me no choice but to proceed with foreclosure."

"Very well." The words were torn from her in a ragged, whispering breath. "I believe I can find…the white waratah."

Sawyer finally spoke. "It is in the company's interest to allow a small amount of time to find such a prize. The world is already mad for the famous red waratah, and Australia itself is in a sway of nationalist fervor, now we are indeed a federated country. We are looking at our own extraordinary plants and animals for all manner of designs and ornamentation."

Lilwen opened her mouth to retort that she didn't need his help but pushed her lips together. She was never yet a fool.

Mr. Thane said, "And precisely how will this white waratah bring you fortune?"

Lilwen judged that though the man was vain, patronizing, and possibly evil, his greed topped all. He subsumed his thoughts of revenging himself on her to the lure of profit.

"Collectors will pay good money for samples. If I can establish how to propagate and cultivate the species, we can sell it in a special rare plants catalogue, which will garner interest from all over Australia and indeed the world."

"And why this particular plant?"

"It has only rarely been located, in Tasmania. Its flowers smell divine, and it looks quite regal, the blooms occurring in branches like lit candelabra. It is large and flamboyant, unlike some of Australia's other beautiful, but tiny flora. Because we are in the colder zone, I have high hopes of being able to grow and sell it."

"Very well."

"Pardon?" The slap of astonishment made her blink.

"I said very well, but there are conditions. You have just three months, not six. The arrears will continue to accumulate at compound interest while you are away."

"No, sir, that is unfair."

"They were the terms agreed to by your father."

"What was the money for?" she hissed in desperation.

"He said for medicine, for the ailment that plagued him."

Lilwen was silent. The wasting disease that had claimed her father had no cure. She supposed she could not blame him for trying everything.

Mr. Thane continued, "And by repute, for gambling. In the clubs and on the stock exchange."

Lilwen winced. "Sir, if we agree on this, I must enjoin you to reticence. I do not want rival collectors to arrive before me. Collecting plants can be much like gold or opals in the ground: news of their occurrence can create a fever in people wild to discover it, almost unhinged in their desperate greed to locate it. They will rip it up, kill it with ignorant approaches to cultivation, or smuggle it away. They will destroy whole areas of the plant so they control the monopoly."

"This tells me you are ignorant of business. Of course I will be discreet, to protect my investment."

"*Your* investment?"

"It must be so. To forego the immediate payments due to me, the principal of the nursery itself…"

Lilwen decided to ignore this. "Once I view this paperwork—and have a lawyer look through it—we can proceed with an agreement."

"There is another condition."

"What can this be, sir?

"I wish to ensure you do not just disappear. My son will accompany you."

The office reverberated with silence.

As Lilwen choked on her reply, her brain seizing up, the door slammed shut. Sawyer was gone. She stared at the closed door.

"Show me the papers."

****

Much later, Lilwen stood in the quiet of her nursery, her former haven, her refuge, her creation, as her world shattered around her. It was all true. The astronomical sum her father owed to the Thanes weighed on her spirits like convict fetters. He had pledged the nursery, so the debt did not die with him. Lilwen had negotiated hard for a stay on the arrears, to be back paid on her return.

A terrible choice: marry Mr. Partridge or borrow more from the Thanes to go on an impossible mission with no guarantee of return. A high-stakes gamble.

Maybe she was more her father's daughter than she had ever believed possible.

If she failed…thoughts of crawling to Mr. Partridge in supplication filled her mind. She shuddered. No. Far better to die scrambling up a cliff face in Tasmania, wild and free in a beautiful landscape, her lungs full of cold fresh air, and glorious nature filling her soul.

Now she had made this last desperate throw of the dice, a wild elation possessed her.

It was all or nothing.

She had nothing left to lose.

****

Flora put down her delicate china cup. "That will never do, to go with this Sawyer Thane. A single man, and quite wild, by repute."

"Those are the terms."

"Nonsense. My brother Donald and I have been saving all the bye, and we have bought ourselves a wee craft. We learned to sail as children on the wild west coast of bonny Scotland. The Bass Strait holds no fears for us. We will sail with you to Tasmania."

Lilwen took a big gulp of her tea and plonked down the cup in its floral saucer with a rattle. She stared openmouthed at Flora. Would the woman never cease to surprise her?

Flora had been a most unusual governess when her mother was still alive and they were rich. Much of her horticultural knowledge had been kindled and fanned by Flora. Flora remembered the infamous Clearances on her native Isle of Lewis, and she had survived the gold rushes in Ballarat. She was hardworking, tough, opinionated—and an absolute godsend.

Donald often lent a hand for the hard labor in the nursery. He was enormous and painfully shy, with very large hands and feet, as tall, solid, and gentle as Flora was small, lean, and fierce. He had rosy cheeks, gray in his hair, hard muscles through his body, and the peace and wildness of his lost Isles in his bright blue eyes.

"Flora, this is my family's shame. My duty to repair. I can't have you and Donald involved. Why, you have suffered hardship after hardship yourself and now deserve a little respite in your elder years. I cannot, *must not*, ask you to help me in any way."

"Lilwen, my bonny lass, enduring hardship teaches us to look after the ones we love, for there is nothing else in this world that matters so much." Flora stretched out a hand, holding a tiny lace handkerchief, the lace tatted by her own hand, Lilwen knew. "Whist now, my bonny. Tears! I've never seen the like from you, not with all your troubles. And you cry now!"

Lilwen made a kind of gulping, sobbing laugh. "It's just that I seem to be getting my heart's desire, in the strangest way. As though things are arranging themselves so that I have no choice. As though I am being compelled to do that which I have always said I wanted."

She rubbed a forearm across her damp face and muffled the shameful words in her sleeve. "I imagine that I am an adventurer and that I have only been prevented because of my father…but the truth is I am perhaps a coward! I fear exploring, at the same time as I desperately want to go. I fear failure and the terrible consequences. All I have known since I was a young girl is this nursery."

Flora tactfully drank tea while she recovered herself. The familiar Scots burr wrapped around her like a warm tartan rug. "It takes much courage to set out on the path which we have always said we wanted. We stare truth in the face then."

Lilwen nodded. "Never did such a valiant heart beat so truly as yours, Flora MacNeil!"

"Now, now, there's enough of that. I've been thinking about who will look after the nursery in our absence…and there's poor Ayla McFee and her daughter would be glad of the work."

"That's true. Since their menfolk went on strike with the wharfies and shearers in the early '90s, they have been in a bad way. No one will employ union shearers now." Lilwen looked at her friend. "It seems you have it all worked out."

"As you say, hardship upon hardship gives one the sight toward fixing the present and a little of the future."

They fell to talking and planning. By the evening's end, Lilwen was well satisfied with both her friend and her own hopes for a positive future. She just had to somehow impress upon the Thanes the necessary change of plan.

Chapter Five

Sawyer strode around the Melbourne docks, choosing his ship and crew for his voyage to Tasmania. He grinned as he savored the image in his mind: the utterly astonished expression on charming Lilwen's face when his father instructed her to take Sawyer on the plant-collecting expedition to the Tasmanian wilderness.

He still had not got to the bottom of the wily old villain's plan. He suspected…but no. Sawyer dragged his thoughts away. One must honor one's family.

Fists in his coat pockets, he assessed a tough old boat; it would be suitable for a rough nut like him, but not the gently bred Miss Lilwen Jones. He walked on, a fresh wind whipping his face and the thick salt smell of seaweed, tar, coal, and seabirds heralding new horizons.

The coup had been neat and complete, and now he would spend the next few months enjoying the fascinating company of lovely Lilwen. He stopped pacing and groaned. He would be facing some terrible and torturous times in self-control.

His senses pulsed with alertness. His mind and body hummed with excitement, akin to the fear and thrill of tracking his first leopard, rescuing three leopard clubs, and then unearthing the black opals that had made him rich. He would not disclose his personal wealth. He wanted her to have all the joy of a plant hunt with the attendant excitements, perils, and adventure.

Nothing gave life quite as much spice as knowing it was *do or die*. He absolutely couldn't wait to guide her through it.

At approximately the same time that he became aware his face was plastered with a foolish grin, the cries and racket of a feverish bustle at an older-style sailing ship snared his attention. Brawny dock hands tossed loaded trunks and packages to each other, cursing and jesting as they loaded the ship with provisions, goods, stores, and all the tackle for an imminent expedition.

Interested, he strolled closer, his thoughts still occupied with fanciful imaginings about his future adventures with luscious Lilwen.

So he wasn't altogether surprised when a woman with a shape very like hers, and yes, a very similar energy of walking and moving, appeared from a coach and began gesturing and making orders. He chuckled. Now he saw her everywhere.

The truth was he could not get that woman out of his mind. Her pliable, strong body. Her directness. Her courage in adversity. Her lovely face made beautiful by the candid expression of those large gray eyes. The plump mouth he yearned to taste.

A stab of lust—and soft, painful yearning—spiked him so hard he stumbled.

And then his skin shrieked as though he had been doused in freezing seawater.

That woman at the docks, supervising the loading of the ship, was in fact Miss Lilwen Jones herself. The ship looked very much like a seagoing craft about to depart for far seas and perilous waters.

Sawyer lengthened his stride, temper sparking like the new electric lights from every cell. How *dare* she? And who was she trusting with her person, her life, her passionate nature, if not him?

And then the infuriating woman turned and looked him directly in the face.

"What do you think you are doing?" he roared, across at least a hundred yards of shipyard, with sun-darkened sailors throwing ropes, burly wharfies carting goods, and ships and boats of all kinds creaking against their moorings.

The wench had the temerity to place her hands on her hips and stand very straight, while she waited for him to come to her.

"You care for your nursery so little?" he grated.

"I care for my good name and my reputation, sir."

"You are to accompany *me*! Else your nursery is forfeit, your debts reanimated, and the doors of the debtors' prison loom open for you!"

"No, sir. That is not true. I am to collect a rare plant that will bring me fortune. Your family has given me a stay of payment."

Sawyer mangled a few words of frustrated rage and paced around the slippery dock. Her calmness was a counterpoint to his own very bad, quite unacceptable behavior.

He turned and faced her once more. "There were conditions. As I am sure you are well aware."

"Conditions, sir, which I cannot accept. You are a single man, and I am a single woman. This is the new century, a new federation, but even so, the world would not believe us friends."

Friends? Damn the woman. With one word, she

flipped his fury upside down. Extraordinary, when they barely knew each other. He pitched his voice low. "Are we friends, then?"

She smiled at him, and his heart squeezed in his chest. She was adorable.

"I hope so, Sawyer Thane. I hope so."

He stared at her for a long moment. He would not be beaten in this, although the battle loomed large. He would not give her up. Could not. All his hopes had been pinned on making this journey with her, watching her delight in sparkling seas and star-studded skies, protecting her from every hazard with his body and his attention…

He said, "There is a simple remedy for the single state."

"Not one I wish to entertain in this present moment," she replied tartly. "You may have noticed I am preparing for a long and arduous journey."

The beautiful darling. He could have kissed her. He could have strangled her. His hands twitched.

"I will see this craft in which you are proposing to cross the Bass Strait." Terror built within him, exploding into harsh words. "Do you know how treacherous those seas can be? Even experienced sailors lose their lives in those wild oceans."

"Then it is well that I travel with some of the most skilled sailors in the world. They come from the outer isles of the west coast of Scotland. The sea is their mother and their heritage. They are descended from mermaids and selkies, the sealmen. They can call weather and ride the fiercest storms."

"What nonsense is this?" Sawyer said, and then his tirade was cut off, stillborn before it could breathe life, as a veritable giant unfolded himself from somewhere in the ship.

"Is everything well?" mumbled the giant, in a voice like rocks breaking.

Lilwen put a hand on the giant's muscular arm, and Sawyer felt jealousy bite in his guts.

"This is a man," he began.

"Really?" asked Lilwen, a mischievous grin playing over her face. "How can you tell?

Sawyer growled, long and hard. The giant raised his eyebrows and continued staring stolidly through a pair of the healthiest, bluest eyes Sawyer had ever seen. Sailors' eyes.

"I mean," said Sawyer, glaring, "that if it is inappropriate for you to travel with me, how does it differ with this man?"

"Because," said a sharp, female Scots voice, with a kind of unusual music in it, "that great man is my wee brither, and we together will be caring for Miss Lilwen. She must not go alone with you, Mr. Sawyer Thane, and that is an end to it."

Lilwen's plump lips parted in a delighted grin.

Sawyer clenched his fists, locked his jaw, and glared from the tiny Scots woman to Lilwen's glowing countenance.

"We will see," he said and knew it to be a pathetic riposte. He turned and then swung back to face her. "There is very little difference between 'shrewd' and 'shrew,' you know."

Lilwen laughed. How he loved to see her eyes sparkle, as brightly as the sun making diamonds on the blue water before them. Even if she made fun at his expense.

She said, "Some would not allow a woman to be one without the other. Frankly, it worries me not."

He bowed jerkily and strode away, collecting what tattered dignity he could muster, with Lilwen's laughter ringing in his ears.

Concern for Miss Lilwen Jones hammered in his brain. Nobody else should be taking her on that treacherous voyage. He must sail too, at the same time as them, or before.

They appeared almost ready to sail on the next tide.

He broke into a run.

****

Sawyer muscled his way through the crowd milling and squawking about the purser of the grand steamship *Sea Princess*, the passenger ferry between Melbourne and Tasmania. He would purchase suitable staterooms and cabins to tempt Lilwen and the MacNeils into consenting to sail on the magnificent vessel—under his protection. The great ship could do the journey in fewer than twenty hours. The thought of such speed exhilarated him.

His traitorous mind flooded with images of him and lovely Lilwen, trapped in romantic proximity, under a sky heavy with stars, cool wind in their hair, talking…He cursed himself, wishing he had thought of this scheme much earlier.

As he engaged in a heated, very one-sided conversation with the harassed purser, which consisted of Sawyer half shouting, terrified out of his usual polite charm, and the purser shaking his head—"No, no, I'm sorry, sir, we are fully booked tonight"—a docks urchin ran up to Sawyer and presented him with a folded note.

The bold handwriting, with its vigorous, slanting

form, recalled just one person. He caught the urchin's wrist.

"Where is the woman who gave this to you?"

The boy squirmed. "She said no answer required, sir."

"Which hotel? Tea room?" A horrible thought struck him. "Which boat?"

"The Rising Sun Hotel, sir."

Sawyer tossed the child a coin and, turning away from the purser, hastily ripped open the note. Could she have changed her mind? Had she seen him and decided the great passenger ferry was the best idea? The note quivered in shaking hands.

As Sawyer digested the contents, the words blurred before him. The note contained just one copperplate line: "As little difference between 'friend' and 'fiend.' "

He crumpled the note in his fist and threw it hard at a nearby bollard.

Sawyer stood there, racked with unaccustomed indecision, his nostrils flaring. He faintly registered the purser issuing orders, deflecting enquiries, and soothing the throng of agitated customers. The breeze rose, whipping his hair around his face and stinging his cheeks. A faint underlying banshee scream lurked in the wind, as though gathering strength for sustained and damaging violence.

A sailor in the *Sea Princess* uniform clanged down the gangplank and strode to the purser. "Cap'n says wind is getting up. Big storm tonight over the Strait. We are making sure everything is battened down. Cap'n says take care with the passengers."

Sawyer's imagination instantly filled with visions of gigantic wall-like waves, Lilwen's craft capsizing, she and the Scots spilling into the icy maw of Bass Strait. The Strait was reputedly so cold, one would freeze before there was any chance for rescue. Panic gripped his throat like a vise. He screwed his sight toward the far end of the docks. Was Lilwen's ship still berthed? Or had it left already?

A tall, expensively dressed woman turned her head. "Oh dear," she said to the purser, in a musical, modulated voice. "I am afraid that will not do at all. You must remove all of our luggage. I do not wish to sail in a storm. I must ask you for a return of funds. A storm at sea is not to be born."

A harassed, peevish expression appeared on the purser's face. Sawyer saw his chance and took it.

"Please, madam! Do allow me to assist. Are you wishful of selling your passage? You have a stateroom perhaps? Rooms for your servants?"

"Indeed, I do! A large luxury stateroom and two rooms, for my footman and my personal maid."

The transaction was swiftly negotiated, for a sum which made Sawyer's eyes water, and a gratuity on top for the purser, who rapidly became friendly when he saw both the size of the gratuity and how simply it was all arranged.

The woman stood, holding Sawyer's hands in both of hers. She leaned forward, permitting him a waft of her French perfume and a glimpse of her white cleavage, looking up at him under black curling lashes. "Too, too sweet of you to arrange everything for me so wonderfully. So masterful. Perhaps you will care to take tea *avec moi*, on your return?"

Sawyer's ears suddenly burned, and the back of his neck prickled. He wrenched his gaze away from the woman.

Lilwen stood less than three yards distant, watching him with her face blazing.

****

So much for Sawyer's so-called concern, Lilwen thought in fury. Look at him, holding onto both of that woman's hands, smiling into her face.

The woman looked expensive, rich, and spoiled, soft and seductive in a way Lilwen could never be. No, she herself was all spikes and hurry, with too much honest pride for those tricks with eyelashes and cleavage, coquettish shoulder and breathy whisper.

Frustrated with his lack of success with her, no doubt Sawyer was setting up his shipside flirtation with which he would beguile the weary hours to Tasmania.

Bitter disappointment lanced her. She had thought Sawyer a different species of man to her father and Mr. Partridge. She had believed he treated her as though she had intelligence and agency, honor and ideas. As though he had a respect for those qualities in women too.

The woman's beautifully made-up face glowed as she fluttered at Sawyer, arching her back and leaning close. Lilwen gritted her teeth. She could hardly blame the woman; Sawyer stood tall and firm as a ship's mast in the wind, exceedingly handsome, with that devil-may-care air, hard lean limbs built for action and grace, commanding and yet profoundly gentle.

An object of desire, a perfect man for a dangerously thrilling flirtation. Her stomach twisted, and her throat closed. Was that a spike of jealousy? She hadn't thought herself prone to envy.

She looked down at her practical dress, black for

mourning and created for daily work, her sensible shoes, chosen to walk amongst all the litter and dirt of the docks. Not for her to carelessly ruin elegant shoes more suited to the dancing hall, or a frippery frock fluttering around Sawyer's legs in the wind, as though the woman herself was tickling and teasing him.

At that moment, Sawyer tore his attention from the woman with a visible effort. He nailed Lilwen with a sizzling tawny stare. Furious. And…embarrassed? He dropped the woman's hands and gave her a quick, polite bow.

Lilwen stood straight and jutted her chin. The thought of trying to be pleasing and coquettish made her feel sick.

He loped over, put long fingers against her jaw, and studied her with an amused expression. His sardonic smile was back in place.

Her heart leaped in her breast. Traitorous organ. And it wasn't the only part of her responding to Sawyer's proximity, as though the surge of jealousy had released something hotter, wilder, hungry, and urgent, deep in her core.

She sucked in a breath. "I'm sure your father said *you* are to accompany *me*, thus giving the responsibility for the journey planning to me!"

He growled wordlessly, his flexible lips curling up in a snarl. "There is a storm coming that even the sailors are dreading. I've bought your safety. A luxury stateroom, no less, and rooms for your faithful attendants."

"I suppose you will be sharing with that exotic creature over there, who is still staring at you, by the way."

"What?" He sounded genuinely puzzled. He turned around, saw the rich woman, who winked and waved at him. He appeared so taken aback that Lilwen smothered a snort of laughter.

"No." He shook his head, frowning at her.

She anticipated him. "How very noble of you to consider my safety, particularly without reference to my wishes! So extremely *manly*."

"You are a sensible woman. Stop this charade. These seas can be life-threatening."

"And I have perfect confidence in the navigation and craft skills of my friends."

"Lilwen…" A thread of anguished panic slipped through his control and thrummed in his voice. Her resolve softened. The man could charm a leopard!

For a long moment, they traded silent, fulminating glares.

Unexpectedly, Sawyer found an ally in the tall, hitherto silent Scotsman, Donald MacNeil. He and his sister had been loitering nearby, behaving as though they were not listening with all their ears.

He stepped forward and rumbled, "Aye, lassie, this is a bonny sure vessel. You'll be finding yourself more comfortable here than on my wee craft."

"Donald! Such treachery!"

The Scot gave her one of his rare smiles, which made him look quite beautiful, lighting up his face.

"Storm tonight," he said. "You'd best be going with Mr. Thane there. I'm in the way of thinking there will be music and dancing and such like, which of late you have not had your fill of enjoying. You are a young lassie and not made to be working every hour known to God and man."

Lilwen kicked at a coiled rope and fisted her hands on her hips. How dare Sawyer grin at her like a loon! Because this was a new century and she was her own woman, she relieved some of her temper and stamped her foot down hard, deliberately just missing his boot. She shot a look to Flora, and what she saw there made her exclaim, "Flora? Oh, not you too!" She had to laugh.

Sawyer laughed too and shook Donald's hand with gusto. "As is respectable, I have procured passage for your two companions too. Unfortunately not in the first class—they were the servants' rooms our benefactor had reserved—but Mr. Purser assures me that although small, they are all that is comfortable."

Flora clapped her hands. "Och then, it is decided. I've ever had a mind to sail on one of these large ships."

Lilwen made a final, laughing protest. "So much for the famous Scots stubborn independence! I thought you would both be determined to sail yourselves."

Flora winked at Sawyer, with a very roguish smile on her face. "You have forgotten our even more famous thrift, my dear! We will travel in comfort and style, by this gentleman's grace, and see you reach your destination safely."

The smile left Flora MacNeil's face as she shot a searching glance skyward, her eyes shining silver in the strange light of the gathering storm. "The old gods willing."

A spear of premonition stabbed Lilwen. She shook it off and went to give the orders to move her luggage, travel clothes, plant presses, seed cases, small drawing kits, color charts, and blank notebooks to the steamship.

She needed physical action, to remove herself from Sawyer's magnetic presence, so she could think. And yet, as soon as she was alone once more, she felt strangely bereft.

Not for long; the man was back by her side in minutes, helping her supervise the movement and loading of her luggage and equipment from the MacNeil's vessel into the great steamship, as though he could not trust her not to foil his plans once more.

All those hours in his company on the ship! Her chest seized, and she pressed a palm to her throat to strangle an involuntary moan. And yet, her muscles tingled with excited warmth.

Her mind raced, spinning fast in fractured rainbow circles, not adhering to any sensible plan, thoughts flitting like butterflies alighting on her clothes, to suitable dancing slippers, to images of eating supper together, to Sawyer's warm presence in a waltz under the stars…his hard warm body close to hers…talking in low voices, making her skin shiver, and maybe…another kiss…She faltered in her stride, nearly stumbling.

Stop this right now! Fool! Her breath jerked fast and shallow under her ribs. Her thoughts were so scattered she accidentally let Sawyer take over all the arrangements.

So much for that strong independent woman she strove to be.

Chapter Six

The steamship was gorgeous. Utterly, completely beautiful. As Sawyer escorted Lilwen through the ship, she savored one marvel after another. “It’s exquisite!” she breathed.

“It is one of the new passenger ships,” he informed her. “No expense spared.”

Sawyer steered her through palatial public rooms walled in angular mirrored glass and painted panels, the latter depicting long-haired maidens in floating dresses cavorting with elongated pink flamingos and impossible spring flowers.

They strolled up a grand circular staircase, its carved banisters gleaming with light from ornate chandeliers. Lilwen kept her hand on his arm; he pressed it gently to keep it there. Sawyer’s tall, decisive presence was a bastion of strength as she nodded and politely greeted men and women who assessed her worth in one gimlet-eyed scan.

Their gaze lingered on Sawyer: he was an enigma. His clothes were the best quality but worn, his attitude polite but distant; he displayed no trace whatsoever of awestruck admiration of wealth. Lilwen was glad of it; and despite herself, Sawyer went up several notches in her esteem of him. It seemed a very seesawing thing!

When she saw her stateroom, she didn’t know whether to burst into tears, hug Sawyer in hysterical gratitude, or refuse the whole thing and demand a more modest room.

"Oh my goodness. This cabin…it is utterly divine." Lilwen let go of Sawyer's arm and stretched her arms above her head, spinning around, trying to take in all the sumptuous luxury and decorative detail. The fine fabrics, the rich colors, the easeful furniture called out to her art- and beauty-starved heart, her hard-worked body.

She could unlace the tight restraints she habitually kept on her mind, impulses, and desires.

Here was beauty; here was art; here was comfort, fun, and leisure. Light exploded in her mind. How she yearned for this life! How she wanted it! How she wished to surround herself with decorative interiors and graceful living.

She desired it all so much it hurt.

For the next twenty hours, it would be hers.

Sawyer missed nothing. His dark honey eyes burnt hot and possessive. He watched her want this room, this life, this beauty. He saw her passion, her need, and her lack of these things.

"Is your room similar? May I see it?"

"Later. Let me show you the dining rooms and the Grand Ballroom."

Lilwen couldn't wait.

****

In the glittering ship's ballroom, Lilwen and Sawyer whirled in the dance. His arms enclosed her; his grace and athletic power entranced her. She tilted her face to his shoulder and breathed his clean male smell of bitter herbs and citrus and the faint lavender scent of his fresh linen.

Their proximity shocked her nerves: too intense for comfort, too physical, present, virile, and male. And yet, to move away was to feel cleaved in half. So she clung to him, riding out wave after wave of sensation with him the life buoy.

The musicians struck the next tune, and they danced side to side, arms across each other's shoulders. His hip and thighs pressed to hers, heat stealing through her dress; they moved as one. Her insides seared hot and fluid. She couldn't stop or let go. Their bodies sought each other with a mad hunger, melding into that delicious fizz of recognition each time they touched.

Lilwen looked up at him: the same present magic softened the harsh lines of his face. Candlelight gleamed on his smoothed-down dark curls and sparkled in his golden-toffee eyes. His body leaned into hers, possessive and protective. She let her thoughts swoop away and succumbed to the enjoyment of the dance, that special joyful trance of moving with another person through clouds of soaring music.

With his arms, chest, and legs, he listened to her body's wishes and delight and directed their united movements. His firm hands wrapped hers with gentle pressure. His shoulder lunged in a smooth dive, and his strong arm bore her weight in a dip and eased her up again.

He twirled her under his arm, clasped hands held high. He dipped her low, caught her again, and then waltzed through the dancing crowd, expertly guiding them without missing a beat or an impulse of her body.

Lilwen floated away in a dream of harmony of movement, a perfect prayer to the glorious music soaring through the ballroom of the ship. Candlelight, painted wall panels, mirrored images of herself and Sawyer, and the other dancers, whirled past in a riot of color.

The song ended. The musicians paused. Their gaze locked in mutual accord—and something deeper. A thought flashed: was this man bent on ruining her? But she squashed it down. Not now.

"Let's go and see the storm rise, if it pleases you." Sawyer's breath warmed her neck, his deep voice intimate and tickling in her ear.

Suddenly, that was exactly what she needed: to be outside in the salt air, to merge the violence of her feelings with the great fathomless seas and the immense echoing space of the horizon. No boundaries, no restrictions, but admixing her hammering emotions with untrammeled nature. How had Sawyer known this, without the need for words? No matter. She nodded her acceptance, serious faced. She felt too passionate about everything for smiling just now.

Sawyer scooped his arm around her, simultaneously gentle and possessive. He steered them toward a crewman with a tray, nabbed two bubbling glasses with his free hand, backed the doors open into the passageway, and stepped them out onto the decking.

Wild white spray smashed into Lilwen, the freezing drops like tiny icy whips, stimulating and arousing her skin and mind after the calm warmth of the ballroom. Sawyer pushed her to the leeward side of his body to shelter her from the worst of it. They drank their wine, laughing, and then he hustled her along the wet deck toward the front of the great steamship.

Sawyer bustled her up steep slippery ladder after ladder, holding on close behind her, protecting her from the elements and from falling, with the weight and solidity of his body. They reached the highest deck. He barreled them through the wild wind and the slicing sea spray, guiding her toward the front of the ship.

A few hardy souls were taking in the view, huddled in coats and blankets. As they arrived, a man muttered an oath, wiped spray from his face, and staggered and slipped his way back to the warmth of the ship's interior.

Sawyer escorted Lilwen to the front point of the vessel. As she gripped the railing, he enfolded his warm body around her so that the fierce spray barely touched her. Held safe in this cocoon, she absorbed the stunning drama of the storm unfolding on the horizon. It was like lying in bed, listening to rain thrumming outside on an iron roof, or feeling warm and dry beside a hearth fire while a storm shrieked outside.

"Look!"

Lilwen followed the line of Sawyer's long finger. A group of sleek dark heads and gleaming bodies arrowed through the waves, taking turns to leap and spin in the air, and then dive once again.

"Oh, how beautiful! A school of dolphins! They are serenading us!" She stared, fascinated, as the dolphins leaped and played with joyful antics until the ship soared past.

"Oooh!" The gasp tore from her throat. The skies before them flickered and glowed with sheets of green and violet light, like an electric tapestry stretched across the heavens. "What…?"

"The Southern Aurora." He grinned from ear to ear, as though he had himself orchestrated this unbelievable sight just for Lilwen's entertainment.

"Incredible. Stunning," she breathed. "Words fail me."

"Is that what it takes?" Sawyer teased, and Lilwen laughed into the wind. Her spirits soared; she had never known such happiness. Flora's warning accents pierced her mind, but she didn't care that she was "too happy," that it couldn't last, that such an elevated mood could only presage disaster. She clung to the jeweled moment and determined to wrench every bit of feeling she could from it. Who knew what tomorrow may bring? Tonight, she basked in bliss.

The aurora faltered, flickered, and began to fray in colored streamers across the sky, as dark drifts of clouds came thudding through, eating all the glowing stars in their path and leaving trails of darkness. On the distant horizon, large dark clouds roiled, growing in size like boulders in a furious celestial avalanche. Fingers of sudden bright lightning forked through the sky, stabbing from horizon to horizon. All the tiny hairs on her arms stood to attention, and her hair frizzed and curled in the electric atmosphere.

A roaring white-capped wave the size of the new Parliament House sloshed against the ship, with an impact like a truck overturning. Lilwen screamed and laughed, the sound torn from her lungs by the shrieking wind.

Sawyer indicated that they should return inside.

"A little more!" Lilwen shouted, and Sawyer's teeth shone in a feral grin.

They huddled together as sheets of spray and rain drove horizontally into the night, the wind a high-pitched banshee scream. Enormous glass waves reared and crashed on the ship, which rocked and shuddered against the strain. Lightning flashed. Lilwen yelped and laughed. Every part of her sang and roared in the wild storm. She wanted to leap off the boat and fling herself into its center, to be whirled and smashed and suffocated. She *was* the storm.

They were soaked, frozen except where they clung together. Her lovely dancing dress was ruined, but she didn't care one iota. She couldn't tear herself away, not yet, not while Sawyer stood like a stanchion behind and around her, laughing with her in the maw of the storm, loving its wildness just as she did.

He finally turned her, and holding her face with frozen fingers, bent his head and put his lips on hers.

The railing stung her back with cold; all was ice, except for the live coals of his lips on hers, melting and thawing. His cold hands held her face and then that warmed too. He pressed against her, brushing her wet hair away from her cheeks, staring into her face, reading everything he could see there.

They stood together at the center of the turbulence, which radiated around them as if their fierce passion had summoned the storm.

Sawyer pulled her to him more tightly. They were both drenched.

He shepherded her back down a level and took her, shivering hard now in his embrace, along the walkways to her cabin.

He shut the door behind her. "Now—a warm bath for you, my lady."

He opened a small side door to reveal a tiny, perfect bathroom, with hot and cold running water in a shell-shaped bath.

"You…you know your way around a woman's

stateroom!" Lilwen said, but the intended teasing scorn was lost in her shaking voice.

"Now!" Sawyer turned on the taps in the bath, threw in huge amounts of stuff that instantly frothed up into rainbow bubbles. "Get in! I will see you when you are warm and changed, in the Society Bar. You will need hot drinks too."

He paused with his fist on the door. Turned to her. Lilwen blew him a kiss, and then she was alone.

She ripped off her sodden, freezing dress and almost screamed with the pain of sensation returning as she lowered herself into water. Soon, though, she was floating like a happy mermaid, warm and blissful, and admiring the gorgeous painted panels of her own bathroom.

As she wallowed, she saw again Sawyer's angular cheekbones slanting across his handsome face, his eyes like lamps in the storm, his dark hair, whipped by the wind, felt the muscular length of his leg as it pressed between hers. She stroked her skin and imagined his large hands on her body, and a fire ignited and burned through her.

The MacNeils! She must check they were accommodated comfortably. And...Sawyer hadn't said which stateroom he was in.

Had he deliberately omitted to tell her? So he could entertain chance-met women? She shrugged the thought away. What they had just shared was precious and private. She hugged her arms to herself and relived the press of Sawyer's warm body against hers. His hot mouth. The heated expression as his eyes traveled down her form, with her dress plastered to every curve and hollow of her body.

This would never do! As magnetic, as wonderful as Sawyer was, the last thing she needed was another man determining her life, ordering her days, and fashioning her thoughts.

He is not like that.

She couldn't risk it.

Lilwen sloshed herself out from her bath, bubbles trailing and sliding down her skin. Such soft fluffy towels! But she rubbed harder, to scrub away any lingering, delightful, craven longing for Sawyer's hands on her body.

How delicious it was to bask in Sawyer's admiration. Could she permit herself a shipboard flirtation? But no more than that. Her independence and pride, her glorious imaginary future, so close she could smell and taste it, depended on it.

She had to find out. She had to know if she could carve out a life for herself, the kind of life for which she hungered with every fiber of her being. Men, even a lovely one, just meant compromise, duty, and a narrowing of one's horizons.

She wanted to flame with life, to roar like a storm, to create herself anew in an image of her own making. She dared to dream.

And she had a huge financial debt to dissolve, to that same man and his tiresome father.

****

Sawyer had to get himself out of her stateroom—and fast. Her body, with that light, sparkling dancing dress cleaving to her form. The swell of her hips and buttocks, with the dress hugging the sweet peachy crease between her buttocks. The pointed pink nipples protruding through her wet dress, offering themselves to be tweaked and licked. The shape of her strong shoulders, her lovely arms, her shapely legs showing against the clinging fabric. Her hot, clever tongue as he kissed her.

Despite his frozen state, Sawyer's body knew what it wanted. Every cell in his blood and muscle screamed at him to turn that handle and open the bathroom door. Tantalizing images of her rising from that perfumed bath, clad only in smooth, slippery froth sliding from her body in lacy trickles, tormented him. His forearms strained as he pressed his arms hard against the wall. His body throbbed in a kind of delicious sensory torture. He unclenched his jaw before he shattered teeth.

He could not—would not—take advantage of her. She had no one in the world to protect her, barring the gallant MacNeils, and she remained heavily indebted to his father. He burned to change that situation for her. She deserved the independence she sought so valiantly. He wanted to know that she chose him for himself, not for his wealth, or his ability to cancel her debts. And he wanted her to come to him, free and equal, not a debtor paying a duty.

It was just a pity that his body refused to listen.

Sawyer had turned the topic when she mentioned his stateroom, for in fact, he didn't have one. He had agreed with the purser that he would travel on one of the deck chairs set out in the viewing room, there being no more rooms available. It was warm and dry, and it wouldn't kill him.

Shaking now with cold, Sawyer grabbed a change of clothes from his locker and made an awkward change in the small public male washroom. The washroom was tiny in every direction, and he banged fingers, elbows, knees, and hips trying to get dried and dressed. His skin felt sticky and damp rather than soaking wet, and he now had dry garments on. An enormous improvement.

Miss Lilwen Jones. What a woman. She had loved the fury of that storm, drank in all the sights and sensations of nature putting on a show. She laughed in the teeth of the wild wind and reveled in the power of nature.

In Tasmania, he would have weeks of her company almost to himself—weeks of hideous self-restraint. His thighs bunched. She was so sweet and trusting. His arms shaped around an imaginary Lilwen's curving warmth…and her passionate, fervent response. He shuddered, desire wracking him.

As though sharing his passion, an enormous bang shook the ship, and the whole thing gave an almighty lurch.

Sawyer leaped up.

Chapter Seven

The wind howled around the decks with an unholy wail. The vessel shuddered with increasing velocity. Crash! The ship lurched with a sickening heave almost onto its side. People screamed and smashing sounds echoed through the ship: flying plates, chairs, unsecured luggage, cups, and glasses.

Lilwen! She should be safe in her stateroom, but she would wish him to check the welfare of the MacNeils housed below the waterline with the other steerage passengers. They would be the most vulnerable if the ship had taken damage.

Sawyer struggled through the vessel, holding onto banisters and bars, anything that was fixed and not moving. The ship groaned as it slowly came upright. Half the lights snapped out. Curses and yells split the murky half-light. Loud thumps and sharp splintering, cracking sounds resonated like fired bullets in the heart of the ship. People around him retched and moaned, affected by seasickness with the extreme rolling motion of the distressed ship. Sawyer battled on in the gloom, trying to sort high-pitched wailing from the scream of the wind and the shrill laboring of the ship's engines.

Just before he descended from the upper decks, he narrowly missed being hit by a human missile, as a man pitched headlong down a companionway. Sawyer slammed himself over to the wall, just in time, which gave him a view through to the helmsman on the bridge. Crash! The ship listed heavily; the helmsman was taken by surprise, his hands wrenched from the wheel as he was thrown bodily into a corner.

The ship still steamed ahead, but appeared out of control, slewing about, traveling almost on its side. His heartbeat slammed out of rhythm; the whole thing might capsize. He didn't like anyone's chances if that happened. The deathly, freezing waters of Bass Strait were notorious for swallowing human offerings and refusing to spit them back alive.

Wait! Through the flickering otherworld, the captain plowed through wind and flying debris, swimming his arms to propel himself forward, to finally grab the wildly spinning wheel and take control. Slowly, painfully, the ship righted itself.

Sawyer flicked fear-sweat from his forehead with shaky fingers.

Hand over hand, he headed down to the steerage passenger quarters. He descended into chaos. With each heave of the ship, loud thumps and yells penetrated the darkness, as passengers were pitched from their bunks and hurled around their cabins. Unsecured doors flew open, and luggage and other detritus of living spilled out and rolled through the hallways, mutating into tangled trip hazards, lining floors and hanging from ship lights. He helped two stunned passengers back into their rooms and forged onward.

A shouted conversation through the MacNeils' adjoining cabin doors, Sawyer with arms outstretched to anchor his swaying body against the passage walls, assured him that they were unharmed. They chose to remain below at present rather than risk injury trying to ascend above.

Sawyer surveyed the carnage around him. There was little of practical use he could do here. He would return to the upper deck, locate the crew, and offer assistance. He climbed the narrow stairs again, his body smashing against the walls on either side of the staircase with each rock of the ship.

Just as he arrived back on the upper boat deck, the ship listed heavily. A roaring wave smashed over the rolling deck—as if the sea had opened its hungry maw to swallow them all.

Sawyer froze as another wall of water reared above the boat deck, more than forty feet above the waterline. A wild beat of his heart saved him, fueling his body with instant vigor. He ducked back into the companionway, clinging hard to the handrail of the constricted staircase. Helplessness flooded him as the water swept two men away in the semi-darkness, their hands and feet scrabbling futilely for purchase on the slippery-slick deck, their screams fading to threads of sound as they dropped down a far stairwell.

The ship hiccupped and jerked. The boiler rooms! They must keep the ship steaming forward through the storm toward land and safety, if everyone, crew and passengers, were to survive this. An image of Lilwen's face, drowning in a raging sea, flashed before him.

He fought his way down once more to the bowels of the ship. A sight like Hades itself greeted him as he used all his strength to crash open the engine room door.

Two stokers in the boiler room were pinned against the bulkheads by heavy barrels, sturdy barrows, shovels, and piles of loose coal. One huge boiler blazed bright through its untended, open door, glowing coals and flaming combustibles rolling around in the great furnace, spewing sparks out onto the hot metal floor. Three men hastily shoveled fuel into two other furnaces, leaping out of the way with every lurch and jolt of the boat. The noise was terrible, the heat extreme; Sawyer's entire body burst into a hot sweat, water pouring from every part of his frame, his face, his back, in streaming rivulets.

Sawyer pulled and forced his way to the trapped stokers, staggering with every lurch of the ship, gasping hard in the thick smoke-laden air. Lights flashed off, with just the hellish flames of boilers for illumination, flickering red and orange in the heat. Straining, he wrenched one barrel away from a stoker, only to have it slam back into his right hip and leg, robbing him of breath and sending sharp spikes of pain through his body. He waited, working with the lurch and listing of the ship, heaving on the great barrel as the ship rolled to the other side.

One stoker sprang loose and assisted Sawyer to free the other man. The second man's left arm dangled uselessly by his side, his face a rictus of pain. Once they pulled him out, Sawyer sent the injured man stumbling away, cradling his arm, out of the heat and danger of the boiler room, to find somewhere safer to wait until medics could strap and set his arm and ply him with some sort of pain relief.

Sawyer tore off his jacket and cast it to one side. Heedless of the danger of burns, he strode into the fray. Right now, the ship had to be kept going, the furnaces burning, the steam powering the ship through the dark and danger. It was a priority over helping one man to find a medic.

The head stoker regarded him in the flickering darkness for a short time, gave a curt nod, and got back to stoking the boilers and powering the ship through the ragged seas.

****

Lilwen dressed in deliciously clean clothes and spent several minutes examining the delightful stylized Rennie Mackintosh roses adorning the stained-glass panels in her stateroom. If her botanical drawings left a lot to be desired, perhaps she could develop a stylized form of plant illustration for her nursery catalogues? These images were stunning, and so appealing, communicating the essence of the flower while uniting it with fashionable Art Nouveau design.

Her quick mind leaped forward into possibilities and planning, envisioning just how her new catalogues would look, all artful design and sumptuous color, calling forth the shillings and pounds from garden lovers' pockets and purses.

Lilwen sat herself in the velvety armchair, wriggling her warm bare toes in an ecstasy of privacy and comfort. In a minute, a little minute, she must check on the MacNeils. She did not want to admit to herself that she might be awaiting another visitor: one who would know just what to do with her warmed and perfumed skin, the soft fabrics draping her frame, and the sensuous, languorous feeling drifting through her relaxed body like spiced wine.

Bang! The entire stateroom tilted. Lilwen's chair tipped, spilling her to the floor in a heap of limbs, tingling and shocked. Luggage careened around the cabin as though thrown by a giant hand. The small chair at the desk flew across the room and crashed into the opposite wall. Over the screams of the ship trying to right itself, she heard bottles and tins, the paraphernalia of her personal toilette, sliding and crashing in the tiny bathroom. In the corridor outside, women screamed and called out, babies and children babbled in terror, and deeper male voices tore the air with startled profanities.

The ship's engines were grinding and shrilling, as slowly, slowly, the great vessel began to right itself. Unsecured items slid and crashed once more.

Just outside her door, a woman's astonished voice colored the air with rich invective. Despite herself, Lilwen had to laugh. She crawled to her feet, and lurching and staggering as though drunk, she made it to the door and pulled it open with main strength.

The scene which greeted her resembled one of Bruegel's paintings: all distorted people, busy in their own private hells, unravelling themselves from deformed and knotted postures, with luggage, clothing, books, candlesticks, strewn and tangled about like a demon's lair. The inventively swearing woman hung just outside her room, clinging to the opposite cabin door.

Lilwen grabbed her and pulled her inside, pushing her onto the bed. They clung together, Lilwen finding some relief from her fright in the woman's stoic cursing.

The woman said, "This blasted, blighted Bass Strait passage is often wild and dangerous. Last time I traveled, saw a woman and two children washed overboard with my own eyes. When the storm died down, they searched for hours, but no trace was ever found."

"Good Lord."

"Nothing to do with the Lord, my dear. The farther south we get, the farther from civilization and the closer we arrive to Mother Nature in all her majesty and power. We find less and less of the Lord in men's black hearts too."

The ship lurched again, and the women clung to each other. Lilwen's new acquaintance was cultured and beautifully dressed, of medium height, pale haired, and a little older than her own age, possibly in her early thirties. The scorching Australian sun had already kissed her skin with tiny wrinkles and dotted her dainty nose with freckles. Lilwen sensed that the woman was steel tough in the way that women can be hardy inside, despite her groomed exterior. She wanted to know more.

The ship lurched again, tumbling the women, still clutching each other, on the floor. Both shook with giggles. Warmth flowed through her. Had she possibly met a friend, in this most unusual of circumstances?

The woman heard her thought. "This is one way to get over the boring social preliminaries, is it not?" She struggled up from the carpet, carefully untangling herself from Lilwen. "I'm Mrs. Fraser, Dolly Fraser. I fell in love with that devil's whelp Rory Fraser and, feeling compelled to follow him anywhere, now find myself living at the literal end of the earth, with few services, almost no women, and just a near-savage husband for companion." Dolly smiled so sweetly that Lilwen laughed. The woman was clearly still devoted to her maligned husband.

How tough she must be! Tough to go with a husband she loved to the ends of the earth, to face solitude and a lack of amenities, to endure an absence of family, friends, and society.

The ship screamed again and righted itself. A bubble of expectant silence hung in the air, while everything and everyone held their respective breaths. The ship's engine's ground, and the vessel lurched forward, apparently upright for the present.

"I am on a journey of discovery," Lilwen informed Dolly. "I am seeking rare plants for my nursery; but more: I am seeking liberty, independence, and my future." She blinked in surprise. She had spoken aloud a deeper truth.

"Bravo!" Dolly laughed, and they smiled at each other, mutually delighted in their blossoming friendship. "And tell me, do you have your journey all planned out?"

"Well, not as yet. I had thought to seek advice and equip myself further once I arrive in Hobart town."

"This may be presumptuous—and your pardon, my dear, if it is—but I do wonder if you would be so very kind as to accompany me back to Strahan, where I live with that small-town-loving Rory Fraser. The area is famed for its wilderness and beauty. I so seldom have the opportunity to enjoy cultured female company. I may even be able to cease swearing and profaning in every second sentence during this frightful trip."

Lilwen grinned. "Far be it from me to try to teach a sister better ways, for I am just as liable to lead you on a merry dance of rebellion and social misbehavior. However, I am already grateful for your company, and I really had no idea how to proceed once we arrived in Hobart. The wilderness sounds perfect for gathering new plant species and materials. Perhaps we can talk about this further, if this ship actually recovers!"

Dolly's eyes gleamed. She had picked up a key word. "We?"

Lilwen shrugged and huffed a sigh. "That is a long story, perhaps best related under a starry sky and calm sea. I have several companions, including a rather singular man who refuses to let me travel alone. But now, immediately, I must check on my nursery assistants: doughty Scots, both of them, but elderly and maybe needing my help, all the same. Perhaps I will see you later."

They embraced, Dolly kissing both Lilwen's cheeks in the fervor of new friendship. "Do be careful, my dear. I shall follow your brave example and check on other passengers myself. I will look to the people on this deck first."

Lilwen cautiously made her way along the stateroom hallway toward the staircases leading to the steerage cabins. She stared at doors as she passed: which was Sawyer Thane's stateroom? How had he weathered this storm?

She considered his love of action and danger.

Something as icy as a Bass Strait barnacle clutched her heart.

Lilwen began to hurry, ignoring the ship's pitching and rolling, dismissing the bashes and knocks to her skin and body as she pulled her way through the ship, hand over hand along the narrow passages.

She let her heart lead her, down and down.

"I'm looking for Sawyer Thane." She was tired of asking, of pushing her way through thickets of panicked people, through hallways awash with seasickness and tangled junk, smashed possessions, and detritus.

"Do you know Sawyer Thane?"

Ridiculous, but she could not stop. Alarmed passion bloomed in her heart, blotting out every other impulse. A connection twanged between them, impossible to sever.

She wanted to ensure Sawyer Thane was safe and not engaging in mad heroics. Then, she would check on the MacNeils, and then retire to her cabin to wait out the storm.

Once she had found him.

A filthy, exhausted man grabbed her by the waist, physically restraining her. "What are you doing all the way down here? No, madam, that direction is the boiler room, dangerous in this storm, with the ship all about. Go back to your cabin. You are just making it difficult. Do as you are told."

Lilwen jerked and her vision constricted. Panic made her fierce. She raged at him, right in his face. "So I'm difficult! Now let me go." The man's head reared back, and he loosened his hold, enough to wriggle free.

The metal corridor clanged as she stumbled and ran down its length. Two thick metal doors, heavy with iron studs, stretched across the passage at the end. She used all her weight and body strength to wrench open one door, a great heave of the ship lending gravity to her effort.

There, inside. A flickering, red-infused, flame-dancing half-darkness. A mirage of hell, shifting and shining, and at its center, a form she knew with her whole being. The way he moved. His ferocious, focused energy on the task at hand.

Sawyer Thane, his sweat-drenched shirt plastered to his body, smeared all over with dark streaks of ash and coal. All bulky, corded muscle, moving rhythmically as he loaded and heaved great shovels of coal into huge hot furnaces: shoulders like boulders, arms rippling with strength and stomach ribbed with effort, all tapering into a narrow waist. Ridged biceps pumping with work.

He tore off his damp shirt and wiped his forehead and arms with it, then threw it aside. His sweat-slick skin danced with red and gold firelight as though his very body flamed. His dark blue work pants hung low on his hips and clung to taut thighs as he lifted and heaved. His hair hung in curling locks over his left eye.

He looked like a god of fire, Vulcan, all male virility and strength.

Lilwen sucked in air, her mouth and throat dry, the searing air burning and starving her lungs.

The ship lurched. Sawyer looked up, met her gaze. Amazement swiftly followed by fury kindled in his eyes as he threw down the shovel and took three great strides toward her. He flung moisture from his face with the back of a furious hand.

"Get out," he roared through the ship's wild keening.

His body shouted something different. His hard urgent form pressed her body to his own, grinding her to him. Her dress dampened from his sweat. She smelt his sooty, sweat-sweet, effort-laden skin. The heat from the furnaces pounded her face and exposed skin. The hot air shriveled and seared her lungs. His skin was puckered with small scores, and he had yellow burn blisters on the back of his hands.

"Come with me," she said. "Come now."

Sawyer staggered with more than the ship's

movement. He was spent, his eyes smeared with coal dust and dark with fatigue. As she held him, his body began to shake.

"Must…keep…ship moving."

Through the noise, a stoker, also covered in black-smeared muck, yelled, "Have a break, man. Get some water and food into him, miss. I don't know who you are, mate, but thanks. We've just about got through this storm. Now get some tucker into you. Go on, get out of here!"

Sawyer turned as though to resume work.

Lilwen grabbed him. She did the only thing she could think of to stop him, to bring him with her.

There, in the heat-ridden, red flaming half-darkness, full of the smell of fire and metal and work, she pulled his face to hers and kissed him.

His body under her hands was slick and wet, grainy with coal dust. His lips were cracked and dry, so she licked them. He pulsed with muscle under her fingers. He pressed a thick thigh between hers. His hands held her now, urgent, pulling her tight to him as he kissed her in return. She dimly heard catcalls and ribald laughter from the stokers, but she couldn't care. What mattered was that she got him out of there, even for a brief rest.

"Drink. Food," she ordered.

He groaned. Shook his head. His mouth on hers scorched as if he had swallowed the fire and was breathing it back into her. He licked her lips, the moisture a shock in the heated atmosphere, and tangled her tongue with his.

Externally, all was searing, burning heat; inside her mouth and body she burnt too, with the wet molten heat of lava bubbling up in a volcano.

She slid her hands over his slippery, bare torso, the springing hair wiry and damp under her fingertips, his smooth shoulders, his ridged back. More fire ignited inside her, sparks rushing through her core in a spurting, aching sensation. She ground her body onto his, rubbing and demanding with her hands and fingers, lips and tongue. The shape of him, the power, the hard, agile strength of his whole body.

The ship screamed, bucked, and lurched sideways. She flew across the room, toppling over, and suddenly Sawyer was there, his body an iron cage over hers. His face hovered over hers, his eyes dark, his lips parted. Heavy tools bounced and pounded on his back and buttocks. He barely flinched, but instead stared steadily, seriously, into her eyes. His chest pressed against her breasts, but just barely, as he held himself like a shield above her. His arms held taut on either side of her shoulders. His hips, his pelvis, locked tight above hers, close, but not touching. Drops of sweat dripped from him onto her cheeks; a drop landed in her mouth, and she tasted the salty, masculine tang of him.

The ship righted itself. Plowed ahead with a steady chug.

"You all right, miss?" asked the stoker, as they struggled to their feet, Sawyer pulling her up with his sweat-slick but firm hand.

"Yes, yes, I am," she replied, hating the quake in her voice.

She only had a moment.

She had to think of something to get Sawyer out of there, before he chose to be a hero, staying and feeding those hungry engines, harming himself, burning himself in an accident.

His own actions earlier, which now seemed a lifetime ago, gave her the idea.

"Bath," she said into his mouth. "My stateroom."

Sawyer stepped back, scouring her anew with a blazing amber gaze. Then through all the dark smeared dust and sweat, he smirked evilly. He touched her, his hands and fingers promising pleasure with every stroke. Her insides melted.

Sawyer bundled her up like a kitten against his hot slippery skin and took her away, heading back to the upper decks.

Chapter Eight

Sawyer ached in every muscle of his body, but the ache in his male parts as he half carried Lilwen along was an intent raging beast with a single pulsing call.

It was a good thing that the way back to her stateroom was so far, and so strewn with distressed people calling for aid, information, and loved ones. He and Lilwen helped where they could, and it became a long journey up the few levels to the stateroom deck.

Gradually, his rational brain reasserted itself. Yes, there would be a bath, but the bathroom barely accommodated all his body and limbs, let alone hers too.

Reluctantly, he let go of those delicious images which had burnt a hole in his brain with the vividness of his imaginings: of Miss Lilwen Jones clad only in bubbles, emerging…

Stop it. Now. She was a lady, vulnerable and alone, who deserved his respect and protection. And, by hell, he would treat her as she deserved, whether she teased him unknowingly with her innocent, passionate responses or not.

His nostrils flared as he willed away his fancy. Later, he promised himself. Later, with a fully willing and complicit Lilwen, in a room designed for seduction, not with a sweaty stinking beast in a bath the size of a thimble.

Nobility had never felt so painful.

****

Lilwen pushed Sawyer into the bathroom and firmly closed the door, pressing her back and palms against it. Her mind, that generally reliable organ, was exercising the most peculiar somersaults and performing contortions worthy of a traveling music hall.

She wanted nothing more than to open that door again and…check his burns? Ensure he had everything he needed? Bring him some cool water to drink? His fire-bright, sweat-slick muscles played over and over in her brain like a cinema reel about to shoot into flame. His scorching gaze. His tiger-like, athletic motion, his quickness and pace.

So who cared about reputation? Who would know, if she just opened the door, and went in and let events unfold? She was a New Woman, as young as this shiny new century, and a bright fresh future beckoned.

But…what did she know of him, really? She was alone in the world. She must fend for herself, more than ever. She could not let emotion rule her.

Not that she wanted anything more from him than a brief skirmish, a satisfying of her wild attraction, her intense curiosity. *Just once.*

"Lilwen?" His voice, calling soft and intimate from the bathroom door.

Her heart jetted into her throat. Should she…?

"Yes?"

"Why are you still there?"

"Because…" Lilwen swallowed. Courage was her new maxim. Truth demanded more courage than did an easy evasion. And Sawyer deserved her truth.

"Because I am discussing with myself…whether to come in there."

She faced the door, inhaled, and opened it a crack. Took a fascinated peek. Humph. Only misty light and an innocent slice of wall tiles.

She put her mouth to the tiny space. "In that boiler room…all I could see was your extreme beauty, in that intense heat, in that strange reddish light. Your grace and strength as you moved through a nightmare. Your courage."

She took a breath. Listened to the heavy silence in the bathroom. Not a drip of water. Not a splash. Just now, his breath, in long inhales and exhales. "Like a tiger in dappled jungle. Perfect form, perfect muscles, gleaming and glowing with the sweat of your labor. I wanted…"

"Yes?" The growl.

"When you were protecting me, your body crouched above me, I craved…your…"

"Yes?" Louder now. Deeper. Spiced with desire. Tension.

She softened her voice. Almost whispered. This strange intimacy through a part-closed door thrilled her to her toes. The sound of her own voice, telling him things she had never even dreamed of feeling or thinking—every connection with this man stripped her of false layers.

"Sawyer Thane, I don't actually know what I wanted, exactly. But I suspect you know how to show me."

A huge splash resounded, followed by a peculiar noise, as though Sawyer groaned and choked underwater.

Lilwen shot the door open. Her eyes widened; she gulped, her skin scalding pink all over. She shut the door again.

Opened it.

Sawyer met her gaze, held it. He sat up in the small bath, his long bare legs dangling over the side, the black hair curling with water. He leaned back, made a gesture with his hand. Look at me, if you want.

A fierce blush mantled her cheeks, but there was trust between them. She swallowed against the lump in her throat and allowed her eyes to rove over his body: his rugged face, with the blazing amber eyes and slanting cheekbones, blue-black stubble stretching across his jaw. His perfect torso. Elegant legs dangled over the side of the bath, flapping large, shapely feet. The rest of him was submerged in the bath.

Magnificent! A strange hunger caught her.

Holding her gaze, Sawyer rose and stepped out, water sloshing over the tiled floor. His thick manhood bounced with the movement and aimed right at her. Water streamed down its silky length, and it gave a firm pulse under her fascinated gaze. He reached for a towel.

Her throat tightened. Heat licked over her skin. Her heart clanged in her ribs.

Suddenly, she had no idea what to do next.

She fled.

She stood in the stateroom, quivering, a burbling, shocked laugh exploding from her throat. She was filled with elation, shock, desire, fear, she knew not what. She wanted him. She was terrified. Her brain was mush. There was no room for decision. Her hands went to her face, her chest, her thighs.

And then, a knock on the door and the well-loved

tones of Flora MacNeil floated into the stateroom.

Lilwen blinked. She opened the bathroom door a crack, averting her eyes from Sawyer lest she lose all brain function once more. "Stay in there! Flora is here!" she hissed.

"But I'm very hungry and thirsty. And have no clothes except my dirty, smoky traveling clothes, now quite ruined. I shall have to get more from my locker. While wearing a towel."

"Oh no!" Lilwen giggled and then couldn't stop, laughter bubbling from her belly and flowing into salty tears. "Let me get them. But I just have to get Flora somewhere else."

She opened her stateroom door, Flora stepped in, and as they were embracing, she saw Sawyer creep around behind Flora and disappear.

****

The storm settled during the night. Crews were detailed to clean up the mess, soothe distressed passengers, attend to those requiring medical assistance, and generally restore confidence, calm, and order.

Lilwen admired both the crews and passengers. Everyone showed a great deal of fortitude, although the pale-faced, trembling people consuming breakfast the next morning were mere shadows of the ebullient passengers who had embarked the previous evening. Flora and Donald MacNeil ate eggs and toast with their usual stoic composure.

She had weathered more than one kind of storm. She could hardly explain her own behavior, her own shouting desires to herself. They seemed to have vanished along with the man who caused them, and now, as she sipped tea and turned over a piece of marmalade toast, she hardly knew what to think.

An answer presented itself in the shape of Mrs. Dolly Fraser and her husband. Lilwen buzzed with curiosity about the so-called devil-spawned husband, Rory, but saw little to discommode one. A humorous pair of dark, intelligent eyes enlivened a handsome face. He was tall and commanding, full of good cheer, and clearly relished the company of his vivacious and witty wife.

Within a bare few minutes, Dolly and Lilwen had reestablished their previous accord and mutual liking.

She gladly accepted Dolly's renewed offer of hospitality. That removed the twin immediate problems of where to go next and what to do or think about Sawyer Thane, and promised a veritable wilderness blooming with known and new plant species. A haven.

Dolly chattered with excitement, planning all the wonderful things they would enjoy during Lilwen's visit. Walking. Taking tea. A sail around the harbor. A trip on the famous Mt. Lyell railway, a unique system which permitted trains to peg their way up mountains and through the Tasmanian wilderness: a journey not to be missed.

The world settled around Lilwen in a steady fashion once again. This excitement about exploring and new plants was a commonplace emotion, as comforting in its familiarity as the marmalade toast in her hand. She regarded it almost with surprise and took a healthy bite.

She could leave those unaccustomed, passionate, riotous emotions of the storm, which made her feel both full to bursting and hollowed out, wrung out.

New plants. New horizons to explore. New friends.

Little by little, she shaped her future with a careful hand. It was all arranged. All wrapped up in a bow. She just had to inform Mr. Sawyer Thane, if he ever turned up, that she would form her own direction from here.

She would see him back in Melbourne.

****

All Sawyer's experienced and cultivated charm, his effortless gallantry, deserted him the moment he interacted with Miss Lilwen Jones.

She engendered an alarming mix of emotions in him. He yearned to protect and support her…until he saw her in the flesh, and then his brain became possessed with images of taking her, holding her, kissing her with the savagery he generally reserved for hunting illegal poachers. He hungered to show her where her own beautiful, wonderful body could take her, where her passion could take her, together with him. His cock pulsed.

Enough! To business. He would arrange every detail of their expedition before seeing her in person, and then he would be able to remember what he had planned and what he would talk to her about, instead of being stricken with such all-consuming desire that all his sense fled. He would make it all easy for her, to achieve her heart's desire. And then…

Sawyer busied himself, talking with crew, gaining recommendations for accommodations and supplies, sending off wires from the ship's communications room. He had gained himself some credit with the ship's crew. The head stoker had personally gone to the captain to describe Sawyer's help in the crisis. The captain expressed a pleased willingness to assist him with his travel arrangements.

Sawyer strode to the breakfast room, his usual assurance quite restored, when he encountered Miss Lilwen Jones, as though by accident, enjoying her breakfast repast. A rosy blush stained her cheeks as pink as one of her ripe peaches, though her clear gray eyes were as direct and frank as ever. Her bud of a mouth trembled between a smile and a mischievous remark.

She appeared angelic this morning, her lacy black bodice swelling sweetly, narrowing to reveal her slim waist. A long crepe skirt covered her hips and legs. She had dangling pearls in her ears and more pearls around her neck, with a golden locket attached.

Sawyer attempted bravado. "Well, it is all arranged."

Lilwen's fine high forehead creased in a frown. "To what arrangements do you refer, pray?"

"Our travel. We have accommodation in Hobart, supplies from Ferguson's, a small team of handy explorers who can direct our steps. I hope that is to your satisfaction, my lady." He performed his best regal flourish, his attempted stateliness marred somewhat by a wicked grin that refused to be suppressed.

Her mouth did tremble then. Sawyer tore his gaze away from its rich plumpness, remembering the taste of her…to note the glare in those remarkable eyes.

"Why would it be to my satisfaction, if I have not been consulted as to the smallest detail?" Her face flamed, her tone acid.

Sawyer's blood sang in his ears. The hunter in him awoke with a snarl. *Does she wish to escape me again?* The manifold perils of the wilderness flashed in his inflamed brain like comets.

"What do you know of exploring, of travel, of Tasmania, for that matter? Why should you be consulted? This is not some weekend stay in a fashionable resort. You would only find yourself in trouble."

Lilwen pushed out of her chair and stood so that she was close to him, glaring straight at him. Rage radiated from her, making those silver eyes gleam like sun on water, those plump rosebud lips pout and tremble as she formed exactly the correct choice of excoriating words with which to metaphorically lash the skin from his frame.

"Oh, would I? Well, as it happens, I will be visiting Mrs. Fraser in Strahan, in the remote southwest. So you can cancel all these arrangements you have so *kindly* made on my behalf and return to your own project forthwith. Mrs. Fraser will show me how to go on."

Sawyer directed a fulminating glare to the vivacious blonde, who watched them both with great interest.

"You don't know the woman," Sawyer ground out. "Strahan is nowhere. Anything could happen to you—and no doubt will!"

He was shocked at his own rudeness. "I beg your pardon," he said abruptly to the woman. "I am overset." He gave a short formal bow, turned on his heel, and marched away from them.

Sawyer stopped and leaned holding the rail, gulping in salt air. His chest rose and fell as heavy and fast as if he had been stoking the boilers once more. An intense, hot frustration beat in his brain.

His mind busily spun and rejected plans. She could not be left to travel with people she had only just met, to the very ends of civilization. Tasmania was full of hard, desperate men, and especially all along the west and southwest corner. Descendants of convicts and criminals. Wild miners and foresters working in isolated camps for weeks, years at a time. No roads to speak of.

A disgruntled growl rumbled in his chest. He allowed it full voice, releasing it in an agonized, painful howl. He didn't apologize to the passing matron, who reared back in fright then gripped her husband's arm tightly, hurrying them away.

He must find a way to ensure she stayed safe. He *would* find a way.

And as it happened, Strahan perfectly suited his own mission: finding the last wild Tasmanian tiger, the mysterious thylacine.

****

It was for the best, Sawyer going on to Hobart without her. So why did she feel so mutinous? She had escaped the shackles of living with and caring for her father, and she would not abide a new man dominating her life and narrowing her horizons. She could not order Sawyer as she pleased—he was not a meek-willed man. No.

She hardly knew yet what she wanted from her life. She had to find out for herself. And while being with Sawyer felt like being attached to a generator, live-wired and fully awake, existing in showers of sparks, there could be no doubt, if she spent more time with him, she would find herself bent to his will and living a life shaped by him. He was strong, opinionated, and forceful. Also gentle, considerate, and imaginative, she added in a spirit of fairness, but that was neither here nor there.

Where was the man, anyway? They were nearly arrived. People had been shouting about sighting Launceston for an hour: "Land ahoy!"

Lilwen closed her eyes, imagining their kiss goodbye—flaming, passionate, and with Sawyer creating those incredible stabbing sensations of pleasure and wanting within her. She wanted it in private, so she could abandon herself to the extreme pleasure of his lips on hers, playing with her, flicking and flirting with her, one final time. She had been lurking in her stateroom for too long, inventing excuse after flimsy excuse to remain.

She had expected him to find her. To come to her. To press her once more, for everything and more that she would give him. He was a hunter. If he couldn't locate his prey in its lair, it could only mean one thing: he had tired of the chase.

A surge of pride and anger came now. To hell with the man.

She would wait no longer.

Chapter Nine

The boat decks filled with people, all pointing excitedly at the slice of land slowly heaving into view: Launceston, Tasmania's northernmost port. The storm had blown them off-course from their original destination of Hobart, the southern capital city.

Bodies hemmed and pressed against Lilwen as they jostled for a welcome sight of land. She struggled for space amidst all the chattering, excited people. Despite herself, she turned her head, seeking a tall profile, a negligent stance, a loping stride. *Stop it! Where's your pride? Find some backbone, girl.* It was her father's voice in her mind, and it had the desired effect, like a dousing in chilly Bass Strait water.

Dolly's coiffed blonde curls appeared in a magic space within a group of porters, so Lilwen pushed and scrambled her way through the crowd to her side.

"Darling! You found us!" Dolly air-kissed her cheeks and held both her hands as Rory the devil-spawn gave her a grin and a wink. Lilwen smiled at them both, her spirits lifting. Who cared about a dominating adventurer, anyway?

Dolly didn't appear to notice Lilwen's uncharacteristic silence. She chatted gaily about the journey ahead and the fun activities waiting for them in Strahan. She devoted a large part of her conversation to expressing how very delighted she was to have Lilwen coming as a houseguest.

Even Lilwen's dour mood could not withstand such joyous enthusiasm, and she began to smile and talk with genuine interest, looking forward in earnest to her next experiences of a remote destination and a romantic and beautiful wilderness.

She suddenly tuned in fully to Dolly's artless prattle. "And so I said to Rory that it was a good thing he was to have extra male company, as I assured him I would be far too busy to attend to his trivial needs, with all that we have planned. He has his work, naturally, but men do seem to need each other's company and their clubs and whiskey, no?"

A dark suspicion entered Lilwen's breast, but there was little time to enquire further. The ship was pulling into port. The passengers cheered with one rousing voice, with prayers, curses, and grim humor floating on the air like grateful streamers.

With a great crunching and screeching, the ship docked against the Launceston terminal pier. All crew on deck had sprung into action, hurling ropes, tying them to bollards, jumping lithely from deck to pier and back, and shepherding the passengers into more orderly lines and groups, preparatory to disembarkation.

Before too many minutes had elapsed, Lilwen found herself ensconced in a luxurious tearoom in the Mountain Hotel, with a delightful suite reserved for her on the third floor. As she sipped her tea and tried to summon appropriate responses to Dolly's repartee and banter, she squashed down a growing fury.

How dare he importune her so? How dare he stir up thoughts, emotions, and desires shockingly new, profoundly uncomfortable, and most socially unsuitable for a single woman in her twenties? And then, vanish, like a ghost of her fevered imaginings.

She raised her cup to take a sip, and her hand froze midair. Surely he would have come to her, if he could. Terrible imaginings flashed and jumbled in her brain. Had he, like those poor men, been washed overboard, even though the storm had passed by morning?

She shook her head. Nonsense. She merely sought excuses for his execrable behavior. The evidence all pointed to the reprehensible actions of a cad.

So. She was better off without him. She turned her full attention back to Dolly.

Arm in arm, Dolly and Lilwen strolled around Launceston, admiring the impressive new stone buildings. Such solidity, style, and largess had been wrought with money from the Victorian gold rushes and the new riches brought from Tasmanian mining. Lilwen kept her chin up and her eyes straight ahead and cursed the absent Sawyer in her soul.

****

Early the next morning, all was in readiness for an exciting rail journey across wild country all down the west of Tasmania. The traveling party would change rail three times: Launceston to Burnie in the northwest, and then take the new train line from Burnie all the way down the untamed west coast to Zeehan. They would change trains once more at Zeehan, and finally arrive in Strahan in the remote southwest, late in the afternoon.

Rory Fraser was executive director there of the huge railway system which moved all the products of mining out to Tasmanian ports and beyond. “Strahan is the third largest rail center on the island,” Dolly informed Lilwen, with indulgent pride in her voice as she regarded her husband.

The stalwart MacNeils decided they would explore Launceston for several days and then take a steamship back to Melbourne. "Enjoy your adventures, my darling," said Flora MacNeil. "You are well chaperoned by Mrs. Fraser. My wee brither and I are too old to leave our comforts for too long. We will keep an eye on things for ye at home."

The rail journey was pleasant, the regular chugging of the train lulling Lilwen into a torpor. They enjoyed refreshments at the tiny port town of Burnie, prior to relaxing in the most comfortable carriages in the recently opened Burnie to Zeehan line. Lilwen opened her *Women's Sphere* magazine, anticipating stirring suffragette news, but found herself too excited to read.

She pressed her forehead to the cold window. The stunningly beautiful countryside flew past: wild, rich, green, filled with strange trees bearing unfamiliar silhouettes, sculpting the skyline with astonishingly bizarre forms. Her familiar Australian landscape, yet so deeply, so profoundly different in Tasmania.

The mining towns came as something of a shock. "These towns look very bare and rough," she observed to Dolly. "So hard-scraped."

"Like horrid cold sores on the skin of the earth," Dolly answered crisply. "Don't make eye contact with any of the men that board the train." She patted the seat next to her. "Come, sit here next to me, away from the corridor window."

Lilwen peered around Dolly's shoulder. "They do look tough and dirty, and their faces are very hard too, as though their minds are small and greedy." The mining men reeked with a definite whiff of danger and lawlessness, worlds away from mannered Melbourne and Hobart.

She studied her friend Dolly with new eyes, wondering just who her society was and what indignities she might be forced to suffer.

Sudden shouting split the air. The train whistled and braked with screaming steel protesting. Their carriage shook as aftershocks rippled through the train. Lilwen cast a glance out of the window and gasped a petrified breath; the view sheered away in a dramatic fall cascading hundreds of feet below. Mountains and trees in a deep valley marched into a blue distance.

The yelling intensified. Rory Fraser stood up, rooted in his satchel, and produced a revolver, which he calmly began to prime.

"Don't worry, my dear. There are policemen on this train," Dolly had only just enunciated when the door to their carriage slammed open. Four men burst in, black masks covering the lower half of their faces, checked shirts old and worn hanging above dirty, ragged trousers tied up with string. Old cracked boots braced themselves on the floor, against sudden movements of the train. In seconds, they had pistols aimed straight at Rory and Dolly's heads.

"Hand it all over, me lovelies," said the first man.

In her shock, Lilwen had risen, as though to snatch the pistol from the leader's grip.

"No!" she gasped.

Perhaps it was her worry over Sawyer's nonappearance for so many hours, or the shock of all the new experiences; perhaps she had worked so extremely long and hard for everything she owned, that the thought of giving these robbers anything filled her with a blazing fury so intense she wanted to fell them with a touch.

"How dare you!" she yelled. "To deprive a hardworking woman of all she has earned. No! No, I tell you! Go back to your mines and your holes, and chew on worms!"

"Ah, Miss Jones," Rory Fraser said, a nervous quaver hitching his voice. "Best not…"

The leader put his gun alongside Lilwen's jaw. "Oh, feisty! Nice. We'll be taking this one with us. Need a cook, and sumptin else!" All the men laughed like a chorus of croaky, half-sick crows.

"Well, do please laugh, won't you, and share with us your disgusting lack of dental hygiene!" Lilwen ripped out.

Rory was shaking his head, lips pursed, no, no. Dolly stared at her in delight.

Three things happened at once: The leader grabbed Lilwen, she sidestepped and punched him in the jaw so hard his gun went off with an ear-splitting roar, and from the corridor, a lithe dark tigerish shape cannonballed through the carriage. Two robbers were knocked out with heads smashed together by a pair of steely hands. One robber was tripped and kicked hard in the head, and by the time the leader was held tight in a painful headlock, Lilwen held the pistol, pointing it at his face with a steady hand.

"You should listen to the lady," said Sawyer.

****

Lilwen shook with laughter, in a kind of hysterical relief. Tears poured from her eyes. Sawyer sat next to her in the carriage, his arm around her shoulders, holding her while she laughed the fright and shock from her nervous system.

Rory Fraser, revolver in hand, had gone in search of the police purported to be on the train, and Dolly had decided to accompany him, hanging hard to his arm and cleaving her body to his, belying her pretended insouciance.

The robbers were tied up and held in the end of the train carriage, a terrified conductor watching over them, baton held like a threatening cricket bat in his arms.

She hiccupped and stopped laughing abruptly. Sawyer gazed earnestly into her face, studying her reactions. His hand touched her brow, smoothed back the tiny curling hairs there. His lips brushed hers. Warm, intimate.

Lilwen jerked back.

"Interesting way to get to Hobart," she said tartly. She wiped the last frightened tear from her left eye and glared at him.

"I heard society was both fascinating and unusual down this way."

"If you prefer your social interactions violent, with menace and intent to steal. Or kill us with gum disease."

Sawyer let out a shout of laughter.

"If you will persist in making such remarks to men such as those, I think I cannot let you out of my sight, Miss Lilwen Jones. You are lucky you didn't get a bullet through that beautiful skull."

"Which does not address the question of what exactly you are doing here, Mr. Sawyer Thane?"

"Protecting my investment."

Was the man trying to make her furious? If so, it was working. Lilwen bit her lip to suppress an explosion of demented words. She opened her eyes wide and glared at him. "I suggest those fiends were allies of yours to allow you to make a most spectacular entrance."

Still seated, Sawyer gave her a flourishing bow, circling his right hand in the air. His left arm stretched along the top of the seat behind her, his fingertips barely touching the small curls at her hairline. "I am all happiness that my arrival met with your approval." He looked deep into her eyes. Lifted his brows. "But you malign me. Scum like those men will never be on terms with me."

He took her chin gently in his hand. "Lilwen. You punched a man holding a gun. By the merest luck, the bullet fired into the roof. It could have been you. Promise me you will never do anything so foolish again."

"You are inordinately fond of that descriptor for me. A fool I am not, nor never have been."

"Hasty, then. Impetuous. Impulsive. Emotional." Sawyer's voice husked as though sand grains scratched his throat.

She could look at him forever. His solid, reassuring bulk, so close, warmed her. He was so handsome as he remonstrated with her, pleading almost. His wild dark hair curled over his forehead and behind his ears. His dark eyebrows frowned over flashing eyes. His mobile lips, that she had kissed, parted with the intense passion of his words to her. She longed to flatten her fingertips on his cheeks.

To disguise another frightened shiver, she rose and paced the few steps around the carriage. Sawyer leaned back, watching her with steely focus.

She said, “You know I cannot promise any such thing. In fact, you would do better to teach me how to punch effectively, how to shoot, and to find me a pistol from your no-doubt-extensive collection.”

Sawyer snorted in derision but swallowed the noise into a cough when the full force of her outraged stare hit him.

“Why not?” she demanded, hands on hips now, chest jutting forward, chin out. “This seems a wild place. Wild and very, very beautiful.”

He nodded. “Very well. At Strahan, I will give you some lessons. But! On the condition that should you prove a less than apt pupil, there will be no guns—and no punching!”

Lilwen lit up inside. She had never handled a gun and had always wished to be able to defend herself. “A most necessary attribute for a female explorer and plant collector!” she declared.

Sawyer’s eyes narrowed to slits. His lips parted and set themselves again, as though she was a dish he couldn’t wait to consume.

She blinked at him, repressing a smile. “So. You are coming to Strahan then?”

He laughed. “Rory Fraser finds he is in need of cultivated male company. So yes, I am invited and will attend you there.”

“Hateful man, you did it deliberately.”

“Of course I did, Miss Lilwen Jones. We will hunt for the white waratah, the elusive *Agastachys odorata*, together.”

She shot a look at him from the corner of her eyes.

Life had suddenly regained its spice and shine.

****

Sawyer clenched rigid fingers on his thighs as Lilwen bent with customary grace to peer out at the infernal scenery.

He couldn't rip his eyes from her; he could hardly resist grabbing her and hog-tying her to the seat. When she punched that punk! His whole world had frozen in one dreadful moment. Lucky his reflexes were faster than his brain.

"The scenery is so incredibly beautiful, is it not?" she was saying, in a cool, conversational tone, blast her! He could hardly absorb her words. His body was still firing and his heart mashing against his ribs. He snapped his brows into a frown, forcing down the most overpowering urge to smother and protect that had ever cursed him.

She chirruped on. "The wilderness is almost terrifying, and yet it calls to me so strongly, I want to leap from the train and walk into the forest and just walk and walk, imbibing the deep green smell, filling my sight with all the variety of leaf shapes, touching soft new ferns and dainty rainforest moss, walking forever until I am consumed by it."

Like hell! his protective urge shouted.

He managed a grunt in affirmation. Why wasn't she prostrate with shock?

He made an effort. "There is a special magic about Tasmania. An island cut off from everywhere for so long, it has birthed plants and animals which cannot be found anywhere else in the world."

He couldn't keep still any longer: he had to *feel* she was safe. He rose and stood behind her, blocking the doorway. He cleared the thick choking sensation in his throat with a rasping cough. "Many of its inhabitants have turned the freedom of isolation into the reverse of civilization. As you have seen, the worst types of men dwell here. It is both paradise and hell."

She turned to face him, her face all fascinated inquiry. "You have been here before?"

"To several of the mining townships. My family has business interests here. Mortgage defaulters have gifted us mine shares, land reserves, and fishing interests." He hesitated. "It was an interesting exercise for my father and me in collecting those debts."

Her gaze flashed silver hard. "I have little chance then, of defaulting on my own debt, or extending the loan period, if mining trolls and Tasmanian hard men still pay your father."

Sawyer struggled with himself. Not now. "Come with me. We can watch the forest from the observation deck at the end of the train—not, I hasten to add, where our uninvited guests are secured."

She allowed him to guide her through the narrow rocking corridors with his hand in the small of her back, his whole being alert to danger. At the observation platform, Lilwen leaned on the barrier. "I adore these heart-shaped patterns in the wrought iron!"

She might be still afraid. She pressed quite close to him. Not as close as he wanted, however.

The train slowed as it traversed the mountainous country, with sheer drops and steep curves affording views of miles of virgin, untrammeled forest. Colorful flocks of birds launched themselves from the canopies of forest giants. Kangaroos and wallabies jumped away from the train with jerking diagonal movements. Echidnas nosed for ants along the railway tracks, curling themselves in prickled balls as the train rushed noisily by. Her face, so entranced, roused his protective urges as fast as whiplash. He pressed his lips together, swallowing the unwelcome emotion.

"Tell me what you know of the Tasmanian flora." She smiled up at him with a deliciously sweet expression. *She is happy.* Being close to nature made her happy.

"I read about the forests to understand the Tasmanian tiger, its habitat and behavior." He amended his gruff tone and produced a lopsided smile. "I know only a little about this beautiful place."

He racked his memory for the plant information he had gleaned, seeking to know more about the location of Lilwen's white waratah. And, it must be admitted, to impress Miss Lilwen Jones. "There are many endemics, flora which grows only here. There are large tracts in the wild southwest where many plants have not yet even been named. I believe that the alpine plateaus, at this time of year when everything is in flower, are so breathtakingly beautiful that hardened men shed tears and reanimate a belief in an all-powerful Creator."

"I must go there. I must see all these beauties." She spoke with such yearning, such passion and conviction. He wished she would desire him in that way.

She mused, "It is strange. It is amazing how a small turn of fate, a decision here or there, and one's life is suddenly turned over, to experience marvels and to have within one's grasp a future full of exciting possibilities—of which I have never dared dream. If you take the first steps, reach out your hand, it seems the universe arranges things to assist."

She removed her hands from the barrier and stretched her lovely arms in the air. "I cannot wait for

Strahan!"

Sawyer grabbed her hips and finally found a grin. Was Strahan ready for the redoubtable Miss Jones?

Chapter Ten

In all the bustle of arrival, settling, washing, changing, and ordering herself to be Dolly's guest, Lilwen didn't see Sawyer until the tea bell chimed in the early evening.

Dolly and Rory lived in a mansion a short carriage ride halfway up the mountainside overlooking the stunning port of Strahan.

Tea was laid in a sumptuous room in the mansion. Lilwen cast a covetous eye around: rich reds, blues, and greens glowed in tapestry scenes, couches rioted in William Morris florals, and English china gleamed in display cabinets. Her normally impervious heart spiked with envy when she beheld the collection of Art Nouveau pendants by Rene Lalique, displayed in a small glass-topped table, and two stained-glass Tiffany lamps patterned with dragonflies.

How she would adore to possess such a room and such beautiful treasures!

While Lilwen had been coveting the decor, it seemed some of Dolly's guests were likewise eyeing Sawyer with possessive intent.

"Lilwen! Do come and sit down," Dolly called. "You may study my trinkets and fancies whenever you choose. Here! A lovely cup of English tea and some of Mrs. Dicker's scones and tiny cakes. She is my absolutely irreplaceable cook, you know. In fact, Mrs.

Dicker is the reason I married my wild Rory—Mrs. Dicker was his. I had to marry him to gain ascendancy over the woman, as she wouldn't hear of leaving him! Addled in her wits, clearly, but what is a woman to do, if there is no other maker of tiny tea cakes quite so expert in the entire southern hemisphere, and for all I know, in the civilized world?"

Lilwen was laughing long before the end of this speech.

Rory Fraser, clearly accustomed to this type of discourse, merely chuckled and piled his plate with the dainty cakes.

Two other guests smiled in welcome, a couple titled Minnie and Rupert Brigg. Minnie was a blonde in her late twenties, slender to the point of emaciation. Perhaps she had been ill. Her very thin limbs were disposed about her person in gracious attitudes. She was perfectly coiffed and groomed, with subtle makeup which enhanced her fairy-like features.

Minnie exuded a kind of false charm which set Lilwen's teeth on edge. The husband Rupert appeared several decades older than Minnie, short in stature, making up in girth what he lacked in height, liver-spotted across his balding pate, and tending to blot a sweaty brow regularly with a large handkerchief, which he kept in his top pocket for the purpose. Minnie referred to him as "Roo."

Minnie was teasing Rory about the extent of his mining interest, with much casting of glances over a frilly shoulder and artificial tittering. Lilwen cast a look at Dolly: could the woman who curated such a beautiful room be so blind to the strangeness of her friends? Perhaps she herself was just tired and out of sorts, and

Minnie would improve with acquaintance.

The women maintained dutifully polite conversation until Sawyer Thane strode into the room. Lilwen happened to be regarding Minnie at the time of his entrance; she could not miss the flare of interest in her eyes, which widened until they were blue pools fringed with long dark eyelashes. As Sawyer was introduced, Minnie lowered her long lashes and smiled up at him, stretching her wide pink mouth in a curving smile. He bent over her hand, looking more than interested. Perfectly charmed, in fact.

A knife of jealousy sliced through her ribs. She had not seen Sawyer in company. Perhaps he treated all women as he did her: full of gallantry, teasing humor, interest, and—it must be admitted—a very flattering attention.

As the party sipped their teas and nibbled on cakes, each silently testing the atmosphere and assessing their new acquaintance, Lilwen became aware that Minnie was subjecting her to a thoughtful, silent interrogation.

She lifted her brows in inquiry. The woman lowered her lashes to hide their expression, but not before Lilwen caught the flash of malice.

Minnie turned to Dolly and said brightly, with a sideways smile for Sawyer, "And so, darling Dolly, do share your news of the city. Tell me, did you see any of the fearsome New Women on your travels?" She gave a fastidious feminine shudder, while her husband smiled dotingly upon her, and she cast those blue eyes around the group, lingering longest on Sawyer.

"Here in Strahan," she continued, placing a dainty cake on her plate, "we are protected from these terribly modern notions." Minnie tittered. "There are far too many *manly* men around here to need women pretending to be men. I feel sorry for them: who would want such unfeminine women, wearing men's clothing, smoking cigarettes, thinking they know everything, so raucous and graceless. Who would want to marry *them*?"

Lilwen hardly dared to glance at Dolly. Their friendship weighed in the balance.

Sawyer surprised her by joining the conversation. He said to Minnie, "Do you not wish to be able to vote? To engage in employment, in athletic sports, to enjoy the vigor of open debate? To exercise and sharpen your intellectual faculties on our poor male scaffolding?"

Lilwen snorted a laugh. "Because you yourself are such a pushover, Mr. Thane, so prone to negotiation and compromise, so willing to consult the wishes of your female attachments, to acknowledge that they may have thoughts in their heads actually worth hearing?"

Sawyer grinned, with a flash of his dark honey eyes.

Lilwen caught, with some shock, a glance of decided interest from Roo. Minnie also noted her husband's regard, and a tiny frown and mulish tightening of her pretty mouth marred her countenance.

Minnie was clearly the feted reigning beauty of Strahan, seeing any newcomer as a threat and a challenge.

Lilwen wasn't interested; the whole battle for male approval made her feel weary and impatient. However, she wasn't going to sit and calmly take the stings and barbs of Minnie's conversation, either. Or Sawyer's provoking remarks.

Sawyer said, his eyes now lit with a most unholy

amusement, "And you, Miss Jones, do you consider yourself a New Woman? Wanting to vote, and smoke, and wear men's clothing?" The teasing, caressing note was plain in his voice. A traitorous curl of lust and desire snaked within Lilwen's abdomen.

"All of it. Absolutely all of it. The men's clothing, the uglier the better, the working, the voting, and most particularly, the smoking." Sawyer was laughing.

Before she could say more, Minnie interjected in a shrill voice, "Oh, how horrid. But you would *stink*."

Roo began to explain to his wife, a note of strained and embarrassed patience in his voice, "She is joking, I apprehend," just as Lilwen said, "And we must endeavor to smell like flowers for our menfolk, must we not. God forbid we might smell as though we had been walking, or working…" She caught sight of Dolly and stopped, mortified. "Dolly, I do beg your pardon. I don't mean to foster argument and discord in your lovely home."

Another glance at her hostess's face reassured her. It was alive with laughter and enjoyment.

Dolly reached over and patted Lilwen's hand. "You are a tonic, my dear. We need some new ideas here in the wilderness to spark our minds and stimulate our social interactions. Just be yourself. In fact, that is the very benefit of being in the wilderness. There is space here for everybody, of all views, persuasions, and preferences. Not always beneficial, not always socially accepted, but it makes for a fascinating place in which to live."

Her eyes moved to Minnie. "Naturally, in some ways, there is also extreme pressure to be very conservative, to fit a very narrow model of how to go on, in a small society. We retain the ideas which were in currency when we left what we knew of as civilization. We have not the benefit of experiencing the slow growth of ideas, of having the exposure and the time to get our minds used to change. You must accept us all as we are and make allowance."

Dolly sipped her tea. She had everyone's attention, so she added, "We are a small society and must value everyone in it. In the wilderness, we rely on each other in times of trouble. We know our neighbors in a deep way, and we are grateful for every one of them."

Sawyer was grinning at Dolly now. "Masterful!" Lilwen thought he said under his breath. She grinned back at him.

Rory joined the conversation. "There's no debate, is there? Don't know about the New Woman. Reckon they've always been the same, whatever you call them. The sooner you learn to do exactly as they say, the better for all, hey, Rupert?"

Rupert's response was less than enthusiastic. He frowned, lips tightening as he regarded his wife. "Like a pretty, feminine woman, myself," he grunted.

Minnie preened, but Lilwen wondered: did Rupert admire his wife, or keep her in a state of ignorance to better impose his will? Whatever the case, the atmosphere in the room made her appreciate Sawyer's healthy frankness.

Suddenly, she longed to escape both the room and everyone in it. She felt stifled, as though the air was stale. Such small-town attitudes clamped her mind in convict chains.

Her body was accustomed to hard nursery work. Her limbs, aching with the stiff postures of travel, screamed to move and stretch. She longed to breathe the fresh salt air sparkling above the shining blue harbor and calm her restless soul with natural landscapes.

"So is it possible now to venture down to Strahan township, of which I have heard so much from my lovely Dolly? An utterly glorious view beckons from this gorgeous picture window, and I believe I can restrain myself no longer. Surely there is an hour or so left of daylight, with which I can see the town and admire the harbor?"

"Perhaps you would allow me to escort you," said Sawyer, at the same time as Rupert Brigg said, "I'd be delighted," and his wife whined, "Oh dear, Rupert, the mosquitoes."

"Nonsense!" said Dolly. "A marvelous idea! We will all take our guests to view our magnificent harbor as the sun turns it to fire. Strahan is the most beautiful anchorage in the world, and Strahan the most gracious small city."

And with that last remark, Dolly appeared to achieve accord with all her guests, except Lilwen, who was in reality chafing to be alone, striding through a landscape of blues and greens, redolent with the fresh smells of glorious nature and discovering wonders as yet unknown.

Or, at worst, walking in the sole company of either Dolly or Sawyer. Plenty of time yet to spend with each of them. She hoped.

****

Arm in arm, Dolly and Lilwen strolled along the curving harbor frontage, leading the rest of the group. Voices behind them were loudly heaping praise, as though in competition, on the elegance and style of all the new Strahan architecture. The houses and shops were built with the grace and solidity wrought by a rich seam of mining wealth pouring into the town. Lilwen added her words of admiration, sensing that it was important to Dolly.

"I am expecting another guest in coming days." Her companion's voice lilted as she smiled. "My sister."

"Dolly! I must find other accommodation. I do not wish to intrude—"

"You will do no such thing! We have plenty of room, and she is not able to visit for long." Dolly's eyes creased in amusement. "I expect you will like each other a great deal."

"Well, if you are sure. I am enjoying your company and your magnificent hospitality very much."

"And I yours, my dear." Her new friend's words sent a flood of warmth through Lilwen as they matched their strides more closely.

Strahan glowed in the evening light. The coastline curved in a generous arc, embracing a sparkling azure sea, and opening out to the great, wild Southern Ocean. Brick and stone cottages and shops lined the foreshore, with larger residences and cobbled streets nestling back in the foothills. The whole was enclosed in the clasp of jagged mountains clad in the rich greens of virgin Tasmanian forest, all of this sumptuously echoed in shimmering reflections in the bay.

Having traversed the length of the harbor, stopping on the way to admire a fisherman's catch of giant peach-colored lobsters which temporarily distracted even Lilwen from her restlessness, they reached a small dirt path which beckoned up a steep hillside.

It was too much. Lilwen turned to her host. "Dolly, I beseech you. I must explore this enticing path leading to thicker forest just up the hill there. Where does it go? Surely it is safe, for a short while, ten minutes only, to walk here? I am overwhelmed by all this beauty in your gorgeous town. I would adore just a few minutes to take it all, alone. Please don't think me strange or rude!"

Dolly smiled at her. "I know you have a love of plants and nature even greater than my own. But…this is the frontier, my dear. People from all walks of life *literally* wash up here. Lonely men, violent men, with no pretenses to social graces…perhaps take Sawyer with you?"

Lilwen looked over Dolly's shoulder to Sawyer's profile, defined and masculine, outlined with gleaming gold in the evening light. He was smiling at Minnie, leaning forward to her, as Minnie pouted those bow lips and whispered something to him.

But it wasn't a misplaced jealousy that made her spirit rebel. It was the idea that she couldn't even stroll up a beautiful cliff path on the edge of a major settlement, without fearing for her virtue or her person, subject to the ever-present threat of violence from men. The social constraints that demanded a man's constant attendance, just in case.

A pulse of fear jigged in her heart. *The men on the train.* She resolutely squashed down the flare of panic. It would not do.

"No," Lilwen said, her voice a thread in the evening air. "Dolly, say nothing, just turn about, and maybe no one will notice I am missing for a few short moments. Surely I can take a very short walk and scream sufficiently loudly, if required, to summon help from the promenade just there. Come and find me if I am not back within twenty minutes. I beg you."

Dolly pressed her hand and nodded. Chattering gaily, Dolly ushered the group around to return to the Fraser mansion. Lilwen took her chance and vanished with swift, silent feet up the path, ducking behind thick trees and shrubs to begin her ascent out of sight of the others.

The narrow path dripped with moisture, and the multicolored soils gleamed red, black, and ochre. Wild plants spilled and scrambled along each verge: purple flowers of *Dianella* lilies, bright green mosses, and curling baby ferns. A magnificent yellow and red Christmas bells lily blazed out like a beacon. She had only before seen them in Tasmanian botany books. She stretched a hand toward the huge, bright bell flowers, her heart flooding with happiness and gratitude that she was actually here to see such beauty. This mad adventure would be full of marvels!

Sizzling with renewed vigor, Lilwen lengthened her stride and picked up the pace. She loved how her heartbeat accelerated with the exercise, swinging her arms freely and feeling the strength in her legs. She gasped in huge lungsful of brisk, pure mountain air until she felt dizzy and jubilant.

As the path meandered, she caught tantalizing glimpses of the blue ocean winking with diamonds of sunlight far below, and mountain peaks soaring above, clad in wisps of multi-colored cloud floating in the sunset-streaked sky. A great wedge-tailed eagle hovered overhead.

At the summit, Lilwen succumbed to delicious

temptation and lay on the ground, listening to trees growing and the great earth turning. The wildness of her environment was calling to her deepest self.

Her body rushed with blood, waking every vein and artery, every muscle, every soft and secret place. Tears of joy dampened her cheeks. She stopped thinking and permitted herself to just be, in this perfect place, at this perfect moment.

****

At last, she raised her head. She strained her eyes into the gray shadows, which stretched in the twilight and morphed into darkness.

She was alone on a mountain.

Chapter Eleven

Sawyer lurked in the dining room of the Fraser mansion, leaning against the ornate mantelpiece, an untasted whiskey warming in his hand. His fingers tightened around the glass, itching to squeeze the blasted glass until it shattered, dashing the whiskey across the lovely William Morris floral carpet.

The talk flittered over him like dancing butterflies—but engaging him not one whit.

"Where is Miss Lilwen Jones?" he had asked Mrs. Fraser, Dolly, at least fifteen minutes before, and she had given a laughing, evasive answer and began to talk of something else.

The wife of Rupert Brigg fluttered over. Again. Brigg, the head of the Oceana Silver mine in nearby Zeehan, seemed a decent enough fellow, becoming animated and informative when discussing his mining or the markets for silver. Sawyer seemed to be ending up talking to the wife more often than the man. He steeled himself to be courteous. Again.

"Such a brooding presence, Mr. Thane. Too reminiscent of one of my literary heroes, Lord Byron."

Sawyer's attention caught. The woman may not be as silly as he had thought. He must not be so quick to judge. "Oh? You read the classics?"

The woman tittered and preened herself at him, fixing him with those protuberant pale blue eyes. "Oh!

Well, that is…who has time for such things?"

He made an effort. "Mining then? Do you share your husband's interests, Mrs. Brigg?"

Minnie pouted prettily. "Roo prefers a restful home, an escape from always talking of business." She blinked up at Sawyer and her mouth curved. "He likes me pretty and womanly."

A suffocating sensation of boredom immediately began to creep over him. He was hopeless at these drawing room exchanges, able to sustain such shallow interactions for mere minutes rather than hours. One person, however, could keep him in evening dress, observing a semblance of social niceties, but where was the infuriating woman? His instincts, which had saved him again and again in the wilds of Africa and Asia, informed him that she was up to something.

"…?" The blue eyes had a hint of steel now. If steel could be petulant.

"I beg your pardon, Mrs. Brigg?"

"Minnie, please." She placed a small hand on his arm. Sawyer tensed, trying desperately not to rudely shrug it off. The sensation made his flesh crawl.

The woman rubbed his bicep slightly. Blinked up at him from under her lashes. Sawyer clenched his jaw. The woman's wide mouth parted, the tip of a pink tongue licking her lower lip.

Sawyer looked up, his gaze tracking across the room, seeking some male help. Rupert Brigg watched them, a hurt, lost look engraved on his saggy face. As Sawyer met his gaze, Brigg glanced away. A prickle of anger surged. But it was no business of his. Hard to judge other people's relationships from the outside—nor did he wish to.

Rory Fraser was oblivious to personal byplay as usual, his dominant, sunny, and simple personality engaging in swapping a quiet joke with his wife, who was the exact opposite; she saw everything.

Sawyer turned and kicked the hearth savagely. Give him tigers or panthers any day. Nature had rules: eat or be eaten. Survive or die. It all seemed so much simpler than a typical drawing room. In nature, survival rested on knowing a great deal about his environment, about his prey, and about those hunting him. He kept the odds in his favor by preparation, maintaining excellent reflexes, whipcord muscles, and the peak of physical fitness. Listening to one's gut instincts could mean life over death.

Right now, his instincts screamed at him.

Find Lilwen. Fresh, and natural, and courageous, and pig-headed, and impulsive, and she had probably trusted someone else she shouldn't, or done something naive and totally dangerous.

"Excuse me," he said to Mrs. Brigg, handing her the whiskey glass. She flashed him a look full of disappointed spite, looked dismally at the glass, and then tipped the contents down her throat in one swallow.

He was already barreling out of the door.

****

The day was folding into night's embrace as Lilwen racewalked back down the path. Shadows assumed mysterious shapes, of men and monsters, only resolving themselves into shrubs or rocks as she halted, cautiously edged past, and then walked fast again.

Fear elevated her heart rate now, but her mood still tingled with the radiant joy she had experienced alone in wild nature. The feeling was a secret to hug within, a tiny treasure to keep her firm of purpose, fired up to fight for the life she wanted.

A figure flashed in her mind: Sawyer. What to do? No time now to think about it. Maybe she would come back tomorrow and really sort through all the confusing things in her heart and mind. Make some sort of final decision, instead of allowing herself to rock from emotion to emotion, being led by her feelings, instead of her brain and will.

She stopped abruptly, fright zinging through her like sherbet fizz when she saw the blocky shape of a man striding upward.

"Lilwen." As though her thought had called him, Sawyer emerged from the shadows. Relief flooded her. She halted and smiled at him.

Perhaps it was the steep climb which rendered his cheeks rosy and his eyes spitting fire. "You are unhurt?" His voice rasped with tension and anger, although the tone strove to be pleasant.

"Unmolested, not kidnapped, as you see, despite Dolly's dire warnings." She spoke lightly, her heart still singing with awe, and yes, it must be admitted, with the sight of Sawyer and his vital male presence here in this half-dark wonderland. Her heart did a somersault. No need for that, she remonstrated with it, but it didn't seem to be listening.

If she could have wished for something more, it was for Sawyer to share the moment, now she had had her fill of solitude. Sawyer, with his love for nature, his courage, and frankness.

"It's not a joke," he said. "This is a frontier. Full of men of the most dangerous kind. Lonely men, rough, uncivilized, brutal men. You saw them on the train."

Sawyer came close to her. His body warmed her, enveloped her in the clean sweat scent of his fast walk uphill. In the half dark, he came alive, like a panther, defined by shadow, a creature of dark spaces and the outside. He simmered with fury and wanting. Not touching her. Not yet.

She strained toward him. His Sawyer-ness was a perfect complement to wild nature and the darkness, in accord with her exultant mood. "I felt like Eve, in the First Garden."

He made a noise in his throat, like a groan. He put out his hands to her, laid them gently on her upper arms, her shoulders, lightly squeezing the place where her neck met her shoulders. Thrills spiked through her.

"I lay on the ground and embraced the earth. I was so happy to finally be outside and alone."

Sawyer nodded in the dark. She had known he would understand. Something visceral hummed between them, like their bodies and secret selves already knew and loved each other, but their minds could not catch up.

"I am fanciful tonight, sir," she said.

"Lilwen." Her name was the shape of wanting in his mouth. The sound of need.

She put her hands on the warm, hard muscles of his arms. "Our bodies understand something our minds struggle to catch. As though..." She hesitated, but the mood of the evening bespelled her. He had somehow known to come to her in this perfect moment, and she had to honor that with truth. "As though we...belong together..."

Sawyer looked shocked in the dark, and then a tide

of savage joy suffused his expression.

She put out a hand, palm up. *Stop!*

"I'm sorry, that was very wild," she said. "And don't mistake me. I'm just trying to think things through. I had such an intense experience this evening, filled with wonder. Oh, that all sounds so mad!"

"Lilwen," he said again, and this time his voice shook with a kind of anguish, like he was in emotional pain. "Can we go back up there? Show me what you saw?"

"I think it will all be different now. It was just me, and the landscape, and beauty." She paused. "You know, you are the only possible person on earth I could have expressed any of this to."

Sawyer finally found his voice. "I am honored to be of service." His sardonic tone was back.

"Please, pay me no heed. Tomorrow, my mind will catch up with me and tell me off for being an unguarded little twit. We had better go back. At least I had better. You, a man, can naturally please yourself. Dolly will probably be frantic. I have been away much too long."

"Yes." Sawyer put his arm around her. "Let me guide you."

Lilwen shrugged him off. "I'm fine. I have very good eyes and can see in this twilight perfectly well. But I would be very glad if you would stay close. I must admit I was beginning to be a little unnerved, returning by myself with the dark closing in."

"You know," he said conversationally, as they strolled, squeezing awkwardly together on the narrow path, ducking low branches and shrubs on either side, "Someone else rubbed my biceps tonight and curled her little hand around my triceps, as you were before."

Lilwen stopped, and Sawyer bumped into her, grabbing her to stop himself from falling and tugging her with him. He put his lips next to her ear, her back to him, within his arms. "It was horrible. It made me make up my mind to find you. I simply couldn't wait there, being polite and stewing, any longer."

"Should you be boasting of your conquests, sir? I thought you a gentleman."

"Merely a very thin veneer, believe me. I am closer to a savage beast. Most particularly at this moment."

Sawyer's words, his fluttering breath on the delicate skin behind her ear, thrilled Lilwen to the core. Her legs trembled and her skin skipped, sensitive to his every touch.

She sank into his strength. "I know you are a beast. A nature lover, a wild person. Just like I am." She blinked, shocked at herself. But he was so easy to talk to. He understood her. And yet—there were so many things to consider.

She turned within his arms. "Sawyer Thane, I am so very confused about you. I need to think, and then we must talk."

Sawyer replied, in a cautious, horrified tone, "Talk?"

He walked in silence for several paces, and then said, with the air of someone bestowing a gift, "I am decided. You will have your time to think. Rupert Brigg tonight told me of a man at his silver mine who is a hunter. He has heard of a sighting of the Tasmanian tiger, a wild one. In a few days, I go with him to seek it."

A sharp tear ripped in her chest, as though her

rapidly beating heart had divided in two. She imagined herself here in Strahan without him, and her stomach knotted. She had wanted time to sort her feelings and desires. So why did everything within her rebel at the notion of him leaving? She had imagined him waiting somehow just in the background, ready to be there as soon as she wanted him.

This was a clarion example of how Sawyer muddied her thinking and compromised her bid for independence and freedom. How could she be a whole, developed woman, with her mental architecture collapsing at the very thought of him leaving?

She turned and led the way back to Dolly's house, talking of inconsequential things, while her emotions churned and her mind shied away from thoughts and plans, for this night, at least.

****

Lilwen slept restlessly all night, images of glorious nature superseded by dark dreams of being alone in a strange closeted society, hemming her in until she clawed to escape. She awoke with a start in pitch darkness, her heart hammering and sweat covering her body, thoughts churning. Sawyer was right. She knew nothing of these people. For that matter, very little of Sawyer himself. What on earth was she doing here?

There had been no way she could have remained working diligently at her nursery—her father's debts were too deep to steadily work one's way out of the morass. No, there had to be a magnificent coup, a do-or-die effort. It wasn't only for herself; the MacNeils relied on her to keep them in work, and now Ayla McFee and her daughter depended on her too. Flora had written that they had taken to the nursery trade wonderfully well and that Ayla had even laughed on several occasions.

The thought calmed her. Fresh determination to pursue her quest grew like a solid core within her.

A riot of bird calls heralded the morning, with bands of light slowly creeping under and around the thick bedroom drapes. Lilwen lay for some moments, enjoying the birdsong, the warmth and comfort, reveling in the beauty of Dolly's furnishings as they emerged in the half-light.

Another Art Nouveau Tiffany lamp adorned the small writing desk, the early morning light eliciting glowing color through its stained-glass peony rose pattern. A small loveseat couch was upholstered in William Morris's strawberry-thief design. A stained-glass bay window had curvilinear peony roses over a deep window seat.

Lilwen wiggled her toes in the warmth of the bed.

Finally, she got up, the chill Tasmanian air enlivening her cheeks, fingers, and toes. She had a quick wash in the flower-patterned jug and dish, dressed in a fresh morning gown of dark gray with sheer white linen collar and cuffs, and went to find the breakfast room.

The smell of lamb chops, kidneys, toast, and coffee led her to a tiny, attractive room set with small tables covered with white lace cloths, English breakfast china, and heavy silver cutlery. Pretty floral-patterned curtains were held back with gold-tasseled ties, to permit bright golden streams of morning sun to fill the room with cheer.

Lilwen checked on the threshold.

Sawyer was before her, seated at a table nearest the

window, a dainty floral coffee cup resembling a child's toy in his large brown hand. He halted in the middle of raising it to his lips. As he surveyed her, a spear of sunshine called golden lights from his dark tawny hair. A large plate of toast, eggs, kidneys, bacon, and spinach was almost demolished.

Sawyer rose. "May I help you to coffee, eggs, toast?"

She was starving! "Yes, all of it! But do we have to abide by these old conventions, that the gentlemen wait on the ladies at breakfast? Please, sir, finish your own repast, and I shall collect my own."

Sawyer smiled. "It is a pleasure to do you any service, I assure you."

Lilwen regarded him as he carefully arranged a delicious breakfast on her plate. Something fluttered in her stomach, extra to her hunger. He was gorgeous. His movements were so fluid and athletic, his muscled buttocks tensing and firming as he bent and moved, his long, strong legs in their moleskins, the strength of his upright back. He placed her plate at his own table and smiled at her in invitation.

She swallowed. He must have seen the interest, nay, lust in her eyes. She knew that he had when he met her gaze, his wicked smile appearing, heat flooding his lean cheeks. Lilwen studied her plate. His stare burnt the top of her head. She began to cut up her bacon and eggs, speared a small amount into her mouth.

Sawyer said, "Someone may come in at any minute. We must discuss our arrangements."

She jerked her gaze upward. His tone simmered with suppressed anger. Clanged with resolve.

She put down her fork. Better to face down this

tiger than to run. "So you are abandoning me to chase a mirage of a Tasmanian tiger? They have not been sighted in the wild for decades, Dolly informs me. Killed off completely by farmers and hunters. Like you. The last one is a sickly specimen grieving its heart out in the Hobart zoo."

Sawyer showed his teeth in a caustic smile. His eyes flashed fire. "You busily altered our arrangements. I had organized a perfectly fitting, not to mention expert, expedition party which was planned to start from Hobart, with adequate travel gear and knowledgeable guides. But now? I'm not cooling my heels here in Strahan while you sup tea and admire soft furnishings. Indeed, Lilwen, what was I thinking coming here?"

"I'm not here to admire soft furnishings either. Dolly told me that Strahan borders the wilderness, and indeed the town seems barely to have made a dent in the lush virgin forest. I am here to explore too. Find plants. Change my life."

"Make sure you make the best of it. Here, alone, with just-met people you barely know, perhaps you can pick up some dangerous guides who will lead you into the forest and assault you, possibly murder you, and at the very least rob and abandon you."

"It is your own family who drives me to extremes. I must have a coup, a product, a special plant, to make me a small fortune, so I can pay off my heavy debts to your father. To your family. In just three months."

Sawyer rose and strode around the room. "Lilwen. I want you to consider something. An offer."

Lilwen had commenced eating a small amount, but now her fork clattered onto her plate. She rose too, to face him. "No!" she exclaimed. "I cannot, will not marry, until I have some idea of who I am and what I want; what I can achieve. I feel barely formed, a clay model, brimming with possibility, but so far not able to have shaped any kind of future. Who will this woman be, in what will she be clothed, what will her talents make her? And," she added, pitching venom in her tone, feeling the rosy flush staining her cheeks, "not to your family! Marry to expunge my debts! Appalling!"

"Thank you for that polite rejection. Especially when it was not marriage I was proposing."

Embarrassed shock hit her like a slap. Her face burnt red, and guilty dismay squeezed her stomach.

Sawyer clamped his mobile lips tight, creases forming along the sides of his mouth, and a heavy frown descended on a thunderous brow. His eyes blazed dark honey fire.

How totally mortifying! She burst into sudden laughter, tears of mirth streaming down her cheeks. Every time she looked at Sawyer's fury, giggles bubbled up and spilled over unrestrained. She doubled over, hand over her mouth, trying desperately to stop. Like all men, Sawyer clearly hated to be mocked.

"Listen to me!" he hissed. "I will buy your debts, and then I can be free of you."

Lilwen stopped laughing. Rage filled her, consumed her. Pride held her head up.

"Fine! You do not need to buy my debts—I will resolve them myself. However, consider yourself free of me from this very moment! I have no need of a Lothario who thinks me incapable of even filling my own breakfast plate!" Weak, she knew, but it was the only example she could think of at this instant. "Get to your hunting. I will arrange my own plant expedition."

Lilwen clenched her fists in her dress as Sawyer, overcome with rage, banged his way out of the dainty room.

He didn't belong in this homely environment.

But perhaps, neither did she.

So she would get her wish for freedom and independence, after all. Sooner than she bargained for. She deliberately chewed some more bacon, its smoke flavor making her feel nauseous now.

She would show him. Free of her, indeed. She would organize her own expedition this very day. It was time she focused on her task, anyway, instead of dallying and wallowing in male admiration. See where that got her: feeling cleaved in two, and close to tears.

Grow a spine, Clementine, she told herself fiercely.

Time to go and do what you say you want to.

Chapter Twelve

Sawyer flung his way out of Dolly's mansion, marched along the drive, and strode along the harbor promenade. Greetings from fishermen and shopkeepers met curt replies. He had been confined too much indoors lately, subject to the dictates of drawing room manners. It had made him brusque, his natural courtesy deserting him. He nodded a quick apology to a shopkeeper who had leapt back, startled, out of his way. No doubt his expression was thunderous.

He took the hill path where he had found Lilwen—curse the woman!—yesterday evening. The vigorous uphill walk amid lush southern rainforest trees began to wreak its magic. He calmed as he inhaled the cool, sweet, pristine mountain air. The exercise whisked his blood around his body and cleared his head.

Blast the minx for disturbing his peace! It could never work between them.

His own restlessness would ruin it; his own uncertain temper and the compelling urge to travel and explore, to never remain for long in one place, would be the fault line that fractured a domestic peace. He would end by resenting the one who corralled and restricted him with womanly snares of domesticity.

But what a woman she was. An incredible, unique woman, one in a thousand, a million. If ever a woman was designed to be the woman for him…

And he hadn't had a chance to broach his proposal.

A reluctant grin tugged at Sawyer's mouth, and a bark of laughter escaped him, startling a bird on a nearby branch. He thought of her embarrassed laughter after his "proposal." She was right. It had been funny.

Was there any way in this world he could have both Lilwen, that unreachable goddess, and his lifestyle? He shook his head. She would eventually want a stable home and children. A pang smote him at the thought. Pain and desire, both.

He hadn't told her the truth. She would be furious when she found him out. First, he wanted to give her the exhilaration of finding the freedoms she so desperately sought.

Calmer now, he made his way back to Strahan harbor, to ready himself for the hunt: for the famous and elusive Tasmanian tiger. Dangerous, challenging, and enlivening: very much like hunting the affections of the fascinating Miss Lilwen Jones.

****

Lilwen and Dolly strolled along the promenade, arm in arm.

"You are thoughtful, Lilwen?"

"Dolly, I don't know how to *be*. None of the lives of the women I know fit my shape. I'm not domestic, not yet, although I *adore* visiting your beautiful home. Not for me the small social rounds of many women's lives, finding happiness in children, house, and garden." The very thought made Lilwen feel as though her mind was in a vise, squeezed tight, her ankle caught in a trap to hinder flight.

They paused to watch the sun sparkle on the blue water and the white-topped lacy waves rush into shore.

Her spirits lifted. It was impossible to be gloomy in this remote paradise.

Dolly squeezed her hand. “If you take that little path there, you will discover the side entrance to my garden. You will enjoy looking at the plants, and I long to have your opinion of the design. I must go now and oversee Rory’s packing.” She smiled and kissed Lilwen’s cheek. “You know, it is entirely possible you will find your answers here in Tasmania. It does have a special magic in that way.”

Lilwen followed the charming little path up the hill, trying to sort out her turbulent emotions. Sawyer’s words in the breakfast room had been uncomfortably true. She *had* changed all their arrangements. She was stuck in the wilderness with chance-met strangers. What had she done?

How could she tell him that she had been behaving very impulsively since her father died? It was as though her growth had been frozen sometime in her early youth by his strictures and bullying. Now, finally free of the old tyrant, she had begun to grow again—but her behavior more resembled a silly young woman, as though she was trying to find an early youth, which she had lost to hard work and money worries.

Curse Sawyer, with his handsome face and gorgeous body, his deep and lovely voice which never failed to thrill her to her core. Damn his pride and independence and charm! And double damn his proposal, to buy the debt as a gift.

A thought speared her like an arrow point, halting her in her tracks. *Why shouldn’t she take Sawyer up on his offer?* Tantalizing freedom floated before her like a shimmering mirage.

Her pride rose up in a red fury. No, and no again. *Especially* not Sawyer Thane. It would give him too much power over her, just like her father held over her mother. Planning, attention to reality, and hard work had saved her before, and that is what she must rely on once more.

An elaborate Art Nouveau arch marking the garden entrance was covered in a riot of climbing roses, exuding a sweet scent that immediately cheered her. Glad to cease torturing herself with impossible choices, Lilwen stepped through a long vine-covered arbor to find acres of pretty gardens stretching out before her.

Tall, convict-made red-brick walls enclosed kitchen gardens and revealed peeks of fruiting orchards through enticing archways. The pleasure gardens were divided into garden "rooms" in the English way, defined by walls, clipped borders, and changes in level.

All was scented and peaceful. Bees buzzed, the gentle Tasmanian summer sun warmed her face, and a light cool breeze gently rocked myriad blooms bursting in all varieties of form and color from the garden beds.

She wove her way along the gravel path toward red and pink hollyhocks blooming in a far garden. How she loved hollyhocks! She adored their happy faces and fairytale flower spikes reaching for the sun.

Lilwen stopped dead. An older but athletic woman—in trousers!—was tending the plants, pulling small weeds from around their stems.

The woman saw her, straightened up, and smiled. A pair of twinkling hazel eyes enlivened a leathery face creased with laugh wrinkles. She wore an old, but quality-made shirt, leather gardening gloves, worn cotton trousers, and men's work boots. She removed her right-hand glove and stuck out her hand.

"Edna Heathorn. Third generation Tasmanian, landscape designer, gardener."

"Lilwen Jones." They shook, and Lilwen added mischievously, "Nursery owner, plant collector. Aspiring."

"Well met, Miss Jones, nursery owner, plant collector, aspiring." Miss Heathorn took off her man's cotton sun hat and wiped a hand across her brow, smearing a line of dirt across it. Her grin was friendly and sunny. "It's time for me to have a drink. I'd love you to come with me to the potting shed, share a morning refreshment, and tell me all about your interesting life. Please do call me Edna."

Edna Heathorn led the way to a building which seemed to be half submerging itself into the garden and was cool and dark inside. Small leaded windows gave views into a sunken garden with a tiny, very pretty lake.

Edna opened a decorated tin on the mantelpiece of the tiny brick fireplace, delivered several spoonsful of tea into a large brown teapot brightly dressed in a knitted cozy, and grabbed the kettle hissing merrily over the small fire, poured water over the leaves, then carefully turned the teapot several times. She popped the lid on a tin of homemade biscuits and arranged them on dainty floral china plates.

As they ate and drank, Lilwen rhapsodized about the garden, about the rose arbor and the hollyhocks in particular. As she talked, Lilwen found herself staring at the gardener's trousers more and more.

"You know, Edna," she finally burst out, "what you are wearing would be perfect for a rugged plant-collecting expedition. Where do you purchase your trousers, or have them made? Here in Strahan?"

Edna grinned. "I knew you were a brave soul, with a good imagination, as soon as I laid eyes on you." She took a huge bite of her oatmeal biscuit, brushing the crumbs from her shirt.

"Tasmanian society tolerates me and my trousers, now. There is so much space in Tasmania, and so few people. Sometimes society is so very restricting, you can't breathe for your neighbors' condemnation; but other times, once your friends and neighbors get accustomed to something, it just becomes who you are, and they will fight to the death to defend your right to act like it, wear it, be it."

"Oh? Tell me more!"

Edna chuckled. "I was arrested more than once in my youth for wearing trousers. The newspapers called me a 'male impersonator,' and the police charged me with vagrancy. Once I was even charged with lunacy and taken to the asylum in Hobart, but the governor's lady, the redoubtable Harriet Gore Brown, is also a keen gardener, and she became convinced by my submission that male attire freed women, rather than restricted them, that shirt and trousers are far more healthful; indeed, she agreed with my petition that women's dress should 'protect the person, and allow freedom of motion and circulation, and not make the wearer a slave to it.' "

Lilwen could feel her eyes popping. Admiration and delighted kinship with this remarkable woman blossomed within her. Had she found a friend, a true friend of the soul, in this unlikely outpost of the very edges of the civilized world? Dolly made her laugh and filled her envy with all she owned and had created, but she would never *be* her. Not for Lilwen the staid, domestic, rich woman's life. In a flash of insight, Lilwen suddenly understood that marriage to a wealthy man could be as confining as any other.

Edna was saying, "You are too young to remember the famous Ellen Tremayne, who lived as Edward De Lacy Evans, are you not? She even wore a false moustache. She featured in all the papers, in the late 1870s and early '80s. Poor woman was institutionalized for insanity, but even in the Kew asylum in Melbourne town, she refused to get out of bed if they dressed her in women's clothing! She had lived for more than twenty years as a man before she was discovered."

"Astonishing! The poor woman! I have no wish to live as a man, however. I do covet the freedom of movement, the ease, which I can see wearing male attire bequeaths the wearer. If I am to undertake a perilous expedition into the Tasmanian wilds, it seems more than sensible to me."

"Very true, my dear!" Edna's eyes sparkled. "You sound as though you are preparing arguments…for someone in particular?"

Lilwen laughed. "Well, yes, perhaps. But I have a better idea! I do not need a particular overbearing male of the species if I can find assistance elsewhere. Tell me, do you know a sturdy team of men who could guide my plant exploration?"

"But naturally, my dear. Any amount of them! Tasmania breeds hardy exploring types. It is the cultivated ones we lack!" They both laughed.

Edna stretched out an arm and shut one eye, measuring her. "I will kit you out in suitable clothes—I believe we are of a size, and I have a genius sempstress who can make any alterations required."

She flung her arms around the gardener. "How very lucky I am to have found you. Indeed, Tasmania is full of surprises. I have high hopes of more!"

Lilwen and Edna spent a happy hour chatting about plants and gardening. Finally, Edna squinted through the leaded-paned window. "Time I was back to it. Lilwen, are you aware that the famous Burnley Horticultural College in Melbourne is taking women students now? That's what I'd do, if I had your youth and freedom."

Lilwen simmered with incandescent glee. Edna called to the adventurer within, showed her how to be herself, how to carve a life in this world. She hoped they were deep friends already. No matter the age difference: nothing compared to how Edna's ideas and yes, her very life made her heart leap and her brain fizz. A whole new world out there called.

Lilwen said, "Things are changing for women, and I am so excited by all the new ideas. I want to be part of that change. Did you hear about the hospital for women in Melbourne? Dr. Constance Stone had to get her medical degree overseas because they wouldn't accept her in Melbourne, and then she started a little women's hospital in a church hall. Just two years ago, in 1899, the facility opened: a hospital for women by women. The money was raised by collection: every woman in Victoria was asked to donate one shilling! I was so proud to give my shilling. The total amounted to more than three thousand pounds! Can you imagine?"

"We had best ensure you are fitted out for the future, then! Dolly won't mind if I take a little time off this morning. Come, let's go to my cottage, which is very nearby. We will try on shirts and trousers suitable for adventures!"

****

Lilwen couldn't stop giggling. She felt wicked. Her breasts were wrapped in a kind of modified, shortened corset, with just the top pieces covering her breasts, leaving air against her ribs under the cool linen shirt. Stiff bands underneath the corselette gave support, and thick, soft, gathered lace covered her breasts. She had not worn a corset very often since her father died, but she had never donned a *shirt*! There was only semi-transparent lace between her skin and the shirt, giving a sensory rasp of lace on skin with every movement.

Her legs though—the sensation was incredible. She strode around the room in her new trousers, laughing, making poses, flinging herself down in a chair, with legs apart and speaking in a deep voice, only to stride around again and assume a pose against the mantelpiece, one leg cocked and resting behind her on the brickwork.

Edna watched her antics, applauding, a twinkle alight in her hazel eyes and a huge smile on her face.

"How *dare* men deprive us of this particular liberty!" Lilwen exclaimed. "It is so very freeing! I want to stride up hills and sit on the ground, uncaring! I want to shove things in my pockets. But…are trousers hot to wear during summer? And how does one…?" Lilwen made an exaggerated grimace and waved her hand in circles.

"That is the easiest of all. One simply unbuttons the trousers and pushes them down, either sitting on the commode or squatting down in the forest, holding the pants out of the way. Not quite, perhaps, as simple as holding up one's skirts—there is a little *breeze* on one's exposed bare nether region, you understand, but very easy to accommodate one's natural functions, even so."

Lilwen effected a few jumps and twirls. "How to be free, by Lilwen Jones. One day, when I am a famous, intrepid plant collector, admired and feted the world over, I shall pen my small contribution to feminine philosophical musings. And it shall start with trousers! As shall all my adventures!"

"Hear, hear, my dear! I am so glad to be able to assist you in this simple, but important transformative matter."

Lilwen grabbed Edna's hands, and they danced around the room.

Tomorrow, she would meet two brothers, known to Miss Heathorn, to discuss details for her plant-collecting expedition.

And someone, Lilwen thought, *has no need to know* anything*, until it is all arranged.*

Chapter Thirteen

"What in the blazingest of burning *hells* do you think you are doing?"

"I am proceeding toward the house and thence into dinner. Is that so very strange, sir?"

Sawyer's incendiary gaze might incinerate her clothes. He glared, his face a mask of horror, at her shirt. His blazing eyes met her challenging stare, and slowly, as though savoring, as though not missing a single detail, his gaze traversed her shape. He stared at her neck, where her top shirt button was negligently undone, and then slowly ranged down to stare fixedly at her breasts, propped and supported, and yes, possibly boosted, by the modified corselette.

A surge of heat thrummed low in her body. She wriggled to contain it a little. As she moved her chest and swayed her hips, the movement jerked Sawyer's eyes to her hips like a magnet. She saw him swallow a sudden lump in his throat. He coughed out a sharp breath.

"What...have...you...got...on?"

"Trousers. My plant-collection expedition is almost arranged. I shall be wearing these for practicality and comfort."

The hitherto calm, sardonic Sawyer Thane appeared to be about to suffer an apoplexy. His face flushed deep red. His fists clenched. His jaw clenched, and his lips curled back from his teeth in a feral snarl.

Lilwen put a hand on her hip, jutted one hip to the side. “Like them?” she asked, the innocent tone barely hiding her bubbling laughter.

Sawyer coughed and made a choking sound. “*Like* them?” he shouted. She sucked in her cheeks as he visibly tried to calm himself, taking a deep breath, and another. Clenching and unclenching his fists. “Do you want every man in Tasmania following you like a pack of rabid dogs? Have you any *idea*…what you look like…in those *things*?”

“Trousers, Mr. Thane. Whether you or I wear them, they are still called trousers. Would you seriously have me traipsing around the wilderness in skirts? How very romantic of you. But impossible, I am afraid. So, trousers. I am wearing them in, to check for comfort and wearability.”

“Oh, you are, are you?” The deep growl was back. The predatory air. The intense, sizzling focus. Lilwen’s skin shivered. She could feel every breath of air, every touch of fabric, the cool linen of the shirt, the soft clinging fabric of the moleskins.

Sawyer took hold of her arm and shook her, but very gently, restraining his strength. His eyes widened as the closeness permitted him a glimpse down her shirt. He swallowed again and looked up and around, staring blindly at the rose-covered garden wall next to them.

Lilwen had been walking through the garden preparatory to dinner, when she had been intercepted by Sawyer. Now, his attention sharpened, taking in their outdoor surroundings, making a quick reconnaissance of options around him, and he began to pull her with him along a small gravel path into a small, secluded garden house, with open sides, decorative iron lacework ornamenting its roofline, and a long rattan bench positioned so that one could rest and view the delights of the garden.

"Oh!" Lilwen said as Sawyer bundled her inside. She shook herself free and faced him. Ire flamed in her cheeks and her heart pounded uncomfortably in her chest. She took two fast, angry breaths. "What are you about, to be manhandling me so? It is very disrespectful of my person and my wishes, to use your superior strength to compel me to your will."

Sawyer released her as though branded. He shook his head muzzily, paced the few steps from one end to the other of the tiny garden house. "Arrrgh. Sorry. Sorry. You look so…" He sank his hands in the thick, curly, dark brown hair springing from above his temples and visibly pulled it.

Lilwen watched, half amused, half appalled.

Sawyer stopped pacing and looked at her. His eyes were melting, burning amber. His hands, when they took her face, were as gentle as a cloud. "You look so…" His voice hitched and rasped. He cleared his throat and tried again. "You look so…damned *feminine* in those male clothes. The shape of you, the curve of your hips, your buttocks, your legs…" Sawyer slowly, slowly, took his hands from her face and placed them lightly on her ribs, the top ones just under her breasts. His intent gaze locked on hers, he moved his hands deliberately down her sides until they rested on her waist. The warmth of his fingers spread and moved down inch by scalding inch until he cupped her hips. Squeezed.

Lilwen's breath came in short, jerky breaths. His blazing eyes, the wanting expressed in his firm, parted lips, mesmerized her. The heat of his hands on her left trails of fire and sparks on her skin.

His sensitive fingers, his warm hands began their insistent traveling once more, down, around, until they rested just on the swell at the top of her buttocks. Listening to her body's pleading, she moved experimentally within his grasp, setting off tiny rockets of desire shooting through her and eliciting a long moan from Sawyer.

He turned her around so that her back pressed lightly to his chest. Hard planes of muscle, his pounding heart under his white evening shirt, pressed against her. His hands came around again, to stroke down the front of her thighs, and with a sudden movement, he pulled her to him; the long hardness of his member pressed into her buttocks. Lilwen gasped.

"Promise me," Sawyer said huskily, "you will not go anywhere, dressed like that, without me." His deep voice shivered in her ear, sending more shivers down her neck and spine.

"In that case, Sawyer Thane, you will be welded to my side, as I intend to wear these garments for the foreseeable future. Is that indeed your desire?"

He made a muffled groaning sound which sounded a lot like a "Yes."

Lilwen pulled herself free and turned to face him. She wanted this man, she knew that. He was the most handsome beast she had ever seen, with a wildness that echoed her own, called to that part of her, sending her mad with a kind of joy. But! She could never have a man on those terms, where she did his bidding. Not ever, no more. Her father had tried to force her to submission and obedience, and she had done her duty, but somehow along the way she had instead learned pride and a desperate need for independence.

She thought of a flippant answer but decided Sawyer was a quality person, if temporarily deranged by the sight of her in male attire, who deserved the respect of seriousness.

"Sawyer Thane, I must find my own freedoms. I have never had this chance before. I have not elected you my protector, and maybe it is foolish, but I cannot travel with you if you insist on making all the decisions. I must travel and explore as your equal, or not at all."

"Lilwen. Listen to me. I have not told you this—yet—but I have considerable wealth of my own. I will buy your debts from my father. You do not have to reduce yourself to these straits but can return in safety to tend your nursery and your life."

"What?!" She took a long moment to think this through. Her outrage only increased. Her cheeks scalded, her chest heaved; she pressed her lips in a vain effort to hold back the tide of fury. "Be beholden to you, instead of your father? Never, Sawyer Thane! Did you not hear a word I said? How could that make us equal? No! I am more than ever determined to do this my way. The devil take all men!" Lilwen shouted this last, trying to stem the hot, angry tears sprouting from her eyes. She dashed an impatient hand across them, shaking away saltwater, and turned and marched away from the little garden house.

Sawyer came after her, fast. She could hear the gravel crunching under heavy, rapid feet. "Lilwen, wait!" Sawyer shouted after her. "I mean, I will tear your debts up! You will be free!"

His words somehow penetrated the clouds in her mind. She stopped, turned, and glared with all the venom and bitter anger of the captive years with her father.

She hissed, "That would make the debt even worse! Always there, hanging over me, to be repaid in some way, if not in actual money. No, Sawyer Thane. I will see you, before the due date, with the receipts in my hand to pay you in full." She stepped closer and added, her tone dripping with as much poison as she could muster, "So do you please take care you are not eaten by tigers in the meantime. I mean to pay your family back for my father's folly, and you must not deprive me of my determination to do so."

Without another glance back, Lilwen hiked toward the mansion. As soon as she believed Sawyer was no longer on her tail, she stepped sideways into a small, rose-scented alcove, and allowed the tears of shock, confusion, and jangling emotion to pour out unchecked, until shaking and somewhat satiated, she stumbled into the house and sought quieter back staircases to her room. Tonight, she would have her dinner sent up. She could not face her hosts and their friends tonight.

Dolly came up briefly, much later, to check on her, and seemed content with Lilwen's excuse of a small headache brought on by too much excitement.

Dolly had only known her a short time, Lilwen reasoned, so could not know that a headache was as rare for Lilwen as was her earlier complete loss of control.

It would not happen again, she resolved. The sooner she departed on her expedition, the better.

****

Sawyer trembled in every cell of his body. Lilwen in those men's clothes! He was completely undone. Her breasts under that shirt, clad only in foamy lace. Her small, firm waist, swelling into her high, round, muscled hips, which promised athleticism and strength. Sawyer sucked in air.

Her derriere! Round and ripe and both muscular and soft at the same time. He wanted to bite it. Squeeze it hard in his fists until she bucked and squealed.

Never had he wanted a woman more.

That fire between them, that absolute compelling attraction. He had no doubt Lilwen burned with it too. And then they kept coming up against the wall of her will, her determination to be her "own woman." Why did she behave like this, the epitome of pigheaded, when they both knew it could be so good between them?

And how did he manage to keep saying the wrong thing?

He kept trying to second guess what she wanted, so he could lay it out for her, like a gift, an offering, a prayer. Why couldn't she see? Why couldn't she accept what he had to offer? What did he have to do to win her?

Sawyer itched and shifted in his chair all through the seemingly interminable dinner. Conversation buzzed around him like so many summer cicadas, with as little meaning.

All he could think was that Lilwen was absent. He glanced frequently at her empty chair. His mind kept wandering to possible locations where she might be, weaving fantasies and plans: if he just lingered by the lake in the moonlight, she would suddenly appear, or he was wandering in the orchard, and there she was, the moonlight glinting on her midnight hair, as she half lay along a blossom-covered branch. In his imagination, she wore lacy, silky, billowing dresses in both his scenarios. He dutifully corrected his mental image of her until she was smiling, cheekily jutting her hip at him as she had earlier, the trousers defining her slim form.

Sawyer choked on a mouthful—what was he even eating? It resembled some kind of red jelly with cream. He put down the spoon. He hated desserts.

"I beg your pardon?" he said hastily, as Rupert Brigg was clearly repeating himself, addressing Sawyer directly. "A visit to your silver mine at Zeehan? Tomorrow, early? Of course, be delighted, very interesting…"

Dolly smiled at him. "Please do come, Sawyer. Zeehan is known as the 'Silver City of the West'! One of Rory's lovely trains will take us in style, and we will visit the new Gaiety Theatre—it is as grand as a palace!"

Sawyer nodded, helpless before this stream of enthusiastic information. As soon as talk resumed around him again, he returned to his mental images, pleasure and torture both.

Much, much later, after drifting around the ornamental lake several times, wandering in the orchard, and even retracing his steps from earlier today, all with no Lilwen, Sawyer returned to his room. He was cold to his core from the stiff wind blowing all the way from the Antarctic, and chilled too from the self-knowledge that he was behaving like a lovestruck fool.

He was still befuddled when a servant called him the next morning, which was how he came to be part of the party making the trip to the Briggs' silver mine, via carriages and then the train all the way to Zeehan.

The excited traveling group had progressed a considerable way in well-upholstered train carriages, when he realized, with a sinking heart, that the party lacked one sprightly female, in the adorable form of Miss Lilwen Jones. Curse the woman!

If this excursion did not return early tomorrow, he would borrow or buy a horse and gallop back to the mansion.

Sawyer sank back into the carriage squabs, feeling thunderous and as though only murdering some unfortunate person with his bare hands would relieve his feelings. Perhaps he looked it too, for even Minnie Brigg took one look at him and wisely directed her prattle elsewhere.

****

Lilwen clutched the sill of her bedroom window, brisk morning air nipping her curious nose, while below, the silver-mine expedition departed amidst noise and laughter and flurry.

She did feel a little pique, having noticed that the party included one Sawyer Thane. Clearly he did not care at all about their altercation in the garden house. He was fixed on enjoying himself. She wished him all the best. No doubt he would find a more *feminine* woman to amuse him in Zeehan.

She flamed with self-righteousness as she pulled on her trousers and marched out to the garden.

Edna Heathorn's botanic tour guides turned out to be twin brothers about five years older than Lilwen.

Wild, dark curls snaked around alert faces crackling with humor. Both men stood with balanced, athletic postures, which augured well for traipsing through dense forests. Their clean, study work clothes molded to work-hard frames and their boots had shaped to their feet with long wear.

Edna said, “Meet Welcome and Wallace River. They grew up in the wild southwest forests—”

“—With our logger dad and eleven siblings. The old man’s a joker. Named the lot of us for Tassie’s great rivers. Crammed into a two-room loggers’ hut like snakes in a log.” Welcome’s slow drawl curled around Lilwen like gum-scented smoke. His blue eyes shone as he grinned at her. He wore the blue checked shirt.

“Nothing to do but run wild.” Wallace chimed in, echoing the blurry consonants and flat vowels of his brother. “No room indoors for grubby lads.” Green checked shirt.

Welcome quirked his eyebrows at her. “Got a bit of tutoring from Aboriginal mates and the Elders. Our mum made us read and figure, with slap-ready hands! But we learned most of everything from the bush.”

Lilwen shook their hands, blinking and laughing at this onslaught of goodwill. She looked around them, blushed and grimaced.

“Am I to accompany you…alone? Are you coming too, Edna?”

“No, my dear. You’ll be safe with Welcome and Wallace. Nobody knows the forest better.”

Lilwen repressed a pang of unease. Accompany two strange men, even botanic guides, into the wilderness? She stiffened her spine. She was a professional plant hunter now. So be it.

The Rivers had already equipped and prepared for a botanic expedition. They planned to leave on the morrow, after Lilwen had ensured good supplies of foodstuffs, tea, cooked pies, hard bread, vegetables, fruit, and flour were prepared and collected. She packed a shotgun, after Edna taught her how to load and use it.

She also carefully packed her plant presses with lots of newspaper for new pressings, specimen jars, seed containers, notebooks, pens, pencils, and paints. Although she was but an indifferent botanical artist, it was important to capture the precise color of a flower, to be reproduced in later paintings and future catalogues.

Lilwen forgot all else: excitement hummed in her throat. She was going! She would see the true wilderness and discover who knew what wonderful plants!

****

Ouch! Lilwen's behind and inner thighs chafed from hours in the saddle. She swallowed against a dry throat and scrabbled behind for her water flask. Hunger hollowed her ribs and stole energy from her muscles—and yet her mind leapt with ardor and every sense gloried as she absorbed the breathtaking, unique beauty of the lush Tasmanian wilderness.

It was like traveling through a poem, as each emotion, each individual experience, each moment was pure, perfect, and sublime. Tears of wonder and happiness dampened her cheeks.

They were in the true wilderness now. This was dinosaur land: the land that had been part of the ancient Gondwana forests. All around her, ancient, megalith trees towered, creating a green canopy through which filtered golden light made everything magical. Spongy bright green moss grew everywhere. The delicious, softly astringent smell of Huon pines assailed her nostrils. Celery-topped pines cut lobed silhouettes in the sky. Like gold at the end of the rainbow, Lilwen caught orange glints of the spectacular deciduous beech, *Nothofagus gunnii*, showing early color change.

In a few days, they would be on the alpine plateau. And it was there, or in the forests edging the plateau, that Lilwen hoped to find her own holy grail: the white waratah. *Agastachys odorata.*

As they ventured deeper into the forest, the brothers spoke little. Their softer consonants and longer vowels melted into the landscape and became part of the song of nature all around them.

Welcome River stopped to show her a sassafras tree, pointing out the shiny green color and distinctive serrated edges of the leaves. “Sassafras stops bleeding. If you ever hurt yourself in the bush, this grand lady will see you right,” he said. “Wrap it on the wound. Sassafras. Remember.”

“Really?” Her grin almost split her cheeks. How exciting. These men knew plant lore. Forest lore. She could have danced for joy. Their progress slowed somewhat, as Lilwen asked question after question about every plant. They told her all about each one. She took careful note of the native cherry, which resembled a small cypress tree with small, juicy red fruits.

Welcome said, “You can eat this fruit. Nutritious. And the sap is good for snake bite. Smear it on, and the poison won’t spread.”

How Sawyer would have loved this, Lilwen thought and quickly caught herself.

"Does your brother Wallace know forest plants too?"

"Yes, Miss Lily, he knows some bush tucker and bush medicine—but he's a ripper at tracking. I'm a tracker too, though not as good as him."

Wallace sauntered over. "Welcome remembers every flaming thing anyone ever tells him about bush medicine. That's his gift."

Welcome gave his brother an affectionate punch on the shoulder. "You've got a kangaroo loose in the top paddock, mate." But he smiled.

That night, around the campfire, Lilwen scrunched and released her shoulders and raised her arms high to the starry sky as an incredible surge of happiness blasted through her. Embraced by the forest. Safe with the Rivers. On her own right path to liberty.

Outside the circle of light, the night shifted with dark spaces. Eyes caught by the firelight shone golden and disappeared away.

One pair stayed. Crept closer.

A thin, yellow dog crept forward on its belly, its ribs hollow and shadowed in the firelight, pleading golden eyes fixed on hers.

"Come here, sweet thing," she crooned. It crept closer, stopping at the border of flickering firelight.

"That's a wild dog, Miss Lily," said Welcome quietly. "Looks like a dingo."

"Dingo!" breathed Lilwen. She picked up a small piece of leftover kangaroo the men had roasted for dinner. Delicious it had been too. She placed the piece of tender meat on the ground nearby. She sat very still, talking to the dog in a high, soft, singing voice.

The dog crept closer, snatched up the kangaroo,

and wolfed it down.

"It seems very hungry for a wild dog. Are you sure it hasn't been someone's pet?"

"Maybe, miss. Dingoes are good dogs. Intelligent, learn quickly. Very loyal. There are no dingoes in Tasmania. Someone brought this girl from the mainland."

She placed more pieces of the kangaroo on the ground, closer and closer to where she sat. Finally, she was sufficiently close to stretch out a hand, gently touch the dog's matted fur. The dog froze, its quivering frame tensed to run away. Lilwen kept talking in a low voice and stroking it. After a long, long time, the bunched muscles begin to relax.

"It has scars on its ribs, look."

Welcome bent to examine it, but the dog shrank back.

"She doesn't like men. Escaped someone who has been mistreating her, I reckon. She likes you because you are a woman."

Lilwen asked Welcome to bring a dish of water for the dog, which it lapped up thirstily. "Poor thing," she crooned. The dog stared up at her, adoration in its face. Her face split in a grin, mirrored by her guides, when the dog snuggled up next to her and fell into an exhausted sleep.

When Lilwen retired to her tent, she let the dog creep in with her and lie across the entrance. Contentment settled in her belly as she reclined, safe, warm, and thrilled about what tomorrow would bring.

It was the dog who warned them when the wild men came.

Chapter Fourteen

Lilwen sprang awake. The dog was snarling and barking, holding off someone salting the air with a stream of expletives and attempting to get into her tent.

She could smell the man from where she half lay. A funky, deep odor of unwashed clothes, rancid sweat, and alcohol fumes. Not one of her guides.

Things happened all at once. The dog howled out a yelp, snarled and lunged. Sank its teeth into a leg visible in the tent opening. Lilwen leaped up, half crouching in the tent, grabbed the shotgun by her bed, and struggled toward the entrance. A man screeched and swore, and she saw a fist swing out to hit the dog. Lilwen fired into the leg. The man bellowed and half her tent collapsed as a body fell heavily on the canvas.

The dog burst out of the tent, Lilwen following with some difficulty from the half-collapsed tent. The dog stood braced with fangs bared, Lilwen with gun cocked.

Two ragged men were dragging their wounded comrade from the top of her tent. He was alive, holding his leg, which poured blood.

"Bitch!" he shouted when he saw her. She looked around wildly, swinging the gun. Her two guides battled four wild men, with their telltale matted, filthy hair, shredded clothes, and patched boots. No help there.

She stood her ground. “Be off!” she screamed.

One man stepped toward her, and the dog sprang, teeth wrapping his ankle. “Blasted dog!”

Everything unrolled as though in slow motion, her vision unable to take it all in while terror pulsed and sparked in her chest. One of the wild men holding up the wounded man pulled a pistol from his pocket and moved it around to point at the dog. He would shoot the poor thing!

The man shouted, “Fang, let go, you goddamned mangy cur!”

Lilwen stared in disbelief, then yelled in fury. “This is your dog? This dog is totally mistreated! How could you treat an animal like this?”

The man leered, revealing blackened stumps of rotten teeth. A once-red bandana knotted into a dirty cravat flopped around his soiled neck. “This is a wild dog. Dingoes do what they like, answer to no man. But I’ve tamed this one. She knows to obey me, or it will be the worse for her.”

He rubbed his groin, smiling evilly. “It will be mild compared to what I’ll do with you, my lovely. My last bitch just died. I need a replacement.”

Lilwen could feel her eyes bug out as the man began to remove his trousers. The other men were jeering and commenting in thick thieves’ cant. She was grateful she couldn’t understand them, but there was no mistaking their tone.

The dog was slinking and snaking around the men. The man with the red bandana, possibly the leader, if a leader existed in this wild pack of men, snapped his fingers, and the dog crept upon its belly toward him, haunted eyes begging and pleading.

When the man had turned his back on the dog, the dog looked at Lilwen and regarded her for a long moment, as though communicating something, and leapt suddenly onto the man's back, sinking its teeth into the man's neck.

The man screamed in shock and pain, and as his trousers were halfway down, he tripped and fell over. Some of the other men laughed. The one Lilwen had shot still swore and held onto his bleeding leg, cursing his comrades for failing to aid him. Her guides still fought the other wild men, rolling over and over in a cloud of dirt and fists. She could hardly tell who was winning.

The dog leapt off the man and ran to her side. She patted its head, then strode into the center of the clearing, cocked the gun, and held it pointed toward the fallen leader, who froze in the act of repairing his trousers.

"Everybody stop fighting now!" she screamed. "Get lost all of you. You won't find anything you want here! Go back to whatever hellhole you came from."

The leader vaulted to his feet. Three wild men now held one of the Rivers captive. Blue shirt—Welcome. Wallace had vanished. Two other men came and stood next to the leader. Lust, revenge, and greed simmered in their expressions.

I'm done for.

She raised the gun.

The man barked, "Get that shotgun, grab that woman, and take her. We are getting out of here."

"What about him, boss?" grunted one of the men, kicking Welcome, who shifted against the ropes securely binding him to a tree.

The leader hefted his own gun in his hands, looking thoughtfully at the bushman. Welcome stared back with dull eyes.

Lilwen couldn't help it. "No!" she squeaked.

The leader turned his dark eyes on her and grinned. "Come quietly, sweetheart, and he can come too." She stared at Welcome, who shook his head urgently at her, blue eyes wide and alert now.

Lilwen swallowed. What could she do?

"Give up the gun, bitch, or he gets it."

She sucked in air. Could she somehow shoot the leader, trusting the dog to get another man? How many guns did the men have? Could Welcome somehow break free? And where was Wallace?

The leader laughed at her as she weighed the odds. She put up her chin. "Why would I submit myself to you? Your men have already threatened me with harm."

The leader smirked. "Ooh, a fiery one then, is she? And she is one of the quality, lads. Not for your grubby hands. This one is mine, understand? Mine only."

Lilwen stared at his tall, filthy person. He was broad and strong, with long matted dark hair, held back by a band around his head. He wore good quality clothes fashionable a decade or more ago, now tattered and battered almost beyond recognition. Lace edged his shirt cuffs, filthy and frayed, and two gold buttons remained on his waistcoat. Might he have been a gentleman once?

"Hurry up, my lovely. Drop the gun, and he comes. Stay there, resisting, and we kill him, get your gun, and take you anyway."

Lilwen dropped the gun with a thud. Her mind fogged with terror. Her limbs had frozen to the spot.

Two men grabbed her. The dog snarled. A man raised his pistol.

"No!" she screamed. She bent and looked at the dog. "Get lost! Go! Run, now!" She pushed at the dog, who stayed, staring at her with love and loyalty. A rock came from somewhere behind her, hitting the dog, who yelped and ran away. Lilwen whirled. *Welcome.* He nodded.

The leader said, "Bring him too. The bushie. In case the other tries anything. Be handy to have him alive." He smirked at Lilwen. "We were always gonna bring him, love. But I like your guts."

They tied Lilwen's hands together and bundled her onto one of their small, fast mountain ponies, tying her to the saddle, leaving a small amount of movement so she could cling to the horse's mane.

"I can't ride," she said, but the men just laughed more.

They tied Welcome to another horse by a noose around his neck and slapped the horse hard, leaving Welcome to try to run behind the horse as it galloped away. Lilwen watched him stumbling and running, the noose choking him as he tried to get up. Good God. How long could he keep that up?

Panicky chills stabbed through her body. There were no rules out here. These people had a whole different way of living, where only strength was king.

She had to escape, she had to. She would watch for her chance. Wallace was still out there somewhere and the dog.

As she jolted along on the horse, absolutely petrified about her future, a volcano of anger began to broil deep within her.

It warmed her through her cold terror; it kept her brain functioning.

How she hated prisons of any sort. How she detested being constrained against her will. If her father was a tyrant, this leader of the wild men was so much more.

She galloped up to the leader, slipping and swaying on her horse. "Let him ride!" she commanded with everything she had within her. "You'll kill him."

The leader grinned sideways at her. "Why? What do you care? He's just a bushie, isn't he?"

"He is under my protection."

The leader laughed. "Ridiculous! But I like you!" He shouted something behind in thieves' cant. They all slowed the horses, pulled Welcome from where he had fallen, retied his bonds, and sat him on a horse in front of one of the men.

Then, the group picked up the pace, galloping fast and hard through the dense wilderness. Lilwen's mind almost gave up from the terror that possessed her. Only her fury kept her conscious.

The day darkened into evening. Thick rainforest obscured the moon. The men galloped in a long line through hidden pathways, ever inward, ever upward, toward the mountains. Lilwen feared she would never be found again.

Civilization and sanity were far away. She tried not to rehearse in her mind her likely fate, tried not to dwell on unwelcome images of mistreatment, despoilment, imprisonment. Years of being hidden, a captive, slowly degenerating into a wild man's plaything, a slave, glad of scraps of food or kindness. She shuddered. Bitter tears sprang hot to her eyes.

The world was indeed full of strange and wonderful things. But also people so embittered, so hard, so cruel, they were almost a different species. She had no way of navigating these worlds, hitherto unknown and barely imagined.

Sawyer's face and body came into her mind, as it had often since they had parted. How different were the feelings he engendered in her. How very different was the way he treated her. Suddenly, she longed for him with her whole mind and body. "Help me, Sawyer Thane," her mind urged, her spirit throwing itself out into the universe. "If you have ever loved me, help me now. I need you. I need your hunting ability. Don't give up. Find me. I'm here."

A terrible thought smote her. Would Sawyer still want her, after she had been held captive by wild men? Wouldn't he think her despoiled, ruined? She shuddered away from her own imaginings.

She knew the chances of being rescued became more remote as the landscape became ever more wild and uninhabited. She had to save herself. Just like always. She vowed she would escape, somehow, even if she had to walk every long mile back to a town. She must be free. She must.

Or die in the attempt.

****

They had been riding for hours. Lilwen was sore and thirsty, and wavered between an extreme pitch of shattering fear and numb acceptance. Her anger seemed to have died with the miles. All that remained was cold, discomfort, hunger, and thirst.

They galloped now, heading uphill along narrow mountain passes, the horses breathing hard, the men cursing and kicking them to further effort. Even in the dark night, the men never hesitated with their direction on meagre tracks and paths.

Every now and again, Welcome had burst into frenzied song, hallooing a loud, yodeling chorus. She admired his efforts to keep their spirits up—but each time, one of the bandits rode close and cuffed him hard. Now they gagged him. The poor man's head jerked as he sucked in air through his nose and coughed into the gag.

Finally, the leader shouted an order and the group slowed, stopping in a flattened clearing near a large, dark cave in the side of the mountain.

They untied Lilwen, she staggered and fell. She pulled herself up, standing and hopping on legs and feet filled with pins and needles.

"I need to…" she said to the leader. She hated her own subservient tone. *Stop that now. Be proud and hard.* Very difficult when she was held in the sharp jaws of terror. She staggered toward a cluster of thick leafy shrubs. The leader strode with her.

Lilwen stopped. "I need some privacy, just for a few moments."

"No. No privacy."

She had no choice. She walked to the clump of bushes. He stood facing her, watching, as she undid the trousers and bent over as much as she could to obscure his view of her while she made water. Anger and shame burned within her. How many more unexpected, unimagined humiliations would she have to face? And what would she have given for the privacy of skirts now?

She wiped herself with a handful of moss, still very

bent over, then did up her trousers and pulled them back up. At least she would be able to run in them, when she got the chance. She had to run. Or die. She could not stay here at these men's mercy.

The leader dragged her back to the camp and tied her to a nearby tree. Several wild men leered at her body, and a deeper chill went through her. How powerful was the leader? What if his men decided a different fate for her?

She desperately rubbed the bonds up and down the tree, wiggled her wrists to check for room. There was a tiny bit of give. If she could just squeeze her hands into a tiny ball…She carefully kept her face impassive. Yes. The skin of her hands burnt and scraped on the rope, and the small bones in her hand throbbed with pain as they almost dislocated—but she was so close…

Face stiff and blank, she rubbed at her bonds while the men set up a traveling camp and started a campfire.

****

The violence came as suddenly as a thunderstorm.

Three men tugged out pistols. One shot the leader right through the head.

One ran to her and cut through her ties.

A small shape burst out of the shadows behind the tree, leaping onto the man that had hold of her, snarling and growling.

The dog. The poor, faithful dog had somehow followed them all the way.

And now someone was about to shoot it.

Chapter Fifteen

Lilwen threw herself onto the man, pushing them both over as the gunshot rang out in the night air. The dog lunged for the man's throat as he fell to the ground and held him there.

And then, all of a sudden, a great noise of racing hoofbeats echoed through the mountains. The remaining wild men started up in surprise as a figure bolted into the clearing. A man clung to a driving horse's back, gun arm held high, firing bullets high into the air. Four other men followed in rapid succession.

The man wheeled his horse around. The horse reared, hoofs flailing, crushing a running wild man as he tried to run away.

The horse and man were a twinned creature of lethal fury, of athletic grace and power.

In the flickering red and gold firelight, it turned into the enraged form of Sawyer Thane.

****

Wild men ran about in panicked disarray; Sawyer had dismounted and his fists were everywhere, sending men sprawling unconscious into the dirt like ninepins.

One wild man pulled a pistol. Sawyer didn't hesitate and shot him through the heart.

Lilwen held another gun and cleared a space around her and the dog as she ran to untie Welcome. A flying shape got to him before her.

Wallace, tears pouring down his cheeks, hugging Welcome.

Lilwen turned to see where she was needed next. Sawyer waited as a wild man ran toward him, and Lilwen gasped as Sawyer easily picked the man up with sheer brute strength, and casually walked him over to a tree, where he smashed the wild man's head until he fell, unconscious.

Everything stilled. Every wild man was dead or captured.

Across the space of the clearing, in the flickering golden and red light, lit by the full silver moon, Lilwen and Sawyer's eyes met.

Terrible cold shaking began deep in her bones. She gripped her last shreds of courage and clamped it back down.

Right this moment, all she wanted was to devour the sight of Sawyer Thane. Sweating, dirty, clearly having ridden nonstop through the day and night in search of her. His shirt and breeches were soaked in sweat. Mud and leaves adhered to his trousers, wet to the thighs. The tail of his shirt hung loose from under a torn waistcoat. His wild, dark hair curled and stuck up everywhere. Dark stubble lined his jaw, cheeks, and neck. His shadowed eyes now lit with a fierce light that burned her all the way across the clearing.

Something unfurled within her in feminine, lustful greed.

Magnificent! Gorgeous! Every cell in her body shouted. *Mine!*

A blinding realization smote her so hard she staggered, stardust exploding in her vision.

She was safe. And she was free. Both, at once.

At that precise moment, Lilwen finally admitted to herself that she wanted Sawyer Thane. Now and forever.

Her eyes drank him in as he strode across the clearing toward her. He reached her, took her shoulders gently in hands that shook.

“Lilwen. Thank all the gods.” He held her to him, and finally, at last, her shocked tears flowed. Her body went weak. She collapsed into his strong arms. The familiar, male, vital smell of him. His heat. His certainty.

“Did they harm you?” Harsh voice, gritted, strained through agony.

“No. I am completely unharmed. Just terrified. I thought my mind would crack with fear. I have never been so afraid.”

Sawyer held her there as she shook and wept in his arms. She couldn’t hold it in any longer. She was safe, and she was free, so she just cried and cried with enormous gulping, shattering sobs.

He spoke softly to her in soft crooning words, as though she was an injured, terrified leopard cub, and slowly, after an eternity, her sobs quietened and she could almost breathe again.

When she came to herself, Sawyer’s men had taken the last of the wild men away, and Wallace and Welcome had vanished.

They were alone in the wilderness, under the huge night sky studded with heavy stars, surrounded by deep darkness and the silent creatures of the night.

****

She was utterly magnificent.

What a woman in a million!

The way she had freed herself and stood there, gun pointed, arm outstretched, face blazing, as she went to save Welcome. No thought for herself, the mad, impulsive, fiery, beautiful, courageous fool.

He thought he had lost her. A day ago when Wallace River found him…! He was so angry, so afraid, he had nearly shaken Wal half to death, to shake free answers of which the poor man had no knowledge. Poor Wallace had taken it well, worried himself about his brother Welcome.

Wallace had followed after the wild men, hidden in the bush, tracking them and listening for his brother's yodeling song, until the wild men gagged Welcome into silence. Once Wal worked out their direction, he'd ridden hard for Strahan.

And then Wal led the rescue party, tracking the wild men. On the mountain path, consumed with impatient fear, Sawyer had ridden fast the last hour, his instinct compelling him, as if she was calling for him, seeking him, desperate and afraid and alone.

If those bandits had touched a hair! But she was saying no, the leader had protected her until they killed him.

He had come in the nick of time.

His face felt like stone as he held her, his mouth a hard line of determination. His throat choked up and his heart burned for revenge, for satiation, for justice. He would hunt out every last one of them and either destroy them or haul them into police custody.

Wallace had told him they were men who had come to work in the mines, and during the stock market crashes of '93 and the closure of some silver and copper mines, the men were laid off. Some had gone back to wherever they came from; others found work in other mines around Tasmania.

But many had taken to the wilderness, roaming in ungoverned bands, preying on travelers, and raiding remote outposts and farms and businesses on the edges of towns. Sometimes they descended on a rural outpost to drink into the night, carousing, taking whores, or smashing property and attacking women, stealing whatever they could carry away.

They were already hard men, many of the miners, and these, the scum who floated to the top, were the worst. They took to banditry with enthusiasm. Tasmania was still one of the wildest places in Australia. Federation and all it meant had no meaning at all on the wrong end of a loaded gun.

Lilwen still sobbed in his arms. His shirt stuck to his skin, damp with her tears. His muscles cramped after his long, terrifying ride, but he could hold her forever. Her strong, lithe body. The sweet, herby scent of her skin, even here, even after all that had happened. Her beautiful dark hair, tumbling now in midnight waves over her shoulders and chest. Her white, luminous skin, glowing in the moonlight.

Her fierce, courageous heart and quick brain.

He never wanted to let her go.

Be damned to anyone who tried to make him.

****

Lilwen collapsed gratefully into the cozy nest Sawyer made for her from a saddle and blankets. She nodded dumbly, too exhausted to speak, while he assured her he would not be far away.

"Welcome and Wallace River said goodbye. They wanted to persist with your botanical hunt, despite

Welcome's battered body. But he needs to heal, so I sent them home. I assured them you'd be safe in my care."

She rested in a passive heap, hollowed out from crying, the skin on her face tight and stinging from long exposure to salt tears. Her limbs flopped weak and rubbery as though they would never function properly again, except in jerky marionette movements, driven by a different brain from hers. Her stomach clenched with emptiness. She had no fight left in her.

In a moment, Sawyer returned. He dabbed a cool cloth against her swollen, burning eyes. How very good that felt. Next, he trickled a cool waterskin against her lips, relieving sore dry cracks wrought by exposure and hours of fear.

"Try to rest. Close your eyes. Here, pat this infernal hound who won't leave you alone."

Lilwen opened her eyes. "The dog! What a little hero! She wouldn't leave me. She even pretended to do what the bandit said, so she could trick him and jump on his back. Such a ball of courage! Here, sweet dog, come here."

Sawyer's gaze drilled her cheek.

"Yes?" It wasn't quite her old sparky tone, but she was getting there.

"I'm not sure that's a dog."

"Of course she's a dog! A beautiful, heroic, loyal dog. Oh well, maybe a dingo, Welcome said."

Sawyer laughed. "A wild dog. That's fine then."

She sat bolt upright. "Have you got any food? The poor thing is half starved. We must reward her for her valiant efforts."

"Not to mention a certain intrepid, or perhaps

foolhardy, plant collector, who no doubt is also starving."

Lilwen jumped up. "Now we come to it! Why don't you yell at me now I am quite recovered, and tell me how very foolish I was to venture *without you* into the wilderness, with only two *very experienced* bush guides who know the area like they know their own hands!" She put her hands on her hips in her characteristic fighting pose, but her legs wobbled, and a fresh sheen of tears streaked her hands as she wiped them across her face. She sat again, covered her face, and began to weep anew.

"Lilwen, Lilwen Jones. Oh, my darling. Please don't cry. Can you stay with the dratted dingo for a few minutes while I trap us something to eat? You will feel better directly if you can have some hot food and a hot drink." Strong, gentle hands smoothed her hair, touched her hands. That touch…from the first moment he had held her at the Melbourne Zoo, it was as though her body knew his, recognized it, thrilled to his touch, as though they had been lovers together in other lives, other times. She shook her head. She was being fanciful. Must be shock. Probably starvation.

Lilwen clung to Sawyer in a shamefully weak manner, but fright and fear still trembled in her bones and muscles—perhaps forever. Finally, she released her hold. She gulped, sniffed, and said, "And you too, Sawyer Thane, hero of the hour, are probably ravenous. Please, do catch something if you can. Did these disgusting bandits not carry any food?"

"Not anything we would want to eat. Provenance unknown. Tasmania has a terrible history of foodstuffs which no civilized man would want to eat."

"What can you mean?"

"Some of the brutally mistreated convicts in the very old days escaped and stayed alive by eating their fellow plotters."

"You are suggesting…these men…?" Lilwen's voice shrilled in horror.

"No, not really." Sawyer laughed. "Just trying to distract you. But I will provide your food. Scream loudly if you need me. I will return as soon as I can."

"So forceful and manly," murmured Lilwen as she watched his dear silhouette recede into the blackness.

A strong pulse of fear nearly knocked her sideways. She darted her head around, anxious to penetrate the deep shadows. Shrubs and trees distorted and moved in strange shifting shapes, as though giants and monsters had awakened and were taking steps closer every time she wasn't looking.

Yellow eyes peered at her from the black depths, shining in the reflected firelight. Her dingo kept up a faint growling, just under the level of sound, which seemed effective at keeping them at bay. Unnamed things rustled in the forest litter. Birds called in the treetops.

She called the dingo close to her, holding the thin, shivering thing against her side until it relaxed. "Not long, little hero," Lilwen whispered, "and you shall enjoy the victor's feast." She pondered the right name for her new pet. She would not abandon her brave friend, dingo or no.

"Valery, for valor?" she said, pulling its soft ears. "Liberty, for my favorite obsession? Libby?" She patted the dog some more as it panted, red tongue lolling from its mouth. "Hero. I think that will do." The dog looked up at her with adoring eyes.

"Yes, then, you like Hero, don't you?" She cuddled the dog to her side.

Together, they waited for Sawyer to return, Lilwen comforted by the dingo's nearness.

****

For once, Lilwen wallowed in Sawyer's cosseting and protecting as she sat snuggled in the blanket and saddle, propped against the side of a large fallen tree. Sawyer had returned with a possum dangling from one hand and a wallaby borne over his shoulder. He skinned and gutted the game with his hunting knife, wrapped the meat in soft pale bark tied with vines, and arranged the parcels on coals raked from the fire with a sturdy stick.

He chopped handfuls of small round plant roots, rubbed them with fat from the wallaby skin, and placed them on hot flat rocks on the edge of the campfire to roast. He added handfuls of thick green leaves, which he said was a type of settlers' spinach, into more wrapped parcels. He had refilled the waterbags from a nearby stream, and he handed her one with such a caressing smile that tingles erupted over her skin.

The enticing wafts of cooking food was making her salivate—but that wasn't the only cause. Lilwen luxuriated in gloating over Sawyer's elegant form, admiring his muscles working, bulging in his shirt and moleskins. He was so quick and graceful and sturdy, with a lovely economy of movement as he wrestled with the game, bending and stretching while he prepared the meal for her.

He threw the dog some slices of bleeding meat. Hungry as Hero was, she turned an enquiring, starving face to Lilwen's, as though seeking permission.

"Yes! Yes, of course! That is for you," she said, marveling at the dog's loyalty and intelligence. The dog leapt forward to wolf down the meat. Hero edged closer to Sawyer now, watching him alertly, hoping for more. Sawyer threw her some more offcuts. He found a metal dish in the wild men's campsite and filled it with water for the dog, who lapped it thirstily.

Before long, the smell of the cooking meat made Lilwen's stomach rumble. The dog lay with ears pricked and eyes searching the darkness, but Sawyer seemed as laconic as ever. He retrieved a billy and metal cups from his saddlebag, picked the tips from a nearby *Melaleuca* shrub, and made her a delicious cup of hot fragrant tea with a fresh bush tang. The hot liquid continued to thaw out muscles which had been clamped in both exhaustion and fear. Everything—mind, body, emotion—slowly began to relax and soften into the beautiful Tasmanian night.

Sawyer cut off succulent sections of the cooked meat, assembled the bush vegetables, and served it all to her with a flourish on plates made of more of the soft bark.

"If one is ever going to be lost in the bush, make sure it is with a hunter," she said.

"Even better, if you must insist on getting lost in the bush as a regular practice, you make sure that it is only with *this* hunter."

"Oh, I don't know." Lilwen pretended to consider. "I haven't tried any other sort of hunters."

Sawyer answered with a growl, quickly repeated by Hero. She laughed.

"Did that damn dog just snarl at me?"

"Well, you did growl at me."

"I did nothing of the sort." Sawyer looked at the dog, who peeled a top lip back in the beginnings of a snarl, which made Lilwen laugh even more.

"Now, Hero, no ugly faces," she said in a singsong tone. Sawyer scrunched his face in exaggerated disgust. "Sawyer is caring for us at present. We are not fighting. Yet."

The astonished expression on Sawyer's face when the dog obediently stopped snarling and lay down next to her was priceless.

"Would you like to wash?" Sawyer asked. "I can show you where the stream forms a sweet pool near a gentle, grassed slope. I warn you, Tasmanian streams are utterly freezing! The moon is almost full. I can wait nearby if you are afraid."

"I would love to wash! And please do come and wait nearby. I am…I must admit to…feeling quite afraid and nervous."

"Don't be ashamed. It is natural to be shaken by your horrible experience. You are a woman in a million: most would be prostrate with nervous shock, and yet you are already bandying words with me. I am myself still very shocked. Lilwen…I nearly lost you…"

She went to him and ran her hands over his face, his shoulders, his chest. He bent to her and clasped her to him. "Wash," she said into his chest, the words muffled by his waistcoat and shirt. She needed to clean off every touch of those filthy men, every terror seared into her skin.

Sawyer grabbed a couple of warm, clean blankets from his saddle roll and led her down to a stream running through the forest. A pool had been formed by a natural billabong in a curve of the stream. It was as round and perfect as a bubble, edged with lacy ferns trailing their tips in the reflections, the water glinting silver in the bright moonlight. Insects buzzed on the surface, and small rings formed and faded in the water as fish jumped and snapped, rippling the reflected moon into pale golden circles.

They stood in the silver-tinged light, facing each other.

Lilwen said, "I am going to take off every stitch of my clothes. You may watch, or not, as you please. But don't leave me."

"Lilwen…" He sucked in a breath, and his chest rose and fell under her hands. "What a woman you are. But I cannot take advantage of your fear. When you choose to show yourself to me—if—I want it to be with full knowledge, with full courage. A gift from strength, from want and need, not from gratitude or fear."

They locked eyes.

"I want you to watch me," she said. "I want your eyes to be the first man's that sees me in my skin, who sees all of me. Then, no matter what happens to me in the future, it was you who saw me first."

Sawyer stuttered, but no discernible words came out, so Lilwen stepped two paces away from him.

Keeping her eyes on his, she began to undress.

Chapter Sixteen

Sawyer's mouth dried. All the blood rushed from his head straight to his groin. His cock hardened. He opened his mouth to argue once more, but only stuttering sounds emerged, so he closed his mouth before she decided he was just a fool and sent him away.

God, Lilwen. He had come so close to losing her. And now she was here, showing herself to him.

He should be a gentleman and turn away. She was distressed. She hardly knew what she was saying. He would be a cad to take advantage of her.

Her eyes were burning his, challenging him, forbidding him to break contact and turn away. She wanted him to see her, she said. Him, to be the first man to see her naked.

All he could do was see her, as she asked, and use every bit of willpower he possessed not to ravish her right here at the edge of the stream.

Sawyer swallowed. His lips dried. Desire rushed around his body like a grass fire in the parched, hot days of February. He clenched his fists. Clenched his jaw. His lips. His stomach muscles. To no avail. Despite himself, an agonized groan escaped him.

Lilwen discarded the coat he had earlier placed on her shoulders. With lithe flexibility, she crossed her arms and peeled off her woolen jumper. She began to unbutton that man-style shirt, which somehow made her look even more feminine, top to bottom, one button at a time. The shirt hung loose. With a wriggle, it too was cast aside. She stood there in a soft white lacy corselette, which just covered her upper torso, leaving her slender waist quite bare above those double be-damned trousers. Her white skin gleamed ivory, and darkness pooled where her belly pitched in to her belly button. Sleek muscles defined her waist, tightening and flexing with every movement, and ran down into her trousers, curving out into rounded hips. Sawyer's hands twitched and clenched. How he would love to hold those shapely, elastic hips and press her body to his.

Her pitch-black hair spiraled down over her shoulders and breasts like curls of night. The smooth, slick skin of her neck, shoulders, and arms glowed ivory and pearl in the moonlight. Through the lace of her corselette, he could see the pale flesh of her breasts, the pink nubs hardened in the cold and pushing against the lace.

Sawyer stretched out a hand. "Lilwen," he whispered.

"Watch," she said. He obeyed, mesmerized, barely holding himself at bay, as her chest rose and fell. With emotion, with desire? Her rounded flesh pressed against the lace cups, filling and stretching them to bursting as she breathed.

His eyes were trapped by her hand, as it slowly moved down her body to the top of her trousers. Her gaze locked on his, her eyes huge dark pools in the moonlight, as she began to undo the trouser buttons. Every male part of Sawyer was aroused, transfixed, on high alert. He could not move away now, could not turn his gaze. All his willpower was on staying still, watching, as she had asked.

The trousers were undone. She pushed them down, stepped out. Underneath, she sported a tiny pair of very lacy pants, very brief, frilled and beribboned on the lace edges. Transparent.

Sawyer's mouth was arid. His heart pounded under his ribs, a pulse beat in his neck and somewhere in his brain. His balls were like rocks.

Lilwen stood there for a long moment in nothing but the lacy corselette and the tiny white transparent bloomers. Quick hands pulled off the corselette and the knickers and dropped them to the ground.

Lilwen stood there, fully naked, nipples pink and erect as she shivered in the cold, clothed only in silver moonlight and sparkling starlight. She let him look at her for long seconds, watching him from under her lashes. Then she turned and ran lightly down to the swimming hole, her slender buttocks bunching and quivering as she moved.

Sawyer stayed, utterly transfixed, as she plunged into the pool. She leapt up with a piercing shriek and shouted curse which made him smile. Giggling, she began slapping her skin warm and jumping in the pool. Her skin blushed pink from the freezing mountain water and flushed pinker on shoulders and hips where she smacked herself. Sawyer marveled at her rosy red cheeks and glowing eyes, the water pouring from her long hair, her shoulders, her white arms and round breasts in silver-rimmed droplets. She was a creature of color in a monochrome landscape, a water goddess, a sprite made of men's fantasies and the ancient joy of elemental beings cavorting in nature.

She dived and rose again; she was an enchanted water nymph, a mermaid, sent to torment him and drive him wild with desire.

She laughed with delight, with the sheer pleasure of swimming in the cool fresh water in the middle of the wilderness. He stared, mesmerized, as she swam and dived, upending that peach-like bottom, and then surfaced again, with toes held just above the surface. He wanted to suck them. She rose up, her arms crossed over her breasts, which somehow was even more enticing, as rounded, nippled skin peeked out through her fingers.

"Don't heroes wash, then?" she called out mockingly.

Sawyer froze, lips parted, for one unbelieving instant, and then with fumbling, hasty fingers, half ripped the clothes from his body. In record time, he stripped completely naked and ran toward the pool. Lilwen rose up out of the water and studied his form. Fair was fair. He halted on the edge of the pool, allowing her greedy, marveling gaze to see all of him.

And then he dived in the water, gasping with the cold of the pool, and the wicked nymph was laughing, swimming away from him, splashing water over him.

He dived, and swam, and took hold of her waist, bringing both their torsos out of the water. For a long, long, moment, he simply stared, glorying in her beauty, her warmth through cold flesh, her gleaming, ivory skin, and then he clutched her to him, embracing her.

His mouth sought hers. First, lips meeting sweetly and then harder, hotter. His tongue darted into her mouth, around her lips, probing and dancing. All was the kiss, intense, deep, and arousing. Her body pressed against his felt chilled where the air kissed her skin, and heating where they rubbed and pressed together, Lilwen moving against him with increasing urgency.

He couldn't bear the agony, sweet as it was, any longer. Sawyer scooped her up and took her to where he had placed the blankets, laid her gently down, and rolled her in the soft wool until she was dry and warm. Her skin glowed pink where he rubbed her with the blanket. He quickly dried himself and lay next to her. She reached for him, and they tangled together in the blankets, kissing and touching, stroking and squeezing, feeling and nuzzling.

She froze in his embrace. "What was *that*?" she whispered.

"What?" he murmured, his hand squeezing a round, plump buttock.

She pushed him away and sat up. "A kind of brown, striped blur. An animal. It stared at me with yellow eyes. Like a small tiger."

Sawyer leapt up, naked as he was, staring around into the bush all around them.

"Describe it again!" he looked down at Lilwen, who stared at him with interest, her gaze traveling down his body to his very erect member, down his legs to his toes, and back up. He gasped out a bark of laughter. "Did you just want me to stop? Did you invent that creature?" He collected himself. "And you are right. What am I doing? Hardly protecting you, keeping you in this chilly air, naked as you are." His throat closed, choking on the word *naked*. "Here." He bent and handed her the trousers and shirt. "Get yourself dressed and warm. We will go back to the fire."

Lilwen looked a protest. He ripped his gaze from

her curves, shapely and tempting under the blanket, and stared up at the night sky. "Quick. Please."

After a drawn-out pause, Lilwen began to dress, her movements rapid. "I did see something. Striped, like a small tiger."

Sawyer was torn. He wanted to rush into the night, find traces of the beast. Could this be his quarry, the fabled Tasmanian tiger? Already thought to be extinct in the wild, with only a few sad specimens dying of grief and loneliness in the Hobart Zoo?

He couldn't leave her. Not after what had happened to her. She would be terrified all over again. And he had promised to safeguard her.

An owl hooted into the night. Sawyer snapped back into himself. He had nearly taken her, ravished her, here in the wilderness, far from civilization. His cock pulsed again at the thought, but he was back—or almost back—in his right mind now. Not now, when she was vulnerable and afraid.

"Come," he said, and he heard the husk of thwarted, controlled desire in his own voice as he spoke. "Let's go back to the fire. You need to get warm."

Lilwen took his proffered arm, and they stumbled and staggered back to the fire as best they could, with arms wound tight around each other.

But Sawyer's mind raced—how soon could he deliver her back to Strahan and safety, and return to track the beast?

****

Sawyer arranged the blanket next to the fire, ensuring Lilwen was well wrapped up and warm, and they lay down together. The huge velvet sky hung heavy with twinkling stars; the Milky Way wound sinuously through the glittering mass, as thick and white as a river of cream studded with silver cake decorations.

The moon floated in the clouds, casting a ghostly light over the camp. The fire had died down. Fantastic shapes danced in the red coals glowing in the heart of the fire.

She couldn't stop touching Sawyer. At the moment, her body rested against his tall, solid shape, protecting her from the cool tickling breeze.

She was so warm, full of food, and content: desire still coursed through her veins, blunted now, a simmer rather than a burn, waiting to flare into incandescence. The peace and beauty of the night, the cessation of fear, and Sawyer's staunch, capable presence gave her a kind of floating happiness.

She was very aware of him. Him as a person: his valor, his fight, his determination. His body, strong and reassuring, keeping her safe. What he had done for her!

His large, gentle hands. His long, athletic legs. The sight of him naked, laughing, and chasing her in the pool. A shot of heat spiked into her core, and her female parts softened and went slick.

His hand moved and curled around her, pulling her closer to him. He too seemed affected by the night, as though they had all the time in the world, could explore every moment, every sensation, every emotion to the fullest.

She wondered if he would begin again to kiss and stroke her, until her mind blurred, her breath hitched in an urgent struggle for air and the fever of desire possessed her once more. She lay in suspenseful anticipation, every cell of her body aware of every atom of his: his limbs, the expressions dancing across his features, every shift of his body and touch of his fingers. Craving his touch. Burning for his attention.

Sawyer spoke, his voice low, the rumbling consonants tracking right through her body and igniting small bursts of desire all through her blood. At first she listened only to the rich sound of his black coffee voice, fascinated by the effect it had on her. Then she quickly tuned into his words.

He murmured, "This feels utterly wonderful. I'm used to nature, camping under huge night skies and traveling through rugged and spectacular scenery. But now, here, with you? This is another layer of extraordinary."

His hand rested on her stomach and then slowly, slowly crept higher to rest just under her right breast. Everything in her screamed for him to move his hand higher, to cup her breast, to tweak and tease her nipple. Did he know the effect he was having on her? He must, the horrid man!

She felt so close to him, here, alone in this perfect moment, in beautiful nature. Content, clean, cared for. Aroused. Protected.

"When you saved me…" It came out much shakier than she had intended.

He heard her fear, still there. "Shhh. You don't have to talk about it yet. Later."

Lilwen reached for his safe strong presence right next to her. "No, I want to tell you." The enormous indigo sky glimmered with the infinite stars. They gave her comfort, made her feel part of a giant plan, connected to an always changing and yet constant world of natural beauty.

She swallowed. “When you burst into the scene, on your horse, gun blazing, everything in me thrilled and rejoiced. When you rescued me, I felt so free. And so safe. Both. I didn’t think they went together. I always thought it was one or the other. Freedom *or* safety. That you had to choose which path your life would take.”

Sawyer stroked her hair, teased his fingertips around to her neck. It felt wonderful. Tickly and tingly, sending tiny sparks through her body, through her drowsy tranquility.

“You see,” she said, “All my life I have wanted to feel free and never felt so. I want to be free. I *crave* liberty.”

Sawyer’s hand stilled on her neck. He froze for a moment, and then he sat up, gently loosing himself from her. Firelight flickered on his stiff cheeks and flat mouth.

“What?” she asked.

“I understand you.” Huffy. Hurt.

He thinks I am saying I don’t want him.

She laughed and squeezed his bicep. “You know very well I want you.”

“But?”

How to assuage the pain in his voice?

She shook his arm. “I just can’t work out how to be free and have you in my life. I almost saw it when you saved me from those terrible men. I was brimful of joy and life—both safe *and* free.”

“How to be free?” he answered, his voice cold. “Live every day as though it is your last. Speaking of which…” He snaked out a long arm and pulled her back into him. With the other hand, he traced the side of her face, the shape of her lips. Her heart began to pound, her awareness of him increasing to fever pitch. His lips met hers, gently.

"Oh!" she said, and then all the day's fear and pain, and relief, took her, and she kissed him with all her fervor, all her gratitude, and yes, her love.

Her mind hazed into sensation, her body aching and yearning for him.

She pulled away. Her voice choked. She coughed a little, tried again. The husky tone was plain even to herself. "Living every day as though it is your last…yes, that does sound lovely. Fun. How I wish we could live like that. But I disagree."

"Naturally," Sawyer said, his tone so dry it could have cut bone. He shifted his position, lying back on the blanket, hands clasped behind his head, staring up at the night sky, his whole pose saying he was ready to listen.

She fiddled with a twig. "I know from my childhood and youth, many years spent in poverty, you can't live like that, with no regard for the morrow, or you will never be free." She paused.

"Mmm?"

She watched in fascination as he licked his lips, and then kissed him lightly.

Sawyer growled, "Do you want to kiss? Or finish talking?"

"Are you just waiting for me to finish so you can kiss me again, the niceties having been properly observed?"

He grinned, the cheekiness of it stealing her heart all over again. "But naturally."

"Well, you will just have to listen."

Sawyer turned on his side, a hand propping up his

head as he regarded her. “So speak, my goddess.”

“Maybe this is women’s knowledge. We know you need to do the sensible things, the work, the provision for the future, at least some of the time. That is the only way your future self can be free.”

“You might get bitten by a snake at any moment. Run over by an electric tram. Felled by disease.” Sawyer’s toffee eyes shone serious. The lustrous moonlight cast silvery shadows all around them. His finger stretched out, began stroking the side of her thigh, sending blazing fire through her once more.

He said softly, “Find your hard-won nursery has been gambled away and you have nothing, after all those years of labor.”

Lilwen sat up, pushed his hands away. “But those years of labor taught me much. That work can get you places. To never give up. I’ve been poor and worked my way out. I know I can do it again. That is the only way for self-respect.”

He caressed the hair from her face. “So what are we doing here, my practical, hardworking woman of my dreams? You lie here thick in the Tasmanian wilderness, having barely escaped with your virtue, your much-vaunted freedom, and quite probably your life, lecturing me on behaving sensibly?”

A peal of laughter bubbled up and burst from her throat. “Such adventures certainly give one perspective!” She smiled at him. “One does have to attend to one’s dreams, or what is life about? You make your own future by what you do in the present moment. And at this moment…”

“Yes?”

“I couldn’t wish I was anywhere else, with anyone

else. Since I met you…"

The full force of Sawyer's attention beamed on her. His beautiful face looked vulnerable, almost afraid, full of a complex emotion, as though he was peeling wide open.

She said, "Life has a shine, a lustrous glow, a looking forward. I have never been so happy." She squeezed his upper arm. "While I was captured, I had plenty of time to think about liberty, that elusive concept: as elusive and hard to trap as your tiger!" She waited for his grin, and then added, "I believe now that true liberty is also about the courage to take a risk—not a gamble! A leap of faith into a desired future."

The question burst into Sawyer's mind, "…and am I in that future?" But he bit his lip and kept silent. How else to keep her safe?

His chosen life would only cast her into further danger.

****

Lilwen slept curled in the blanket. The dog lay not far away, watching him.

Sawyer had listened to her with everything he had. To her words. To the unsaid words. The soft, honest, wondering tone. What her body told him.

Sawyer hardly knew what to say. His heart had swelled within him. Emotion such as he had never known, or not since childhood, had grown within him until he felt his skin would burst with it. A bubbling joy, clamoring to break free. If he let it.

He poked the fire with a stick. He understood exactly what she meant. How could one have both freedom and spend a life with somebody? How could someone like him, in his dangerous occupation, deserve a wife and family, having to abandon them for long periods? What kind of life was that?

A family. His thoughts hiccuped and shattered. A deep kind of longing burst in his chest and stomach. He instantly repressed it. Not for him.

Not for him.

No. Whatever thoughts he had entertained before, it was not possible. Her first foray into the wilderness, the first time he had taken his vigilance and his protection from her for a second, and look what happened. And what had occurred on the train even getting here. No, he could not expose her to this life, no matter what she said about wanting to be an explorer. The world was simply too wild and too dangerous. There were too many evil men.

He imagined her fury if he told her his thoughts, and a wry grin twisted on his face. No doubt there would be fireworks such as Tasmania had never before seen. A thunderstorm to rock the sky.

He had to plan how to get her back to safety. Perhaps he could convince her to return to Strahan, to find more guides, and then accompany her on her search for the white waratah, the *Agastachys odorata*. Send her home when they found it.

And—a Tasmanian tiger could be lurking in the bush nearby. His stomach lurched with impatience and longing. Lilwen's sleeping face was soft and composed now. Could he quietly go for a look? He imagined her waking and seeing he was not there. Imagined her fear. No, he could not.

Soon.

Chapter Seventeen

Lilwen opened her eyes to a huge dawn sky, pale gray streaked with iridescent pink, apricot, and purple. Birds trilled and screeched, and the surrounding forest crackled and rustled as unseen wild creatures welcomed the new day. Hero had gone.

Sawyer lay dead asleep, his body on the other side of hers, between her and the forest. He must be freezing. She would have had all the fire's heat through the night, Sawyer only the cold wind. Still protecting her.

She bent closer, stealing the opportunity to study him. He had ridiculously long, curling, dark eyelashes shadowing his cheeks. In sleep, he looked younger, almost angelic without his trademark sardonic glint in his eye or satiric smile. His cheeks glowed soft and rosy. Dark brown curls rioted from his forehead and across his brow and down his neck. His relaxed body took up space, huge and masculine, his robust frame all angles and muscle under his blanket.

Lilwen got up quietly and crept into the forest to relieve herself, all her senses on high alert. She had just finished and was taking a few tentative steps toward the pool for a quick wash, when a joyful, wagging bundle burst out of nearby shrubs, leaping on her and licking her.

"Hero!" She gave the dog a huge cuddle, enjoying

her lively presence, warm fur, and her joy in the fresh day. "Good morning to you too!"

They went down to the pool together. Lilwen splashed her face, and they sat there, the dog leaning against her, both breathing in the glorious morning. The brisk air seared her nose and throat with cold as she inhaled, but it filled her with exhilaration. Bright sun caught ripples in the little creek which fed the pool, turning it into a glittering crystal snake.

Vivid-colored parrots flew screeching past in a whirl of bright carnival colors: green, orange, red, purple. A brown furry shape surfaced on the edge of the pool. Lilwen held her breath: a platypus! Its brown duckbill rooted in the soil for grubs, its small furred body wiggling busily.

A low growl from Hero made her turn swiftly. A black and white creature stood there, thick-shouldered and squat, more than a foot high, its huge teeth bared in a ferocious grin in a wide red mouth. A Tasmanian devil! A carnivorous marsupial, just like Sawyer's fabled Tasmanian tiger.

It crept down to the river to drink. Lilwen's heart almost stopped; two small devils tagged along behind. They were the cutest, fiercest-looking things she had ever seen. The tiny devils snarled and wrestled with each other, running and returning to their scary mother. Lilwen kept her hand on Hero's back, holding the dingo beside her, and Hero seemed to understand.

The devils regarded her warily while they lapped from the pool. She held her breath, stock still, until they had drunk their fill. They made for the forest canopy, running fast and low to the ground. Every now and again, the mother would nip one of her recalcitrant babies back into line, who would respond with tiny growls.

Suddenly, an immense howling and snarling came from the forest. It sounded like War of the Devils. To her horror, Hero took off toward it.

She leapt to her feet. "Hero!" she screamed. The mad dog. It didn't stand a chance against those huge jaws, like a shark's, bred to hold on and to crunch through bone.

Lilwen ran toward the noise. Maybe she could beat the creatures away with a branch. The dog had saved her life. She couldn't just let it be injured, or even eaten, by a devil.

The sight that greeted her startled gaze halted her in her tracks. Her eyes widened until they felt as though they would burst out of her head.

There was the famed Tasmanian tiger! Fighting with the she-devil, who was protecting her young.

The beasts growled and snarled, the fierce sound ripping through the forest like hounds from hell. The tiger and devil rolled on the ground, biting and snapping, trying to grab each other's throats. One moment it looked as though the tiger was winning, then the devil. The young devils grumbled and yipped, running in and out of the battle, probably biting their mother as much as the tiger.

Hero, she was glad to see, stood away from the battle, also growling and snarling, teeth bared, hair all along her back standing up in a ridge of brown-yellow fur.

"What the…?" Sawyer burst into the scene, arm stretched out, gun pointed, hair awry, and eyes dark and wild. "Bloody hell! You've found the tiger!"

"Sawyer, don't shoot it! Please, don't shoot!"

He lowered the gun. "I wasn't going to."

The devil began to rip into the tiger's neck. Sawyer fired into the air. Hero emitted a high-pitched, terrified bark and scampered away into the forest.

The devil released its fearsome jaws from around the tiger's neck, swiveled its great head around to check for danger, picked up one of its young by the scruff, and darted on fast legs into the thick undergrowth with the other tiny devil racing behind.

For a fleeting moment, the tiger stood, its yellow glare reflecting Sawyer's dark toffee gaze. Man and beast looked eerily similar, tense with imminent action. Sawyer's fawn leather coat, streaked with dirt, echoed the tiger's yellow-striped dark fur. The tiger stared for stretched seconds, long muzzled and sad-eyed, and then it turned and melted back into the darkness.

****

"The tiger was just hungry. We should leave some food for it," Lilwen said again.

Sawyer shook his head, again. "It's a wild animal. Possibly injured, which makes it more dangerous. I will have to find it. Capture it for the zoo. Might even have to put it out of its misery."

"No! It seemed fine. Bit of blood on its neck maybe." Lilwen toed a stick poking out of the campfire. "Please don't take it to the zoo. Did you see how sad its eyes were? Can't you leave it to die in the wild?"

Sawyer's mouth thinned. He wasn't looking at her. "Sentimental foolishness."

Her stomach wrenched. Misery hitched in her throat. "Taking it to the zoo is cruel."

"How so? It could become part of a mating

program. Ensure the creature's survival." Sawyer finally met her eyes.

Lilwen almost shrank back a step. There was anger there, and pain. Resolve. Hardness.

He said, "This might be the last wild Tasmanian tiger. It might be our last chance."

She had to convince him. The words were urgent in her mouth. "I've seen the tiger now. Seen it wild and free. You would cage this creature, to leave it to die in sadness, longing for its forest home? Pining for its free life, for the feel of running fast with the wind on strong, wild legs? Yes, yearning even for the glory of fighting in the forest, blood surging, feeling fully alive and free?"

Silence. Then he said, "I know how you feel about freedom. You are putting your own emotions in the head of a wild animal."

"Do you deny it would feel like that?"

Sawyer shook his head. "What about this dog of yours? You are compelling it to your will. It is a dingo, a wild dog. How is that free?"

"Don't you see? The dog stays with me and seems to do as I ask because it loves me. Not because it is afraid I will hurt it if it doesn't. There is a world of difference. So like a man! You think only of the actions, the results, not the inner motivations, which to me, can be the most important."

Sawyer humphed—impatient with her? With wanting to hunt the tiger?

"Go then," she said. "Try to find the beast in case it is injured. Maybe you can help it. Promise me you won't shoot it."

"You will feel safe? I will be gone only for a short

time. I will try to track the beast before it gets too far away. But I don't want to leave you…"

"Go! Hero will stay with me. I will scream if I need you."

"Yes. That hound of hell will keep you safe."

"She is not a…!"

But Sawyer had gone.

****

Lilwen occupied herself to prevent thoughts of wild men returning while Sawyer was away from the camp. She scooped up remains of the game they had eaten last night. She gave some to Hero and then crept cautiously into the forest clearing where the tiger and the devil had fought.

She placed the remains of the cooked wallaby and possum in the clearing and walked back until she could only just see the clearing. She sat and rested her back against a tree. Time passed slowly, as though hours drifted by as she dozed. Hero wriggled, restless with the lack of action, and wandered off.

Lilwen sat bolt upright. A striped yellow shape was slinking out of the forest, its long muzzle close to the ground. Blood still dripped from a gash on its neck. The injury looked severe. Lilwen held her breath as the creature crept closer. Suddenly, it made a dive for the food, crunching bones and ripping skin from meat and muscle. It kept its eyes trained on her, checking every now and again that she had not come closer, had not moved. The creature was weak and bleeding from the neck but consumed the food in ravenous gulps.

Finally, it loped off toward the pool. Lilwen crept closer on hands and knees, peering through a gap in a thick shrub as it drank thirstily. With a last sniff in her direction, the tiger melded into the forest, the light and shade playing and changing under the great trees: one moment there, the next gone, faded away.

Like an omen of its uncertain future.

The Tasmanian tiger had been hunted almost to extinction, marked with a bounty, and hated by sheep farmers. Now she had seen the magnificent creature for herself, wild and free in the forest, she ached to help the poor thing.

****

Sawyer returned crankier than she had ever seen him, silent, preoccupied, and short-tempered.

"Were you successful in your hunt?" She offered him a fresh-made bush tea.

"I was not."

He ignored the tea, so she placed the cup on the ground.

She decided not to tell him, for the present, that she had fed the creature.

He cleaned and chopped two rabbits, which he cooked in a large pot with water from the stream, adding wild green herbs growing nearby. "I hope you are ready to return to civilization."

"Of course not! We have barely begun."

"No."

Lilwen studied him—the averted eyes, the clenched jaw, the abrupt movements as he prepared their food. The atmosphere emanating from his turned back was almost a solid thing. He had clearly come to some decision about her. Without asking her.

"I feel perfectly safe with you," she began.

He turned to face her, and the anger in his face speared her with shock. "No. This kind of exploring is not suited to gently reared women. Any women."

The old, slow anger kindled deep within her. Who were they, this other race, these men, who always, *always*, sought to curtail her, constrain her, order her and shape the matter of her days? Why did they always think they were the boss? Had they no imagination?

"I am a person," she began shakily, trying to control her burgeoning anger, her sense of deep betrayal that Sawyer acted like all the rest. Like her father. "Not just a woman, to be lumped together as a formless, helpless bunch of useless dolls, pretty and decorative, weak and spineless."

She stood facing him, staring up at him even though her neck began to hurt, slanted up like that. Trying to hold her ground, hold her line, not be swayed or persuaded. "I am not a fool, either."

He blew a loud raspberry. "I know you are not."

"Then why treat me like one?"

Sawyer turned away, and bending, began to do something to the rabbit stew, unnecessarily, she suspected.

When he stood up, she could see he had his speech all prepared.

She tried to forestall him, but for once he had abandoned his gentleman-like manners and talked over her. "You know nothing of the dangers of this environment," he said viciously. "Bad enough deadly snakes, spiders, and plants, but wild men too? No. Who knows how many bands of criminals and rapists are roaming these wilds? Next time, I may not be able to protect you. To get there in time…" He swallowed, groaned, and looked up at the sky, as he took a few deep breaths.

"I think this experience has affected you more than it has me!" Lilwen tried for levity. Her joke fell like a rock in a pond. "We are here now. Let's search for your tiger, find my *Agastachys*, and then we can return home."

"No. I am taking you back to Dolly's house. I will find your *Agastachys* myself."

As Lilwen's temper rose again, he added in a low voice, "Or die in the attempt."

"Don't be so ridiculous."

"The only ridiculous thing is keeping you here for one more night. Prepare yourself. We are leaving at first light."

"And if I refuse?"

"I will tie you to the saddle and take you anyway."

"You will not! I will explore by myself." Even as she said it, she knew it was childish. She wouldn't even try. She knew little about the bush and would soon be both terrified and starving. Even if she found her treasured flower, she would have serious trouble finding her way back to Strahan. Or any civilization. There were many miles of wilderness in the southwest of Tasmania, and they were probably right in the heart of it.

"Which way *is* Dolly's?" she asked in a friendly, conversational tone.

Sawyer snorted like an angry horse. "You will find out when I deliver you there in a day or two, depending on how fast this horse can take two of us."

In desperation, Lilwen tried something softer. "What happened to our idyll in the wilderness? Just you and me?"

Sawyer reddened and lowered his brows over

amber eyes flashing danger. He jerked out the words. "That too was most ungentlemanly of me. I cannot keep you here, just you and me. As it is, we will have trouble explaining ourselves."

Lilwen fixed on him the hottest glare she could summon and pushed up her chin. "Oh, is that all you are worried about? That you will be compelled to marry me, because of your *gentlemanly* manners? Be assured, I would not marry such an autocratic boor as you are turning out to be. I thought you were different, Sawyer Thane, not more of the same. Orders, orders, orders, morning, noon, and night. Don't break the mold, don't let your behavior stray. Stay in your corset, wear your long skirts to ensure you trip instead of stride. Stay in rooms, like a decoration, don't run and breathe the free air, don't have ideas, or dreams, or desires!"

Hot tears pricked her eyes and cheeks. A drum pounded in her head.

Sawyer's nostrils flared, and the skin tightened over his cheekbones. He clenched his fists, then spread his fingers wide.

A long silence ensued, her words echoing in the still, starry night.

He coughed and said in a strangled voice, "I cannot marry you. Be ready at first light."

He put food on a plate for her, disappeared briefly to collect water in his waterskin, and placed it by her plate. He fetched his blanket and walked to the other side of the fire, curling up in a long, heavy heap with his back to her and the fire.

Lilwen sat there. The only sounds were the fire glowing and hissing, a faraway owl hooting a mournful song, the quiet rustlings and hissings of the forest as the creatures began once again to go about their business, and…a snore.

She couldn't believe it. Sawyer had actually just fallen asleep, despite all the emotional turmoil plunging her into disarray.

Men!

****

The atmosphere on the ride back to Strahan thrummed with screaming-pitch tension.

Sawyer put Lilwen behind him on the saddle, and as they rode, she clutched him around his waist. Hero ran beside them until the paths grew clearer and straighter, and then, as they increased their pace, Hero permitted Sawyer to balance her in front of him on the saddle.

At first, Lilwen had proudly tried hard not to even touch him, but within a few yards of them starting off, she realized she would fall off unless she held onto him.

So a weird mix of emotions assailed her on the long journey back to Strahan. On one hand, his masculine, virile presence attracted and drew her; the strength in his back, shoulders, and thighs as he rode, and his easy handling of the horse, fascinated her as always. She hated him at the same time for not acceding to her wishes, for making her forego her great adventure, even though a tiny bossy voice inside her repeated that he was right, this time. And most of all, because Lilwen was deeply feminine, his words the night before, dropped into the night as though they were nothing, scored into her like corroding acid, circling again and again in her mind.

"I cannot marry you."

Chapter Eighteen

If Sawyer had been overbearing in his unnecessary cosseting of her, Dolly was positively claustrophobic. Dolly seemed to feel it was all her fault. She had imprisoned Lilwen in the sunny morning room, ensconced on a squishy sofa suitable for an invalid, surrounded by plump embroidered cushions, blankets, back rolls, and silk shawls, ordering her not to move and bringing her an unending succession of teas, delicacies, and restoratives until even Lilwen was laughing.

"Dolly! There is nothing wrong with me! Now I am here with you in your lovely house, I am completely recovered." A shaft of guilt lanced her, and her stomach curdled. "In fact, I have thoroughly enjoyed your fabulous hospitality for many days now…"

"Lilwen! Don't you dare think of leaving for at least another six weeks. I treasure your friendship and society. You know how I adore having guests. Promise me you will honor me with a few more weeks yet. You must stay and find your elusive flower." Lilwen could only laughingly comply.

She and Sawyer were still at loggerheads, icily polite when they spoke at all. Minnie Brigg had watched them for much of the previous evening, her curious, spiteful eyes locking on first one then the other, and making her own conclusions, had returned to her assault on winning Sawyer's admiration. The woman could have him. So why did she feel so out of sorts at the thought?

He was handsome, yes, clever and funny too, and yes, very caring while she needed him there in the wilderness. An exceptional man. But! Unforgivably, irredeemably overbearing and controlling.

Had she lost her only chance to find the white waratah? She tapped her cheeks with spiky knuckles, grimacing with the little shock of pain. She faced dire consequences if she faltered now. She would have to return to Melbourne and sell the nursery. To pay the rest of the debt, she would take some horrible job pouring beer in a public house or working as a domestic for someone else: slaving from before dawn to after dark, never seeing the sky. Plenty of other women worked in jobs like that, why should she be different? And the elderly MacNeils? Who would look after them? Or she could go crawling back to Mr. Partridge, who would make sure that she suffered for her rejection of him.

She was becoming blue-deviled, that was the problem. When Dolly danced away to attend to one of her myriad household concerns, Lilwen bodily flung the pillows, blankets, cushions, and covering from her and took several deep breaths.

She was being strangled, suffocated, hedged in, and confined; all her worst fears, and by her friends too. Enough! She had to get some air. She had to stretch her legs, move her body, feel the sun on her face.

Lilwen walked into the garden and checking that nobody observed her, began to stretch and dance in the sunlight. How she loved to move! How she loved to feel free and unrestricted. She danced around a corner and stopped short.

A nun sat on the grass by the fishpond, clad in full convent regalia: habit, black veil, white forehead covering, white collar, flowing black robes, and long silver chain dangling a heavy cross. The nun had cast aside her heavy shoes, her habit was pulled up to her calves and she wriggled bare toes in the fishpond with a look of absolute ecstasy on her face. One of her smooth pale hands rested lightly on Hero's back. Hero smiled at Lilwen and thumped her tail in welcome.

She took all this in within a few seconds, and the startled exclamation burst from her: "Good God, a nun! Oh dear, I mean…"

The nun opened eyes as blue as cornflowers and smiled. "Hello! You must be the famous Lilwen!" The nun cocked her head. "You don't look too traumatized to me."

"I'm not! I've just escaped the most serious cosseting of my life to date! Please don't let them find me again, Sister. I could hardly breathe."

"That's more the idea I had formed of your character. Lilwen Jones, the intrepid plant collector."

"I wish."

Something about the nun's cheerful insouciance, her blue eyes, her careless disregard for her habit, rapidly dampening along the edges, and smearing with soil where she brushed the ground, called to something within Lilwen and made her smile. She sat down next to Hero. They both patted the dingo, who panted happily.

The nun's sweet, humorous face glowed from the confines of her habit. She was young, much younger than Dolly, perhaps a few years younger than Lilwen herself.

The nun said, “I’m Dolly’s sister, Sinead Kelly. I’ve got a nun name—a male saint’s name—but please do call me Sinead.”

“A nun! Of all people! Oh dear, I am so sorry. You are an unusual family. Is your convent in Tasmania? I thought once locked inside those high walls…” Lilwen shivered. “Sorry, I am being rude. But sticking my toes in the fishpond is exactly the sort of thing I do! And get into terrible trouble for it!”

Sister Sinead laughed. “I’m a missionary. It’s very exciting. I run a small orphanage in French Indochina, in the northern city of Hanoi, teaching English and the rudiments of mathematics to orphan children, so that they can get some kind of start in life. And yes, some nuns stay inside those convent walls their whole lives. I am a Loreto nun. One of our founders said, ‘Go set the world on fire.’ I prefer to regard that as my divine instruction.”

The nun grinned, and in her sheer exuberance, Lilwen saw the resemblance to Dolly. A small pang smote her. Here was a nun, preaching a message her heart yearned to hear. How extraordinary, hearing it come from such a source. She grinned back.

Lilwen said, “Are your feet refreshed now? Would you like to walk along the bay to a pretty, secluded beach with lovely views, and tell more about your life? I am intrigued, but fear that one or other of my minders will recapture me soon if I dally too long here.”

Sinead winked and confided, “Ah, you have picked the very best person to aid you. I am an old hand at escaping various kinds of captors. In fact, becoming a nun was another, I must say, brilliant stroke toward freedom."

The nun rose, dried her feet with her long habit, clearly uncaring about any new stains, and put her shoes back on. Arm in arm, they sauntered the length of the garden and escaped through the side gate, Hero scampering with them.

Sawyer's deep tones called "Lilwen" somewhere on the air.

Let him call.

****

Lilwen and Sister Sinead sat in the curve of a rock face, the sea pulsing and heaving just below. Small, warm pools lay scattered in the smooth rock shelf on which they sat. In the pools, bright red long-fingered anemones opened and closed in time with each breath of the sea, tiny crabs scuttled hither and thither, and small iridescent fish darted and leapt in the sun.

Cool salt spray hit their faces with tiny sticky fingers. The ocean before them stretched on forever, in shades of blue and green, turquoise, emerald, and sapphire, all the way to the great Antarctic. Hero wandered among the dunes and chased flying sea birds along the shore.

Sister Sinead and Lilwen talked of this and that, enjoying a newfound friendship and the beauty of the day.

Lilwen threw a pebble into the air, watching until it landed with a tiny plume of water into the ocean. Sinead's story intrigued her. As they giggled together after a particularly drenching splash of salt spray, Lilwen found herself asking, "Forgive me. You are a most unlikely nun. Do you not find living in a convent like a prison? Telling you how to behave, how to think?"

"Yes, sometimes," Sinead answered gravely. "But it is also sometimes so very beautiful, when we sing or pray together, all voices lifted up to praise God and the world he has made. And you see, a very good reason to become a nun, is exactly for that reason—to become free."

"You mean in a religious way."

"No, Lilwen, I mean the world. Did you not know that nuns are educated very well, if they have the ability? I have been to university, even! To me, education, and the capacity to travel the world, is the greatest freedom I could wish for. As a nun, I can do these things. Nuns are women who can be freer in their choices and actions than almost any other woman in our world today, married or single."

Lilwen's heart jumped with excitement. "Tell me more!"

"My family could not afford to educate us past a certain level of school. Our parents are Irish, coming out to Australia during the gold rushes. They had no sons to give to the priesthood, and Dolly, so beautiful, was always going to make an advantageous marriage. So I chose to go to a convent—once a wise old nun told me how I could live my life. She said the best way to praise God was to develop and use our talents and to help other women to be strong and brave. She has inspired me so much. And so, here I am."

"You look happy." Lilwen couldn't hide her doubtful tone.

Sinead laughed, like a tinkling, clear bell. "Yes, I am happy. My life is very busy and interesting. At my orphanage in Hanoi, in French Indochina, we especially ensure the girls are educated. We teach them to speak English, to read and write, and how to figure accurate mathematics. When we find girls with special talent, we send them to a Catholic boarding school for a good education. Then they can return and share their skills with their whole community."

"And the God bit? Pardon my bluntness."

Sinead laughed again. "Yes, there is a bit about God. But I'm not Dolly's sister for nothing. Our mother was Irish, and I must say, there is quite a lot about Mary in my teachings, who can be understood as another image of the goddess Brigid, who is so important for fertility, healing, poetry, and smithcraft. All the important things. And there is the Roman goddess Minerva, who is for arts, trade, and strategy. Women are fighting to be free and equal all over the world. This is how I choose to do it."

"You are amazing."

"Why don't you come with me when I return to Indochina? You could help in the orphanage, see what we do there. And there are the most beautiful, fabulous jungles and forests, filled with the most achingly beautiful plants and flowers: huge colored orchids, bright rhododendrons, sweet-scented tropical flowers of all kinds. I suspect my kind of freedom may suit you too."

"Yes! Probably. But I think I need to invent my own kind of freedom." A giant wave curled toward them, translucent aqua edged with lace, as fragile as crystal, yet as strong and unstoppable as birth itself. It broke itself on the rocks below them, surging up in watery fingers throwing bubbles of many-colored froth, and it was echoed by another wave, and another.

Lilwen said, "How I would love to see those plants you describe. The tropical jungles of the near East. The people, the food. Ah, I am a restless spirit! I know not how I managed to stay working, working in my father's plant nursery all these years, with the song of travel pulling in my veins."

"I am perfectly serious in my offer. I feel a bright kinship with you, in a way I don't have with Dolly, or many of the nuns. I would see you again, if I could."

They clasped hands and stared eagerly into each other's eyes. They embraced on that cold rock, laughing as the shock of the freezing spray hit them again and again with the rising tide. Finally Lilwen said, "I must return, or either Sawyer or Dolly will have every able-bodied man out in search for me."

Sinead laughed. "Come, then. I will treasure the time we spent together this afternoon. Thank you. It means much to me that I have found a sister of the adventurous heart, and to whom I extend an eternal welcome."

"And thank you, too," Lilwen answered. "I have only met one other woman whose life I would emulate, and she can be found in Dolly's garden! Your life—you make it sound so vivid and exciting—offers the wide horizons, the adventure, the purpose, that I seek. If I can, I will visit you. Sometime."

****

Sawyer was pacing around the garden when they arrived back, half drenched with spray, laughing and elated. His face darkened and his brows snapped down when he saw her.

"Oh no," she whispered to Sister Sinead. "Thunder

at four o'clock!"

Sinead smiled at them both and gave an airy wave as she tripped back up the path toward Dolly's mansion. She had barely reached the back door before Dolly's amused tones floated out on the air, exclaiming and fussing.

Sawyer stepped in front of her, blocking her view. He was trying to master his countenance. She gazed at him from underneath her eyelashes, repressing a smile at his expression when he took in her wet clothes, her wild hair, the tiny shells she clasped in her hand for remembrance of the day she met the redoubtable Sister Sinead Kelly.

"You look glowing," Sawyer ground out. "Elated. Did something happen?"

"Maybe." All her mischief rose up. "I am thinking of becoming a nun."

Nothing could have been more satisfying than the absolutely stupefied expression on Sawyer's face. He stood there, frozen, his jaw dropped, his eyes wide in shocked amazement. His mouth opened and closed, and a few mangled words emerged in tattered shreds of sound.

Her lips compressed, she ran away from him, inside the mansion and up the staircase to her room, before he could catch her. Once inside, she laughed with the happy abandon of a child.

Chapter Nineteen

Sawyer could barely choke down any of the delicious repast placed in front of him, course after delicious course, one delicacy after another. He struggled manfully to keep his eyes from boring into Lilwen, as she sat, talking and laughing, as spirited and charming as ever.

Why hadn't he ravished her in the forest when he had the chance? At least then, she would have to consent to be with him. Horrified, he caught the direction of his thoughts and took a large gulp of the ruby wine in his glass. The business part of him noticed as an aside that the wine was rich and fruit-filled; Tasmanian wine would hold up well as a potential future export.

A nun! Surely she jested. The author of this latest dispute between him and Lilwen sat there, demure in her all-over sober nun's habit, but young and pink-cheeked, merrily laughing at one of Lilwen's conversational sallies. Dolly joined in with a remark of her own. All three were lovely, sparkling, enjoying the moment and each other. He felt like a great male clod, unable to keep up with feminine sparring and jokes, the women tripping lightly as mayflies from one subject to the next, all happily talking over each other, exclaiming, and seeming to be able to listen and talk at the same time, in perfect accord.

A most unsocial thundercloud weighted his face, his jaw tight, his lowered brows as heavy as disappointment.

Minnie Brigg chose that inauspicious moment to resume her one-sided flirtation with him. She appeared to believe that making Lilwen look questionable would endear Sawyer to herself. Perhaps she felt left out of the other women's quick, affectionate banter.

Minnie said, with revolting archness, a petulant glance toward Lilwen and a fluttering glance at Sawyer, "But everyone is so mysterious! Why have we not heard more of your explorations? Surely, Miss Jones, you did not fail to find that plant you were seeking? Perhaps it was just a reason to be alone with…"

Sawyer put down his fork. Lilwen gave a slow, exaggerated blink. Her plump bottom lip shot out; she clearly held her temper in with a tight but fraying rein. A silver-eyed glare pulverized Minnie, as liquid and dangerous as mercury in a hot thermometer. Minnie faltered in her flow and ceased talking. Not, alas, for long.

"I heard *so much* about your plans for your exciting adventures," Minnie continued, false-interested. "How you were so different to other women. How the *conventional* life could not be yours, quite shocking for my poor Roo to hear, indeed."

"We were not successful in our endeavors," Lilwen snapped.

Minnie's expression underwent a gamut of emotions, none of them edifying, Sawyer thought. She clapped her hands coquettishly and produced a tinkling laugh which made her "poor Roo" gaze at her with evident embarrassment.

Sawyer winced as Minnie said, "But I have it! Miss Jones will remain here with her friends, having discovered the sad truth that the Tasmanian wilderness is not for gently bred women, and that she is, in fact, an ordinary mortal like the rest of us. And Mr. Sawyer Thane will go himself into the wilderness, and finding the plant, will bring it back and lay it as an offering at her feet!"

Lilwen blanched as though she was about to vomit. The nun held a laugh behind her hand, and Dolly had put on her hostess face, and was about to intervene—not a moment too soon, Sawyer thought, for the future harmony of the Frasers' friendship with the Briggs.

Sawyer took in Lilwen's outraged countenance. "I think you will discover that, far from perceiving such an action on my part as a romantic offering, Miss Jones would cram said offering down my throat and immediately set out to find the plant herself."

Lilwen rewarded him with the first genuine smile he had seen since the forest, her expression warm with approbation. Her foot sought his under the table and pressed.

Sawyer spoke, drowning himself in the silver lake of her eyes, magnetized by her warmth as though he had been out in the cold for weeks, "You see, she *is* quite unlike all other women. Lilwen Jones wants to find the plant herself. She is a true collector. She wants to see where it grows, and how, and what grows with it. Does it prosper on a north slope or a south, in wet boggy areas or well-drained soils? She wants to record it in her mind and in her plant presses, in her drawings and her memory, so that when she cultivates it, tames it, she can keep that core of wildness that first spoke to her."

Lilwen stared at him with delighted amazement. His blood hurtled in his veins. Finally, he had got something right.

Sawyer was nothing if not a disgraceful opportunist. "That was a sensational dinner, Dolly. So marvelous that I feel the need for a stroll in your lovely gardens."

Minnie Brigg half rose from her chair, but Sawyer barely had any emotion to register her. He could not tear his gaze from his lovely Lilwen.

She regarded him with a laugh in her eyes, her plump lips pursed to keep the smile in.

Dolly said, in an amused tone, "So delightful a dinner, Mr. Thane, that you barely tasted any of it. Perhaps a walk is a good idea so that you will be in more of an eating frame of mind on the morrow."

"Excellent!" enthused Minnie. "Just the thing! My poor Roo does need some more exercise," and the execrable woman patted her long-suffering husband mock-playfully on his distended stomach. But Minnie wasn't his concern.

Sawyer stood and, going around the table to Lilwen, proffered his arm.

Her eyes sparked diamond-gray satire, and ignoring the arm, she pushed herself out from the table. "After that speech, I had understood you did not think me weak—that I could actually manage to walk without the assistance of the male of the species."

Her smile sent ripples through him. His bright brain melted. She dangled him on a string; his will functioned only to serve her.

He coughed and pulled himself together. If he

understood her personality at all, she wouldn't want an obedient paramour, but one whose wit matched her own, whose armor could withstand her sharpened claws. Obedience wasn't his style anyway. He wanted a woman who could give as good as she got. Who had a mind, and a will, and spirit. And in Lilwen's case, those qualities just happened to come in a package of stunning, intriguing, and spectacular beauty.

Once outside under the benevolent shine of the moon, Sawyer captured Lilwen's hand and placed it under his arm, the better to stroll together in the romantic light. She permitted this. They both ignored the other members of the party, who Minnie had jealously rounded up in order that Lilwen and Sawyer could not stroll alone.

At last, he had got her close to him again. At last. The long ride home had been pure torment, Lilwen so physically close, her anger practically incinerating his shirt as she sat behind him on the saddle. He would not change a thing: she had to be protected, but he had been missing her company, her smiles, her wit, their badinage, their mutual accord.

He must take care. He must proceed as warily as stalking a leopard in the wild. He would not jeopardize this reanimation of her regard.

For a short while, they spoke of this and that, pausing to enjoy the perfumed flowers which opened at night to attract moths and the other night pollinators.

Sawyer could bear it no longer. They leaned together on the outside of a tall, vine-covered garden wall, gazing out over the orchards and mountains, which were blue-gray and hazy with shadow in the evening light.

"Those men affected you badly. I promise you, not all men are like that! You need to take time to recover. Not make important, life-changing decisions now."

Lilwen looked up at him from under curling eyelashes, the amused irony in her expression signaling that he had made yet another misstep.

"You know best, of course." Her voice sang smooth and cold.

Familiar frustrated rage turned his blood to fire. How did she—so ridiculously easily—disturb his own detached calm, his independence from ordinary mortals? How did she bump him back to the current moment, the present, where he had to be fully attentive, fully present, to survive her wicked banter and sharp mind? She always forced him to be aware of the real woman alive and vibrant before him, not some half-imagined creature of male expectation and social convention.

He groaned. "Lilwen," he almost begged. "What then?"

"That's better," she riposted, adding one of her trademark grins. "Why do you assume? Why not just ask me?"

He stared at her. "As easy as that?" She laughed at his no-doubt incredulous expression. Even he could hear the surprise in his voice.

She smiled at him. "I'm not so complicated, surely. Just talk to me as though I were a man."

He choked and then recovered himself. Her smile melted his heart all over again. This woman could do anything with him. He loved it and hated it. Just like Lilwen, he had to feel free. But he wanted her too. Treat her like a man! What nonsense.

"Lilwen, tell me. You plan to become a nun?" He heard the pain in his voice but plowed on. He had to know. "Why? Did the experiences with those men…? Have they changed how you feel?"

Lilwen smiled again and took a few steps forward, twirling herself around in the night. Sawyer's throat dried. She couldn't have any idea what she looked like, almost dancing under the pale moon, her floating dinner dress revealing tantalizing glimpses of her shape while simultaneously concealing it, her midnight hair flowing and curling in the cool air, which was spiced with a lick of cold now.

She stopped and stood in front of Sawyer, her silver eyes huge in the moonlight, the shine playing on her hair and picking out the gleam of her alabaster skin on throat and shoulder. She said, "No. I didn't understand before. Nuns have freedom other women do not. The freedom to be your own person. They are protected by the habit to go where they will. A nun doesn't need some overprotective, virile male hunter, to hustle her back to safety."

Sawyer made a strangled half laugh. "Ouch!" And then said, under his breath, "Virile?"

He swallowed. "Can that be why you seemed so happy tonight at dinner? Thinking about freedom in a nun's garb?"

She laughed. "I was just enjoying the company of my friends."

He caught her hand. "Marriage can give you both freedom and protection."

She stared at him. "I remember your words very clearly. You said, 'I cannot marry you.' "

Sawyer dropped her hand, took a few paces, his

agitation making him feel very disturbed and restless. "That is true. I cannot."

"Well, I could ask what are we doing here then, but you see, I do not want to get married either. So it does not matter whether you can marry me or not." She whirled, angry once more. "Or were you helpfully suggesting I marry some as yet unknown but fine example of manhood so that I can be *safe*?" She spat the last word. "Who you will be so kind as to select and approve? Then what was the meaning of all your fine words at dinner?"

He groaned. "No! Lilwen! I am confused. I do not want to inflict a half-life on you, leaving you in some fine house while I spend months away tracking game. And I cannot, *cannot* have some routine clerkish job in my father's business. You understand me."

"I do." The chill in her voice and manner froze him to the marrow. "Excuse me."

Sawyer watched, helplessly, as she strode away back to the house.

Of all the cloddish idiots! He was never this clumsy with women. The truth was, he hardly knew what he wanted. He wanted Lilwen, but he couldn't envision the life they would lead. How could they be together and both be happy? Lilwen spoke the truth. What did marriage offer her, but another cage?

He shook his head, and far more slowly, made his way back to the house, where he endured the inane banter and febrile chatter of the Briggs as punishment for upsetting Lilwen and for being such a poor guest for Dolly.

Once abed, he spent the night tossing and turning in sweaty, tortured dreams.

****

The next day, morning light brought only one solution.

He waited at breakfast until Lilwen came down.

"All right!" he said, as she bit into her toast and jam. "We will go exploring once more. Just promise me, please! Don't go and be a nun yet."

He waited while she chewed and swallowed her toast. He felt dreadful, his teeth aching with lack of sleep, his mind fuzzy. Only one thing shone clear: He could not lose Lilwen Jones, or his life would have no meaning any longer.

Somehow, by spending time together, they had to work out how to have a life.

When she finally nodded, the great rock of despair lodged in his stomach dissolved and his desperate mood lightened.

Tomorrow was another day.

And Lilwen Jones would be in it with him.

****

To everyone's surprise, Dolly put her tiny, fashionable, well-shod foot down.

"Absolutely not. Lilwen, you are *not* going into the wilderness with only Mr. Sawyer Thane for company. When Sawyer went to rescue you, we told everyone that Rory's men and one of the wives were there too. This may be a new century, but we have not advanced so far. I doubt we ever will. And certainly not here in Tasmania. I remind you that you are in a social backwater and also, that scandal travels as fast here as it ever does."

Sawyer looked immediately contrite, the blush mantling his bronzed cheeks. "Of course," he said.

"How could I be so remiss."

Lilwen spat her fury. "That is not your decision, Sawyer Thane. I have talked to you about *protecting* me. I don't need it. I will never grow up, but be kept in some girlish, infantile state, if I cannot make my own decisions, for good or evil, like a mature woman."

Sawyer's eyes told her that he thought her a mature woman already, but she resolutely ignored him and turned to her friend. "I traveled before with only Welcome and Wallace."

Dolly wore sympathy in her lovely eyes. "They are renowned botanical guides. Plus, you left without any of us knowing. I must admit I let it be known that my gardener Edna and a female cook accompanied you." She paused. "I am your hostess and your friend. I will not allow you to do this. Don't look so mutinous. Think how your impulsive, ungoverned actions will reflect on my own reputation, should you do such a scandalous thing."

Horrified repentance filled Lilwen. "Dolly, no! I would not harm you for the world." Impulsive! Ungoverned. Was that how Dolly perceived her? A flush of shame burnt through her body.

She said, "I will move out, and then in a few days, Sawyer and I will travel as planned."

"No!" said Sawyer and Dolly in one voice. Dolly added in a sprightly, no-nonsense tone, "As if I care for my reputation. I was just trying a little blackmail!" She smiled so sunnily that Lilwen had to laugh. Dolly continued, "And you will not take yourself away from my house. I love having you here."

Lilwen began shaking her head, but Dolly ended by stating most firmly, "In fact, you will be married from this house, and then you are free to travel as wildly as you wish."

The charged silence that met this extraordinary statement threatened to shatter Dolly's crystal chandeliers.

Sawyer's tawny eyes were on her, warm and melting. He stretched out a long brown hand, a hand which she loved to see, to touch.

Lilwen swallowed. She grabbed all her courage. "He cannot. He will not marry me. And I will not marry him." She turned away.

Dolly's trilling laugh was like a caress on her neck. "But why? So silly! You two are clearly made for each other. I haven't seen a more perfect pair since the day Rory and I walked down the aisle together."

Dolly's gaze moved from one to the other. "There is nothing to fear, you know. A good marriage helps one to be twice the person you once were. Nobody knows who they are inside; it is a process of discovery. The important thing is that you choose wisely who to do that discovering with!"

Lilwen replied, "Brave words, my lovely Dolly. But I will not be married because of convention. Because of mealy-mouthed scruples about possession and ownership. That is all marriage is really. Ensuring women are controlled by one male or another."

Dolly said, "Oh, Lilwen, no…" She rallied. "No respectable woman will buy your plants."

Lilwen froze, halfway to the door. She swiveled. Fear swirled inside her like an evil fog about to corrupt all her dreams and crumble them to dust.

"Really?" she gasped. She fought down the panic. She turned to Sister Sinead, who had arrived some minutes ago, and who was unashamedly watching, eyes bright with interest. “Do nuns take fallen women?”

Sinead laughed. “That’s one of our main business lines.”

“Well, that’s all right then. Problem solved. Sawyer, we leave on the morrow. Make sure you are ready.”

And finally, she managed to escape from the room, head held up proudly during the long walk to the door and down the passageway.

She didn’t want to look at Sawyer, see the relief on his face that he didn’t have to marry her. Or the frown, for her intentions to be a nun, to do what she wanted.

He could do exactly as he wanted, whenever he wanted. So why not her? Just because of her gender.

In the safety of her room, an outrageous thought struck her. She would be damned as a fallen woman anyway, so why not enjoy it?

Her mood circled right back up.

She would seduce Sawyer Thane in the forest, heart to heart, man to woman, as natural as love was meant to be.

After that? Let the future take care of itself.

She knew she was strong enough to endure anything.

Chapter Twenty

They had been deep in the forest for three sexually charged days and nights. They had not so far found either the tiger or the white waratah.

Back at Dolly's, Sinead had expressed a fascinated affection for Hero, so Lilwen had left the dingo for the nun to pet and enjoy while they were away. So in all the miles of forest, there was only the two of them, without even a clever dingo to mediate between them.

Sawyer maintained a pleasant, exceedingly polite manner, careful to keep his distance from her person. An occasional grin split his watchful silence, enlivening his laconic responses to her conversational sallies.

She grew increasingly, frustratingly aware of him—his strength and grace, his strapping physique as he set up camp and strode around carrying bundles of firewood. Currently he was chopping wood, shirt off, ridged abdominals and back bunching and stretching, his skin covered with a light sheen of perspiration.

She forcibly restrained herself from drawing close to him. A shocking urge clamored in her breast, to slide a hand down his ruggedness, to put her mouth on his skin, licking and tasting his salty, slick, sweat-covered back and stomach.

Never had any man made her feel so magnetized, so out of her senses.

His long lashes curled over chiseled cheeks and

stubbled jaw as he studied the wood. Now, he allowed her to linger close to him, his jaw and body tense, his eyes urgent and hot, sliding to hers, to her mouth, to her breasts, and away again to the trees all around them. His throat moved as he swallowed, lips tight and then parting as though he wanted to groan in frustration. He stepped away, making space.

So far, they had not revisited their previous conversations, preferring instead to remark on neutral topics, the forest, the animals and birds inhabiting it. The incredible beauty all around them, with surprises in every nook and stunning views at every turn. All so rich, so lush, smelling of outdoors, of pristine air, of leaves, and minerals, and the memory of recent rain. Lilwen repressed her fantasies and assisted Sawyer with the campfire and dinner.

****

Tonight, all was dark and quiet, the sky drowsy with sparkling stars and the heavy creamy twist of the Milky Way. They sat next to the campfire, which had burnt down to glowing embers. A tiny tickling cool breeze made the warmth of the fire all the more enticing.

“I adore the smell of Huon pine,” Lilwen said. “It seems amazing that they can live for thousands of years. There is a special feeling in these forests, of ancient memories, of the earth as it once was, long, long ago.”

Sawyer regarded her. His face, in the ruby glow from the fire, looked soft and youthful instead of his usual hard decisiveness. “You feel it too.” The quiet and peace of the night smoothed his voice. He took a breath. “You are a very special woman, Lilwen Jones.

The things you feel, I feel too. The things you love, I love too."

For once, Lilwen hardly knew what to say. Horticulture! Her safe place. "And I am absolutely in awe of the *Nothofagus gunnii* forests, the deciduous beech. I would love to see the colors when they change with the cold."

Sawyer laughed softly. "That is a strange kind of answer. What is it? Can you hear the bars of a cage coming down around you when I speak of my deep accord with you?"

"No." Lilwen licked her lips.

Sawyer watched her.

She said, "The very opposite."

The night twanged with tension as stretched as a high note in a song.

Sawyer spoke, and his voice was the ripple of thunder in the distance, the heavy drone of a bee replete with nectar, the crash of an ocean wave in a wild sea. "You give me a wild hope that I cannot control. Please, explain. I do not want to *assume*, as you accused me of doing. I must understand you."

She flipped a twig into the coals and watched a tiny flame blaze and dance. "I love this, here with you. This makes more sense than anything I have ever experienced in my life. I don't care about that other life. The more time I spend with you, the more artificial layers I cast away. You are peeling me back, all the social facades and protective layers, to some kind of essential version of myself. I feel distilled into what matters, what I love. I feel such joy."

Sawyer hadn't moved. He sat as still as an ancient pine himself. On guard. Had she misjudged him?

Mistaken this conversation, this situation?

Be brave. You cannot be truly free if you are afraid to speak the truth.

"Marriage," she said. "Marriage feels to me like another corset, another awkward bustle, a shape to squeeze my body and brain into. A social shape that does me no favors."

Sawyer shifted and slumped, as though in defeat. She hurried on, words tumbling and falling out like a stream down a hill, like a young bird trying to fly. The last thing she wanted was for him to feel sad.

"I am already damned as a fallen woman. Why don't we throw convention to the wild winds and yield to our desires? To explore each other, as we have this wilderness." Her heart beat as loud and wildly as a Scottish reel. The blush seared her body. She was terrified of her own daring, and his reaction. *Courage!* She would be free, to speak and love as she wished. She watched him for his reaction, her breath strangling in her throat.

Sawyer jerked up and sat straight. His jaw dropped. His gaze widened and riveted on a tree in the distance. A strangled sound emerged from his throat.

And then he said the thing she least expected.

Sawyer turned his gaze on her. "Lilwen Jones, I will not lay a hand on you until we are married. In a church," he added hastily as she opened her mouth to snap a response.

It was her turn to stare in shock, her mouth a rictus of shocked dismay. How very embarrassing. She had actually propositioned a man, and he turned her down.

The hurt engulfed her. Pain lanced as though she had been fatally stabbed, blood spurting from her mortal wounds.

"Lilwen, I want you more than any man ever wanted a woman. I want you—body, soul, and mind."

A great buzzing in her brain obscured his voice—but at last his words registered. He wanted her. She knew it, really. Somewhere, deep, deep within, the part that knew this wilderness too and welcomed it with joy.

He said, "But I will not ruin you. I will not permit you to ruin your fledgling business, shatter your dreams, destroy all your hard work. You heard Dolly. No woman will buy your plants if your reputation is besmirched. I'm sorry. It will be difficult enough for a woman to create and run a business. I only took you into the forest so you didn't run away and become a nun. It was ill-judged of me. You will marry me the day we return."

"I don't know if I am more embarrassed or more angry! There! You are doing it again. Making my decisions for me. Hedging me in, like the worst of social arbiters. I doubt you really do want me so much. You refuse me so easily."

"It is the most difficult thing I have had to do in my life." He might be speaking truth. He had turned away from her. His profile, face, neck, shoulders, back were ridged with tension like the hard slope of a small mountain.

She said, "It is different for a man. You can take a woman as you please, or not. I have never before lowered my pride to ask a man to love me. You shame me with your answer, Sawyer Thane." Lilwen rose to her feet.

Sawyer rose too, stepped in close. He put one gentle finger under her jaw, tilting it up to him. With the other hand, he gently wiped a hot tear which insisted on squeezing from her eye, no matter how hard she tried to hold it in. "Never. I would never shame you. Let me take you back to Strahan now, and we will be married. *That* is how much I want you."

"No. You told me you could not marry me, and so I shall not. I will not ruin *your* life, Sawyer Thane, by becoming the millstone around your neck that you fear so much. I will not be a drag for anyone. I prize freedom and autonomy far too much."

She pushed his hands off her, though everything hurt where he touched her, calling, screaming, for his touch once more. "Leave me now to walk off my embarrassment."

"Lilwen, you must marry me now. You cannot return to social shame. I will be a good husband to you."

Anger, embarrassment, hurt pride, and frustrated lust all boiled up in Lilwen like a geyser in a hot spring. "If you are going to marry me anyway, why not make love to me, now? What can it possibly matter?"

"It matters to me, to show respect—"

"This is not respect. You say we feel what each other feels, so how can you get it so wrong? Tonight was such a beautiful moment, in a richly natural, glorious place. We could have given each other our love here. Now you have ruined it. Ruined everything. I wasn't serious about becoming a nun before, but now I am."

Sawyer strode over to her and gripped her shoulders in his hands. He vibrated with the urge to shake her, to compel her to his will. His mouth was an angry slash.

"If I am going to be a nun," she said, making her voice as drowsy and silky as she could, "then I want to taste love before I take the veil. Will you love me now?"

Sawyer gripped her harder; then he wrested his hands from her and strode away a few paces. His shoulders shook. He radiated such desire Lilwen was magnetized, every cell longing to cleave to him.

"You are destroying me," he groaned, his face in his hands. "I want nothing more on heaven and earth." He took his hands away and looked at her, his face working. "I must not. Cannot."

The devil danced in Lilwen now. She had nothing more to lose, mentally stripped down as she was. "Is there a physical problem?" she asked sweetly.

"No, there is not!" Sawyer roared. To her thrilled delight, he marched over to her, picked her up, and carried her over to the fleeces by the saddles. He threw her down and landed heavily on top of her. He began to kiss her until her mouth stung, hard and punishing and bruising. Then soft, enticing, tasting.

"Can you feel how much I want you now?" he growled, pressing a huge erection through his trousers into her groin. "Does this feel like there is anything wrong to you?"

Lilwen laughed with lightheaded abandon. "I do not know. I have nothing with which to compare. I have it! When I return to Strahan, I must seek informed experience."

"You will not!"

"There you are again. You must cease this masterful behavior. It does not become you, and I certainly am not cowed by it."

“Are you not?” he growled again and proceeded to kiss her so thoroughly and demandingly that she completely melted into a luscious, soft, wanting ball of lust. Had he asked her to marry him again, she would have consented then and there. But fortunately for Lilwen, he did not. Once he had kissed her into a thoroughly aroused, soft, and malleable version of herself, Sawyer called a halt.

This time, she let him go.

She was a jellyfish. Completely at his mercy.

****

The morning sun shone clear and silver-golden in that special Tasmanian light. Lilwen wished she was a better landscape artist, to capture with fast and clever strokes the vivid yellows and greens of the forest, the streaky blue sky layered with thin fluffy clouds, the lingering apricot and brilliant pink of the sunrise, the tall pale wood of the Huon pines, and the brown soil made of millennia of shed leaves, bark, insects, and all the life of the forest, forever cycling and renewing itself.

The scenes with Sawyer last night had enlivened her skin, her mind, all her blood and vessels. She felt super-alive, super-awake, prone to bubbling laughter. Joy sang within her like an orchestra.

She had better do something with all this energy, all this love and zest. She scrambled out of her camp bed and went to retrieve her pencils and paints. She could use this glorious light, this wonderful day, this beautiful mood to transcribe the intricate beauty of plants onto the page, practice for when she found her *Agastachys*.

There was no sign of Sawyer, but a pot of hot

coffee nestled by the campfire, together with fresh bread damper sliced ready to toast and a pot of jam. A small handful of tiny, bright-red berries shone from their soft bark wrapping. Welcome had told her the berry was sweet *Coprosma*, edible and juicy.

Lilwen ate and drank, then washed in the freezing stream, allowing herself to shriek aloud in the still morning, causing a flock of colorful parrots to rise up, squawking, as though showing her how to screech properly. She sprayed water at them, and they wheeled away in a blur of color, shrieking into the heavens.

Lilwen returned to the campsite, pink and glowing from her wash.

Sawyer stood at the edge of the clearing, looking extremely self-conscious.

She smiled at him. He didn't move.

"Hello, Sawyer Thane. A beautiful day, is it not?"

He gave her a lopsided grin which made her heart flutter. He stayed there, just in the shadow of the trees. Lilwen couldn't see his hands.

They stared at each other for a while. His eyes glowed like honey in front of a fire, and a high color lit his cheeks. He was clearly primed for mischief, tense shoulders radiating bottled-up anticipation kept in check with an iron will. She waited for him to make the first move. A kind of scared grin broke free once or twice from twitching lips.

She took the opportunity to study him more deeply, as he was so kindly standing still for her.

Dark stubble stretched across his jaw and up the lower part of his cheeks, mingling with sideburns into that dark tousled mane of hair. A line of dark hair traveled down the front of his throat into the open neck of his shirt. The shirt itself barely stretched over a muscular chest and was soft with wear. Only three random buttons were done up; the rest of the shirt hung loose, streaked with dirt here and there, partly tucked into his trousers and partly hanging out. His trousers hung low on his hips and were streaked with dirt across knees, calves, and one hip, as though he had been crawling through damp, muddy undergrowth.

His boots shouted Sawyer Thane as much as any part of him; molded to his feet, soft, cared for, well-worn in, they radiated his capable, outdoor, physical, athletic personality.

Lilwen's examination returned to his face, and now he had Sardonic Sawyer back in place, a slight curl to his lip, eyes dark and watching her intently.

"About to do some botanic painting?"

"Why not?" she asked cautiously.

"Don't kill me."

"You kill me every day. It would be nothing but what you deserve."

Sawyer laughed.

Now, he looked as bashful as a sheepdog caught napping on a tapestry chair. He stepped forward, stopped. Stepped forward again, his eyes never leaving hers.

She waited.

Sawyer walked close to her, hands behind his back. Slowly, he pulled his arms out from behind his body. He was clasping a bunch of candelabra-like flowers, vivid white and cream, tiny flowers piled on top of each other on long branching stems, smelling of dreams and wishes and love.

Shock and quick envy lanced through her. "*You*

found them! The white waratah! It should have been *me*. And *you picked* them?"

Sawyer's face fell. "I didn't know whether to…bring them, or…"

"Or!" she said, temper rising. "Or! You should have left them and taken me to them!"

Lilwen grabbed them from him, feasting her sight on their rich beauty. They were everything she could have hoped for.

He was saying, "There is a bit of a problem…" but she hardly listened, except to retort, "Yes, you shouldn't have picked them! I need to see how they grow, check for seeds or other means of propagation potential, inspect the soil and aspect."

Lilwen examined the flowers. They were exactly like candelabra, each thick stem branching into multiple upright branchlets, and each of those holding a long candle of creamy butter-white tiny flowers, which formed the appearance of a single long spike of delicious bloom. The perfume smelt as sweet and heady as a gardenia.

"Where are they?" she asked. She could feel her eyes were wild, and her heart banged under her breastbone as savagely as when Sawyer kissed her.

"There is a problem." He gestured down to the streaks of mud on his clothes.

"As if I care for a little mud."

"It's a bit more than a little mud. They are growing near the base of a sheer cliff, in the middle of very thick prickly shrubs." He rubbed at his head and removed a long spike of something with small and prickly leaves. "This sample was very difficult to get to, but the bigger population? Almost impossible. You will need an air balloon."

"Nonsense! How you infuriate me! When will you decide, when will you *realize*, I am not made of porcelain? In fact, my smaller frame may be able to squeeze through shrubbery more easily. I may be able to scale cliffs more easily with my lighter body weight."

Sawyer shook his head. "No, no, Lilwen. It is very perilous. One slip would be death."

She studied the plants in her hand. All was not lost. There were more plants still in the place he had found them. Belatedly, she remembered her manners.

"Thank you for bringing them," she said stiffly.

"It seems I would have been better not." The growl was back. "I hardly want to take you there, as you will insist on endangering yourself. Where some grow, there will be others. Can you not draw these ones, press them or whatever, and we continue the search for more accessible flowers." Sawyer's tawny eyes pleaded. He was frightened for her. He knew what her answer would be.

"Better to die in this beautiful place, than eke out some gray half-existence forever in debt to your father," she answered lightly. His face twisted in an agonized grimace.

Naughty Lilwen took hold of her. "If I am like to die, will you not assuage my desperate curiosity before we leave?"

Sawyer stared in confusion, and then a thrill spiked through her as an actual blush spread over his features. His eyes turned hot. "Lilwen, you know I cannot grant you that either."

She stepped very close. Placed a hand on his warm,

muscular chest, feeling his solid heartbeat beneath her palm, smelling his warm male scent. His firm arm enclosed her. He cocooned her, kept her safe from all the world in his embrace, whenever she wished, and yet together they hovered on the threshold of a great adventure.

She pitched her voice low and soft and teasing. "Who would have thought you so very starched up? I thought you were a wild man, answering to no person, living easily on physical power and instinct."

"If I could run up that cliff for you, on all fours, I would."

"I know it. But you won't need to. You will take me there, and we will design a solution. Both our brains together should make something of this dilemma. And if we can't, I promise you, we will go to look for other communities of this fabled plant. But first, I should reward you for finding them."

"Lilwen…."

Her voice became throaty. "Or punish you. Those plants are mine. How dare you pick them."

Sawyer stared, his gaze locked on her mouth shaping the words. She lowered her right hand, reaching around to squeeze and rub his firm left buttock. "Mmmmm," she said on a long exhale. "Or perhaps we could take off our clothes and roll around in them, uncaring, Adam and Eve in paradise."

Sawyer swallowed and his throat worked. His eyes scorched her. His body temperature, radiating onto her, seemed to have increased ten degrees.

She relented from teasing him—although she was only half teasing—and tried to explain. "I can't sit here like a calm person and just draw these lovely plants. I was full of fizz this morning, and now I know why. It's a lucky day. You found my dream. Take me there, now, please. Or have a drink, something to eat, whatever you need, but impatience is roaring through me. I feel as though I have to run shrieking through the forest, leaping and screaming. Take me there. Now. Please, Sawyer."

He bent and kissed her, this time his lips soft and lingering. She melted inside.

"You are right. I was civilized before. At least the outward semblance. But you have called out the wild man lurking deep within me. I am consumed by bestial appetites. When we are married, I will eat you."

Lilwen shivered.

"But right now, I'll take you to your flora-dream."

So it was her fault when the accident happened.

Chapter Twenty-One

Lilwen had sticks in her hair, mud from buttocks to ankle, and despair in her heart.

Yellow-cream white waratahs waved their lit-candle flowers at her less than three yards away, but it was only one bush, and that single bush sprouted on the cliff face three vertical yards upward. She adjusted the focus on Sawyer's pocket telescope. A fresh wound on the side of the main stem was testament to where he had carefully picked the branch for her.

Her chin rose as her vision, through the telescope, followed the sheer cliff face a hundred yards up to a wide ledge, opening into a small escarpment. There, she could see a wide swath of the rare blooms, glowing cream and pale yellow in the sun. Huge, stunning flowers, all tantalizingly out of reach.

She studied the cliff face. "It's kind of corrugated, isn't it? Surely I climbed worse when I was a wild girl, running around the gardens and jumping off the roofs of our family home."

Sawyer made a threatening rumble, akin to thunder in the distance. "We are miles from civilization, miles from help. An injury could mean death." He lay next to her, his curling hair equally full of sticks and leaves, his elbows sunk in mud.

She removed the scope from her eye. "Are you always this cautious? Somehow, I had a different idea of Sawyer Thane, wild animal hunter."

A reluctant laugh escaped him. "Not cautious at all. Usually, I just leap into whatever it is." His expression sobered. "Usually, I don't have gently bred women with mad ideas as part of my baggage."

"Show me how you got the first sample."

Sawyer raised his brows at her. "The first time was bad enough."

"All right. I'm going. I'm fit and strong. If you can do it, so can I."

"I'm considerably taller, with a longer reach and longer legs. You, however, are a lovely, but tiny, package of sheltered girl."

"There you go again. I don't need your permission. I think I can get to the first plant, and then up, up, up to the rest!"

Sawyer rolled himself on top of her. Soft, damp soil squelched underneath her. He took her wrists in his and held them above her head. She wriggled a little under his weight. She felt trapped and suddenly pushed at him, her hands under his chest, bucking with her legs. "No, no, *no*! Let me go. This is not right at all."

Sawyer rolled off as though he had been shot.

Lilwen slithered away. She slid through the shrubs and pulled herself out when she reached the foot of the cliff. Carefully selecting handholds and footholds, she began to climb. At first it was fine, with the ground only a little way below, but the cracks in the rocks seemed to get thinner and shallower and farther apart.

She froze for a moment but shrugged off the feeling. Her body was hardy. It never let her down. And if she focused her mind, it would be strong too. This kept her going for another two yards. She reached the first white waratah and paused next to it, her breathing heavy and fast, her heart thudding hard against the rock. A light sweat coated her face and shoulders. She hadn't exerted herself that much. It was a fear sweat.

Thankfully, she spied Sawyer's disreputable hat, with Sawyer underneath it, proceeding up the cliff face behind her. He joined her in seconds. "How do you feel?"

"I'm fine," she said and realized that she spoke truth now Sawyer was near.

She began to edge her careful way up the cliff face, fingers clinging to crevices, lodging her boot in small ledges. Small plants and twisted shrubs gave her purchase.

She had scaled some way up, gaining in confidence, when a small woody shrub on which she rested her foot suddenly gave way in a shower of dirt and pebbles, leaving her off-balance and scrabbling with her foot for purchase.

She clung to the cliff, and everything froze. Her body pressed itself against the cliff face. Her mind swam. Her hands clenched into claws, and she couldn't move a single muscle, not a finger, nor a toe. Terror nailed her brain fast to the spot to which she gripped. Her limbs shook, and fear such as she had almost never known flooded her body, paralyzing her further.

And then Sawyer's body and breath and voice were there. His body cradled over hers, not quite touching, protecting her from falling. He spoke in low, crooning tones, such as one would use to a frightened, injured animal. "Now move this finger, that's right. I've got you. You won't fall. Now your hand. Very good. Very, very good. Yes, now this foot. Keep going. We are closer to the top than the bottom. Can you keep going?"

Lilwen still trembled in paralyzed fear, but somehow his voice gave her fingers, her hands, her feet the courage to move. Slowly, her mind unfroze enough to listen, to see the next hand hold, the next toe hold. *Don't look down. Don't look down. Keep your eyes straight.*

Slowly, slowly they crept up the cliff, Sawyer talking to Lilwen in his smooth, calm, coaxing voice. She looked up. The top beckoned! She made a jerky grab for the cliff; soil crumbled in her fingers, and she lost her grip. A heavy weight slammed her against the cliff, and then heaved her up, hard, so that she almost flew the last few yards, and lay, half on, half off, the top of the cliff. Pulling and scrabbling, yanking at anything she could find, full of fury and determination now, she pulled herself up and over and lay there, gasping, feasting her unbelieving eyes on the field of yellow-cream candles in which she had landed.

But the heave had unbalanced Sawyer. She looked over the edge. Under her horrified gaze, he began to slide down the cliff. She could see all the way down to the bottom, and it made her dizzy just to look at it. The ground was far, far below. She couldn't believe they had managed to climb all the way up here.

Sawyer grabbed holds, plants, shrubs, anything, but his balance was off, and he was sliding and scraping; he began to fall.

"Nooooo!" Lilwen screamed, as with a slowly turning motion, his body left the cliff face and began bumping and smashing its way down.

It seemed to take forever, and then Sawyer Thane was lying, all the way at the bottom of this thrice-cursed cliff, in a tangled heap of limbs, clothes, dirt, rocks, and branches.

Lying as still as her heart.

She closed her eyes. Opened them again.

Nothing moved.

"You great fool!" Lilwen yelled down. "Why didn't you let me fall?"

Shocked tears streaked down her cheeks. Every muscle trembled, and all her nerves twitched, her exhausted body going into spasms after the long-endured state of terror of climbing the cliff face. She lay on the ground, weak and helpless, in an agony of emotional torment. Her dirt-blackened fingers scrabbled on the soil with scored and broken nails. Her boots were half destroyed, large gouges scraped in the leather. The ripped knees of her trousers gaped, edged in her own blood where they had dragged against the rock. More blood seeped from grazes under the torn places.

When she could think again, she moved back from the cliff edge, stood up shakily, and looked all around her. Was she close to any habitation? Any human presence?

She turned in a slow circle. Nothing but sky, mountains, hills, forest canopy, blue tarns, and shadowy valleys. Button grass plains, subalpine to alpine flora. If Sawyer were here with her, it would have been gorgeous.

There was no choice.

It was up to her.

She had to go back down the cliff, praying Sawyer still lived, and then get him back to Strahan.

Do it, Lilwen Jones! Just get yourself down there and do it.

She looked over the cliff edge once more. “Sawyer!” she yelled at the top of her lungs. “Sawyer, Sawyer, Saw-yer,” the hills echoed back. “Sawyer Thane!” she screamed. “Thane, Thane, insane,” said the hills.

The tangled heap below didn’t stir. Lilwen swallowed bile.

She took a long, regretful look at the *Agastachys*. This group of flora was truly marvelous. The candles grew as long as her forearms. The shrubs rose taller than she was. She sucked in a breath. Well, it would be stupid to do all this for nothing. She selected a few stems and leaves and snapped them off. She dug a few layered horizontal branches from where they had grown little roots into the soil and collected some of those too. She put it all into pockets in her clothes. If she fell and died too, and someone eventually found their bodies, maybe they would find the *Agastachys* and the plant would make its way into a nursery somewhere.

Stop it! You need to stay alive for Sawyer. Get back down there, woman, and see to him. The best man you have ever met, ever known, and you throw him off a cliff.

She tried once more, leaning over the cliff edge. “Sawyer? Hold on! I’m coming!”

Was that a sound? A groan?

“Sawyer, hang on my love. I will marry you! I will go back to Strahan and marry you in a church. Just don’t you dare die on me! I’m coming now.”

Lilwen hooked her mind fiercely on that one thing. Hold on! Get to Sawyer. Help him.

You must get down, save Sawyer.

Get down, save Sawyer.

Down. Save.

Lilwen's mind was black. She was only a creature of broken fingernails, holding crevices. Feet, stretching down, stepping, moving down the next time. A body, hugging the cliff. Get down. Save. Move.

It went on for years. She moved like a snail, a sloth, a congealing drop of blood from a wound. Her shoulders screamed. Her hands cramped. Her thighs shook with pain and exertion. At last, feeling with numb toes, her foot struck hard, solid ground. She risked a peek down, clinging tight.

She had made it. She unhooked hands that were frozen into stiff talons and leaned away from the cliff that had been her life. She looked around for the heap of clothes and limbs.

There! She staggered over. She was crying, probably had been for ages, as her swollen face itched and her eyes stung, but it didn't matter. Fear drove her.

Sawyer looked as pale as death. She bent down with her shaking legs and brushed dirt and rocks away. She touched his face. Cold or warm?

"Sawyer?" her voice croaked. "Lover. Friend." Fresh tears spurted, burning her cheeks.

She knew nothing about medicine or healing. She wasn't one of those women always talking about illness. Not one of those capable women with remedies for every ailment. She touched him again. Blood! There was blood! All over his thigh.

Quickly, she bent and felt for the pulse in his neck. And there it was, thready and weak, merely a tiny pump against her desperate fingers.

She pushed the rest of the dirt, leaves, sticks, and small rocks and other debris from his body. She adjusted his clothes and gently, slowly, pulled his limbs straight.

His face had the extreme pallor of death, his dark bristles standing out against the paleness like ebony and ivory keys on a piano. Dark shadows lurked under his eyes. His face had relaxed completely, his cheeks sucked in. Without his habitual amused, sardonic expression, his mouth looked vulnerable. Voluptuous. His arms lay where she had placed them, the hands relaxed, palms open to the sky.

His legs. A terrible, long dirty tear split the fabric of his right thigh. Blood still pulsed through, quite fast. A huge sticky pool widened underneath him. How much blood had he lost? She had heard of people bleeding to death, women in childbirth and such like. What did one do? Think, think!

The only thing she could remember was that one must stop the bleeding, and Welcome saying sassafras was an old bush medicine. Stopped the bleeding. *Was it sassafras?* Think!

"Sawyer! I'm going to find something to patch you up! I'm coming back."

No answer. Just that faint, thready breathing, a minuscule raising and lowering of the chest. She suddenly remembered: if someone was unconscious, make sure their tongue wasn't blocking the throat. She thanked all the stars that Sheila O'Donohue who worked in the Flower Hotel near to the nursery had fits. Lilwen had checked her more than once, pulling out her tongue and rolling her on her side.

Now she carefully opened Sawyer's mouth and gently flipped his tongue to make sure it lay forward in his mouth. He made a sound that made her leap in the air, a wordless, growling, grunting noise. But that was all. A tear splashed on his face. Her tear. She wiped it away with her thumb.

The thought flashed—people must drink water when they were losing blood. Doubt assailed her, gripping her throat as she regarded his pale, lax cheeks. He might choke.

Stop the bleeding first.

Feeling sick, she peeled back the blood-matted fabric all down his right thigh. The wound was a long, deep tear in the flesh, filled with dirt and pebbles. She would have to get that out too, or it might fester. Fester. Gangrene. Amputation. The unwilling vision of Sawyer with one leg made her start to shake. She must save him, she must! Or he would want her to kill him. He would hate to live a half-life. But her imagination was running away with her, thinking of amputations. He had to live first.

"Oh my God!" she screamed out loud. "Help me! Somebody, help me!" But there was no living soul for miles except Lilwen Jones.

Get to work, woman. Do what you can. What you have to. Do it, now.

Which tree was the sassafras? Welcome had shown her so many plants. She must get it right. She was used to studying plants, noting unusual characteristics, their identifying features like leaf color and shape, flower structure. She pictured Welcome pointing out the tall, conical tree with shiny dark-lime-green, toothed leaves that smelt like aniseed. His fingers turning the leaves to show the undersides—hairy and grayish-white.

She walked rapidly into the forest, turning back regularly to check her position in relation to Sawyer and the cliff.

Here! The lower branches and leaves were easily at her height. She pulled off several small branches and some soft pink bark from a nearby shrub and ran back to where Sawyer lay. She squatted down next to him, exposed the wound, and crushed the leaves in her hand. She washed the wound as best she could with a little water in the water skin Sawyer always carried. She dug around in his jacket until she found the small hip flask and poured some whiskey on her fingers and then into the wound, swishing it around inside. She pulled the deep edges of the wound together, holding it tight with fingers stretched across his thigh, fingers white with effort, blood seeping through her grip.

She crushed more leaves in her other hand, chewed some of them to make a mashed consistency, and packed the improvised compress over his wound. She finished it off with layers of soft young bark and tied it all together as firmly as possible with long, thin, pliable bark strips of the bootlace bush. She watched, her heart in her mouth, for many agonizing minutes. No more blood.

****

She trickled the last of their water into his mouth, drop by patient drop. His eyes opened.

"Oh!" she said, shocked. She bent closer. "Sawyer. Sawyer Thane. Are you with me?"

"Lilwen? What the hell?" He shifted his body and cried out when he tried to move his leg.

She pressed both hands on his chest. "Don't move! You are injured. A massive wound in your thigh."

"What? What happened?"

"You fell off a cliff. Lucky you are a mountain

tiger. Not many mortals could have survived it." Her tears started again, a huge rush of weakness overtaking her for a moment, her terror reanimating now she had someone to share the decisions, and no longer had to be so tough.

"How long…have I been like this?"

Lilwen looked at the sky. Massing pale gray clouds were lit with purple and gold, heralding the evening. "A few hours? Half a day?"

Sawyer tried to sit up. She managed to support him. "Have you been with me all this time? It hurts like the devil, by the way."

"Here, drink the water. You need it for the blood loss."

Sawyer drank and looked at his leg. "What in blazes…?"

"It's sassafras. At least I hope it's sassafras. And bark. Tied with bootlace bush—you know, *Pimelea.* Welcome told me that Aboriginal people use sassafras leaves to stop bleeding. I don't know how exactly, but I crushed the leaves, and chewed some, and put whiskey in the wound, and then packed it, and put bark on too, and the bleeding stopped, and…"

Sawyer grinned through his pallor. "If I live through this, remind me to tell you that you are a bloody marvel!" He drank some more water. Shook the water skin. "Have you had any of this?"

She shook her head. "I couldn't leave you. Sawyer, I was terrified. I didn't know what to do, and night was coming…I was going to make a fire to keep the animals away and find more water. I thought…I thought…you were going to…"

"Shhh. You've done brilliantly. I'm a hard man to

kill. Now, damn this leg, I'm stuck here, but you will have to find water. Our base camp is too far away." He studied the landscape around them. "I'm surveying the lines of trees and shrubs, noting the way the ground falls in certain places. Looking for animal tracks. See that fairly wide animal path just there?"

It took a while for Lilwen to see it, but suddenly she did.

"See how it dips down and widens? I bet it goes to a water source. Take the water skin and follow it. I'm just within calling distance; you can't get lost. Will you do it?"

Her dry, parched mouth craved moisture. Her skin felt as shriveled as an Egyptian mummy. She had given it all to Sawyer and hadn't had a drink for hours. Of course she would do it! Her confidence grew again now Sawyer could tell her what to do, with his expert knowledge. They might even survive this ordeal.

Lilwen followed track after track, blundering through thick spiky button grass and horizontal shrubs. At least the ground was becoming spongier, back into the wet rainforest vegetation. At last she came to a small waterfall, pouring out of a dirt face into a tiny gurgling stream, rushing through the rainforest. She drank thirstily, uncaring about water running down her neck and wetting her clothes. She filled the water skin, made wet cloths torn from her damaged trousers, and as she walked back to the sound of Sawyer's calls, made cuts in the trees so she could find the way to water again.

Sawyer drank thirstily, shifting his body in restless discomfort. She must—somehow—get him to civilization before he succumbed to wound fever.

"Hungry?" he asked her.

"No, I'm fine."

"Don't lie. Here, help me get my knives out."

Lilwen extracted two long knives from his boots, another strapped to the side of his injured right thigh, two shorter knives from his belt, and one in his coat. She was laughing by the time he had a pile of gleaming knives resting on a sheet of bark next to him.

"Ready?" His grin held a spark of the old Sawyer, and her heart turned over.

Dusk mantled the forest, shadows deepened, and the rustling, calling, and scrabbling of nocturnal creatures had begun.

A fat possum crawled toward them on a branch. She grabbed Sawyer's hand just as he was about to throw. "No! She has a baby on her back, see?"

"And no doubt one in her pouch. But tonight is her lucky night. Lilwen Jones would rather starve than murder a cute baby possum, and so it shall be."

"Don't be ridiculous!"

From his seated position, propped against a tree, Sawyer threw three knives with alarming accuracy. Lilwen ran to collect the animals, checking that they had been killed instantly. It seemed terrible, but they had to eat. Sawyer had to eat.

Lilwen gathered wood, sticks, and twigs, and before long had a fire going. Sawyer skinned the animals where he sat, wincing now with pain. His pallor had worsened.

"Here, give it to me. Just explain how to do it."

"Is there any of that whiskey left? Or did you pour it all on my wound?"

"A small amount. Here."

Sawyer gulped it down. "Not enough," he said hoarsely. "When it is full dark, I shall explain how you can find our camp, our horses, and best of all, the full bottle of whiskey I have in my saddlebags."

Somehow, between them, they skinned and prepared the food and cooked the animals on long sticks over the fire. Lilwen bit into the warm meat, hunger clawing at her belly. Nothing had ever tasted so incredibly good.

She brought back damp cool cloths from the stream and bathed their faces and hands.

"Lilwen, you have saved us," Sawyer said.

A pleased blush warmed her cheeks, despite the inaccuracy of his words. She had more likely killed them both. As she opened her mouth to retort, he held a hand up.

"I need you to go, tonight, to our camp. We need to clean and retie this wound. Somehow, you will have to bring the horses as close as you can, and then we will find our way back to Strahan. You will be walking through the bush, alone and at night, for some hours. Can you do this?"

No! screamed every cell in Lilwen's body. The dense darkness all around them rustled and scratched, hooted and growled.

Sawyer said, "There is nothing in the Australian bush at night that will hurt you. Nothing fauna or flora, that is. Only humans."

"What if I step on a snake?"

"It's far too cold. They will all be asleep. Just don't poke any hollow logs."

"Spiders?" she whispered. Terror pinched all the way up her spine. Her stomach clenched. She would be insane by the time she got to the camp. If she didn't lose her way. And that was the main problem.

"I don't know the way." She pressed her eyelids with trembling fingers.

"Come here. Sit beside me. That's right. Now. Look up into the sky. Do you know the Southern Cross?"

"Of course! And the two pointers, Alpha Centauri and Beta Centauri."

"Excellent. Now draw one line through the longest part of the Cross. See it there? Can you hold it in your mind? Draw another at ninety degrees from the midsection of the pointers. Straight out from the middle of them. Got it? See where the lines meet?"

"I think so?"

"That point is celestial south. Draw a line straight down to the horizon. That is due south. You walk straight toward it."

"But don't the stars wheel around in the sky?"

"Yes, clever! But you see, the lines always work. No matter where the constellations are in the sky. A line through the longest part of the Southern Cross, keep going until it meets the line coming straight out from the midpoint of the pointers. Draw a line down to the horizon from that point. South."

"How far is camp, Sawyer?"

"You can do it, Lilwen, my brave one. I don't think I can wait until morning. My wound burns and flames—and it's swelling. Hurts like the devil himself breathes on it. But still. Would have pained me a great deal more if you hadn't treated it." He rubbed his temples. "And my mind…my mind grows strange, tormented with fever dreams. I may not make any sense when you return. So. First, you will tie me to this tree."

"But Sawyer, why?"

"Because if I become fevered, I may wander off. You will come back, and I will be gone, wandering like a madman in the forest, until I die of my wounds or I chew the damn leg off."

Lilwen obediently took the rope he pointed to and tied him, securely but not too tightly, to the tree.

"Now, fill the water skin, give me another drink, and fill it again. You are taking it."

"No! I will not! You need it. You have lost a lot of blood."

"My only hope is if you return with the horses. You must take it."

"No. I will find water on the way. You know I can. And this is a very wet rainforest."

Sawyer pondered, then nodded. "Very well. Now, the camp is only about three miles away. It will take you about two hours to walk there in this forest. I don't know how to bring the horses through this thick bush, but just try, will you? Try not to stray too far off your path. You may never find it again."

Lilwen bleated, "Sawyer, I am utterly terrified! Walking through the dark bush alone…"

"You are my brave plant collector. Look how you have saved me already! Actually…" He thought for a while. "When you get to the camp, you could saddle a horse and then ride due west. You will come to Strahan in half a day, by morning. Get Rory Fraser and some bush trackers to find me."

"No, I will come back to you tonight with the horses. Going to Strahan will take too long." Even in the darkness, Lilwen saw his relief. Time was critical then. She could only believe him.

She passed him two clean, wet compresses made from her torn trousers. "Here are cold cloths. Bathe your face when it heats from the fever. Here is your water, and your knives. Be safe, Sawyer Thane. I will return before five hours are gone. Stay alive for me until then. Stay alive."

She kissed him, and it was sweet and scary too. His mouth tasted fever-hot and metallic. His rolling eyes held a kind of white light like the dangerous shimmer which presages a storm. Sweat beaded his forehead and upper lip. He grimaced with pain every time he adjusted his body.

If she returned with whiskey, he could manage the pain. A shame she had not asked Welcome to teach her the pain-killing plants. But now, it was time to go, while the skies were clear, showing her the Southern Cross and pointers bright in the southern sky.

What if clouds came? She repressed the thought, kissed Sawyer thoroughly once more, putting all her hope that it wasn't for the last time. She stood, trying to breathe in courage, her agonized gaze constantly seeking the Southern Cross, drawing the lines again and again, and then tracing the faint animal path before her which had led them to this place.

She knew she would be more terrified than ever before in her life. She clutched her small knife, ready to blaze the trees as she walked, to help her find her way back to this place again.

She put her chin up, drew her coat tight, and stepped out.

Chapter Twenty-Two

Lilwen had never, in all her life, experienced such terror. The bush pulsed full of deep shadows and hunched, black forms, which shifted and changed under her petrified gaze. The moon glimmered in the sky. A little more than half full, it yielded a silvery light, only enough to create shapes and phantoms to startle and confuse her. A whole galaxy of stars blazed overhead, helping to light the path immediately before her. More than a few feet in front simply dissolved into darkness.

She constantly checked and rechecked her position in relation to the stars. What if she missed? What if her lines were just a little out, wouldn't she walk and walk, and never find…

Stop it, Lilwen Jones. All you can do is keep trying; keep hoping.

What was that? She shrieked and curled over, still standing, into a shaking ball of terror. Something had flown at her face. A night bird? A bat? For a long while, she remained curled over as though paralyzed, her arms wrapped over her head, a choking nausea stinging her throat.

Sawyer, she thought. Sawyer. She managed to uncurl and keep walking.

Keep walking.

Just do it.

In the dark, her sense of self blurred; she lost her

edges between skin and night. Always, people built protective shapes around them: houses, gardens, fences, walls, even tents and campfires, caves. The frantic urge hammered in the old part of her brain: hold back the dark, hold away the wild things. Instead, she walked right amongst them.

Lilwen stopped again. What shape hollowed the darkness? A human form, hiding behind a tree, the edge emerging, imperfectly hidden? A native Aboriginal person? A wild man? A monster, from myths and legends? Did ghosts haunt these forests? *Sawyer*, she thought, and moved her feet again. First one, then the other.

Walk, damn you.

At every noise, every movement of the bush, her heart spiked and stilled for a shocked instant, then beat as though it would fly out of her chest. Her blood was full of needles. Bile scored her throat. Her eyes swiveled around, stretched and staring, like those of a frightened animal. Dark thoughts battered at the edge of sanity; soon she would go mad with terror.

But she kept walking.

Through her terror, she held fast to one idea: she loved Sawyer Thane.

She would do *anything* to ensure he lived.

****

Lilwen had stopped thinking. She was only her body, moving in a terrified miasma of fear. Her feet stung; she must have been walking for hours. Where was the camp?

At times, the sky had darkened with cloud; she could barely make out the Southern Cross, and then fresh panic engulfed her. The stars were her only guide.

If clouds covered the sky, obscuring them completely, she and Sawyer were done for.

She had battled through thick shrubberies and detoured around impassable cliffs and huge, tangled forests of dense trees. She didn't remember any of this on the forward journey. Was she still walking in the right direction? Perhaps she had wandered off to the east, where thick forest marched for hundreds of miles? She would never be found again, and Sawyer would die, raving in fever madness, tied to a tree.

"There is nothing in the bush that can hurt." She repeated Sawyer's words over and over, like a prayer, until they had no meaning. The fear stayed constant, except for regular spikes of dread at some new dark shape or sound. But she kept walking. It was all she could do.

At times, sure she was lost in the dark, a half-imagined shape would glide through the shadows, pale amber stripes shimmering for an instant under the unearthly glow of the moon. Always, she turned and followed it, even though she knew not if it was a figment of her panic-stricken brain or something corporeal. It could have been a Tasmanian tiger waiting for her to trip and fall, to plunge its sharp teeth into her soft neck, suck on her warm blood as it pulsed away with her life; but her instincts insisted the animal was *her* tiger, the one she had fed, and it would lead her to safety.

Almost out of her senses, petrified and exhausted, Lilwen at last stumbled on a large cleared space. She gazed around in stunned amazement. This looked horribly like their first camp, several miles south of their current camp.

There! Their old fireplace, marked by a ring of stones. The small pile of firewood left for another traveler. The marks in the soil where they had slept, the small track to the pool.

Lilwen crumpled to the ground and lay like a dead thing. She was beyond crying, beyond fear. All her hopes were destroyed. How had she ever expected to find their current camp, with such a vague way of finding it?

And now the tears came, and her body shook with deep, hurting sobs. She was lost.

They were both dead.

****

Something rushed out of the bush at her. She had barely registered the noise of scampering paws, when a warm, wriggling body was jumping all around her, licking her tear-burnt face with a rough doggy tongue.

She sat up. "Hero? *Hero*? What the…? But I am so very pleased to see you!"

Lilwen wrapped her arms around the dog, hugging it madly, squeezing it again and again to her body, crying into its fur. After some time, she looked up.

Her stomach knotted. Her heart shot into her mouth. Was she going to be attacked? A man stood there. *A wild man?* Her brain shattered in silent screams. And then her eyes traced the shape of his countenance, and she knew.

She was saved. *They* were saved.

Welcome lurked in the shadows, the moonlight gleaming on his grin. Or was he Wallace? No, definitely Well. She knew that crinkle around his eyes, the emotional warmth emanating from him, the brimming laughter held back.

She staggered to her feet. "Welcome! I'm so *glad* to see you!" She flung herself on him, embracing him. She stepped back. "But how did you get here, now, in the dark? What's going on?"

Even in the darkness, she could discern Well's face blushing red after her hug.

"I was in the garden this evening, talking to Edna. Your mad dog here started howling like a bunyip in a trap, Miss Lily. She scratched and yowled in her kennel until she broke right out and leapt the fence. The dog came back when I called her, and the damn thing waited while I saddled the horse. Smart dog! Then she took off like greased lightning. We rode and ran together, for hours. Bloody long way, but she shot straight as an arrow, all the way here."

He paused. "And here you are, all alone?"

"Hero! Did you really? My beautiful, wonderful, amazing dog. Did you sense I was in trouble? I can't believe it! And thank you, Welcome!"

"She knew you had come this way the first time, so she followed the same track to find you. Dingoes are exceptionally smart dogs, Miss Lily."

"They surely are! And this one in particular. Oh Hero, you have saved me twice! A big juicy bone for you, as soon as we get back."

"Best reward for that dog is to keep her with you. Don't leave her behind again. She will look after you always."

"And so I shall. Hero, I owe you my life. And now, we need to save Sawyer Thane."

Welcome found the way back to their current base camp; on her terrifying march, Lilwen had missed it by only a few yards. Well took a small detour out of the direct way to show her the marks she had blazed on the trees not so far away. It had taken them another twenty minutes to get back there. It made her feel sick, how close she had come, and yet missed it. Thank all the gods for Hero and Welcome.

Safe once more—relatively—Lilwen worried and fretted about Sawyer. Exhaustion and her night of terror had leached the vigor from her bones. The food she had eaten with Sawyer was long hours ago. She stumbled, weak and dizzy. She steeled herself for another long trek through the bush, and then they would be back to Sawyer.

They had to walk the three horses most of the way back, and detour around steep ridges and thick tangles of forest. Welcome insisted she sit astride one of the horses whenever she could, while he led the others. Lilwen acceded without much argument, profoundly grateful. After a while, though, she had to get off and walk too; sitting on the horse made her feel full of tears and panic for Sawyer. At least walking, she could assuage her terror in action.

The sky darkened. The stars wheeled in the sky and disappeared at times behind streaks of scattered cloud. Even the nocturnal animals had quietened, and the forest was mostly still, excepting the birds that they startled on their way through. The air had the soft, sleeping smell of night; the exhales of the forest had a different quality to the day.

The moon set, and the sky began to grow the gray light of false dawn. The chill air tasted dead in her lungs. But they were getting closer; she could feel it.

Along the way, Welcome collected many plant samples—leaves, mosses, bark, fragile discs of gray-green lichen, and some small handfuls of thick yellow clay. He put them all in a pouch attached to his belt.

He had questioned her closely about Sawyer's wounds, and what she had done; he was delighted to hear about the sassafras and confirmed she had the correct plant. "It's an excellent tree, sassafras. You did the right thing there, Miss Lily."

At one point, they heard wild howls faintly in the night sky. Lilwen stopped abruptly and turned terrified eyes to Welcome.

"Are there wolves in the bush?" she asked.

"No wolves. Men, I reckon."

"Wild men?" Every atom in Lilwen froze. No! Not again!

"Are they with Sawyer?" she asked, a new terror possessing her now. What if wild men had found him? What would they do to him, injured as he was?

"Coming from that direction."

"What will we do?" she whispered it, the horror strangling her throat so the words had to be forced through a vise.

"Keep going, Miss Lily. We'll think of something. Maybe they aren't exactly where Sawyer Thane is. We'll creep up and see when we get close."

Lilwen moaned aloud. Would this night ever end? Could it get any worse?

The horrible fact was it probably could.

****

Apricot, yellow, vivid pink, and rose-red streaked the eastern sky before the sharp angle of the *Agastachys* cliff appeared in front of them, silhouetted against the bright morning. Pale blue sky gleamed amongst the vivid colors of sunrise in the east, while darkness still clotted the west. The top of the cliff gleamed with cream and gold: her white waratahs shining golden in the dawn.

They found a good place to tether the horses, in case they needed stealth and subterfuge when approaching the camp. Welcome hoisted the saddlebags over his shoulders.

The calls and yowls had ceased. Lilwen's heart was a stone in her chest. She greatly feared what they would find.

Her limbs flopped as though boneless, her nerves more wrung out than she could ever remember. The night of no sleep, horrors, and shocks had taken its toll, but as they neared the makeshift camp at the bottom of the cliff, her weariness of mind, body, and spirit dropped away, and she began to run.

Lilwen burst into the camp, staring wildly around her.

Everything was as she had left it, including Sawyer Thane, tied to a tree.

There was no sign, none at all, of invaders.

Sawyer listed over to his left side, his whole body drooping and hanging off the rope around his waist. His hands lay passive, his body relaxed as in sleep…or…

Lilwen caught a sob in her throat, and ran to him, kneeling down beside him.

"Sawyer," she pleaded in a croak, hardly worth calling a voice at all. "Sawyer Thane. I'm here. *We* are here. Welcome and Hero."

She touched his face. Cold.

Everything in her chest squeezed and hiccupped.

The world went black.

Lilwen made herself move. She touched his neck,

feeling for that pulse—and yes!

He lived.

Welcome untied Sawyer with calm and gentle hands and laid him down on one of the blankets Lilwen fetched from a saddlebag. She also brought whiskey, water skins, hard bread, cheese, and dried fruits.

Sawyer shook and mumbled, jerking suddenly and crying out. His face had been cold from sleeping in the night air, but now he tossed with fever. The strange wild cries had been Sawyer in fever dreams. Not the dreaded wild men at all.

Welcome began gathering wood.

"Let me," said Lilwen.

Well smiled at her. "Do you know how to build a fire?"

"Of course." She hurried about her task. When the fire blazed, she fetched water from the waterfall and filled a billy. Hot water. She guessed they would need that for Sawyer's wounds, and for them to drink.

Hero bounded along with her, happy to be at her side. She patted her, feeling comfort in Hero's smooth fur and warm, beating heart.

When she returned, Welcome had stripped most of Sawyer's clothes from him, leaving a saddlecloth covering his groin, perhaps for her modesty's sake. Together, they washed his body, with particular care for his wounds.

Sick as he was, Lilwen couldn't help admiring the wonderful shape of him, the broad, muscular shoulders and smooth-planed chest; burly arms, now lying passive; his defined stomach tapering into narrow hips. His long, athletic legs. The huge tear in his right thigh, covered with her bush compress, with angry red streaks searing his skin around it.

Welcome gently peeled back the compress. Sawyer leaped and swore. Lilwen had to help to hold him down, her hands pressing on his shoulders as he writhed and mumbled.

Well peered into the wound. It looked terrible, black blood clotting in and all around it, the telltale angry red of infection swelling the muscle and skin.

"You did a brilliant job, Miss Lily." Welcome probed the edges of the wound with his fingertips. "The bleeding has slowed to a trickle. The fester is contained. We'll fix it fresh now."

He washed the wound with water and then whiskey, and then made a hot solution with boiling water and some of the bush plants. Lilwen tried to watch his actions very closely, but she was preoccupied with keeping Sawyer calm and as still as possible. He shouted her name three times. "I'm here, Sawyer Thane, I'm here," she answered each time.

When the solution was very warm but not burning, Welcome poured it over the wound, making Sawyer shout. He rubbed leaves, moss, and clay together and smeared the paste all over. He boiled a long bit of cotton and a needle from the saddlebags and stitched up the wound. He then covered it with a paste made of the ochre clay, crushed leaves, and ground-up bark.

"Will he be all right? Will he recover? Will he walk again?" she asked.

"He should be fine." Well gave her a huge grin. "Bush medicine is often better than a visit to those pricey town quacks. It's been healing people for thousands of years. He'll be a new man."

Lilwen burst into tears, then hugged the bushman

with all that was left in her.

"I'm so glad you and Hero came to find us. You have saved us both. How can I ever thank you?"

"No thanks needed, Miss Lily. My Aboriginal mates always taught me that the forest looks after us. That the earth is our mother. They say we can find everything we need right here, to stay healthy and well—and that we must care for the forest in return."

Lilwen wiped her eyes, and finally, something settled in her heart. A kind of peace.

This moment, right now, she had much to be thankful for. She sat next to Sawyer and stroked his hair, wiped a cool cloth over his forehead.

"He still has fever?" she asked.

Welcome made another hot drink with dried leaves he took from his pouch. When it cooled to tepid, he said, "This one cools fever. Keep dribbling it into his mouth."

Well pulled up his shirt. A puckered pink gouge, long healed, bisected his left pectoral. A row of ridged dots scarred the shoulder.

"What's that?" she said, horrified. "It must have been painful."

"I grew up in a logger's hut with nine brothers. Got these beauties when Wal, Meander, Derwent, and I built our own plane out of scrounged junk and flew it off the side of Frankland Peak into Lake Pedder."

She slopped tea on Sawyer's chin. An amused, appalled snort burst from her.

He peeled back his trouser leg and showed her more scars zigzagging across his calves. "Rafting the mighty Gordon, racing Wal and Meander. Went over the rapids." His trademark grin lit his face. "I won that time, but Wal and Meander had to drag me out of a half-submerged river cave before I drowned. My legs got snagged when the rapids spun me around all which ways."

He patted the pouch at his belt. "Wirarawn people living by Lake Pedder patched me up. Bush medicine. Nothin' better."

Lilwen laughed, a bit hysterically. "I believe you!"

"Here, Miss Lily, drink some of this too. You'll get all calm and sleepy. Eat first, soon as I make you something, then sleep. When Sawyer Thane improves, we'll head on back to Strahan."

"You don't think we should try to go now? Sawyer's life might depend on it."

A strange expression lurked in Welcome's eyes, wary and assessing.

"Depends. We could linger here until Sawyer improves. If we take him back now, those know-nothing docs in Hobart might take his leg off, and charge you double for the privilege." He paused. Scratched his head. "I reckon we wait here in the forest until the infection clears, then we go back. There'll be nothing for a crazed saw-wielding quack to ruin. The bush will have healed him cleanly."

Lilwen stared at him. Her stomach plummeted. She had thought it was all arranged and now she had to make another decision. One that could mean Sawyer's life, or full use of his limbs. Shouldn't she take him back to civilization, to a hospital, to doctors? She swallowed and stared at Sawyer's limp form, struggling to quell the beginnings of panic sparking around the edges of her vision.

She would wait until morning. If his condition had

improved, they would stay a day longer, maybe sending Welcome back to Strahan for help, or until Sawyer could ride a horse or be carried.

If he was worse, they would have to tie him behind Welcome and ride back as fast as they could.

Decision made, she allowed Well to catch and prepare hot food for her. She drank his potion, settled down next to Sawyer, and all of a sudden, sleep reached out sticky hands and pulled her down into mindless oblivion.

Chapter Twenty-Three

"Arrrgh! What the be-damned devil? What's the matter with my leg?"

Lilwen sat bolt upright, sleep fleeing like frost in sun. "Good morning, Sawyer Thane. So you live after all."

"What? Oh, bugger this leg. Argh, sorry for the language." Sawyer rubbed both his hands over his face and through his hair, making the wild curls, now stuck together with sweat and goodness knew what else, clump up in anarchic fashion. He stared in horrified disbelief at the wound on his leg, covered in yellow ochre and bound with stringy bark. He looked so comical that Lilwen had to suppress a laugh.

"You fell off the cliff."

"I *what*?" He looked around him. "Welcome?" He dodged a wildly licking tongue. "And Hero?"

Lilwen rapidly caught him up with all their adventures. He seemed to be most fixated on one particular point. "I *what*?" he repeated. "I sent you walking for hours, in the dark, using only the Southern Cross as a directional guide, to find the base camp and horses? Was I completely insane?"

"You said you wanted whiskey. You'd drunk the hip flask."

Sawyer let out a huge laugh. "I'm sure I did. This hurts like the very devil."

He studied her. "And you went. You walked in the dark, for hours. And somehow, you found not only the camp and the horses but Welcome and Hero too. Are you a witch?"

His eyes blazed hot as he studied her. There was something more than his usual teasing stare in their dark amber depths. She had never seen him look quite like this. She had seen him look tormented and lustful, amused and intrigued by their banter, frustrated by her willfulness, and worried to death about her safety. Now? He regarded her with a profound respect. Like he would look at a man he admired.

"I've learned something about you, Miss Lilwen Jones," he said. "And something about me. I've worried and fretted about keeping you safe, and yet you have completely confounded me with your superb courage and determination. I need to change how I think about you. It's the very least you deserve."

"Come now, Sawyer, this humility doesn't become you at all. You are just feeling a little weak with blood loss and the effects of fever, I assure you. You will be back to your superior, masculine self in no time, once you have had time to recover."

Sawyer laughed again. "No small thanks to you and Welcome, I understand. How soon can I move this leg?"

Lilwen pretended to consider. "Well, there is still an important choice to make. Rather than stay here another moment, we could sever the leg from your body and carry you back to Strahan upon the instant."

"Vixen! Wait until I have the use of my limbs once more!"

"Yes, I don't like your chances if you have to rely

solely on your wits when conversing with me. How much easier to resort to physical intimidation, or looming, or glowering, or all the other tricks in your arsenal, to try to best me."

Sawyer held up his hands. "I surrender at once! And I don't *loom*."

She said, in her sweetest tone, "Don't you? Perhaps I meant standing over with a menacing expression?"

She saw he was becoming pale. Their badinage had tired him, so easily. He said, "I am dreaming of a soft, considerate Lilwen. Was it just a fever dream, that you gently wiped my brow with cool hands, that you spoke softly to me, and your sweet voice brought me back from some shadowy country, where I thought I was lost wandering forever?"

Lilwen's core melted, and she blinked back tears. While she struggled for a response, he turned bright, victorious eyes on her. He grinned, and it was as shark-like as any as he had ever given her.

"I remember! A voice—your voice—shouting, "*I will marry you, Sawyer Thane. I will go back to Strahan and marry you in a church!*" Do you deny it?"

They stared at each other: Sawyer hot-eyed, smiling, fever pale, and sweating; Lilwen stricken, dumbfounded, and tongue-tied. He had heard *that*, out of all the things he could have heard?

He sobered. His expression was hungry and intense, his eyes scorching her. "You called me back from the void. It was you, your voice, your promise. So I came back. For you. I want to marry you, Lilwen Jones. You are a woman in a million, a thousand million."

She choked a little. "I want you down on one knee.

No! It was a joke! Stay where you are! Welcome!" Welcome hurried over.

"Tell this foolish man to keep still, Well. And tell him what you told me about bush medicine."

Sawyer said, "Ha, subject cleverly averted, Lilwen Jones." But he submitted, with tight lips, to the bush medic looking in his eyes, feeling his temperature, and pressing lightly around the wound to check for further swelling. He listened as Well presented the options.

Sawyer said, "We are not staying here any longer. I can ride behind you, man, can't I?" When the bushman nodded, Sawyer continued, "Lilwen has been through enough. She needs rest, and food, and the kind of cosseting Dolly Fraser is famous for. We are not remaining another day in this forest."

"See," Lilwen said in a sighing voice, "not even a day, and your autocratic nature reasserts itself. The very instant you are conscious, you think you have to protect me."

He was right, though. She wanted a proper bed, and proper food, and a bath. How she would adore a bath. She was so very tired of being strong, stalwart, and uncomplaining. She wanted to cry. She wanted to be cared for. She had scaled as many emotional cliffs and valleys as corporeal ones. And now that Sawyer was almost returned to his sardonic, funny, demanding self, she desperately longed for civilization and the easy welcoming friendship, and luxurious house, of Dolly Fraser.

"Welcome? You decide. Is Sawyer's leg fit for riding, or will he damage it more? Surely the pain would be intolerable?"

"Yes, Miss Lily, he'll be pretty cactus with pain.

But not to worry, my special bush tea will make him dopey as a koala. We'll have to bind up that leg tight though, or it will split open like a snakeskin in summer."

"Maybe we should send Welcome back and bring men with a sled or something?" she said uneasily. She couldn't imagine how Sawyer could sit a horse in his condition.

"Nonsense," said Sawyer. "It is simplest, and quickest, for us all to ride back. In a very short time, we will be in Strahan, and I will have plenty of time and every convenience to help me recover." He looked at the bushman. "Thanks to you and Well."

"I suppose we can try it, and if the pain is too bad, or your wound reopens, we can just make camp again." Doubt shaded her tone.

"I'm a hard man to kill," he said again. And so it was decided.

****

Sawyer was a shocking convalescent.

Now returned to Dolly's, he was restless, by turns autocratic and cranky, and searching for a target for his frustrated energy.

He did now indeed resemble a caged tiger—the intelligent gleam, the restlessness, the sense of an athletic, mobile body held against its will in the wrong environment, the yellow glare, which said *set me free*.

Dolly had put Sawyer in a room which was everything comfortable and pleasant, but somehow all the floral chintzes, the plush cushions, and the frilly curtains merely emphasized Sawyer's dangerous masculinity.

His dark, lean length stretched along a high bed,

the cushions meant for propping up an invalid strewn across the carpeted floor. He sat up, resting against the bed head, the quilt tossed aside and a pillow supporting his right knee. He glowered.

He bared his teeth at her. “Come closer, little girl, and I will eat you!”

Lilwen smothered a laugh. “You would do better to eat this soup, which I have brought you.”

“I’m tired of soup. And I never thought you the nursing type.”

“Yes, in your company I seem to be constantly cast into feminine roles which don’t suit me. Yet here I am.”

Sawyer instantly looked contrite. “You are right.” But then his countenance brightened, and his eyes flashed wickedly. “Can you not stroke my fevered brow with your cool, calm hands? I am quite hot.”

Lilwen tugged the curtains further open and released the shutters. Mountain-fresh Tasmanian air flowed into the room. “There! That should cool you.”

A long hand reached for her, but she danced out of the way.

“How are you occupying yourself?” Sawyer asked.

“You know, equipping my next expedition, arranging my guides…”

“No! Lilwen, you must not. I can take you exploring again very soon. What if something happens to you? Wild men, or snakes, or aggressive bunyips!”

“Bunyips are an Aboriginal myth. And you told me yourself that nothing in the bush would hurt me.”

“I’m a fool. Do you want to give me a relapse? I will worry every single minute you are gone.”

“I suppose you would prefer if I donned my corsets once more, perhaps a new sort that covers my face so I can't see, and goes down to my ankles, so I can't walk."

"Well, since you suggest it! Preferably. As long as it isn't one of those nun's habits."

Lilwen shook her head at him. "Hmmm. Those habits are very freeing, you know. People can't tell you how to dress or behave."

Sawyer groaned. "It's this damned immobility. I am fretting myself to flinders. But please, wait for me. We know where the white waratahs are. We can collect some samples. We will take proper equipment next time or find another way around. This damn leg won't be long. Look, I can just about get up now, I don't know why Dolly keeps me lying around…"

"Sawyer. Stop."

This time the hand grabbed her, pulled her close into the side of the bed. "I can't bear to be without you, Lilwen. Come here. Sit by me. I know I'm not much of a specimen at the moment. But it would give me great pleasure to have you close, even for a short while. Hasten my healing, I have no doubt." Suddenly, Sawyer let go of her. "Listen to me, practically begging. Forget it. Do as you will."

Lilwen sat down next to him. "I was only teasing. And in all the excitement, I neglected to tell you that I did collect samples! Really good ones, too; quite a range of plant parts and different specimens. I am going to work with Dolly's gardener, Edna Heathorn, you know, the trousers woman—"

Lilwen waited for Sawyer to finish growling, and continued, "—And try some different propagation methods. Seeing how they grow in nature gave me some ideas: the white waratah may be subject to layering, if not grown easily from cuttings or seed. And actually, I'm very excited. I'm not going anywhere."

Sawyer seemed to crumple with relief. She looked closer. He was still ill, with a waxy sheen on his pale face. She did stroke his forehead then. "I think we better get the physician back."

"No! Tell Dolly—nobody but Welcome. You may send him in."

"Are you sure? Bush medicine is all very well..." She swallowed, and added, her voice barely more than a breath, "And I couldn't bear to lose you, Sawyer Thane. No other man would have expected from me what you asked of me in that dark night; you showed me that I have courage beyond my wildest dreams."

Sawyer sat up again. He took hold of her, hands gentle around her waist, his body twisted toward her. He was close, his dark-toffee eyes hot and melting, the sculpted planes of his face etched with desire. "Does that mean...you will marry me, Lilwen Jones? You promised. On the cliff. I heard you."

Yes! Shouted her traitorous, demanding heart. But instead, she said, "We will see."

"No, don't go! Forget I said anything. You will not want to marry a cripple, so we will wait to see if I am a whole man after this wound heals."

"Nonsense, I—"

"Lilwen, Stay. I have to tell you something."

"I will return. That is Dolly calling me now. I must go to her."

****

Lilwen hurried into Dolly's sumptuous dining room, trailing a little behind all the others. As usual, Dolly had guests. Dolly and Rory were there, Minnie and Rupert Brigg, two men from the Briggs' silver mine, and another older couple who looked mildly clerical. Sinead, the nun, had left two days ago, hugging Lilwen goodbye and inviting her to visit the orphanage one day. She missed her already.

Minnie's animated face shot around, and she stared at Lilwen. The woman rose from the table. Several sets of cutlery clattered onto plates.

Minnie hissed viciously, "Dolly, really. You *cannot* expect me to be seated at table alongside that…that…fallen woman."

Hand on the back of her chair, about to sit down, Lilwen's mouth opened in a stunned *O*. Her entire body froze in shock.

Dolly said in her calm voice, "Minnie, darling, do behave. This is no time for histrionics. We are all very excited, as Cook has prepared a feast, including one of Rory's favorites, lobster meunière, and for dessert, the new fashionable sweet, the famous Pavlova! I am dying to try this delicious-sounding dish."

Minnie said, "Dolly, how *could* you. If you wish to house this strumpet, that is your business, but you cannot expect decent women to visit you, or grace your table. Come, Roo."

Roo half rose, and his bald dome flushed. "Steady on, sweet Minnie, I'm sure if Mrs. Fraser has no qualms, then you need have no such concerns. Bit rude to our lovely hostess, what?"

Minnie's face changed color. Her eyes drilled Lilwen like twin lamps.

Lilwen's blush began in her chest and rushed tingling over her entire body. Her stomach clenched. Sawyer had warned her that Dolly would face criticism for Lilwen's actions, but things were far worse than her friend had let on. She shouldn't respond but should instead quietly depart this room and indeed Dolly's hospitality, but she couldn't resist one small sally. "Mr. Sawyer Thane is also accommodated in this house. Is he beyond polite company too?"

Minnie gasped theatrically and made to swoon. "The creature mentions her paramour in this room, in our hearing? Such abominable daring!" Dolly shook her head at Lilwen, but Lilwen's heart and brain beat such an angry tattoo…

"You have always been jealous, Minnie Brigg, and I do not know why. Your husband Rupert is all that is amiable." Here she stopped and blinked as Rupert actually gave her a shy half smile. "And yet you must try to charm Sawyer Thane as well."

A heavy thumping hit the door, and it banged open. Sawyer stood there, swaying, his weight on an ebony walking stick, its head fashioned into the shape of an eagle.

"I have asked Miss Lilwen Jones to marry me," he announced to the company.

Lilwen locked stares with Sawyer. His eyes blazed with mischief and merriment. His lips, that sometimes revealed his true emotions, quivered with suppressed laughter, and then as he regarded her, they shaped themselves into need. Need for her. In fact, he looked irresistible. His height, his masculine strength, his decisiveness and power, all called to the woman, the lover, within her. She sucked in a breath; if ever she had come close to letting him call the shots, allowing him to fold her into his life, it was now.

The room had burst into female exclamations and deeper male congratulations.

Minnie appeared to have swallowed a frog.

"You see?" said Dolly. "All is as it should be, or will be very soon."

A devil grew inside Lilwen. No, and no again. She would not marry Sawyer because it was expected or to save Dolly embarrassment.

Or because he was the most gorgeous, the most electrifying man she had ever seen, the best friend she had ever known. In fact, it was exactly because of those things, that she would not change and restrict his life, merely because he didn't want her socially embarrassed. He wanted her, yes, she knew that. But he didn't at all want to change his life. He didn't want a millstone wife around his neck, hobbles for his adventuring feet, a drain on his precarious finances.

Plus, she wanted to see Minnie's face when confronted with the scurrilous truth.

"I have not accepted Sawyer's proposal," Lilwen replied in a clear, carrying voice. "In fact, although there has been nothing so far which could be considered scandalous behavior, I have done everything in my power to make it so. I have said to Sawyer he must show me what love is, before I marry him. *Have relations*, in case you misunderstand me."

Minnie flushed red, then green. The guests Lilwen didn't know made shocked exclamations. Dolly covered a loud cough-laugh with her table napkin. The men regarded Sawyer with something like envy, and Sawyer?

Sawyer banged his cane on the floor and emitted a series of huge belly laughs, shaking all the glassware on the table and eliciting shivers from Dolly's precious chandeliers.

When he had apparently regained the power of speech, he said, “Miss Lilwen Jones, I came back from the dead when you called me with your promise of marriage. It was a sacred promise, and I hold you to it!”

“I will not,” replied Lilwen. Her throat closed so that she could not utter another word, so she banged her way from the room.

Chapter Twenty-Four

For the next few days, Lilwen avoided everyone. She sought out activities to temporarily distract her and to stop her circling thoughts, but it was very difficult. As soon as she found herself relaxing, the incredible thought would intrude: marry Sawyer Thane? Nothing else had the power to excite her so much.

But never, never, on the current terms. She must guard herself from temptation. She was within a butterfly's eyelash of succumbing, but the picture of a miserable Sawyer attending a city office every day, or else being absent from her for many months at a time, was too daunting.

Lilwen tried to lose herself in discussing propagation of the white waratah with the trouser-wearing gardener Edna Heathorn.

The woman was a genius. Together, they examined the plant specimens Lilwen had collected. Some plant pieces had fruit attached. The fruit appeared to be a one-seeded winged nut. Some of the seed might be sufficiently mature for germination.

Edna instructed, "I find burning the seeds of some natives works well, or soaking them overnight in hot water. I am experimenting with smoking them, too, to trick them into thinking there has been a bushfire."

"Where we found them didn't really look like fire-adapted flora. It was thick rainforest with huge old

Huon pines nearby. Although they were higher up on a cliff; perhaps there are small fires locally."

"Hmm. Well, there are a few seeds here. What do you think if we soak some, smoke a couple, and just plant a few more in rich, acidic rainforest-type loam?"

"Sounds perfect. I will dry the rest and take them back to my nursery on the mainland." Edna shot her a piercing look, but she didn't comment. Clearly the gossip had wafted even her way, out here in the garden beds and shrubberies. All of Strahan held its breath for the next installment of the enjoyably scandalous affair of Lilwen Jones and Sawyer Thane. Well, let them wait.

Lilwen turned over one of her samples. "I am most fascinated by these small aerial roots growing from the stems. The white waratahs were suckering in their natural habitat, with more plants growing from aerial roots which suckered into the soil nearby. I am very keen to try layering these stems here, and here. Hopefully I wrapped them well enough, and they still live."

"Yes, fascinating. Acidic rainforest loam, do you agree? We can collect some quite near here and use it for growing compost. Would you try growing *Agastachys* from cuttings too?"

"Of course. Here, cut them about six inches long, with three or four of those growing nodes. Lovely!"

As they worked, a surge of happiness bubbled under Lilwen's skin, her familiar keen pleasure near plants, nature, and the natural landscape. Working with plants, her hands in soil, touching growing things, and all her troubles sloughed off. She smiled and hummed, her heart singing along within her.

"I wonder you are not afraid to spend time with

such a scandalous woman as myself," Lilwen eventually said, an eyebrow angled in inquiry.

Edna laughed. "My favorite sort of friend, I assure you. I grow tired of shocking Strahan by myself, with my trousers and my choices. How very warming it is to find I am merely ahead of the world, as I meet more people like you. One day, I hope, the world will catch up, and it will be possible for our daughters, and our daughters' daughters, to live free, independent, and fulfilling lives."

"We will pray for that, but it seems very unlikely within our own lifetimes."

"Little by little, small step by small step. One day the world will look around and see that everyone is wearing trousers and choosing interesting life journeys." Edna shot her a mischievous smile.

Lilwen's heart pinged. Admiration soared for this feisty woman, undaunted by age or society. "Tell me, have you always been so brave?"

"No, Lilwen. Far from it. My husband died of heart failure in his forties, and my three children are grown. I believe I spent more than half my life waiting for everyone's permission, or even approval, to do the things I wanted. Somewhere along the journey, I realized that this life is no one else's but my own; that no one else burns in quite the same way for the things I wish for. That I can choose to shape the life I want, make the friends I want, have the experiences for which my heart hankers, and that the world will not come screeching to a standstill for the bold choices I may make. Nobody can live your life for you. They have their own concerns."

"Yet despite your own experiences, you appear

very confident that the world will change? For my part, I suspect that with every exciting, hard-fought change will come a new way of keeping women repressed, curtailed, and obedient."

Edna examined a handful of seeds. "Very likely. We can only do what is right for ourselves. I prefer the strategy of doing exactly what I wish with an appearance of blithe unconcern. This tends to fool people into thinking one knows what one is doing. My second approach is to make small changes without all the fuss and fanfare. You will be amazed at what you can get away with if you employ those two devices."

Lilwen laughed, resting a muddy hand on a hip as she considered Edna's words. "You are wise, my friend. I seem to create scenes whether I wish it or no. I shall employ your method for a change."

"Ah, but you are young and beautiful. Exactly the sort of woman that the world desires to keep imprisoned the most. Your beauty and youth make you dangerous. Men and women both want to keep you ignorant and locked in your tower."

"Then it is lucky I have made friends like you, Sister Sinead, and Welcome River, who loan me their free shapes to try on while I am escaping."

Edna said, "You fail to mention Mr. Sawyer Thane in your list of allies?"

"That is because I cannot decide if he is blowing away the tower completely—or erecting a new cage so clever that I barely know I am being locked away from other shining futures."

Edna and Lilwen returned to their putting compost in seedling trays and carefully treating and planting the white waratah seeds.

The silence was easy and comfortable.

Lilwen had much to think about.

****

Lilwen renewed her interest in botanical art. These beautiful, perfumed, stunning flowers deserved to be captured and preserved using what skill she could muster through line, detail, and color.

She whiled away several pleasant afternoons, seated at a sunny table under her bedroom window, her feet resting on Hero's warm fur under the desk.

Lilwen bent over her task, fully absorbed as she measured all the parts of the stems, flowers, and leaves with tiny rulers, trying to get all the angles and proportions correct. She had a selection of pencils with different size leads for different effects, and she made a watercolor palette to test for the right shades of leaf, flower, bud, and seed. As well as the natural colors of the plant and its creamy white-yellow flowers, there were all the effects of light and shade to consider, how the plant lay just so, its essence, the story it told her, the song it sang to her heart.

At the conclusion of several days of frantic measuring, drawing, erasing, coloring, painting over, swearing, smearing paint all over herself and through her hair, and pacing around in frustration, Lilwen had five workmanlike drawings of the fabulous *Agastachys odorata*.

The paintings were not perfect by any means. She had seen botanical artists who could convey the sheer beauty of flowers and plants while accurately rendering the scientific structure and size of all the parts. Her efforts were far short of that beautiful intersection of science and art.

But these would do. One painting even had enough personality that she could possibly use it in a future nursery catalogue. It was less accurate than stylized. Lilwen had finally given up trying to be perfect, admitting that detailed focus for days on end did not align with her impatient, active personality. Perhaps all the hours of close observation had helped; but anyway, at one point, tired of narrow focus, she had dashed off a stylized drawing which yet somehow captured all the special beauty and personality of the *Agastachys*, the white waratah.

She could tell immediately that this drawing would sell many plants, if only their propagation experiment yielded good results which could be replicated back in her nursery.

She stood there, immensely proud of herself, holding the drawing up to the light, and smiling.

Soon, it would be time to return home.

She tried not to imagine the life there waiting for her, except for her newfound success with the white waratah.

Plants made her happy. There must be thousands of women out there who would like to find a moment's pleasure regarding a glorious perfumed native blooming in their garden or bursting from a living room vase.

She had her mission now. To help others feel those small moments of contentment and happiness through looking at the intricate, detailed beauty, and smelling the sweet perfume, of this rare and lovely flower.

****

Like any good hunter, Sawyer had been waiting, patient and observant, while his prey frolicked in her accustomed lair, eventually relaxing her nervous vigilance.

He stood in the orchard, leaning on his cane and quite alone, taking in the vastness of the night sky sprinkled with huge stars.

He would wait no longer.

The last few days had been hellish. Lilwen was having meals sent to her room in order that she did not again embarrass her hosts. Dolly protested, insisting Lilwen was always welcome at her table, but Lilwen had been adamant. She had not appeared since the night the remarkably interfering Minnie Brigg had created such a tempest, although Sawyer used his walking stick and his willpower to stagger down every night to sit at table with the other guests.

Lilwen visited him every day in his sick room, but having her so close, witnessing his helpless state, set him growling and rumbling with frustration.

He hated her seeing him like this; he was less than a man until he had full use of his body. The enforced inactivity chafed at him. The urge to leap out of bed and chase her down, make her answer him, consumed him.

Welcome's face creased in concern, displeased with his prognosis.

"You're burning up, man," Well said, feeling his leg with one hand and his face with the other. "Buzzing about like a bloody bee in a bottle, driving your mind to fever. Slow down, friend! Stare at trees, take a paddle in the ocean. Find peace. Then your body will heal itself."

"I want Miss Lilwen Jones," Sawyer admitted. "But she doesn't want me."

"Are you sure about that? That fine woman shines like a star when she's near you. Miss Lily near worried to death when you were carking it in the bush. Not many ladies—non-Aboriginal women—would walk miles in the dark to save a blasted fool like you."

Sawyer laughed. "She's just stubborn. She wouldn't let even a Tasmanian tiger die."

Welcome said gravely, "I have an old bushman remedy for lovesick folk."

"Oh, yes? Give."

"Bush prescription—go and tell that sparky woman that you love her. Then kiss her soft, kiss her hard, kiss her good."

Sawyer laughed. He reached out a hand and patted Welcome on the shoulder. "I like your remedies more and more, my friend."

****

The moon hung low amidst fruiting branches, a pale golden-silver disc beaming soft light in a deep velvet sky studded with millions of stars. The cold, fresh air floated with the perfume of night flowers blending with the salty harmony of the nearby sea.

The night echoed with thick silence; no voices raised in laughter or music sounded from inside the mansion; no ruckus clattered from the wharves down below. Waves crashed and thudded distantly, and an owl hooted invisibly in a tree nearby.

Sawyer had a kinship with that lonely owl. He longed to join it in its tree, hooting forlornly into the night until his chosen mate flew to him with outstretched wings. Like it or no, in a strange unexpected miracle, he had found his mate. An extraordinary, singular, *delectable* woman.

Go along the beach, Well had said. She liked to walk there and then sit up on the cliff, watching the full roar of the ocean, enjoying the spray on her face, even in the night, when the full moon shone.

"She likes things wild, Saw. The power of waves. The secrets in plants. The heartbeat of ancient rocks as the world turns. The infinity of stars."

This damned leg. Every time it twanged, it reminded him of her courage—and his helplessness—while she braved the unknown horrors of her own imagination, and the dark, and the wilderness, to ensure that he lived and that he would walk again. He owed her everything: self-respect, the full use of his body, his pride, even his life.

An idea, a compulsion, flared like a beacon. Lure her in—and then devour her.

He would open himself to her. He would confess the secret he had held so close for so many years it had conditioned into a reflex. To gain Lilwen, he must unpick a scab. Expose his father. Make her see she owed him and his family nothing at all.

As he limped down to the wild ocean searching for her, a realization flowed into him with the surge of the sea over sand. His confession would free him in a way he had not been since he was a gangly, foolhardy, proud twenty-one-year-old, giving everything to protect his father and their family name.

Blast! Wet sand made it hard to walk with a limp and a stick but be damned if he would give up. Lilwen had faced worse, and so could he.

His thigh burned with effort. A sweat broke out over his face, under his arms, and down his back. Curse this unnatural weakness in limb and body!

Such beauty unfurled before him: the particular searing beauty of solitary walking on a wild ocean beach under a fat golden-silver moon. Wet sand stretched out in a long, wide arc. The moon's reflection glimmered in a snaking, broken line all the way to the far, gray-smudged horizon. Enormous translucent blue-green waves, full of sparkling phosphorescent creatures, reared up and smashed into shore, and then pulled themselves back again with much lacy frothing and churning. They sang of far waters, of Antarctica and the ice continent, of penguins and seals, whales and walruses. The sea's breath was fresh, cool, and salty. He inhaled deeply, again and again.

He rounded the rocky escarpment—hellishly trying with a walking stick!—and then spied the white-clad figure seated up on the ledge, hair and garments blowing wildly in the wild, her face raised to the elements, a huge grin across her face, arms spread wide against the rock as though embracing the barbaric savagery of the isolated coast.

She looked like a seraph, a nature witch. She certainly haunted his waking moments and his dreams.

Her vivid face lit up as she met his gaze. She started to her feet, still clinging to the rock face.

"Here, I'll come and get you!" Her voice carried away on the wind like a spell. "This is magnificent! If I wanted to share this perfect moment with anyone, it would be with you, Sawyer Thane."

At least that's what he hoped she said.

And she didn't try to hurry him back to his sick room, to coddle and cosset him, to tell him he couldn't and shouldn't. No. Lilwen was tough and brave and expected the same from her friends. He loved that. He loved *her*.

And now, somehow, he must find a way to tell her

so in a way that would not make her run from him, yet again.

She clambered down the rocks toward him. He used his two good hands and one good leg, his mouth twisting with pain as he jarred his wounded thigh, to pull himself up to the ledge. She met him halfway and they climbed back up to the ledge together.

Lilwen's face shone with delight. Her hair plastered in sticky wet clumps to her face, neck, and shoulders. Her cheeks glowed bright red from the slap of wind, shining wet with wild sea spray. The radiance of her smile rivaled that of the bright moon. His arms burned to embrace her and love her, right there and then.

"You look like a sea witch. Some kind of elemental spirit."

"I think I am, partly. And there are very few people in this world who understand that about me, Sawyer Thane. Isn't this just totally brilliant?"

"It's very beautiful. Special. Wild. Unique. Tough and yet vulnerable." He couldn't tear his gaze from hers; she was so lit from within she resembled a star herself.

Lilwen laughed and then gave him a dark look. "Are we still talking about the view?"

Sawyer took her left hand and held it as they sat there together, high up over the sea, watching the moon, and the waves, and the night seabirds flying as high as his hopes and dreams.

After long, silent minutes, delicious with hand squeezing and smiles, warm with each other's body heat as they pressed closer together, relishing the moment, he said, "Lilwen, I want to tell you something."

"Mmm? Well, then, if it is important, let us move back into this little sheltered cave just along here. We can talk instead of shouting over the roar of the sea."

They crawled into the small cave formed by an overhang of rock. The entrance framed the sparkling waves and the soaring cliffs, but the howl of wind hushed here, and the air caressed his skin more warmly, away from the cold salt spray.

"Look here." Lilwen pointed. A beam of moonlight gleamed on the cave wall, revealing strange paintings and drawings: white dancing stylized figures wearing long tails, dynamic images of kangaroos and running men aiming spears, and hundreds of silhouetted handprints in faded red and yellow.

Sawyer could not speak for a long, spellbound moment. He shivered. "These are ancient Aboriginal images. Older than our own culture can remember. I feel…humbled. Awed. Did you know they were here?"

"Yes, I come and look at them often. Welcome told me it is fine to look, so long as I respect that it is a special and sacred place. It all fits: the wildness, the beautiful savagery of the landscape, the power and siren call of the ocean, the ancient culture who have lived here for untold thousands of years."

They pressed together, sharing wonder.

"Welcome is an interesting man," he said. She nodded. He kept talking before he drowned in those huge silver eyes, fastened on his.

"Just a bushie—but he has healed this very nasty wound in record time. He loves to joke around—partly to hide his keen perception and clever mind, I believe." *Look how he understands this complex woman after such brief acquaintance.* "He rattles with healing knowledge. I have no idea what his education has been, but he is clearly extremely intelligent."

"His brother Wallace says he never forgets any bush medicine, once told."

Sawyer nodded. "How terrible for him to face a life of labor as a logger or similar occupation, letting that bright brain dull with disuse. It is a kind of torture, being expected to mold into a particular shape."

"As we both know!" Lilwen squeezed his hand. "But he loves the bush. Is it for us to judge?"

"True. But I wonder, would it be possible to sponsor Welcome River to medical school? Would they accept him, when they find out what he can do?"

"Sawyer! What an incredible idea!" Lilwen's eyes shone. He had his answer. They felt the same about this, like so many things. "But is that what you came all this way to talk to me about, with your stick sinking into sand, scraping your hands and feet against these rocks, damaging all Welcome's good work?" Her forehead wrinkled in concern as she checked him over.

A wave of bliss washed over him as she leaned in—he could not deny, having this beautiful woman care for him thus enthralled him.

She said, very bossily, charming him further, "In fact, I think we best return to Dolly's and a comfortable environment. Dr. Welcome will be very cross if you succumb to a chill through my mad ideas of immersion in glorious nature."

"Oh ho! Not concerned for me? Only for Welcome's ire?"

"But naturally! You, my Tasmanian tiger, are unkillable. Come now, back to Dolly's."

Tasmanian tiger. Was that how she thought of him? He loved her calling him that.

Putty in her hands.

Chapter Twenty-Five

Sawyer led Lilwen into the library, sneaking her in via a back door and quiet passage. He would hide out with her here until he had coughed out all his secrets. The library, so warm and enticing, afforded the perfect setting for his scheme.

A huge fire roared in the enormous fireplace. Tiffany lamps turned low added to the warm glow of the room. Squashy chairs and couches beckoned near the fire, and hard upright chairs served the study table in the center of the room. Long windows, now cloaked in lace and thick drapes against the night, opened onto a wide veranda.

Sawyer poured them both a small glass of the single malt Islay whiskey kept in the cabinet. Lilwen sank gratefully into a plump chair on the left of the fire and examined the rich color sparking from her whiskey. "I love these dainty engraved whiskey glasses." She held the glass up to the ruby flames leaping in the fireplace. "Look, they have a crown and a white rose with two buds. And the word Rede."

"Rede. That means return, if I remember my Latin grammar correctly."

"They must be Scots! King over the water glasses! The Bonnie Prince Charlie story. How very lovely, and very romantic."

The smile she gave him then nearly dissolved his

bones. He had to get a grip.

"Lilwen, we may not have much time. One of those annoying busybodies might burst in at any moment."

"You mean Dolly's lovely guests?"

"Yes. But at this point, if we are interrupted, they will be nothing but annoying busybodies. Lilwen, I must speak with you."

She smiled again. She had changed again from the elemental sprite, or the mercurial, laughing girl-woman. Now, she was mellowed by the room, the whiskey, the dim, warm light, and the fact she had released all her pent-up physical impatience and activity through her walk and climb around the cliffs. Now, she listened. There could be no better time.

"I want you to know something about the family business. About my father."

The smile fled her face. Her soft cheeks hardened; her plump lips pursed in vexation. She glanced away. "It doesn't matter, whatever it is."

"It matters to me."

"Well, hurry up and tell me, then, so we can talk of this and that and just enjoy this night. You should know that I am quite inured to impossible fathers and do not want to waste my life talking of them more than is needed. I owe your family a burdensome financial debt, and it is not something that can be changed by our friendship. I must feel that I have freed myself and am not beholden. And Sawyer?"

Her eyes lit. "I am close! So very close! We are having success with our white waratah experiments, and though it is far too early to tell if they will work, I entertain the highest hopes."

He swallowed against a gravel throat. How he

hated to watch that light dim once more. Did it really matter? Yes. It did.

"Lilwen I have been less than honorable in my dealings with you."

"The devil take your honor."

Sawyer had to laugh. "Lilwen—"

"What? Are you married, perhaps? Good. We won't have to worry about our union then. It is illegal to marry another woman while your wife is living, perhaps you were not aware?"

"Lilwen, stop—"

"Or perhaps you have absolute litters of bastard children requiring your support? What interest can that be to me, pray?"

She took a large gulp of whiskey, her throat and shoulders tensing as she swallowed. The firelight flickered on tight cheekbones. Her hand shook a little. "Or you are not a wildlife hunter, but a meek clerk in bowler hat and suit, taking the tramways to work every morning and returning for luncheon precisely at noon?"

She spat the words, voice sharp as scissors. Then she was not as blithely unconcerned as she pretended.

"The business. It is mine. *Your debt is to me.*" His words, long held fast within and now released, smashed and crashed and clamored around the room, bouncing from walls and hard surfaces.

Lilwen's body clenched and froze stock-still, her hand holding the whiskey halting mid-lift.

"I'm sorry I did not tell you before. But I wanted—very badly—to accompany you to Tasmania, on whatever pretext presented itself."

Lilwen held her silence for an eternal thirty seconds. She swirled the whiskey in her glass and took a large swallow, and another. She would not meet his gaze. "So I was right. You are not, in fact, a naturalist, a hunter, an explorer."

"Yes, of course I am those things—couldn't you tell, when we were in the wilderness? Here. More whiskey." He poured a good measure this time into her glass. Sat down in the chair facing hers. Leaned forward.

He said, "Like your family, my family lost everything in the crashes of '93. I was aged twenty-one, already established in my wildlife rescue career. I brought in the money that kept us alive. While hunting, I found black opals, which gave me the means to continue. And then, this other business, moneylending, it started small. A loan to a business acquaintance. More loans to other acquaintances. Then, bigger loans for more ambitious projects. I earned a reputation for discretion; more, a good eye for an excellent prospect, who would repay us as agreed, often with bonuses. The moneylending business grew as other men's businesses grew."

Sawyer drank whiskey. The burn enlivened his veins. He did not look at her now. He didn't want to see her disdain, her scorn, until he had finished talking. The fire crackled, sending out its warmth, with the sweet smell of eucalyptus. Yellow and red sparks danced along a log. The heart of the fire glowed red and orange like a sunset in a bushfire. He hoped it didn't herald the ending of his dreams.

He said, "My father is a vain man. He was angry and humiliated when we lost our fortune. It made him mean. He resents that it was me who developed the business. He has always favored my elder brother, who is charming but feckless. According to my father, I am the irresponsible one, going off hunting wildlife because I cannot settle. He conveniently forgets where the money is coming from." He rubbed his jaw while he pondered his next words, the slight scratching sound the underscore itch of a young man who could never please a parent.

"My brother, too, is angry. He wants to spend the money on a larger house for his expensive wife, tutors and governesses for his children, and all those things we had before the crash. My father encourages him.

"To try to give them what they desire—to free myself, too—I made bigger loans, for some really big projects. They came in. I became quite rich. And I could not bear it anymore. I hated the business. I was mortally tired of my father and brother's nagging and niggling.

"I called my father the proprietor of the business, and my brother the manager. My father likes to bully people and throw his weight around. I let people believe that it is his business. Because he is my father. But it is, and remains, mine."

Sawyer finally looked up. Lilwen had shifted and was kneeling before him, tears running down her cheeks. She took his hands. They were warm and firm holding his. Not soft: a gardener's hands. "What a terrible story." But her voice was soft. Her eyes were huge gray pools in the shadowy room. He tried hard to read her tone. Could he hope that there was no condemnation there?

His words came quickly now, before he could hold them back. "I suspect that is why he sent me to Tasmania with you. So he can have free rein of the business decisions. Indulge my brother. And perhaps…something would happen to me…in the wilderness…and I would not return…"

She wiped tears with agitated hands. "Not while I am here to protect you, Sawyer Thane. With my body, and brain, and my life." She rubbed her hands on his good left thigh with angry vigor, setting his skin on fire.

He melted into her courage. Her spirit. Lilwen Jones. The woman he had never imagined—because his imagination lacked power to envision the truth, that a woman could exist who was so perfect for him. Not perfect: just perfect for him. He held her hands again, leaning in closer to her beautiful face, inhaling her Lilwen smell of herbs and salt air and freedom.

She said, "I understand why this is difficult to relate. It is difficult to face the flaws of our parents. To admit them to ourselves, let alone discuss them in public. But Sawyer, what on earth does this have to do with us?"

Sawyer burst out laughing. He couldn't help himself. "Did you not hear me, woman in a million? I am wealthy. Rich. From a despicable business: loaning money to those who sorely need it."

"Sawyer, I was listening. Did you not just tell me that you loan funds to big business projects?"

"Yes, but I allow my father to loan money and bully poor folk. When he is not around, I help them somehow. Also, I ask him, again and again, not to treat people so poorly. But it is a failure. I continue to let him. It is my fault."

"Sawyer Thane, nobody knows better than I that it is impossible to control or direct a wayward parent, especially a father of that ilk, cut from that cloth—very similar to my own father, I comprehend."

Her eyes gleamed silver. A laugh sparkled within them. She repeated, "What, pray, has all that to do with us?"

His heart squeezed with guilt. He gritted out the words, sharp and unwieldy as broken china on his tongue. "Your debt does not exist. I erased it from our records before we left the mainland. I do not want or need your money. Your father incurred the mortgage. Not you."

Sawyer stood, reached down, and lifted her, placing her gently on the sofa. He sat next to her. "Lilwen Jones, I want to marry you. You know the worst of me now. You will want for nothing material. If you wish it, I will sell the business. Perhaps to my gormless brother, so he can get fat on my reputation until his clients realize he is hollow, vain, and lacking in judgement and ideas. His father's son."

"But Sawyer, I do not want your money! I begin to understand what I do want." She leaned back against the plump sofa arm, long-lashed eyes dreamy now, a smile wreathing her lovely face.

"Yes?" he breathed. Would her wish be within his power to grant?

She leaned forward, as sparky as the fire. "I want freedom. Autonomy. The natural world and beautiful landscape around me. Good friends."

He took a sip of whiskey to numb his frustration. This was Lilwen. Of course she didn't want a material boon.

Her fingertips reached for him and traveled over his jaw, probing his neck and shoulders, sending wild pulses of sensation leaping under his skin.

Her tone deepened. "Mostly, I want to experience the act of love. With you."

Sawyer choked on his whiskey.

He stretched out a hand to her face, her hair, her lips—his fingers moved of their own volition—when a loud knocking on the door shattered their privacy.

"Come to my room," Lilwen whispered, and she stood, opened the door, and brushed past Rupert Brigg, Rory Fraser, and two unknown gentlemen.

"Gentlemen. Good night," she said.

She turned back in the doorway and graced Sawyer with such a salacious smile that his whole body almost stood to attention.

He nodded to her.

He barely registered the male conversation around him. As soon as he was sure Lilwen had left the passageways and sufficient time had elapsed not to invite scandal, he stood.

"Excuse me, gentlemen," he said.

He didn't wait to hear their replies.

Chapter Twenty-Six

The moon shone pearl and gold through Lilwen's bedroom window. She waited, her heart in her mouth, to see if Sawyer Thane would forget his scruples and his blasted honor for one night and come to her.

An outrageously bright, floral silk kimono that Dolly had loaned her slithered on her shoulders.

Underneath!...And underneath, she wore an even more outrageous French concoction, a see-through silk and lace corset arrangement which emphasized her soft curves, tightened her waist, showed luminous moon-pale skin in all the right places, and hinted at alluring intimate detail in the few covered places. Below it, she wore tiny French knickers, with frills and tiny bows where they ended high on her thighs. She had never worn anything so naughty in her life. It made her feel breathless, lush, and expectant, like a ripe banana waiting to be peeled.

She sat on the bed and curled her bare feet in the plush rug, squishing its softness between her toes.

The door opened.

Her fingers tightened on the silky bedspread.

Sawyer stepped in.

For a long, long moment, they stared at each other. Sawyer's dark amber gaze burned into her with predatory intent. His rich brown hair curled in wild disorder. A two-day growth stubbled lower cheeks and jaw. His mouth softened with want and need.

He wore a clean shirt and fresh trousers. He had changed his clothes for her. Their fresh sun-and-wind smell, tinged with a note of citrus, floated in the air like a lure. He radiated vital strength and masculinity, like a constrained lion, athletic and wild and dangerous.

She stood, knees suddenly unreliable. They faced each other across the room, the moonlight pooling around her from the window.

They locked eyes. She slowly shed the kimono, and his magnetic gaze darkened. She inhaled small gasping breaths, her breasts pressing and sensitive under silk and lace.

Sawyer muttered an oath under his breath.

Lilwen tingled with heat. She stared at his black boots, a knot of sudden shyness wedged in her throat. In the wilderness, cavorting in nakedness was as elemental as Adam and Eve. Clad in slippery silk and lace, creamy flesh revealed and concealed in tempting slices, she felt exposed.

"Lilwen." He groaned, spilling desire and desperate attraction.

Sawyer deserved her courage. She sucked in a breath and raised her eyes to his.

The intense power of his regard seared her.

"Lilwen. I love you. I love you without this. You do not need to give yourself to me in this way."

Her heart filled with wild joy. Her skin sparked and shivered. She swallowed. "Is that a yes?"

He growled, "If I remain here, feasting my love-starved eyes on your beauty, so miraculously feminine, so available and so unattainable, I will not be responsible for myself." He paced back and forth in jerky strides at his end of the small room.

Something other than the workaday Lilwen Jones impelled her now. Something as old as time itself, something dark and female, who possessed her and showed her what to do.

Her blood spiked in her veins and roared in her brain. She fought for ancient female precepts: the right to choose her man and give herself to him as she wanted, the freedom to select the man who would father her children.

With the moonlight shining on her hair, her skin, her shape, she twirled slowly, showing him her front, her sides, her back, with her strong shoulders, narrow waist, and small, round buttocks.

She glanced at him under her lashes. His eyes simmered molten honey, flaming with desire.

She wriggled, moving her body in time to an internal music that sang with the rhythm of seasons, the cycle of life, the eternal story of man and woman.

Sawyer's whole body flexed taut, fixated on her. He paced toward her. One, two, three strides and then he was right there with her. Gently, tense with constrained desire, he took her into his arms.

His strong arms, his healthy spirit embraced her. His beloved, familiar man-smell of herbs and leather enfolded her entirely. Always, always in his arms she sizzled with life, and yet deep in her bones she knew she was utterly safe. Safe to be free, safe to go searching for her new self, safe to reach eagerly for love.

He bent his head and plucked the gem dangling in her cleavage, his fingers trailing fire on her soft skin. "The tiger's eye! You have made it into a necklace." He half released her and stared with sultry eyes at her chest. "It gleams like mottled fire against your creamy, pearly skin. You are utterly gorgeous, Lilwen Jones."

His kiss teased and explored, hovering on her engorged lips, tasting and caressing. A surge of hot desire shot straight to the core of her, tingling and pulsing at the apex of her thighs. She pressed her lips on his, soft, hard, testing, and savoring his soft firmness. He engulfed her, hot, passionate male.

His hands touched the side of her face, slid down to her neck, tarrying, squeezing, then running down to enfold each shoulder in his steady warmth. He stroked her arms lightly up and down, sending tongues of fire racing on her skin. She pressed herself closer, loving the rasp of lace and shiver of silk as she gyrated against him.

She ran her hands fast and light over his back, absorbing the width of him, his hardness, his power, his flexible spine flanked by ridges of muscle. She rubbed his arms, his firm biceps, the bulge of triceps, back up to broad shoulders, and then spread both hands on his chest.

She unfastened a button on his shirt. He made a rumbling, groaning sound in his throat. She undid the rest slowly, one by one, slipping a hand under the linen to caress warm skin, coarse chest hair, planes of muscle, the surprising sweet softness of a nipple hardening under her questing fingers.

She pulled at his shirt until he obliged and tore it off and threw it on the ground.

"Lilwen Jones, you are magnificent." His voice husked. "Your pearly skin. Your lovely, perfect shape: so strong and yet so soft in all the right places. By all the gods, the sight of your jiggling breasts in that lace is driving me mad!"

Lilwen pushed her torso forward, pressing against silk and the slight scratch of lace. Sawyer stared like a man dazed. He licked his lips. Her nipples hardened to peaks. She looked down and saw them straining against the lace, her left nipple poking through a small hole. Her breasts throbbed and tingled as his gaze devoured her, heavy-lidded eyes dark with want.

A surge of liquid spiked through her insides, coating everything in hot honey, swelling and softening inside, growing hot and tender and slick. She wriggled, consumed with wonder at the desire spiraling in her body.

Sawyer leaned closer, not quite touching. Her skin burned in his heat. Her whole body strained toward him, wanting.

"Sawyer, touch me. I'm bursting for you. You will show me what to do. Guide me. I trust you."

He studied her expression. She didn't know what he saw there, but she felt quite wild.

"Lilwen, I will do nothing to hurt you. We can stop at any time you feel unsure or uncomfortable."

"Kiss me, damn you! Run your hands over me. I want your tiger. Bring him forth! Set him free! Don't be afraid you will hurt me. I am strong and fearless." As she spoke, she knew it was true, and her heart sang with fierce joy.

Sawyer kissed her, this time his lips meeting hers in a kind of fury, devouring her in his passion. He squeezed her to him hard. She grabbed his head, brought it closer, and held him, her fingers pulling in his hair.

They broke apart, breathing heavily, gasping and heaving. His eyes shone black desire. A sheen of sweat coated his body in a slick gleam. He smelt like her Sawyer, clean, male, healthy, vibrant. And there was another scent, too, just below the level of sensation: his desire, his male need, powering toward the unstoppable.

He possessed her lips. His tongue darted into her mouth. She licked his bottom lip, his top lip, and then captured his bottom lip between both of hers and sucked. He licked his tongue in her mouth, and then their tongues slid and danced, and she moaned deep in her throat.

Sawyer detached himself and stroked down her body with fire-licked fingers. Her limbs softened and wobbled as though made of rubber, her legs barely able to support her.

He bent and licked her nipple. A surprised gasp burst out of her, and lightning flickered in a sharp stab straight to her groin.

He put both hot hands on her breasts, testing their weight with soft bounces. He pulled and flicked her nipples under the lace. As she whimpered and moaned, losing control now, he slowly kissed and sucked each nipple, until she was gasping, her legs folding under her, falling backward onto the bed, Sawyer coming with her.

She lay there, and Sawyer stared up and down her body with greedy eyes, dwelling on her white thighs, the frills and bows on the end of the knickers.

She let him. She felt beautiful, crazy, in love, and hungry for everything he would give her.

This—*this*—felt like the greatest adventure of her life. She had no models, no instruction, no idea of what would happen: only delicious sensation, roller-coaster emotion, her body, and her trust in Sawyer.

Her gaze fixed on him as he filled himself with the sight of her, and she pulled her thighs apart.

Sawyer shot one shocked, amazed, and delighted look at her face, and then stared down at her again, eyes wide and stunned.

The French knickers had an open slit in the middle. There were her thighs, clad in their white frilly lace, and in between, on full show, was her swollen, wet, female sex.

Sawyer snarled and bent toward her. He touched her there, lightly, with just a fingertip. Oh! Her body jerked in delicious shock. She wriggled and, her lips parting to take in air, tightened herself over the tip of his finger and squeezed. Oooh.

He began to touch, tickle, and tease her, slipping his finger in and out, tickling lightly along the seam of her, suddenly thrusting in his finger and rubbing.

She was all sensation. There was nothing left but mounting desire, Sawyer's clever fingertips, her own response, her wanting, aching, need for him.

She clenched her muscles to receive him, to feel him there in her center of pleasure. Sawyer thrust and circled and flicked his fingers; her whole body, her mind, her entire being leapt and spun, into some dizzy far universe of joy and pleasure; and then everything shattered into stars and shards all around her.

"What was *that*?" Laughter bubbled from nowhere. Tears streaked her cheeks.

Sawyer smiled, his expression extremely smug. "*That*, my darling, is my love for you. You are very wild."

Lilwen sat up, concerned. “Sorry…am I not meant to be like that?”

Sawyer kissed her. “*Exactly* like that.”

She hesitated. “Women whisper…I want…there is more, yes?”

Sawyer laughed. “My passionate sweetheart. Yes, there is more. That was the prelude. Shall I show you?”

She laughed. “The prelude? You are joking!…Oh? Not joking?” She reveled in his stroking touch on her belly, her legs, her hips. Her impatience grew, a kind of dissatisfied burning ache right through her body. She lifted herself and wriggled under his touch.

“Sawyer, I do not want any other man to be the one who introduces me to this. If that was a mere prelude, then what are you doing, wasting time! Show me what to do! Can I make you feel like that, too?”

“If you are sure. I want you, Lilwen Jones, so very much. Here, feel. You already make me feel like that. This is how much.”

He put her hand on the large bulge pressing hard against the front of his trousers. “I don’t want to hurt you or scare you. You will promise to tell me to stop, if you are afraid, or not comfortable?”

“I want you, Sawyer Thane. I want you to feel what you just made me feel. Get those trousers off and show me.”

She rubbed along the sides of his hard, long legs encased in their moleskins, every now and again rubbing over his enlarged member straining against the fabric, just to hear him gasp. Sawyer had a hand on the back of her neck, kissing her again. As he kissed her, he began to undo all the laces, buttons, hooks, and fastenings of her corset. He peeled it off, and there she stood just in her little French knickers.

"Take them off," Sawyer said, his voice hoarse, and so she wriggled them off too.

Sawyer took a moment to take her in, in all her full nudity. "You are astonishing. I can't stop looking at you. You fill my heart with your beauty." His voice cracked. He sounded as though his heart was breaking.

Lilwen began to undo his trousers, giggling as she tried to maneuver the fabric over his very erect member. He made a grunting laugh and assisted her with impatient hands.

Finally, there he stood, in all his naked male pride. He reached out a long arm and caressed her hair, her arms. "Touch me. Hold my cock, if you wish."

"Cock." She fluttered her eyelashes at him, smiling, then curled an experimental hand around his huge erect manhood. She squeezed a little, fascinated as his cock jumped in her hand.

She stroked the silky sliding skin over the hard column within, a pulse of satisfaction burning in her as Sawyer moaned endearments and curses. She bent and licked him along the shaft, the tip of her tongue flicking the smooth head. His erection pulsed and blushed purple.

Sawyer drew her head up. He gritted, "That feels too incredible. We will leave that until another time." He kissed her again. His liquid copper eyes blazed with dark intent. "I want to join with you. Thrust inside you. Feel you hot and tight all around me. Do you understand? You must tell me if you are uncomfortable."

"Ha! I want you, Sawyer Thane. Stop talking and hurry up."

He commenced kissing and caressing her so thoroughly and expertly that she cried out, so soft and heated and wanting. "This is a miracle," she whispered. "I am flooded with joy."

He positioned himself over her, arms stalwart and safe on either side of her. He bent and kissed her lingeringly. He nudged her seam with the head of his cock, then entered her, giving a gentle thrust.

She pushed her hips up to meet his. A sharp pain lanced her, and she cried out in surprise.

He pulled out. "Does it hurt?"

She blinked. "Only in an amazing way. Do it again!"

He lifted a hand and stroked her hair and cheeks. He slid the hand to her bottom, gripped and squeezed, sending a bolt of urgent desire right to her sex, and then lifted her hips as his shaft possessed her. He held still, inside her, waiting while she flowed and clenched along his thick length.

He moved then, beginning to spear her gently and slowly, waiting until she found the rhythm of their joining. They rocked together, urgent and demanding. Sawyer's huge manhood pounded within her, sending glorious shouting thrills to every cell in her body.

There were no words, only sounds and emotions, so intense she thought she would break into pieces and fly away on the wild winds. She was a creature of feeling, of sensation; together, they connected with each other and every living thing.

Her brain fizzed like firecrackers. Her body contracted and pulsed, every pulse igniting another shower of sparks. Every slam of Sawyer took her closer to the precipice—and then she was falling over, flying outward, smashing into splinters of lightning. Sawyer growled as he collapsed onto her and drove into her with heavy hard pulses, and then his body leapt and wracked. They lay together, the moon's soft light washing all over them.

****

After that, they couldn't keep their hands off each other.

Lilwen and Sawyer mooned around in a distracted fashion, forgetful and inattentive, except when they were in the same room, and then they sneaked looks at each other, made excuses to touch or brush past, or to engage in silly, nonsensical banter which set them snorting with laughter out of all proportion to the conversation.

Lilwen couldn't eat, could hardly sleep, and her brain sizzled and burned. Sawyer didn't seem to be faring much better.

Working in the garden on the white waratahs with Edna, Lilwen was prone to sudden bouts of giggling, long bouts of abstraction, and random non sequiturs in conversation. Lilwen thought Dolly suspected—she had loaned Lilwen the kimono and the French corset and knickers, which she had carefully washed and tried to return, Dolly insisting she keep them—but although Dolly smiled slyly at times, she had so far said nothing.

Longing consumed Lilwen. She and Sawyer could never spend time together without being interrupted. Desperation to be alone with him consumed her. She became obsessed with discovering if he suffered equally.

The terrible Briggs insisted the group make pleasure outings while the inclement Tasmanian weather remained fine. Their hosts Dolly and Rory dragged either Lilwen or Sawyer, or both, to local events, dinners, and lunches.

They met in secret places—the orchard, the garden, along the coast, in the library—but Sawyer remained adamant he could not return to her room.

"No, Lilwen. We have managed to get away with it once. I will not imperil your reputation."

"Too late for that, Tiger!"

He laughed, grew serious. "Your business will rely on your good name. Already there are whispers because of our adventure in the forest. Now you must behave like a model woman."

Lilwen yearned for Sawyer to seduce her again. Stolen kisses were sweet but no longer enough. His self-control worried her: hadn't he enjoyed himself? Had she failed his expectations? He could not be burning for more, as she was, completely unable to resist him.

She wallowed in her wantonness. She hardly cared what other people thought; caring about social conventions felt like a dim memory of another time. She now understood the behavior of those tragic fictional heroines who cast the world aside for the sake of her lover.

Surely one person couldn't feel as glorious as she had, and the other not?

In the end, Sawyer noticed that she was becoming cast down and taxed her with it.

"You don't seem to care," she began, "that we have not had opportunity to make love again."

"Yes, it's damnable. Sorry, I mean dreadful."

She brightened all over. "So you were not

disappointed? Only I have tortured myself wondering…although I was in transports, maybe our…lovemaking…bored you, or left you unmoved?"

Sawyer growled in his throat and hugged her tight to his chest. They perched together on a low, wide bow of an old apple tree, hidden in the orchard. The sun slid slowly into the inky Tasmanian dusk.

"Oh, Lilwen, my flower, my heart. Making love with you was unbelievable: your generosity, your wildness, your naturalness and joy. You gave me such a gift. You make me so happy I am unmanned. I want you to be happy too." He ceased speaking abruptly and scratched his head. "Actually, I need to know what you want. How best to help you be happy." He tenderly caressed her hair. "Since we made love, I have been the happiest man alive, and the most inefficient! I have barely had an intelligible conversation. All I want is you."

He turned toward her on the branch and grasped her hands.

"Lilwen, I ask you again, will you marry me?"

"It is not marriage I want! I want more of you…"

"I am powerless to say no to you. But to find a place we can be alone—"

"Once, we were happy in the forest. Why not go back there?"

Sawyer laughed and studied her face. "The forest it is. Tomorrow, in the late afternoon, when everyone is resting and dozy."

Lilwen hardly slept that night. The images coming into her mind blazed with that special body hunger. All her thoughts went into tomorrow afternoon.

****

Their bodies slammed together. They kissed and stroked, hugged and murmured, driving blazing, tingling need to hungry fire.

Trees and green shrubs cradled their small clearing. Natural sounds gave music for their lovemaking—birdsong, animals rustling, leaves susurrating in the soft breeze.

Both of them tried to make a slow ceremony of it, but they were too desperate. Clothes went flying. Tongues tangled. Bodies rubbed and held, gripped and caressed, until they were two bodies joining and loving, and neither knew where their boundaries began and ended.

Finally, they lay naked on the thick blanket, satiated for the moment.

"Don't move," said Lilwen. "Just look, very, very slowly. It is the tiger. My tiger. My *other* tiger."

A dappled back and two large, dark, sad eyes shone from the shadows on the edge of the forest.

"I never told you. I saw the tiger a few times. Twice, I fed it. When we were first camped in the forest and then, when I walked in the dark seeking help for you, I kept thinking I saw it, on the edge of my vision. I was lost, terrified, and desperate. So every time I saw the tiger, I followed its shape, its shadow. It became like a talisman. I didn't know if it was my imagination or a real tiger. I believe that is why we are both alive today. The tiger saved us."

Sawyer jumped to his feet and stared into the bush. His whole body tensed.

"Please, Sawyer, don't do anything. Leave it be. It is like the line between the past and the future. A future where wild animals are disappearing fast, because we have hunted them all, and because we are building cities where there used to be forest."

Sawyer turned to her and cupped her shoulders. "I begin to understand you, Lilwen Jones. A piece of your heart and your wonderful mind has become my heart and my thoughts, so I can feel and understand the world as you do. You have changed me. I will leave our tiger be."

As though the tiger understood, for a moment it emerged from the shadows. Its eyes locked on Lilwen. She held tight to Sawyer's hand, both spellbound. The tiger had two small, fierce cubs with it. After a long moment, the beast switched its tail and disappeared back into the forest.

"Sawyer, I wondered…"

"Yes?"

Courage. She knew now that she had it. Even though speaking deep feelings could feel more dreadful than walking through the bush at night, in terrible fear.

"Were you…in hunting the tiger, were you seeking yourself? Trying to find the real Sawyer Thane?"

He laughed. Hesitated. His voice pitched low, with a scratch in it. "I believe you are right. I thrive on action and adventure, but at the same time, whenever things get difficult, I itch to go hunting. To escape, to cease thinking. Especially when reminded of my father's shortcomings."

She waited, still and quiet, barely breathing. Still holding her hand, he stared unseeing into the deep forest all around them.

"That night, in the library. The night I told you about it all. Somehow after that, my father stopped being a huge shadow over me. Somehow, now, I feel he is just a man, filled with flaws and virtues, familial love just a warm place in my heart. I don't need to run from my feelings anymore."

He stared at her, his dark brows raised and mouth parted in surprise.

She bit her lips, but the laugh escaped her. "I'm sorry! I'm so glad. But your face…!"

He stared, and then a reluctant laugh burst out. "Wretch! Vixen! Laughing when I am confessing all!"

Her lips quivered into a mortified grimace. "I think I laughed because speaking truth, being close, makes me feel vulnerable too. I'm still learning to expose myself also."

"Mmmm. Let me assist you," he intoned, his voice and face infused with evil intent.

He tumbled her over and began kissing her into submission, smothering her apologies and laughter.

Chapter Twenty-Seven

At Dolly's house, the next day, Lilwen had a rare moment when she wasn't actually thinking about Sawyer. She was examining the cuttings she had made of the *Agastachys*, where she had layered flexible shoots into the soil at intervals. Were these tiny white roots, just breaking the crust of the stem?

Someone coughed politely behind her, breaking her concentration. "Rupert! Hello. What brings you into my personal Eden?" She was still dizzy and happy from her newest adventure with Sawyer and prone to spouting things that sounded eccentric. Rupert smiled perfunctorily, then looked down, blushed, and shuffled his feet.

She stood, wiping her hands on her trousers. "Why, Rupert, whatever is wrong? How can I help?" She felt a rush of sympathy for him. The poor man looked quite ill at ease and self-conscious.

"Errhm. Mmm. Just came to say, have asked my wife to apologize to you."

Lilwen laughed. "Mr. Brigg, Rupert, there is no need, I am sure." Lilwen was so happy, nothing bothered her. She flew above the concerns and slights from one such as Minnie Brigg.

Rupert's expression became slightly mulish. "Can't have it, Minnie criticizing Dolly's guests. Up to Min to help Doll. Admirable woman, admirable." He blushed deeper.

Lilwen screwed up her eyes and regarded him. Was he in love with Dolly? Maybe that went some way to explaining Minnie's flirting and bitterness. He sat down on the low stone wall near her work area. "Not Minnie's fault," he said. "Brought up to believe ladies only behave in certain ways. She gets scared when the rules change. Makes her lash out."

"Oh, Rupert, of course I understand. There is no need for apologies."

"I insist. You can expect her today." He bowed and strode away. The back of his neck reddened. Lilwen laughed to herself. Well, of all the strange conversations!

She bent again to her work, thinking that Minnie was lucky to have a husband who understood her so well. It was rather sweet.

****

The whole conversation had slipped Lilwen's mind as she pricked and potted in the makeshift nursery that she and Edna had created to grow her white waratahs. A sniff alerted her: Minnie appeared, looking about her with her mouth turned down, as though she feared the dirt would leap from the pots and smear her fashionable attire. Hero, lying nearby as usual, growled low in her chest.

Oh no! She steeled herself. Best get it over with. She put a restraining hand on Hero's head, who lay down, but her eyes remained fixed on Minnie Brigg.

"Minnie! Here you see much of my hopes and dreams." Lilwen saw an ugly flash in Minnie's eyes. Oh dear! Surely she wouldn't damage all her hard work. Lilwen stood, alarmed, and ushered Minnie out of the greenhouse, regretting her friendly words, visions of overturned pots and trays and weeks of work destroyed slamming into her mind.

"How can I help you?" she asked, far more stiffly. Her mind whirled in panic. Should she ask a River brother to guard the greenhouse at night?

Minnie stood there, an angry flush on her cheeks. She dug the point of an elegant parasol into the gravel of the garden path. "Rupert says I owe you an apology."

"No need!" Lilwen said as brightly as she could. They both heard the false note.

"I have been slandering you to all who will listen. In fact, it is only Dolly's great standing in the community that has prevented you from being run out of town."

Lilwen took an involuntary step backward, surprised and shocked by the venom in Minnie's expression and tone. She gathered her courage and her resilience. "The truth is, Minnie Brigg, I don't care what you, or others like you, think. I have fought hard against the constraints of my world, especially for women. I have made my choices. They have all been difficult and hard-won. But I find I am a happy woman." As she said it, she knew it was true. A smile bloomed on her lips.

Minnie stared at her, eyes narrowing, mouth turning down once more. "I envy you."

"Again, there is no need. You have much that others would envy."

Minnie was silent. Suddenly she said, "And what of Mr. Sawyer Thane? You don't care if his name is dragged through the mud?"

"I find it is different for men."

"Indeed. You are right."

Lilwen waited.

Minnie glanced away to the left, watching a bird pecking at seeds in one of the trees. She sniffed. "Rupert is right. I do owe you an apology. I feel small-minded and provincial compared to your brilliance, and it has made me jealous." She held up a hand as Lilwen opened her mouth. "I want to be more like you. To try not to care so much what others think. To try not to compare myself, and…and I find myself lacking."

A rush of pity lanced her chest. "Oh, Minnie! You are a very pretty woman. Your husband is a sincere man who cares for you. You really don't want to be like me! I am beyond polite society and likely to only get worse."

Relief swooped through her when Minnie emitted a small laugh, all her tension visibly escaping. Minnie said, "Well perhaps I can think of you when I need courage." She stopped speaking and scuffed her fine shoes, uncaring, on the gravel.

There is hope for her yet!

"In fact," Minnie Brigg continued, her voice so soft Lilwen had to lean forward to hear, "it seems that things are changing for me. I am more interested in women's choices and women's futures. You see," she whispered, "I am expecting a child. I always wanted a boy first; but now, I imagine a little girl, and all the things she will face are swirling in my mind. I want her to have a freer life than I did."

Lilwen dropped the trowel she hadn't realized she still held and impulsively embraced Minnie. "Oh, Minnie! Congratulations! That is such a beautiful thing to say. Yes, please do borrow any amount of my courage."

She hugged her hard, and they parted with Minnie smiling shamefacedly and Lilwen patting her on the back.

"Chin up, my girl," she said. "Imagine what future terrors you will be able to face, with a daughter at your side!"

Minnie even giggled then, looking like a happy girl.

****

Dolly surprised her guests that evening by advocating a short visit to Hobart town on the morrow.

"Rory has business in Hobart over the next few days. I propose that we accompany him. It has been an age since I have had any new dresses made up. I wish to see what fabrics the haberdashers have stocked for autumn and winter. I would love to show you Hobart town, the shops, the cafés, the wharf, the bustle of the Salamanca market, and the history at Battery Point. There is currently a large Federation celebration going on—I feel we cannot miss it."

Lilwen tensed as Minnie's face turned to her, but she needn't have worried. Minnie said, "I have told Lilwen I wish to be more adventurous, like she is, so yes, we would love to come."

"Well, good for you!" Dolly responded, giving Lilwen comically raised brows, followed by a wink.

****

Hobart was lovely, full of interesting buildings built almost a hundred years ago, and redolent with convict and maritime history. Lilwen enjoyed the sights with her friends—a tram car up Mt. Wellington, a visit to the botanic gardens, eating delicious fish and lobster in the pubs, and strolling along the wharves.

She adored the rich hustle and bustle of shopping with Dolly and Minnie but found at the end of the long first day that she had had enough and was pining again for her wild coast and dense, unpopulated forests.

"I really am a savage," she said to Sawyer that night as he walked her back to the hotel. "I am already weary of civilization."

"I have just the remedy." He smoothed a stray ringlet from her cheek. "I have some meetings tomorrow; but if you can endure one more day of your despised shopping, I will take you somewhere I have long wanted to explore: the waterfall at Mt. Field and the alpine plateau."

"Please, Sawyer! Oh yes! I can hardly contain myself until then."

He kissed her lightly and told her to behave herself, or if she couldn't do that, to not get caught. "I suppose you will charm your way out of any trouble," he said with a gloom that made her laugh.

"If that occurs, you may come and rescue me," she said, sparkling up at him until he grinned.

Sawyer collected her at dawn of the third day. Gold, pink, and apricot streaked a magnificent sky and the biting fresh air of southern Tasmania fizzed in her lungs. They rode horses to the Russell Falls and stopped to wander around the area, looking in amazement at the thundering cascades, letting the spray coat their faces and arms with fine mist.

Then they took the winding uphill track which led to Mt. Field. They brushed the horses and tied them to the hitching post, and then walked the rest of the way up the meandering mountain path, through pale-skinned, bent, and stunted eucalypts, which Sawyer called snow gums.

Finally, they reached the alpine plateau. Lilwen stood on the rough track, looking out over what seemed the curve of the world. They were on the top of the mountain: peaks marched away into the distance on all sides, bluer and grayer with every gradation.

Hardy alpine plants covered every surface in a colorful mosaic: pink, yellow, white, and green. The flora was mostly groundcovers, dotted here and there with outcrops of taller plants and wind-flattened shrubs covered in tiny red berries glowing in the sun like little rubies. White snow daisies smiled with straw-like petals and sweet pink hearts. Small stunted evergreens bore green-blue pods. Bizarre-leafed flat shrubs bore large intricate yellow and orange cones. A huge plant with remarkable giant flowers towered over the others.

In the middle distance and farther, mountain tarns sparkled bright blue, reflecting the sky in their still waters.

Everything was pristine and untouched, as though a god had just finished making it, and they were the first humans to set eyes on this paradise. The fresh, cold air chilled the gold hoops in her ears. Her boots, damp now, let in freezing water and mud, but she couldn't have cared less. Exhilaration jumped in her veins. She was transformed, reborn by beauty.

For a while Lilwen just absorbed the scenic wonders, and then she ran around madly, examining first one plant and then another. All were stunning, fabulous in their intricate, unique design. Everything was highly engineered, a perfect poem to the mountains and nature.

Finally she stood still, gulping in huge breaths of the mountain air, and then burst into tears. Sawyer embraced her and held her to him.

"I'm fine! I'm crying because I have never seen such beauty!" She stepped back so she could look at his face. "Sawyer, I want to stay in Tasmania! I have never experienced such wonder, such happiness. The thought of returning to Melbourne! It makes me ill! The MacNeils and Ayla can have my nursery. I shall remember my mother by naming the most beautiful flower after her."

He regarded her steadily for a long while. "Do you think this can be true, my Lilwen? That you really want to remain here in this remote southern island?"

She gulped. She knew he wanted to marry her. She did not know what to say. Her heart wanted him—so badly. And yet, how could she be a drag on his free life? And how could she leave Tasmania? She could grow a business here, she knew it. Maybe Dolly would sponsor her for a while. She hadn't answered him. He deserved her honesty.

"Sawyer, I love you so much. I want you. I feel bereft when you are not there. And this is why I cannot marry you. It will make both of us miserable: me, when you are gone for long periods, dashing my will against yours because of my need for you; and you, because you will lose your liberty and free life, and end with nothing but feelings of frustration."

Sawyer took her hand and led her to a soft clearing, which looked out over a tiny sparkling tarn and distant mountains. Three clumps of the magnificent *Richea pandanus*—of which Edna had shown her drawings—ornamented the clearing. She studied its massive, miraculous red flowers, as she listened to his response.

"Lilwen, you have changed me. You have made me know something. It is not enough to save wounded animals. Now, I would work on keeping the places they live intact. You told me, over and over, what the Tasmanian tiger represents to you. You tell me now that you would stay here in Tasmania." He flicked a curl from her face.

His expression! So soft and tender. A throb of anxiety squeezed her chest. What was coming? What would he say to her? She began to rise. "Time to go back…"

"Lilwen, wait. Yesterday, I accepted two job offers, conditionally. I will assist Mary Grant Roberts to develop her private zoo, here in Hobart. And I have accepted a post as the first Biology Chair at Hobart University."

Emotion welled up and cascaded through her, a rippling waterfall of surprise and joy. Sawyer here, with her! Wanting to stay. Teaching, helping others to love wild, unique landscapes and all the creatures they protected. Her heart gave a pound, and another. Her face split in a massive smile.

"But wait! What do you mean *conditionally*?"

"You have taught me not to make decisions for you. I told them I will take these jobs on one condition only. Lilwen Jones, will you make me the happiest man on this earth, and accept my love, my respect, and my hand in marriage?"

"Yes! Yes, I will marry you, and gladly, Sawyer Thane! Thank all the gods I went to Melbourne Zoo that day."

Sawyer took her face in his hands and kissed her

and kissed her. She felt his joy, his love and rapture as if they were her own. Happy tears ran unchecked down her cheeks.

She stood, pulling Sawyer up with her, and looked all around. "This place is so incredibly beautiful. I will remember this place, and this moment, all my life. Just to know it is here. And to know that in this moment, you have changed the course of my future, Sawyer Thane, to something unbelievably rich." She held her hair back out of the wind, stood on tiptoes; he bent to meet her. They kissed again.

She said, "For I know something now. Love and marriage. These are not things to negotiate over. Not something to make a deal about. They only have value if they are freely given, with no conditions: an unencumbered trust in the person and the future."

He placed warm hands on her hips. "Are you still worried about your freedom?"

She shook her head and smiled mizzily at him again.

"About my freedom then?"

"Mm. Tell me more."

He settled them in a smooth hollow of vegetation. "Yes, I always believed I could never marry. But now I have discovered, thanks to you, Lilwen Jones, that freedom is more about finding people who share your passion and working in that area. Freedom must have meaning, or it is just hollow, empty space. Hence the Hobart zoo and the university. And you, if you will have me."

"The zoo. Tell me you won't hunt the tiger. It has a deep meaning for me, for us. I believe it saved our lives. It is a symbol of our liberty."

Sawyer hugged her to him, the hot furnace of his body shielding her from the tickles of chill alpine wind. “I will do everything I can to save the tiger, but I fear its time is running out. There are very few seen in the wild anymore. But I can help to save the other extraordinary Tasmanian fauna: the devils, the quolls, the possums, the birds, and everything else that depends on their forest home.”

He stroked her hair, squeezed the back of her neck with his large, warm hand. “Come, it is getting cold now. Let us go back down the mountain and enjoy toasty food in front of a comfortable fire. Perhaps your friends will join us in a little bubbly Champagne!”

“Oh, yes, they will love our news! Come, let’s hurry.”

Sawyer couldn’t stop touching Lilwen all the way down the mountain, excepting when the single track narrowed so much that they had to go single file.

And then he filled his senses, glorying in the very sight of her: her beloved back, swaying as she stepped nimbly from rock to rock or leapt small puddles, her midnight hair cascading in rich tumbles to her shoulders, and her hips rocking in her usual athletic stride. Her electric atmosphere, her vigor, her splintering intelligence. And her indomitable, unfaltering courage.

How had he managed to pursue and woo this incredible woman? The most precious thing he had ever hunted, and she had led him a dance indeed, demanding his greatest endeavor, his truest self, the best Sawyer Thane that he could call forth. And somehow, in the process, he had changed and grown.

Victory. Love! The feelings swelled within him. A

kind of happy expansion out into the world, with the twin soul of Lilwen Jones.

And—the family they would create together.

Something warm and solid grew in the black, fractured hollow within his deepest self.

He hardly had words to describe his swelling emotion, but he knew he would have to try. Lilwen would ask this and so much more of him.

Chapter Twenty-Eight

"About time, you two! I think I can speak for Rory, Rupert, and Minnie when I say watching you two together has reanimated our own romances. Bravo, bravo!"

Lilwen was laughing and euphoric, enjoying being the center of a chattering, excited group. Dolly had insisted on the best Champagne and fabulous hors-d'oeuvres nibbled in front of a raging fire. Even Minnie congratulated her with a genuine smile.

Dolly said, "So, Sawyer Thane. Quite the surprise package! Please, do tell us more about this job in Tasmania. Naturally, I am in raptures that you both are to stay here and live not so far away in Hobart."

"My beautiful fiancée has persuaded me that to preserve the wild animal, we must preserve its home. I think she just wants wilderness and botany at every turn!"

"Too right I do! You know you love it. Who—very suspiciously—knows the names of all these remarkable Tasmanian plants, Sawyer Thane? Only the most dedicated plant lovers are familiar with the spectacular and unique Tasmanian flora."

"Ha ha, guilty as charged." Sawyer saluted her with his glass, his enormous grin galvanizing the room. "But really, Lilwen, where is the challenge in hunting static creatures, rooted to the soil?" He smirked and swirled his glass at her.

"Ha! Far more difficult to find a rare plant. It requires the most esoteric knowledge of forest type, soil, climate, and aspect, and even then it can be more guesswork and luck than knowledge. Plants do choose to grow as they will, in the strangest places, against all advice so cleverly given in botany texts."

"I see now!" declaimed Dolly. "The botanic theory Lilwen describes applies to all of us, no? All of us have created unusual lives against all sensible advice. And yet here we are, glowing with health, happiness, and good cheer."

Minnie's face lit up. "But how generous you are, including me in your band of brave adventurers, and yet, perhaps a little, it is indeed true." She was clearly so astonished and impressed with herself that they all laughed.

Lilwen saluted them, her brain as bubbly with delight as the wine swishing in her raised glass. "We must not deceive you all. We will be here, living somewhere wild and stunning in Tasmania, and indeed, where is it not beautiful? But we will also at times be traveling the globe, to exotic and far-flung places, in search of more plants for my nursery, and to increase our knowledge of wilderness." Lilwen and Sawyer clinked glasses.

"You are both quite mad," said Dolly, and the conversation turned general once more.

****

Later, Lilwen and Sawyer walked south of the city until they were strolling along a lonely beach, stopping to admire the stars or to kiss each other.

"I will come to your room tonight," Sawyer

growled. "I cannot wait any longer, wife or no."

"It is important we practice for this important life ahead," she replied gravely, and then laughed and spun away, dancing on the wet sand and allowing the breakers to wash over her bare feet.

This lovemaking was the most romantic. Both knew they were in love. Both knew they had a sparkling future together. Sawyer was tender with her, murmuring loving words in a gravel voice in her ear, making her skin tingle and her heart flutter.

They explored each other with fingers, lips, and tongues. Lilwen tried her tongue on him, with very satisfying results. Sawyer was completely helpless, groaning and growling as she took him to a pinnacle of joy.

After, they lay in each other's arms.

"I have two surprises," he said.

"Mmm?"

"I have arranged with the university that Welcome River can attend medical training, with my support. At first, I did not mention that he grew up in a two-room loggers' hut, far from any college. They were very enthusiastic about this candidate, and only a little deterred when they discovered his unsuitable background. However, they are men of great wisdom and science. They are interested in learning. We will see how he goes. This way, he will have the best of both worlds: traditional bush lore which has stood the test of generations, indeed many thousands of years of human history, and European medical knowledge.

"How wonderful! Does he wish it then? And will patients attend him? Will he not suffer because he is a bushman rather than a gentleman?"

“He is a man of learning, whatever form that education has taken to date! I will find a good tutor for him. He says he is very willing; he wants to be a doctor to serve his own bush folk and other ordinary people who cannot afford to travel into town, let alone consult a medic. They have great need.”

“Oooh. That is truly fabulous. Sawyer, how I love you!”

They were silent for a little.

“And the second surprise?”

“Come. Don warm clothing and bring a thick coat and shawl. We will have a small adventure together.”

****

Lilwen stood, shivering slightly in the chilly darkness, as Sawyer unlocked a tall ornate wrought iron gate, finger to his lips. He held her hand as he led her along newly landscaped pathways, fresh gravel winking diamonds in the starlight. He pulled a small cart with the other arm. Her nostrils clenched with the penetrating aroma of animal droppings, decaying plants, fur, and hide.

“Sawyer! Where…?”

“Shh! Don’t wake the animals. We are at the Hobart Zoo.”

Soon, they stood outside a wire cage. Moving stripes of shadow and night, with ripples of a dull gold gleam, showed them a creature pacing back and forth, around and around. Its head and tail drooped, and the creature’s head moved slowly from side to side as though to blur the monotony of its surroundings.

“We are observing the last Tasmanian tiger in captivity. It has detected our presence.”

Lilwen locked gazes with the blankest, saddest pair

of tawny eyes she had ever seen. “Ohhh.” The sound was wrung from her. Her heart cracked in shocked pity. “He looks half dead with despair.”

“Yes. This is my gift to you. Now, follow my directions exactly.”

Lilwen shut her mouth, which had popped open in startlement.

Sawyer unlocked the cage, and with a few deft movements, muzzled and secured the struggling animal. He held a cloth over its nose; it twitched and was still. “Chloroform. It will wear off in an hour or two. Hurry, now.”

Sawyer hefted the animal with only a grunt to show that though thin, it still weighed a noticeable amount, and wrangled it onto the cart. They took it to the conveyance he had waiting outside the zoo gate. Sawyer took the reins and flicked. More than an hour later, galloping through freezing, rushing darkness, they reached the edge of the western wilderness.

“Sawyer, the tiger is moving! Beginning to struggle and shake its head!”

The creature emitted a long, high-pitched howl, which echoed into the night.

With calm, expert hands, Sawyer laid the trussed creature on the ground and unbound it, carefully freeing its muzzle last and leaping back.

The Tasmanian tiger’s head shot up. Its long snout sniffed the forest and the cold wind. It leapt to shaky feet. Its head was upright now, its tail a plume like a proud flag.

“It will most likely die,” he said, voice quiet. “It has been captive for too long. But it will have this last taste of freedom.”

Tears stung Lilwen's cheeks. "Thank you."

The tiger emitted another long, drawn-out growl, which carried through the deep, silent night.

Sawyer and Lilwen waited. Lilwen's heart thumped in her chest, beating a strong tattoo. Her hand was clenched in his. Her cheeks and ears were frozen with cold, even though she was muffled in coat and shawl. But still, she waited.

The tiger took a few shaky steps, snuffling the air.

"Sawyer, was that an echo of its growl? Listen…"

Finally, the tiger shook off the last of the effects of the chloroform. It found its legs and its freedom and leapt forward into the forest.

Just before it disappeared, an echo of its shape flashed along the forest border: gold and brown stripes and a pair of glowing, feral, honey eyes meeting hers.

She said, "Do you think that tiger may have been *our* tiger's mate? Did I see…?"

"Most unlikely." Sawyer's voice was dry and practical, but the hand still holding hers tightened.

"I shall believe what my heart tells me."

He smiled down at her. "Good for you."

On the long, cold drive back, Lilwen tussled with swirling fierce emotions—how to express them to him?

"What will you tell the zoo?" she asked, to delay matters.

"We will tell the world that the last Tasmanian tiger died in captivity at the Hobart Zoo, of course. Tell me, did you enjoy my present?"

"Oh, Sawyer…I am struggling to find the words. You are wonderful. Perfect. In fact, so perfect, for me, that I in turn have a gift for you."

"Oh?"

Lilwen took a breath in. Time to tell him. Then, if he thought her mad, he could still withdraw from all offers. She huffed out a breath and watched the fog make ring patterns in the air.

"You know the tiger is a talisman for me. Thank you for freeing this one."

Sawyer let go of a rein and reached over and held the back of her neck. Strong. Safe. Warm. "And?"

"Yes, there is an *and*. That day, when we made love in the forest, with all our heart and soul, and the tiger came. She gave us something else."

Sawyer turned toward her in the half dark, his eyes glinting at her. She rubbed a hand over his scrabbly jaw, enjoying the scrape and rasp.

"The tiger has given us our own tiger cub."

Lilwen laughed as his beloved face changed through shock, amazement, astonishment, and finally lit with fierce, mad joy. He dropped the reins and hugged her to him.

She said, into his chest, "I feel as though I have uncovered a profound truth."

"Tell me."

She picked up the reins and flicked the horse.

"Sawyer, my darling. Marriage isn't the end of the game.

"It's only the very beginning."

A word about the author…

Maryanne Ross is totally addicted to reading. She adores writing contemporary and historical romances laced with adventure, sparkle, and spice, featuring independent heroines, swoony heroes, and satisfying endings.

Maryanne has a science degree in horticulture, and many of her stories are set in gardens and gorgeous wild landscapes. Her multiple awards for short crime and romance stories include Romance Writers Australia, Southern Cross Literary, Thunderbolt Crime, and Sisters in Crime. Her romance *How (Not) to Make a Grandchild* is available from The Wild Rose Press and ebook retailers.

She works as a public relations consultant for a major Aboriginal organization, and prior to that did media and communications for National Parks.

She and her family lived for four years in Tasmania and spent many weeks searching for the elusive and lovely White Waratah!

Connect with Maryanne:
Facebook: @MaryanneRossAuthor
Twitter: MaryanneR@big_galaxy2
Amazon Author Central:
https://www.amazon.com/~/e/B083YVP6XV
Goodreads Author Page:
https://www.goodreads.com/author/show/8282646.Maryanne_Ross

Thank you for purchasing
this publication of The Wild Rose Press, Inc.

For questions or more information
contact us at
info@thewildrosepress.com.

The Wild Rose Press, Inc.
www.thewildrosepress.com

www.ingramcontent.com/pod-product-compliance
Lightning Source LLC
LaVergne TN
LVHW020528100826
845148LV00010B/1389